SUMMON THE QUEEN

Also by Jodi McIsaac

The Revolutionary Series

Bury the Living

The Thin Veil Series

Through the Door

Into the Fire

Among the Unseen

Beyond the Pale: A Thin Veil Novella

A Cure for Madness

SUMMON THE QUEEN

I ♡ Calgary Libraries

JODI McISAAC

47NORTH

This is a work of fiction. Names, characters, organizations, places, events, and incidents are either products of the author's imagination or are used fictitiously.

Published by 47North, Seattle

www.apub.com

ISBN-13: 9781503942257
ISBN-10: 1503942252

Cover design by Jason Blackburn

Printed in the United States of America

for my father

Chapter One

The pain threatened to tear muscle from bone, and the drumbeat of her own heart drowned out all other sound. But Nora O'Reilly knew it had worked. She opened her eyes, saw a swirl of gray, and vomited onto the rough stone under her cheek. She pressed her eyes closed again, trying to control the roiling in her stomach. Hands lifted her into the air, the sudden movement sending another cascade of sick from her mouth. She didn't dare open her eyes, but even in her pain-fogged state she could tell it was Fionn who carried her. His heart thundered in his chest. But when she tried to question him, only a moan came out.

"It's okay," he whispered. "I'm here." He held her tighter, and she whimpered. "Can you stand?"

She shook her head ever so slightly. She could barely breathe.

Fionn sank onto the ground, still cradling her in his arms. Bran, his majestic wolfhound, nudged Nora with her wet nose and whined softly. "What happened?" Fionn asked. "You were grand only a moment ago. Does this usually happen when you . . . ?" He left the question hanging, as though unable to say the words "time travel."

Time travel. It seemed impossible, yet she had done it. She had left behind her old life in 2005 to chase a dream. A man with silver hair and eyes the color of the endless ocean had visited her in her sleep, or so she'd thought, and called out to her for help. The ancient goddess Brigid, whom Nora had always believed to be a Catholic saint, had helped Nora travel back in time to 1923 to find this man—the legendary warrior Fionn mac Cumhaill, cursed by the god Aengus Óg with eternal life until he saved Ireland from her enemies. Together, Nora and Fionn had tried to change the outcome of the Irish Civil War, but their efforts had been derailed at the eleventh hour.

And so here they were. They'd gone further back in time to try again to alter the course of Irish history—with the help of the infamous pirate queen, Granuaile, whom the English called Grace O'Malley. Brigid hadn't specified how her old friend Granuaile could help them, but it was a start. If they could free Ireland from the English occupation, they could prevent the Troubles in Northern Ireland from ever happening. Fionn would finally be freed from his curse, and Nora's brother, Eamon, who had died in the fighting, might yet be saved. But for any of this to happen, they first had to find Granuaile.

Nora managed a weak smile, though the muscles in her cheeks burned with the effort. "It's only my second time," she said, her voice thin as vapor. "Don't quite know how it works yet . . ." She tried opening her eyes and was heartened to see the world had stopped spinning. Fionn's stormy gaze crackled down at her, then lifted to sweep their surroundings.

"We need to get you somewhere safe," he said.

"Where are we? Aren't we in the cathedral?" Nora lifted her head, trying to ignore the protest of her muscles and the renewed wave of nausea. Her senses were starting to awaken. Stone walls soared around them, but the windows that had held beautiful stained-glass images were empty. The altar at the front of the cathedral was unadorned. The beautifully tiled floors were chipped, and the entire cathedral—at least as much as she could see—gave the distinct impression of being on the verge of ruin. Her eyes searched for some clue as to when they were.

Fionn took hold of the hem of his jacket and gently wiped her face, which, she realized with horror, must have been splattered with vomit. "Why is the cathedral in this state?" she asked.

"This was a time of religious turmoil, and it took its toll on the cathedrals. The St. Brigid's Cathedral you know wasn't restored until the nineteenth century."

"So, it worked. Brigid sent us back."

"It would seem. We're certainly in some other time. Whether or not it's 1592 is another question."

"The relic . . . Where is it?" Nora said.

He placed the small gilded box in her hand. "You dropped it when you fell."

Nora clutched the box containing the fragment of finger bone, a magical relic from Brigid that had enabled her to travel first to 1923, and now to the sixteenth century. She struggled to sit up. Fionn loosened his arms, and she slid off his lap and onto the floor. The cold stone assaulted her aching body. "How are *you* feeling?" she asked. "Does it affect you like this?"

"No," he said. "I'm a bit gobsmacked that I've just traveled through time. But physically, I'm not harmed."

"Must be nice to have god DNA," Nora said, leaning her head back and closing her eyes. It was still hard to believe that he was *the* Fionn mac Cumhaill, Ireland's most legendary warrior, whose mother had been a granddaughter of Nuadu Airgetlám, High King of the Tuatha Dé Danann, the gods of ancient Ireland.

"Was it this bad last time?"

"It's worse now, so it is. Then, I just felt sore all over. This . . . this is much worse. But I'll manage." Fionn shrugged out of his jacket and slung it over Nora's shoulders. "I suppose we should be moving on," she said halfheartedly.

He nodded, his face grim. "It's a shame we can't travel through space as well as time. 'Tis a long way to Granuaile. We'll need to make our way to Dublin, then find a ship to take us up to County Mayo. The O'Malley clan is near Clew Bay, if I remember."

"Let's get started," Nora said. She gritted her teeth and struggled to her feet, then swayed dangerously.

Fionn steadied her. "First you need rest. We'll not get far with you in this condition. D'you think you need a doctor?"

"I'm grand," Nora insisted. "It'll wear off in a bit. And I don't fancy having a taste of sixteenth-century medicine, ta." She clutched Fionn's arm to keep herself standing and took a few tentative steps forward. Every muscle burned; every bone felt as though it had been shattered. A whimper escaped her lips, but she clamped them shut and attempted another step.

"Should I carry you?" he asked.

Nora didn't answer; all her concentration was focused on putting one foot in front of the other. Bran ran in circles around them. Apparently she, too, had been unaffected by the journey back in time. Fionn pushed the heavy wooden door open with one hand and wrapped the other around Nora's waist.

"Good lord," she breathed. The town of Kildare as she knew it was gone. Even in 1923, it had been recognizable as the place she'd visited in 2005 while searching for the man from her dreams. But in 1592, or whatever year it was now, the bustling main street had yet to be built, and Kildare Castle, a ruin in Nora's time, loomed ominously over the thatched cottages that dotted the narrow dirt road. A wide, open green stood where Nora and Pidge had shopped at the market. For Nora, it had happened weeks ago; for Ireland, it lay centuries in the future. Her head swam just thinking about it.

"C'mon," Fionn said, pulling her along. "Kildare was a market town even then—or now, I should say. That means they'll have an inn, and we can get you looked after."

"I don't need—" Nora started, but Fionn stopped abruptly and gripped her arms.

"Stop," he said.

"What are you—"

"Shh, listen."

She listened, trying to make out something other than the blood pounding in her ears. Hackles rose on Bran's back as she assumed a protective stance in front of them. Then Nora finally heard it—the shouts of men, growing closer and louder. These were not the sounds of celebration, or of a hunting party setting out for the day. They were the sounds of war.

"Back inside the cathedral. Quick!" Fionn said. He scooped her up into his arms and ran back up the narrow path. He kicked open the door and darted inside before setting Nora on her feet again. The shouts grew louder.

"What's going on?" Nora asked, joining Fionn to peer out the crack he'd left between the door and the jamb.

"Just a raid, I reckon. But until I know exactly when we are, it's hard to know for sure. There's a lot of political unrest in this century."

"Well, that's something we've never had to deal with," Nora said, and Fionn's lips twitched.

She pressed her eye to the crack in the doorway. Two dozen men dressed in long belted tunics and brandishing a wide variety of weapons streamed down the road in front of them. A couple of the men had muskets, but most carried swords, axes, or, in one case, a long-handled garden plough. She couldn't make out what they were saying, but she guessed it wasn't words of blessing. Farther down the road, a thatched roof went up in flames.

"Should we stop them?" she asked, withdrawing the revolver from the beaded bag she still wore around her shoulder.

"Hardly," Fionn said, though he, too, had taken a gun out of the waistband of his trousers. "Kildare is on the fringe of the Pale—the center of English control. This raiding party is Irish. They'll be after cattle, grain, and weapons. Unless someone gets in their way, they'll leave the people alone. They're sending a message to the English: 'You're not welcome here.'"

"But when *is* here?"

"We'll soon find out. You're the time-travel expert, not me."

The sixteenth century. It seemed impossible, though she'd already gone back in time eighty-two years. What was another four hundred?

Nora groaned and sank to the floor, unable to stand any longer. Bran curled up beside her, and Nora leaned against her warm side. "This won't do," Fionn muttered. "I have to get you somewhere safer."

Nora shook her head. "You don't have to be my bodyguard."

He gave her an incredulous look, then started moving around the cathedral, peering out the windows where the glass was broken. "Let's see if there's another way out. They've probably some horses and a cart down the road to carry away their booty. Perhaps we can take one."

Nora moaned and waved him away. "You go check. I need to recover. Just give me a minute."

He hesitated, clearly unhappy with the idea. "Is your weapon loaded?" She checked and nodded. "I'll only be a moment," he said. "Bran, stay with Nora."

Bran stood and moved between Nora and the door. It was the first time Nora had been alone with the wolfhound since Fionn had revealed the truth about Bran. She was his cousin, the daughter of his mother's sister Tuiren, who had given birth to two pups after being turned into a hound by her husband's jealous lover. "So . . . you can understand me?" Nora said tentatively. Bran looked at her with deep, shining eyes, then huffed softly before turning her attention back to the door.

At first Nora thought she'd offended Bran, because the wolfhound bared her teeth and emitted a low growl. But then the door slammed open and a man burst in. Bran crouched low and prepared to leap at the intruder, who was wielding a long pole with a pointed metal end. "Bran, no!" Nora shouted, putting one hand on the hound's shaggy back while raising her revolver with the other.

"Get out of here," she said in Irish, dredging the language from the recesses of her memory. "Or I will shoot you."

The man was short and brawny, with a yellow tunic pulled up to his knees and hanging over a leather belt. His feet were bare, and his sandy-blond hair was short, except for a long fringe that fell over his eyes. A loose beige mantle hung around his shoulders. He gaped at Nora, who was lying on the floor of the cathedral in her cream dress, pointing a gun between his eyes. "Who are you?" he asked, gripping his pike tighter.

"None of your business," Nora spat, her arm aching with the effort of keeping the gun raised. She shifted position, and he took a step forward. "Stop!" she cried. "Don't come any closer!"

"You must be English, with your fine clothes and rough Gaelic. Thought you'd be safer in here than in your castle?" He shouted toward the doorway, "Turlough! Get in here! I've got something."

Nora used the split second he was turned to push her way to her feet. She kept her eyes on the pike in his hands and wondered briefly what it would feel like to be run through. She did not lower her gun. Bran's teeth were still bared, but she seemed to be respecting Nora's command—for now.

"If you take another step, either I or my hound will kill you," Nora said firmly. "Drop your weapon."

"Who are you?" the man asked again. He stopped moving but kept his pike firmly in his grasp.

"I told you it's none of your damn business!" Nora said, and she took a painful step forward. "I've nothing to do with you or your clan. Just leave now and forget you ever saw me."

Just then another man burst into the cathedral. He was tall and powerfully built, with black hair that fell to his shoulders and a thick beard. He swore at the sight of Nora, and she swiveled the barrel of her gun in his direction. "What the devil is this?" he bellowed. "Owen, who is this woman?"

The man called Owen took his chance while Nora was distracted. He lunged forward and knocked her to the ground with the shaft of his pike. Nora crashed into the hard floor with a cry of pain, but the fall did not loosen her grip on the gun.

"You bastard!" she screamed, and without further warning shot him through the leg. He howled, clutching his leg, and collapsed beside her on the ground. She kicked the pike away from his outstretched hand and trained the revolver on the newcomer, Turlough, who stared at her in utter shock.

Bran started barking, but not at the men. At Nora. Turlough slowly moved toward Owen and helped him to his feet, then backed toward the door. Red streaks ran down Owen's bare leg. Bran jogged from her to the men, running around them in circles, her tongue hanging out of her mouth. Turlough watched the hound with narrow eyes. "I know this hound. Who the hell are you?" he asked.

"She's English," Owen said.

"I am *not* English," Nora said through gritted teeth. "I'm an O'Reilly." She hoped this clan—whichever one it was—wasn't a sworn enemy of the O'Reillys.

Turlough's eyes narrowed. "And what is an O'Reilly doing down here? Your lot are up in East Breifne. Has The O'Reilly come to lick the boots of the lord deputy again?"

"Fuck you," Nora said. Her Gaelic curses had always been quite good. "Sit down. Against the wall."

The men exchanged a look before doing as she asked, Owen grimacing in pain. Nora got gingerly to her feet, giving herself a better angle on them.

"For Christ's sake, tie your belt around his leg and try to stop the bleeding," she snapped to Turlough. Every fiber in her body felt as though it were on fire, but the adrenaline had at least cleared her mind. Still, she'd no idea what to do with these men. She wanted to shout for

Fionn, but that could attract more of Turlough and Owen's friends. "Who are you?" she demanded. "What are you doing here?"

Owen glared at her. "What do you think? Trying to keep our wives and children alive."

Nora switched the gun to her left hand, letting her right one fall limp at her side.

"The O'Moore will hear about this," Turlough said darkly. "O'Reilly has been an ally of ours."

"I've no quarrel with your clan," Nora said. "And The O'Reilly doesn't have anything to do with this." *Whoever that is.*

Bran straightened up and started to bark in the direction of the back of the cathedral. Fionn burst around the corner, panting. "Nora! Are you all right? I heard—"

He stopped dead at the sight of the men, still in the shadow of one of the cathedral's great archways. Turlough started to rise off the floor, but Nora waved her revolver at him. He sank back down, a heavy scowl on his face.

"What the bloody hell is going on?" Fionn asked. His own weapon was drawn, but he kept it pointed at the floor. "Nora?"

"They attacked me, so I shot one of them."

"Christ on the cross! I can't leave you alone for five minutes without you shooting someone?"

"Would you rather I allowed them to drag me off as some slave?" she shot back. "O'course I defended myself."

"That's not what I meant." He ran a hand through his silver hair, frustration rolling off him in waves. "It's just that we've enough trouble as it is." He turned back toward the men, then leaned in, the expression on his face changing from suspicion to surprise.

"Good God. Turlough O'Moore!" Before Nora could react, Fionn had hauled the dark-haired man to his feet. They pounded each other's backs and gripped each other's arms like long-lost friends. Which, she realized through her shock, they probably were. Owen looked as confused as Nora. She tucked her gun back into her beaded purse.

"What's going on? Who is this?" she demanded. Now that Fionn was here, she slid back onto the floor, unable to stand any longer. Bran returned to her side.

"This is my friend, Turlough," Fionn said, giving her a significant look.

"Robert O'Hanlon! But I thought you were dead," Turlough said, still goggling at Fionn in disbelief. "Word came round last year that you'd been caught and hung by the English."

"Just rumors, my friend. I'm sorry I couldn't set the story straight until now."

"But you cut your hair—and what are these clothes? Where have you been?"

"Spain," Fionn said, as if that explained it all. "But tell me, what has happened here?"

"It'll have to wait. The lads will think we've abandoned them, and we need to see to Owen's leg. Come with us. I want to hear your tale as well."

A pained look crossed Fionn's face. "I haven't the time. I'm sorry. I've urgent business that cannot wait. But God, it's good to see you again. I never thought . . . Tell me, Turlough, what year is it?"

"What year? Don't they keep the same calendar in Spain?"

"I've been traveling a long time. I've lost track."

"Fifteen eighty-seven, by my count."

"Fifteen eighty-seven," Fionn softly repeated. "Brigid was off."

"What?" demanded Turlough.

"Nothing. If it's 1587, then Munster has burned."

"Aye." The two O'Moore men crossed themselves. "English 'settlers' have started claiming the vacant lands."

"And have all the O'Moores revolted?" Fionn asked, his brow deeply furrowed.

"All that's left of us."

Fionn's hand shot out and grabbed Turlough's arm. "You must stop."

Turlough wrenched himself away. "Stop the revolt? Why would you ask such a thing?"

"Maybe he wasn't in Spain, after all," Owen said, speaking for the first time since Fionn and Turlough had been reunited. "Listen to him speaking English with his wife. Maybe he's switched sides."

"Robert O'Hanlon, switch sides?" Turlough said. "Never."

"I haven't," Fionn said. "But being abroad has given me a wider perspective. Petty raids and minor rebellions won't defeat the English. You'll pay for it with your lives."

Even Turlough seemed taken aback. "You *have* changed, friend. The Continent has made you soft."

Fionn pressed his lips together. "I'm only thinking of your safety—and your family."

"My family will be rewarded when we finally drive out the English bastards and the heretic queen. And if we fail, 'tis better than bending the knee, as so many others have done."

He clasped Fionn's arm again and said in a more subdued tone, "We mustn't linger here any longer. Owen and I will rejoin our clansmen. Godspeed to you."

He helped Owen, who was now a pale shade of green, to his feet, and the two of them hobbled to the door. Turlough wrenched it open, and they stumbled out into the daylight.

Fionn exhaled loudly, his hands shaking.

"Are you all right?" Nora asked.

He shook his head, his eyes on the ground. "I never thought . . . It was like seeing a ghost."

She nodded sympathetically. What would it feel like to see Eamon again, alive and laughing? Or her father, whom she could barely remember?

"But you!" he said, suddenly grabbing her by both shoulders. "What were you thinking, going head to head with those men?"

"I told you, they attacked me. I'm just glad I didn't kill your friend."

His face darkened. "You may have done him a favor if you had."

"Why d'you say that?"

"He hangs. He and most of his clan."

"Ach, no. Is that why you told him he should stop fighting?"

"Aye, but I knew he wouldn't listen. He wants the same thing we do, only we know how it ends."

"We'll change it. It'll be different this time."

He couldn't meet her gaze. "Maybe. But I doubt things will change for him. This is the year of his death. The year of so many deaths, as I discovered when I returned from the Continent. His sons are already dead, and his wife and daughters will soon starve. Not even . . ." His voice caught. "Not even selling their bodies to the new English settlers was enough to keep them alive."

Pain blossomed in Nora's gut. "Then let's go," she urged him. "Let's find Granuaile and see how she can help us. Maybe we'll be in time to save Turlough and his family."

Fionn nodded, but his face was hard. "I've a horse waiting outside in the churchyard—one of theirs, no doubt. Can you ride?"

"Do I have a choice?" she asked evasively. She'd never been on a horse.

He gave her an appraising look. "Right. I suppose people in your time don't need horses anymore. With everyone having cars and all." They hadn't talked much about the future, but she *had* bemoaned the lack of paved highways when he'd been transporting her to hospital in 1923, and every rut and pothole had jarred her injured leg, which Brigid had later healed.

"I'll manage. Let's just get out of here. Turlough may be your friend, but Owen didn't seem too fond of us. I don't fancy having his clan coming after us."

She stumbled, and Fionn put his arm around her waist and half-dragged her out of the back of the cathedral. The black mare he'd tied to a tree was bridled but had no saddle. Fionn hoisted Nora onto the mare's back, then leapt nimbly behind her. She wrapped her hands in the horse's mane as Fionn tightened his arms around her. Then, by some unspoken command, the horse whirled around, and they set off at a gallop away from Kildare, and away from the O'Moores' rampage. As they thundered down the rough, muddy road, Bran racing along at their side, Nora chanced a look behind them. The towers of Kildare Castle—only one of which had survived to her time—watched over the hills and meadows and the few thatched cottages, most of which were now engulfed in flame. The men's shouts grew dimmer as the stolen mare took Nora and Fionn away from the village. Nora's entire body screamed in pain as the horse's back moved up and down beneath her. She pressed her lips tightly together so no sound could escape them, concentrating all her will on staying conscious.

Chapter Two

Fionn drove the horse hard for at least half an hour, then veered onto an almost imperceptible track to the east. They passed by a cluster of upright stones, each about four feet tall, forming a rough circle in the clearing to their left. Here was evidence of an even older Ireland, a civilization that knew nothing of King Henry, Queen Elizabeth, or the Normans who had come before them—one that predated even the Vikings and Saint Patrick. These stones were from Fionn's era, or perhaps even earlier. Would they still be standing when she returned to her own time? Or would they be destroyed in the wars and development to come?

"Where are we going?" Nora asked as the horse slowed to a leisurely walking pace. She leaned back against Fionn's chest, unable to keep herself upright any longer.

His voice wavered. "My home."

"Your *home*?"

"Aye. I had a home not far from here."

"But . . . are you there? I mean, the you from this time?"

He hesitated. "I don't think so. I was on the Iberian peninsula during much of the later years of Elizabeth's reign. I should be abroad." But he didn't sound wholly convinced.

Nora closed her eyes, her thoughts swirling. What would it be like to encounter an earlier version of herself? If something happened to his past self, would the Fionn riding behind her continue to exist? *Only he can't die.* "Who were you then?" she asked. "They called you Robert O'Hanlon. What's his story?"

"He, or I, was a wealthy merchant and adventurer. Seldom in one place, which suited me."

"And you're certain you're not here now?"

"Certain? No. You're from 2005, are you not?"

"Aye, but what does that—"

"Then d'you remember exactly where you were on, say, December 10, 1995?"

Nora thought for a moment, then said, "I was in Belfast, with Mick and the lads. I'd just turned twenty, I suppose. But I don't know where I was on that particular day."

"Exactly. And that was only ten years ago for you. Try remembering where you were and what you were doing over three hundred years ago."

"But you told the O'Moores you were in Spain."

"I *am*. Portugal, actually, now that I've thought about it." Silence fell between them for a moment, and then he said, "Here's another question for you: If you lived forever, how would you explain it to the people around you?" The loss in his voice was clear.

"I suppose . . . I'd have to fake my death every so often, then start over somewhere else, where no one knew me."

"Precisely," Fionn said. "If I stay in one place for too long, people start to suspect. That makes it hard to have close friends or a family. I tried, o'course. I couldn't help but fall in love once in a while. I had children. And I even told a few women the truth."

"What happened?"

"Some thought I was mad. Most left. Some reported me to the authorities."

"But some must have believed you. I did."

"Aye, it was easier for you, coming from the future as you did. You knew such things were possible. It's not like people didn't believe in Fionn mac Cumhaill back then, but they didn't believe *I* was Fionn mac Cumhaill. And why would they? I couldn't prove it. I could do none of the deeds that I could in the stories that were passed down. When they started to notice I wasn't aging, they grew afraid I'd made some pact with the devil."

"So no one believed you?"

"There was one," he said, his voice tight. "And I watched her grow old while I stayed young. I watched her die. Then our children died, one by one, followed by *their* children. By then I had hidden myself as a traveling bard, only passing through my old *túath* every year or so. But my grandchildren and great-grandchildren did not know me, and eventually the older folk began to suspect something was not right. I was forced to move on."

"I'm sorry. I can't imagine what you've been through."

He sat up straighter. "I don't mean to be so melancholic. I'm just trying to explain why I'm playing this particular role at this particular time."

"Robert O'Hanlon, you mean?"

"Yes, him. Living forever has some advantages, I suppose. I can take incredible risks without the fear of death, though Aengus Óg wasn't so kind as to make me impervious to pain. Another is that I've had the time to amass a fair amount of wealth. Although transporting and storing it in the days before banks was a wee challenge, to be sure."

Nora had wondered about this, but it would have felt rude to ask. "How *did* you do it?"

"Hid it, sometimes. Transferred it to myself—my newly invented self—in wills. Lost it, occasionally. Invested in lands and ships. Gave a lot of it to whatever resistance movements were currently happening. I thought maybe Aengus Óg would be appeased if I financed a successful rebellion, though obviously that hasn't worked. I had to stay under the radar, o'course. I couldn't become some great chieftain or military leader. There would be too many questions I couldn't answer. Genealogy is everything to the Irish, especially of this era and the generations before. They know who everyone's parents and grandparents and uncles and second cousins and distant relations are. Everyone is connected."

"So you became a vagabond."

"A wealthy vagabond, you could say. I started traveling, spending alternate generations on the Continent to let those who knew me die off. Then I'd come back to try and save Ireland."

"Why d'you think it hasn't worked?"

"If I knew that, I wouldn't be here now."

"You'd be dead." Her chest tightened at the thought.

"Aye, the curse would be broken, and I'd be feasting in the Otherworld with my men, my wives, and my children."

"So why tell *me* the truth? You didn't need to. You could have gone on pretending to be Thomas Heaney."

"You're a kindred spirit. Someone also out of time."

Nora had a thousand more questions but was too shattered to ask them. Bran had caught up with them and was trotting alongside the horse, sniffing the road in front of her.

"Smell familiar, Bran?" Fionn asked, and the hound barked happily. "Do us a favor and go see if I'm home." Bran barked again and bounded off into the wood beside them. After they rode in silence for several more minutes, the wood around them started to thin. Fionn pulled up the horse and dismounted. Through the trees Nora could see a large, three-story stone house. Thick green bushes flourished in the well-kept front garden, and fruit trees ran along the eastern side.

"That's yours?" she asked incredulously.

"It is. My man Cormac runs it with his wife, Katherine, when I'm away, which is most of the time."

"Won't he be suspicious if they think you're abroad?"

"I've been away for some time, so it shouldn't surprise them that I've returned to check on the estate. But I suppose we *will* need a cover story."

Bran bounded back to them, and she and Fionn had a quick, silent conversation. "It's okay," Fionn told Nora. "There's no one here but Cormac."

He led the horse toward the house, and a wide-eyed man ran out to greet them. "Mr. O'Hanlon! What are you—I had no idea—who—" The man stopped stammering and waited for instructions as Fionn helped Nora down. She cringed in pain when her feet met the ground.

"Hello, Cormac. Obviously, I have returned," Fionn said. "This is my cousin, Nora. She's ill and must rest at once."

"Of course!" the servant said, rushing to hold open the door for them. "But where is your luggage?"

"We were robbed on the road."

The servant pressed his hand to his heart.

"We'll need a fire in my room. Bring warm water and fresh clothes. As well as food and drink. Where is Kat?"

"She went to visit her sister; I'll send for her at once. We weren't expecting—"

"It's grand," Fionn said. "We will only be here a day or two, until Nora recovers."

Cormac hurried off, and Nora allowed Fionn to help her up a curving staircase and into a large room. A four-poster bed with deep crimson curtains stood against one wall, and she sank onto it gratefully. Fionn started unlacing her boots, and she was too tired to protest that she could do it herself. "Thank you," she whispered.

"Sleep," he said, his forehead creased. "Hopefully you'll feel better when you awaken."

"Mmm," she said, closing her eyes. She had so many questions—about him, about this time period, about what they were going to do now that they'd landed in the wrong year. But the pounding in her head was growing stronger, as if a horse's hooves were thundering inside her skull. Sleep took her, and she welcomed it gladly.

When Nora awoke, the room was filled with warmth. The bed curtains were drawn shut around her, but flickering shadows danced across the thick fabric, and the soft crackle of a hearth fire drifted toward her. She stayed still, mentally scanning her body. Much better. The time-travel sickness seemed to have mostly passed, but her lower half was sore from the gallop from Kildare. When she'd awoken in Pidge's bed after appearing in 1923, she'd had to convince herself it was real. Now she needed no convincing. She was in 1587, in Fionn mac Cumhaill's bed.

Good Lord.

She sat up, and someone in the room moved.

"Fionn?" She opened the curtains a crack. Bran's shaggy brown face greeted her, and the hound gave a soft bark. Nora patted the hound's head. "Hello, Bran. How was the hunt?" Bran barked again, which Nora took to mean it had been good. The door opened and Fionn came in. Nora did a double take and yanked the curtain all the way open. Fionn had changed from his simple shirt and trousers into something quite . . . outlandish. A yellow tunic of sorts fell to his knees and hung in a great fold over the belt around his waist. The sleeves of the tunic were wide and short, ending at his elbows, and the neckline was low, showing off his sharp collarbones and the sculpting of his chest. Instead of trousers, he wore a pair of tights in an orange-and-brown-checkered pattern. Over his tunic was a short wool jacket, richly decorated with swirls and bands of color, pleated from his sternum to his hips. The sleeves of the jacket were cut to allow the draping sleeves of the tunic to fall through.

"What the hell are you wearing?" Nora asked.

Fionn laughed and spun around, apparently quite comfortable. "Don't you like it?"

"Please tell me I don't have to dress like that."

"I see you're in grand spirits this afternoon."

"Afternoon? How long did I sleep?"

"The whole day and the whole night, and all of the morning. You obviously needed it. How are you feeling?"

"Much better. What have you been doing? What did the servants say? D'you find out—"

"Wait," he said, holding up a hand to forestall her. "First things first. I thought you might like to wash, so I brought some soap and warm water. I found you some clean clothes. And you must be hungry. You just missed dinner, but I'll get Kat to fetch some food and ale. *Then* we can talk."

Nora touched her hacked-off hair, which was matted with sweat and dirt. "Grand so," she agreed, swinging her legs out of the bed.

Fionn took a kettle that had been hanging over the fire and added warm water to a basin on a small side table, beside a neatly folded cloth and a piece of yellow soap on a porcelain dish. Clothes had been laid across the back of a tall chair.

"There's a sitting room just at the bottom of the stairs," he said. "Take your time, and I'll meet you there when you're ready." Then he and Bran left. Nora listened until she could hear their footsteps no longer, then took off the cream dress she'd worn since her release from Kilmainham Gaol. After washing her undergarments and hanging them by the fire to dry, she dipped the cloth into the basin and washed herself all over, from the top of her head to between her toes. The warm, fragrant water felt good, and she took her time, assuming baths were a luxury in this era. Still naked, she examined the clothes on the back of the chair. There was a long, yellow, tunic-type dress—wool, by the feel of it—with a V-shaped neckline. A long, red cloak, lined with fur, lay beside it. She assumed it was intended to go over the simpler garment. Several other pieces were a mystery to her.

Her underclothes were already dry, so she put them back on first, enjoying their warmth against her skin. She then slipped the yellow tunic over her head and pulled her arms through the tight sleeves. The red cloak went on next. After she did up the lacing in the front, she tied what she assumed was a belt around her waist, letting the long embroidered end dangle down the front of her dress. *That's not so bad.* Up until now, Nora's only impression of sixteenth-century fashion had sprung from Queen Elizabeth I's outrageous wardrobe—skirts so large one could barely move and massive ruffs swallowing the neck. But this dress was actually comfortable.

A rectangular piece of white cloth was left over, as well as two draping strips of the same red fabric as the cloak. Nora studied them but couldn't figure out where she was supposed to put them. On the seat of the chair was a hat. At least, she thought it was a hat. The contraption was shaped like a donut, except a bit of linen covered the top and square flaps hung over the ears. She left it on the chair.

Once she was ready, Nora slipped her twentieth-century boots back on and picked up her handbag. Nestled under the revolver was her rosary, which her brother had hand carved for her before his death. She slipped it around her neck for safekeeping, comforted by the weight of the beads. After sliding her fingers from bead to bead and whispering a prayer, she opened the door. The sleep had helped restore her, but it was time to find Granuaile.

Just as he'd said, Fionn was waiting for her in the sitting room. He was leaning against the mantel, looking down into the fire. His clothes didn't look quite so ridiculous now that she, too, was dressed the part. But then again, Fionn could never truly look ridiculous. He belonged in every century.

He turned at the sound of her footsteps. "You look beautiful. The red suits you."

"Ta," she said. "Where d'you get it? Is there a Mrs. O'Hanlon I should know about?" She tried to keep her voice light, but the thought was a punch to the gut.

"I sent Kat to borrow it from her sister's mistress. It fits you well." He didn't answer the second question.

"I don't know what these are," she admitted, holding up the leftover garments.

"Ah. This goes under your *léine*," he said, taking the white rectangle from her.

"My what?"

"Your léine. Like mine." He fingered the long tunic she wore under the red cloak, then wrapped the white fabric around her shoulders and tucked the edges inside the neckline. A slightly ruffled collar now covered the bottom half of her neck. "And these are hanging sleeves—very fashionable, if I remember correctly. You attach them here"—he buttoned the edge of one to her shoulder—"and here." He fastened the other end to a loop near her wrist and then repeated the process with the other sleeve. "And you'll want to tuck the edges of your dress into your belt."

"I'm sorry, what?" Nora didn't know much about sixteenth-century clothing, but she doubted women of this era walked around with their legs exposed.

"Like this," he said, lifting the front corner of the outer garment and tucking the edge into her belt to expose the furred underside. He did the same to the other side, then took a step back to admire his handiwork. "I see you left the hat upstairs."

"That hideous thing? You're lucky I didn't throw it into the fire." That sounded ungrateful. "But thank you for getting these for me. I suppose we'll need to blend in."

"You're just lucky Kat didn't bring the hat that's shaped like an onion. Or the chimney-pot version—I never understood that one."

Both of them sat, and Fionn poured two tall mugs of ale from a pitcher on the table between them. A plate of cheese and cold meats sat beside a still-warm loaf of grainy bread. Nora grabbed a piece of bread and cheese and took a long drink of her ale, her eyes fixed on Fionn over the rim of her mug.

He tore off a chunk of bread and chewed it slowly. "So," he said eventually. "What d'you suppose we're to do once we find Granuaile?"

"Damned if I know," Nora said. "I suppose we'll find out once we talk to her. She must be involved in the rebellion in some way. Perhaps she's one of the leaders." Nora stood, grabbing another piece of cheese. "We should leave straightaway."

Fionn shook his head. "Not today. It's a full day's ride to Dublin, and that's if the weather is fair, which it usually isn't."

"Oh." Her heart sank at the delay. She settled back into the chair and took a bite of the cheese. "Since we're here, you might as well fill me in. I only know the vague outline of what happens in this time. Elizabeth makes war on Ireland, some of the chiefs rebel, others submit . . . and in the end, we lose."

"Aye. We lose."

He looked ready to say more, but just then Kat, the housekeeper, came into the room, looking flustered.

"Begging your pardon, Mr. O'Hanlon, but a messenger has just arrived."

"Oh?" Fionn asked, sitting up straighter. "What's the message?"

Kat wrung her hands. "Well, that's the confusing part, if you don't mind me sayin' so. You told Cormac you didn't have time to send word ahead. But this man says he's a messenger . . . from you. You want us to get the house ready, because you'll be here on the morrow."

Chapter Three

"Thank you, Kat," Fionn said, his voice shaking slightly. He rose to his feet. "It was just a mistake. That will be all."

Kat looked like she had a few more questions for her master but dipped her chin dutifully and left the room. Nora was out of her chair at once. "Shite! We have to get out of here!"

"Wait." Fionn held up a hand to stop her from rushing out of the room. "Just let me think."

"Fionn, we need to go *now*. Who knows how the you from the past will react if he sees you!"

"He won't. And I told you, it's a full day's ride to Dublin, with no real place to stay in between. We'll leave at first light."

"What if he's early?"

"On these roads? Impossible."

"And what about Cormac and Kat? What will you tell them?"

"I'll leave them a letter. Cormac can read. I'll tell them I took advantage of my resemblance to their master for a couple of nights' free lodging."

"You honestly think they'll believe that?"

"What would you tell them? That I'm their master from the future?"

Nora fell silent. There was no easy answer.

"Come," Fionn said, gesturing toward the door. "There's no use staying here and fretting. Let me show you around."

He took her from room to room. It was as though she were in the world's greatest living-history museum.

"So what were you doing in Portugal?" she asked as she examined the books in his library, thinking of the Fionn who was drawing nearer and nearer to them. "Besides staying away from people who might know you?"

"Making friends at the Habsburg court." Fionn picked a book up off the shelf and fanned through the pages, a gentle smile on his lips. "At this point Elizabeth and Philip were enemies, which meant Philip was a potential ally. What did your history books teach you?"

Nora strained to remember. "Well, it's after the Protestant Reformation."

"And welcome to the root of all our troubles. The English have more or less left Ireland alone since the conquest of the twelfth century, leaving the ruling in the hands of the big Anglo-Irish families. But when Henry VIII created himself head of the Church of England, it caused a few wee problems."

Nora snorted. "An understatement if I ever heard one."

"Aye. A Protestant king and an island of Catholics. He bullied or beheaded the old Anglo-Irish lords, dissolved the monasteries, made it treason to practice Catholicism, and started taking land away from the Gaelic clans. He'd give it back to them, but only after they swore their allegiance to him. 'Surrender and regrant,' it was called, and it worked. Through either intimidation or bribery, almost all of the Gaelic chiefs have bent the knee at this point. Elizabeth has continued her father's policies, but with more . . . vigor, shall we say. Come, let me show you the kitchen."

Nora watched in fascination as Kat bustled about, baking bread and marinating meat, all while scolding the kitchen boy. Nora asked so many questions that Fionn finally had to excuse them, saying she'd never been allowed in a kitchen before.

"What d'you mean when you asked Turlough if Munster had burned?" Nora asked as she examined the tapestries on the walls of yet another sitting room.

"The Earl of Desmond rose in rebellion—reluctantly, some say—and Elizabeth's troops decimated his province in return."

Nora chewed her lip, thinking. "If we're in 1587, that means the Battle of Kinsale isn't far away—1601, right? Eamon used to say that was the end of Gaelic Ireland. He said everything changed after that. Were you there?"

Fionn snorted. "Oh, I was there. I helped convince Philip and his councilors to support Ireland, but everything that could go wrong did. The Spanish arrived to help, yes, but the English showed up in Kinsale instead of Ulster, where they were supposed to land. Our soldiers had to march across the whole bloody country through the winter to meet them. The Spanish took Kinsale, but they were besieged by the English, who were in turn besieged by the Irish, who were then attacked from the other side by a relief force of English. Hugh O'Neill and Red Hugh O'Donnell, the two Irish chieftains leading the rebellion, did not coordinate. Nor did the Spanish coordinate with the Irish."

"I remember studying it in school. It was quite the mess."

"It was a rout. A massacre. And your brother was right: it changed everything. O'Neill and O'Donnell and the other Irish chiefs fled Ulster—"

"And the British replaced them with Protestant Scots. Aye, I know the story. The Plantation of Ulster. Evicted all the Irish from their own land and replaced them with boatloads of Scottish Presbyterians." She shook her head in disgust. "The English blame the Irish for the Troubles in Northern Ireland, but they're the ones who caused it."

"So it would seem. They say the English expected all the Irish to leave the country once their chiefs had fled and their land had been taken and given to the new settlers. Instead, they stayed. And fought. And are still fighting, from what you tell me."

"We don't give up that easily."

"No. We don't."

"Was Granuaile involved with the Battle of Kinsale?"

Fionn's forehead wrinkled. "I don't know. We can add it to our list of questions for her."

They spent the rest of the afternoon wandering through the orchard and fields surrounding Fionn's home. Bran returned from a hunt and walked contentedly beside them.

"It's so beautiful here," Nora said, stepping over a twisting root covered in moss. "It's a shame you couldn't stay here most of the time. But I suppose Portugal isn't so bad, either."

She expected him to smile and agree with her, but instead his face grew somber. "It *is* beautiful, right here, right now. But that is precisely because I was away. I gave the English no reason to trouble me—none that they knew of, that is. Otherwise they would have burned this place to the ground and slaughtered Cormac and Kat and anyone else associated with me." There was a long pause. She didn't know what to say, except to repeat her belief that they were here to change the plight of the Irish people. "Let's talk about something else," he said, trying to smile. "Tell me about the future."

"The future? What d'you want to know?"

"Everything! What do I have to look forward to if I live for another hundred years?"

Nora laughed. "Well, things have changed a lot since the nineteen twenties, so they have. Let's see . . . well, there's the Internet."

"The what?"

"The Internet. It's—ach, how to explain it? D'you know what a computer is? I can't remember when they were invented."

Fionn shook his head.

"They're machines that do calculations," she said, struggling to explain. "They started out quite massive, but they're supertiny and powerful now. If I still had my cell phone, I could show you, but it was destroyed in the fire at the Gillieses."

"What's a cell phone? Like a telephone?"

"Aye, but it's this big." She made a rectangular shape with her hands. "And there are no wires. And you can use it to take photographs, listen to music and everything. But the Internet is incredible; it's changed the world. I honestly have no clue how it works. I suppose you'd say it makes it possible for computers to talk to each other. So you can instantly share information and photos and videos with anyone else who has an Internet connection."

Fionn looked absolutely gobsmacked. "Are you serious?"

"I am!" She laughed at the expression on his face. "So if you have a computer and I have a computer, I can send you an instant message no matter how much distance separates us. And we could see each other and talk as if we were sitting next to each other."

"Incredible," he breathed. "What else is there?"

They turned back toward the house, and she told him about the ease of air travel and the Second World War and 9/11. She told him about some of the places she'd worked and why she'd gone there.

"Some areas of the world are still in the Middle Ages in a lot of ways," she said. "Same technology, same life expectancy, same deaths from easily preventable diseases. It's not fair. The people are smart and hardworking. But the Industrial Revolution passed them by."

"You care a lot for these people," Fionn remarked.

"Anyone would, if they'd met them, if they'd heard their stories. People feel bad for me because I grew up in Belfast during the Troubles. But that's nothing compared to some of the suffering these people have been through."

"Will you go back to it, once all this is over?"

Nora bit her lip. "I don't know. I don't even know if I *can* go back. I've just been living one day at a time since I started looking for you." She smiled ruefully. "Sometimes it's hard to believe I actually found you."

They stopped outside the house, lingering. The sun was low in the sky, lighting the stone so it glowed. Fionn took her hand and held it lightly. "Nora," he began. "I want to ask you something."

Her heart hammered furiously in her chest. *What the devil is wrong with me?* "Ach, aye," she said, cursing her voice for shaking. But before he could ask his question, Kat appeared in the doorway, hands on her generous hips.

"There you are!" She spoke as if they were wains. "Your supper is ready." She gave them an appraising look that said she knew full well Nora was not Fionn's cousin, then went back into the house.

"We'd better go in," Fionn said, dropping Nora's hand. "Kat hates it when I let her meals go cold."

Nora's relief was greater than her disappointment. She'd still not worked out her own feelings or intentions toward Fionn, so she was glad to forestall the conversation—if that was indeed what he had been about to bring up.

"How is the food in this century?" she asked as they climbed the steps to the house.

He grimaced. "Occasionally edible. But Kat is a fine cook, which makes up for the scarcity of ingredients. Supper is usually quite small, but I asked her to make an exception for you."

The dining room table had been laid out with a beautifully embroidered cloth and two place settings. The tall, thin candles at the center of the table emitted a soft glow, and a fire had been lit in the hearth at the end of the room. Fionn leaned close to Nora and whispered, "Notice what's missing?"

She studied the table. "Forks!" she exclaimed, then lowered her voice, as Kat was bringing in various dishes. "Have they not been invented yet?"

"I don't know about invented, but they're not widely used here or abroad. Think you can manage?"

"I'm sure," she said with a grin.

The meal was simple: roast mutton with leeks and watercress, a thick, grainy bread spread generously with butter, and pewter mugs of mead.

Nora kept their conversation light and easy, regaling Fionn with stories about Riverdance and Irish football. But she kept a close eye on the door, expecting his former self to burst in on them at any moment. Once Kat had cleared the dishes away, they moved to the chairs by the fire, their mead replaced with whiskey and great bowls of apple cake and fresh cream in their laps.

When Nora had yawned three times in the same minute, Fionn stood. "Bedtime," he said. "We've a long ride ahead of us tomorrow."

Nora nodded like this was no big deal, but her expression must have betrayed her nerves.

"He—I—won't come until after we've left, I promise."

"If you say so."

He escorted her to her room. She hesitated in the doorway. She wasn't sure why, but she didn't want him to leave. "Fionn," she started, not knowing what she would say next.

His gaze met hers, bringing a rush of heat to her cheeks. But then he glanced toward his own room at the end of the hall and said, "Good night, Nora. I'll send Kat in to wake you in the morning."

He walked determinedly down the hall and entered his room, not once looking back.

Chapter Four

As promised, Kat woke her early the next morning, a basin of warm water and a mug of ale waiting for her. Nora thanked her and dressed quickly, then went to the window. The sun was just starting to lighten the sky over the orchard, a pale-blue backdrop that darkened the leaves of the apple trees. Fionn was already in the yard, fastening a leather saddle on a dappled mare. She rapped on the window and waved. He smiled and waved back. She took a couple of gulps of ale—now this was a custom she could get used to—and went down to join him. He wore a heavy furred cloak over his léine and vest and handed her a similar garment.

"I've put a fur on your saddle as well, since you're not used to riding," he said.

"Ta," she said, eyeing the horse nervously. Riding pillion with Fionn had been one thing, but managing her own horse for several hours would be another.

"We'll go slow," he said, "And your horse will follow mine."

"Did you leave the letter?"

"I did." He frowned. "Cormac and Kat are good people. I don't like deceiving them, but I couldn't exactly tell them the truth. I suggested they keep this to themselves, lest they lose their jobs over it. I hope I've done enough."

Bran startled them both with a sharp bark. Fionn's face blanched. "He's coming," he hissed. "Quickly!" He grabbed the reins of both horses and jogged toward the side of the house.

Nora's heart thundered as she followed, straining her neck to see the road behind them. It would be disastrous if the two men saw each other, and yet she had a burning curiosity to see the Fionn from this era. She rounded the corner of the house, then pressed herself against the wall, ready to catch a glimpse of the man Fionn used to be.

"What are you doing?" Fionn's voice was low and urgent.

"I just want to—"

"If Bran is with him, she'll smell us! We have to move now!" Reluctantly, she followed him and the horses around the back of the house and through the orchard. Bran whined as she followed.

"I know it's strange," Fionn told the hound. "But the last thing I want is for you to get in a fight with your former self. You were stronger back then."

Bran huffed indignantly as Fionn helped Nora mount. Nora cast one last look behind them as they galloped through a field. She hoped Cormac had read the letter before his actual master had arrived.

That was too close.

Bran jogged alongside them, helping keep Nora's horse in check whenever it veered off the road. Nora's steering abilities improved as the day wore on, though her legs and arse screamed in protest. But she bit her lip and swallowed her moans, trying to keep up some semblance of conversation with Fionn as they rode, and rode, and rode.

"Are the O'Reillys involved in the conflict here?" she asked, thinking of what the O'Moores had said.

"Everyone is involved, whether they like it or not."

"Did you know any of my ancestors?" All she knew of her distant ancestors was her Aunt Margaret's claim that they'd been kings of Breifne at one point.

"Troublemakers, mostly," he said, flashing her a smile. "Shocking, I know."

"Smart-ass."

"So is Granuaile, of course. You two should get along just fine."

"Tell me more about her."

"The O'Malley clan motto is Powerful by Land and Sea, and Granuaile is the embodiment of it. She has everything—treasure, cattle, sons, influence. Her fleet is the envy of every coastal chieftain in the country." He narrowed his eyes and nodded slowly. "I can see why Brigid wanted us to meet her. She is well suited to help our cause."

"I hope so."

Finally, when Nora was certain she could go no farther, Fionn said, "We're almost there." She sat up straighter. Houses dotted the sides of the road ahead. At the end of the road loomed the city walls, a thick gray barrier that encircled Dublin, no doubt keeping it safe from the Irish. She'd seen only a ruin of this massive wall, a sparse fragment still standing in what was now downtown Dublin. A tall, square spire rose in the distance, and Nora caught her breath.

"Is that Christ Church Cathedral?"

"'Tis," Fionn answered.

"That's incredible," she breathed. "It must be amazing for you, to have lived so long, to have seen everything change so much." He didn't answer. "I'm sorry, I didn't mean—"

"It's grand," he interrupted. "I *have* seen a lot of changes. I only wish they'd been better ones."

Nora's heart beat faster as they drew nearer to the city. Beggars cried out to them from the roadside, poor scrawny souls clothed in rags, their feet bare and blackened with filth.

"It got worse when Henry came to the throne," Fionn noted, watching her. "The church used to care for the poor, but now that the religious houses have been dissolved and most of the priests are in hiding, there's no one left to look after these wretches."

Nora dropped her gaze. She had nothing to give them, only the hope of a better future.

They approached a tall iron gate set into the wall. It was open, but armed sentries stood on either side; others paced on top of the wall. The soldiers gripped long black muskets, and a glint of long steel hung from every belt. "Let me do the talking," Fionn said in a low voice as a soldier approached them.

"What's your name and business here?" the guard asked.

"Robert O'Hanlon and wife. I'm a merchant. My business is with Joseph Wilde."

The guard peered at them each in turn, and Nora averted her eyes. Then he grunted and waved them through. Bran, masterful at avoiding attention for such a large dog, slipped in behind them. A thrill ran through Nora as they passed under the ancient gate and into the city. The street was lined with tall timber houses, the upper floors hanging out over the bottom. Even though it was near dark, the road was crowded with people, carts, and animals. A cart filled with hay took up half of the road in front of them, its owner shouting from the front seat. The deeper they went, the more crowded it got, with bulks and stalls selling everything from live rabbits to piles of cabbages. A brightly dressed street singer stood in one corner, his clear voice carrying even over the considerable din. But the most noticeable difference was the smell: part sewer, part slaughterhouse, with a whiff of fish market thrown in for good measure. Nora lifted a sleeve to her nose and switched to breathing through her mouth.

The horses moved slowly across the uneven paving stones as they made their way through a couple of narrow laneways. Street children skulked in the corners or held up their soiled hands, hoping Nora would give them a coin. She remembered the wains in the refugee camp in Sudan, the ones who had been so fascinated by her red hair. What was her old boss Jan doing now? Was anyone looking for her in 2005?

"Are we really meeting with this Joseph Wilde?" she asked, trying to stay focused.

"Aye," he said. "The gates aren't normally guarded, but after the Desmond Rebellion . . ." He trailed off, his eyes on the road ahead. "Just as I remembered—over a thousand taverns, but try to find a decent inn. I have acquaintances here, other merchants we could stay with. But I'd rather avoid questions. I believe Wilde's wife offers lodging, so we'll stay there if we can. And tomorrow Wilde can help me find us a ship bound for Galway."

He pulled his horse up outside a narrow storefront. A wooden sign hung from an iron peg. Carved on the sign was a picture of a bear holding a large stick. "The Bear and Ragged Staff," he explained, seeing Nora's curious stare. "Home of bookseller Joseph Wilde."

"A bookseller? How can he—?"

"Books aren't the only things Mr. Wilde trades in. He's also a great source of information. And a discreet man, if I remember correctly."

"You know him well?"

"I used to frequent his shop on occasion before I set sail for the Continent. He'll remember me, but not enough to ask any awkward questions."

Fionn helped Nora dismount, which she did with a groan. "I'm grand," she said, forestalling his question.

"We'll rest soon," he promised. "Wait here with the horses. Bran, you stay as well."

Fionn disappeared inside the tiny shop, leaving Nora holding the reins of both horses, who shifted and stamped beside her as a large cart drove past. "This is mad," she whispered to Bran, wondering where this street was in modern Dublin. Had she walked this road in the twenty-first century? Did a smart café or tall office tower stand where she was now? She inched over to the dark window and peered inside. The glass was dirty, and she could just barely make out the figure of a man moving around inside. Behind him, a wooden shelf cradled several rows of thick books. Then the door reopened, and both Fionn and the man she assumed was Joseph Wilde stepped out into the street. Wilde was short and thin, with protruding ears under his crimson hat and dark moles dotting his pale skin. He wore black hose and short, puffed trousers striped with black and gold.

"Here they are," Fionn said, indicating the horses. "You can have them returned to my estate?"

Mr. Wilde admired the horses and took the reins from Nora. "Of course, Mr. O'Hanlon. I'll have them returned on the morrow. But are you sure you won't be needing them?"

"We'll be in Galway for some time," Fionn said. "I don't know when we will return. When we do, I'll hire another pair. But the city is no place for such magnificent beasts."

"Sure and you're right about that," Mr. Wilde agreed.

"Does your wife have lodging available for the night? I'd rather not stay at the inns if I can help it."

"God forbid it!" Mr. Wilde exclaimed with a hearty laugh. "I wouldn't send my dog to such a place. Aye, we've no other lodgers at the moment, and I'm sure she'll be glad to have you. We're on Picot's Lane, sign of the rose."

"I thank you. And about our other business?"

"I'll have news for you in the morrow. One of my lads works down at the docks. He'll know if anyone is bound for Galway."

Fionn doffed his cap to Mr. Wilde and held out his arm to Nora. She hesitated for a moment, but Mr. Wilde was watching them, so she threaded her arm through Fionn's. "A pleasure to meet you, Mrs. O'Hanlon," Wilde said.

"And you," Nora replied, smiling tightly. She and Fionn walked several paces before she nudged him in the side and said, "What happened to cousin? That's twice now you've referred to me as your wife."

"It made more sense to tell Cormac and Kat you were a distant cousin. I'd not just bring a wife home unannounced. But if we're traveling as far as Mayo together, it will be far more convenient to pretend we are married."

Nora flushed, remembering the last lingering kiss they'd shared at Lynch's hideout. Part of her longed to explore the growing connection between them. But he was the Fionn mac Cumhaill of legends, and she was an ex-Provo from Andersonstown. They'd been thrown together by Brigid and had chosen to help each other. Maybe that's all it was. Maybe that's all it should be.

They were welcomed warmly by Mrs. Wilde, who showed them into a narrow room with a plain wooden table and benches on either side. Nora sank gingerly onto one of the hard benches, her muscles screaming in protest. Perhaps it would be better to stand, but she couldn't muster the energy. She laid her head on the table until Mrs. Wilde came in carrying a pot of stew, bowls, and two pewter mugs. They ate quietly, both worn out from the day's ride.

When they had finished, their hostess offered to show them to their room. Fionn rose quickly, but Nora stayed in her seat, suddenly nervous. Of course, if they were pretending to be husband and wife, they'd be expected to share a room.

And a bed.

"Are you all right?" Fionn asked, holding out a hand to help her to her feet.

"Aye," she said with an attempt at laughter as she accepted his hand. "Just worn out, that's all."

"You'll feel better in the morning. And we won't be riding again for a while—not 'til we reach Galway."

He didn't let go of her hand as they followed Mrs. Wilde back into the hall. Fionn had a few whispered words for Bran, who huffed before settling back down in the hallway. Mrs. Wilde showed them into a small, dark room that was empty save for a single narrow bed. Nora eyed it nervously.

"I've brought water and a fresh candle," Mrs. Wilde pointed out, oblivious to Nora's nerves. "Will you be wanting to break your fast in the morning?"

"Aye," Fionn answered. His hand was warming, and he gripped hers firmer than necessary.

"God be with you, then," she said, backing out of the room and closing the door.

While Fionn lit the single candle and sat it on a shelf built into the wall, Nora busied herself with taking off her ridiculous head covering and unlacing her boots. She opened her mouth to say something witty, something distracting, something to alleviate the pressure in her chest.

"I can sleep on the floor," he said, throwing his cloak down onto the wooden slats.

There wasn't even a rug covering the rough slats. "Don't be daft," she said. "You'll get eaten by rats."

"I don't want to make you uncomfortable," he said. He took a step toward her, then stopped. She snorted, and he raised a gray eyebrow in response. "That is, surely you don't *want* me to make you feel uncomfortable?"

She grew serious at once. "You don't," she said softly, her eyes on the floor in front of her.

He came closer, close enough to rest his hand on her shoulder and tilt her chin up so that her gaze was locked with his. "Then how *do* I make you feel, Nora O'Reilly?"

She was trying to formulate an answer when her legs gave out. Fionn caught her around the waist before she completely crumpled. "Shite," she moaned. "I'm sorry."

"Don't be," he said, leading her to the bed. "My God. You're still sick from the time travel. We should have found somewhere else to take shelter for another day."

"Shut up," she whispered.

"What?"

She edged to the far side of the bed to make room for him. "Shut up and come lie next to me." She didn't care that the mattress was stuffed with straw, or that the pillow was thin and lumpy. She tried not to think about bedbugs, or lice, or other vermin of this century. All she wanted was sleep. Fionn took off his mantle, vest, and hose but kept the long léine that fell to his knees. He lifted the covers and settled himself in beside her. She opened her eyes and smiled at him weakly. "I'll be better tomorrow," she whispered.

"Shh. We'll stay here as long as we need to. Sleep now." He slid his arm under her head, and she rested her cheek on his chest, drawing near to his warmth. A rush of pleasure ran through her, but exhaustion overcame it, and she surrendered to sleep.

Chapter Five

When Nora awoke the next morning, she was alone in the bed. She could hear voices outside the door, the sound of small footsteps running, and the bark of a dog. Where was Fionn? Had he gone to look for a ship? A flash of anxiety jolted her to awareness. What if he'd gone on without her? He didn't need her to break his curse—she had no information about this time period that he didn't. But *she* needed *him*. He was her guide and cultural interpreter, and he had all the money. Her mind ran through the scenarios. What would she do, alone and penniless in Tudor Ireland?

She sat up and rubbed her eyes. "Don't be daft," she whispered to herself. "He'll not have left you." Fionn was probably meeting with Mr. Wilde, trying to arrange their passage to Galway.

She stood and adjusted her clothes. Reluctantly, she placed the linen-roll hat back on her head. She wouldn't sit around in this room waiting for Fionn. She opened the door and nearly tripped over Bran.

"Good morning, girl," Nora said. "Help me find Fionn?" Bran sat on her haunches and gave Nora a curious look. "I can't let him have all the fun, can I? Let's go."

She passed Mrs. Wilde in the hallway. "God be with you," the older woman said in greeting.

"Good morning," Nora replied. "Did Mr. O'Hanlon go out this morning?"

"He and Joseph left for the shop together."

Nora let herself and Bran out of the house and onto the street, which was already awash with people and horses and shopping stalls. She ducked around some barefooted wains playing tag on the cobblestones and felt a thrill at the thought of being alone in a strange city, in a strange century. She'd felt this same rush every time she'd been sent on a new assignment to some impoverished or war-torn country, each place so different, so eye-opening for a Belfast girl who had grown up with brick and concrete and the whitest of white people. Her senses had thrilled at the new smells, sights, sounds, and languages. The more unfamiliar the locale, the further away she felt from her old life. And the further the better.

"Lovely roast chicken for dinner?" a man shouted out to her, thrusting a live chicken in her face. The chicken squawked and beat its wings in protest of the man's tight grip. Nora stepped back, startled, then grinned and shook her head.

She turned onto the next street, wishing she'd paid more attention yesterday. "The Bear and the Ragged Staff," she muttered to herself. No such conveniences as house numbers. Finally, when she was starting to wonder if she was lost, the sign loomed up ahead. She pushed open the door and stepped inside, looking for Fionn. The only person in sight was a boy of maybe twelve or thirteen standing behind a long counter.

"Is Mr. Wilde here? I'm looking for a man who came with him this morning. Robert O'Hanlon. Have you seen him?"

"They're in the back," the boy said. "Shall I fetch them?"

"No need, Henry," Fionn's voice said. He had come out of the back room, the merchant on his heels. "What are you doing here, Nora?"

"Is there a printing press back there?" she asked, remembering what he had said about the bookseller's other business activities. "Can I see it?"

Fionn gave her an incredulous look. "No," he said simply. Then he turned to Mr. Wilde. "Most obliged for your advice."

"Best of luck to you, sir," Wilde replied as Fionn grabbed Nora by the elbow and ushered her out of the shop.

"What was that all about?" she asked. He stopped and turned to face her, exasperation written on his face.

"You need to at least try to blend in, instead of gawking at everything like you've never seen it before."

Nora blushed. "Ach, you're right, and I'm sorry. But imagine if you were to go to the future. You'd be walking around with your eyeballs on your cheeks, so you would."

Fionn laughed at this. "Fair enough. Let's go."

"Did Mr. Wilde tell you about a ship?" She followed him down another narrow street, toward the river.

"Aye, he mentioned a couple. Says our best bet is a Captain Deane. Should be setting sail any day now, once the wind is right."

"Everything takes forever, doesn't it? We could have driven to Galway in a couple of hours."

"Well, this is much more of an adventure. Do you sail as well as you ride?"

She narrowed her eyes at him. "Har har. I'm assuming we won't have to sail the ship ourselves."

"No, though I have to say there are few things I enjoy more than being out on the open ocean. I suppose it helps that I have no fear of death."

"Now you're just trying to wind me up. But I don't get seasick, if that's what you mean. At least, I didn't on the ferry. That's the only kind of boat I've been on."

He raised his eyebrows but said nothing.

The smell of fish grew stronger as they made their way past several ramshackle houses. The cobblestones became more and more broken, until they passed through a gate in the city wall and the stones gave way to mud, moss, and a few stubborn tufts of grass that had yet to be trampled.

Nora stopped walking, her mouth open. "This is amazing," she whispered. The River Liffey she knew was lined with warehouses, restaurants, apartment buildings, and a wide, smooth walkway dotted with benches and streetlamps adorned with hanging baskets, all far above the level of the water. Bridges spanned the water every few hundred yards. But none of it existed yet. There was only the great stone wall that surrounded the city, and then a muddy bank, and then water, crossed by a single bridge. A tall stone building surrounded by a wall loomed on the other side, accented by a few other buildings in the distance, but it was mostly grass and trees and shrubbery. Three ships bobbed in the water between the banks, none of which looked particularly seaworthy. Nora felt an uneasiness in her empty stomach. Compared to the sturdy modern ferry she'd taken from Ireland to England, the ships before her seemed like matchsticks stuck together with spit.

Fionn called out to two men walking by, carrying a wooden chest between them. "I'm looking for Captain Deane. Can you tell me where I might find him?"

"Aye, this way," one of the men said. They continued toward the largest of the ships. At least they wouldn't be traveling in what looked like fishing curraghs.

A short, burly man was hauling barrels off a cart and passing them to another man, who loaded them into a small boat tied up at the water's edge. The first man was bald except for a fringe of black hair that grew on the back of his head from ear to ear and fell past his shoulders. A leather jerkin covered his massive chest over a beige léine and dirty orange tights. He grunted with each barrel he hoisted off the cart. The men carrying the wooden chest nodded at him as they passed, then loaded the chest in the small boat alongside several barrels.

"Hello, there!" Fionn called. "Would you be Captain Deane?"

The man grunted again and hoisted another barrel. "Mr. Wilde told me you're the most reliable captain around—and a successful merchant in your own right," Fionn remarked calmly. The captain stopped his work and wiped his forehead with a dirty sleeve.

"Did'e, now? And I wonder what he'll be wanting me to pay'im for that compliment," he said.

"Well, it takes a good merchant to know another, to be sure," Fionn said. "What's your cargo today?"

"Who's asking?"

Fionn smiled and swept him a short bow. "My apologies. Robert O'Hanlon. An old friend of Mr. Wilde's, but my wife and I have been abroad for some time. I told him I was in need of a reliable captain, and he suggested you. Said the *Barke Burre* is a grand ship."

"Uh-huh." The captain's lips parted in a skeptical grin. Several of his teeth were missing. "And what is it you need this 'reliable captain' for? Goods?" He peered at Nora. "Or passengers?"

"Passage for my wife and myself to Galway."

The captain shot Nora a nasty look. "It's bad luck to bring a woman on board."

"Not so bad when the woman has gold," Fionn countered, pulling a full purse out of an inside pocket.

Captain Deane's eyes flicked to the heavy purse, then glowered back at Fionn. "As long as she keeps below and you stay with her."

"When do you set sail?"

"You're lucky we haven't already. The wind has finally shifted in our favor, God be praised. We're just loading the last of the cargo now. D'you have baggage? And does the hound travel with ye?"

"We travel light," Fionn answered, holding up the one sack he'd brought from his home. "And yes, my hound will accompany us. May we board now?"

"Let's see the gold first."

Fionn handed the purse to the captain, who weighed it in his hand carefully, then opened it to examine the contents.

"There will be more when we arrive in Galway, if my wife has not been troubled by your men," Fionn said, his voice hard. Nora's stomach fluttered.

The captain's lip curled in a sneer, and he gave Nora a dark look. "If she causes them no trouble, they'll cause her none." He pocketed Fionn's gold, then hollered at a man who was disembarking from a small boat he'd pulled up onto the muddy shore. "We've passengers. Take these two to MacSweeney."

The sailor looked at Nora in alarm, but then quailed under the captain's reproach. His back was bent, and he walked with a limp as they followed him to the small boat. Nora cursed the long léine and brat as she struggled to climb in and seat herself on one of the narrow boards. Fionn sat beside her, and Bran crouched awkwardly at their feet, her long legs not suited for such a small vessel. "And we're off," Fionn whispered in Nora's ear.

Three tall masts rose from the deck, crisscrossed with yards, the sails still tightly bound. Cannons jutted out from square windows below the main deck. The ship sat low in the water, its cargo already loaded. Nora's stomach squirmed as the sailor rowed them closer. She'd chased adventure all her adult life, but nothing compared with the thrill pulsing through her veins now. This was the golden age of seafaring, and here she was in the midst of it.

The limping sailor reached the long ladder that hung over the side of the ship and hung on to it tightly. "How will Bran get up there?" Nora asked. The hound could hardly climb the ladder.

"We'll send down a net and haul her up," Fionn said. Bran whined, and Nora scratched the wolfhound behind her ears and kissed the top of her head. Then she stood carefully, lifted her hem, which was now sopping wet, and stepped onto the ladder. When she neared the top, she looked down to see Fionn close behind her. Bran was still in the boat, looking mournfully up at them. Ungracefully, Nora swung her leg over the edge and managed to land on the deck without falling on her arse. Fionn leapt nimbly over the side. Without asking for assistance or permission, he grabbed a length of canvas from the deck, checked that the ropes attached to it were secure, and tossed it down to the sailor below. Bran reluctantly stepped into the net once it was unfolded. The sailor tied up the ends, and Fionn started hauling, being careful to not bump her too hard against the side of the ship. Bran stepped haughtily out of the canvas sack onto the deck, as though offended by her mode of transport.

"I guess he won't be showing us to our cabin," Fionn said, nodding toward the departing sailor, already rowing back to shore.

"Who cares?" Nora said. "This is brilliant!" All around her were ropes and rigging and barrels and more things she didn't recognize and couldn't begin to name. She rubbed her feet against the wooden planks and gawked up at the masts. Men dashed about all around them, carrying barrels and throwing ropes to one another and shouting. Some gave Fionn and Nora a cursory glance, but most ignored them. A gray-bearded man with a thick neck stomped over to them. "Who the devil are you?" he demanded.

"We've just paid your captain for passage," Fionn said.

"'Ave you now?" he said, moving to the side of the ship and looking down to where the captain was being rowed toward them.

"Aye," Nora said. "He said to talk to a man named MacSweeney."

"I'm MacSweeney, the quartermaster," the man said. His eyes were set close together, and they narrowed even farther as he took in their fine clothes. "We've only got one spare cabin, so I guess that's yours. I'll show you where it is; then I've work to do."

He led them the length of the deck, then lifted a hook in the floor, exposing a wooden ladder leading down into darkness. Nora followed the men down the ladder, and Bran leapt down after them.

MacSweeney pushed open a faded wooden door and waved them inside. Their "cabin" was excruciatingly small. Two narrow, short bunk-beds were set into one wall. A single square table had been nailed to the floor against another wall, two rickety chairs beside it. MacSweeney thrust an unlit glass-encased lantern into a large wooden box filled with sand that sat atop the table. The room was dimly lit by the daylight filtering in through a small round window.

"Fire's deadly to ships and all who live on them," MacSweeney said sharply. "Only use the lantern when you need it, and never without a cover."

"O'course," Nora answered.

"I'm sorry it's not more grand," Fionn remarked to Nora, casting a nervous look at her. "We could have waited for a bigger ship, but—"

"It's perfectly grand," Nora said. "Believe me, I've stayed in worse."

"As have I," he agreed.

"Will you be needing anything else, then?" MacSweeney asked, obviously keen to get back on top deck.

"No, thank you, Mr. MacSweeney," Nora said. "Only, how long d'you think the journey will be?"

"With these winds, and God with us, two days and nights should do it."

"Grand so," Nora replied, and MacSweeney ducked out of the cabin. Nora perched on the side of the bottom bunk. At least there wouldn't be the question of sharing a bed, for each bunk would barely hold one small person. "So, we're off. D'you think Granuaile will be easy to find?"

"As long as she doesn't think it's the English looking for her. She's given them a fair share of trouble, and vice versa."

"You don't think the captain meant what he said about me staying below the whole time, do ye?"

Fionn looked uneasy. "Women *are* said to be bad luck on a ship, and sailors are some of the most superstitious bastards I've ever met. I don't think they'll take too kindly to you wandering about."

Nora huffed. "It's going to be a long two days."

"Let's hope we don't get blown off course—then it could be three weeks."

"Always the optimist, aren't you?" Nora stretched out on the bunk and closed her eyes. Though she'd slept solidly the night before, she was still so very tired.

"Mind if I go up top for a while?" Fionn asked. "I used to own a ship much like this. That is, my current self owns one. I'd like to look around a bit, ask the captain a few questions once we've set sail and are on course."

"Aye, go on," Nora said. "No need for both of us to be cooped up down here."

"Bran will stay with you. And remember, you've your gun if you need it."

Nora cracked an eye open. "You think I'll need it?"

"If I did, I wouldn't leave you alone," he said. "But best to be careful all the same."

Nora drifted off to sleep, lulled by the movement of the ship and Bran's soft, steady breath on the floor beside her. When she opened her eyes again some time later, Bran was gone from the room. Fionn was sitting on the floor next to her, his back leaning against her bunk, his head tilted onto her mattress, and his eyes closed. She watched him silently, remembering the first time she'd seen him clearly in her dreams, sitting on a low stone wall, his eyes closed as they were now. Slowly, as though her hand was moving of its own accord, she trailed her fingers through his hair. His breath caught, but he didn't open his eyes. *What am I doing?* And yet she couldn't stop. She slid her fingers down to the nape of his neck and over to the base of his ear, letting the back of her hand slide down his neck to his collarbone. She'd never been with a man so handsome. She'd never even *known* a man so handsome. Would it be so bad, really, to fully enjoy the time they had together?

He turned his head, his gaze locking with hers. "Sleeping Beauty awakes," he said, his voice low. He grabbed her hand, which was lingering on his shoulder, and kissed her palm. Her breath quickened as his lips pressed into the soft, sensitive skin.

"How was your inspection of the ship? Is it seaworthy?" she murmured as he moved from her palm to the inside of her wrist. He held it to his nose and inhaled, though she was wearing no perfume.

"'Tis," he said. "And you smell amazing."

He twisted onto his knees so he was facing her. *Just go with it*, her inner voice urged, her defenses melting under the intensity of his gaze. She brought her other hand out from underneath the sheets and pulled him toward her. He lifted his body from the floor and slid on top of her, his gaze boring into hers. Blood and heat rushed through Nora's veins, and her chest tightened, as though she would not be able to fully breathe until she had him. She arched her neck and captured his lips with her own. A blur of sensation enveloped her: his weight pressing into every inch of her body, his warm skin under her fingertips, his lips hungry, pressing, as though he wanted her as much as she wanted him.

Then he pulled away, his eyes suddenly alert.

"What is it?" she asked, reaching up to catch his face in her hands, lest he pull farther away.

"Something's not right," he said. He slid off her so quickly he cracked his head on the bottom of the top bunk.

"What—" she started, but he put a finger to her lips, his head cocked toward the door. Then she heard it, too—the sound of men's voices raised in alarm. This was more than the usual bellow of orders and shouts exchanged between sailors. It was the sound of fear.

Chapter Six

"Stay here," Fionn said at the same time Nora clambered out of bed and reached for her gun.

"Like hell," she retorted.

"I'm serious. You need to stay here," he said, drawing his own weapon.

"I'm not hiding," she said, checking that her gun was loaded and slipping her feet into her boots.

Fionn grabbed both of her shoulders and turned her toward him. His face was intense, angry. "Nora, this isn't a game. If pirates have attacked the ship, they will rape you—all of them. Then they'll take you as a sex slave, and you'll wish you were dead."

Nora quailed at this, but what good would hiding do? If they won, they'd find her eventually. "I'm as good at fighting as any man." She pushed past him out of the room and started to climb the ladder to the top deck. She shoved open the trapdoor and peered out, still balancing on the ladder. The sailors were all lined up against one side of the ship, some firing over the edge, others crouched low and reloading their long guns. Her eyes found their target. Another ship, sails billowing, was advancing toward them. She pushed the door fully open and flung herself onto the deck, revolver raised and ready. Fionn came up behind her just as the deck rumbled beneath them. A cannon fired from the gun deck below, but the shot missed its mark and splashed into the water just short of the enemy.

Fionn grabbed a passing sailor. "Who's attacking us?" he demanded.

"Spanish pirates!" the sailor cried, wrenching his arm out of Fionn's grasp.

"That's good," Fionn muttered.

"Good?" Nora cried.

"They're after our cargo, not our lives," he said. "If they were Barbary pirates, it would be a different story."

Another cannon exploded from the gun deck, this one finding its mark. But now the other ship was close enough to fire as well. The *Bark Burre* lurched sideways, and Nora grabbed the railing as someone yelled, "We're taking on water! I need hands to the gun deck!"

"Let's go," Fionn said, and Nora followed him down another set of stairs to the deck below. A hole had been blown between two of the three huge cannons that pointed out of square windows on either side of the ship. It was just above the water level, but seawater sloshed through the opening in great waves whenever the ship rocked and swayed. The floor was already drenched. Nora grabbed a wooden bucket and started scooping water up from the floor, tossing it out the opposite window. Fionn had joined one of the gunners and was hoisting cannonballs into position when another blast tore through the side of the ship—and through the gunner Fionn had been helping.

"Fionn!" Nora screamed as a torrent of water swept him off his feet. The wave pulled back, dragging him with it. He caught hold of a rope and held it tight just as someone above deck yelled, "They're boarding!" The sailors below roared and started up the ladders. Nora made to follow them, but Fionn had regained his footing and grabbed her around the waist. The water was shin deep now, with more pouring in each time a wave slammed into the side of the ship.

"Take off your brat!" he yelled, tugging at her belt.

"What?"

"We need to disguise you as a man." He tore off the red cloak and the ruff around her neck, leaving only the léine, which he quickly tied tight with his own belt. Nora shoved the bag containing the relic down the front of the léine but kept her revolver gripped in her hand.

"Wear this," Fionn said, shoving his leather vest at her. She shrugged it on and tossed her hat into the water at their feet. By the time they made for the ladder, the roar of guns and the screams of the men had stopped. Fionn motioned for her to back away moments before the trapdoor above them opened and a Spanish sailor peered down. He shouted something to his captain and thundered down the ladder, a short curved sword in his hands.

Fionn stepped in front of Nora as the man screamed at them in Spanish, brandishing the cutlass.

"Drop it!" Nora bellowed, stepping swiftly in front of Fionn. But the pirate roared, and the blade rushed through the air toward her. Nora fired the gun but promptly lost her balance and crashed headfirst into the unforgiving iron of one of the cannons. When she staggered upright, Fionn and their assailant were locked together like warring bulls. The cutlass was nowhere to be seen. In one swift motion, Fionn captured one of the pirate's arms. The ensuing crack sent a jolt though Nora's stomach.

"Shite. I'm out of bullets," Nora said, examining her revolver as Fionn cracked the pirate's head against the cannon.

"It doesn't matter. Come on," Fionn said, heading to the ladder. But before he could climb it, three filthy faces peered down, the muzzle of a musket between them.

There was no choice but to surrender.

The Spanish pirates marched them up the ladder and then shoved them toward the stern with the rest of the crew. The sailors were bruised and beaten and disarmed, but at least most of them were alive. A thin man with a ridiculously plumed hat was strutting around the deck, shouting orders.

"They're searching the ship for anyone else. Then they'll start off-loading the cargo," Fionn whispered to her.

"And what will happen to us?" Nora whispered back. Before Fionn could answer, one of the Spaniards swung the butt of a rifle into his face. Nora stifled a cry, not wanting to reveal that she was female. Would Deane's men hand her over to the pirates? Would they blame the attack on her and throw her overboard as punishment for the bad luck she'd brought them? Pressing her hands together behind her back to mask her trembling, she risked a sideways glance at Fionn.

He can't be killed, she reminded herself. But the sight of his swelling cheekbone and the trickle of blood dripping off his chin drove home the point that he could be hurt, and badly.

It was close to an hour before the Spanish finished transporting the cargo to their own ship. Then, to Nora's immense relief, they sailed off, secure in the knowledge that the *Barke Burre* was unable to follow them. As soon as the crew was freed, every man set about frantically trying to repair the damage done to the ship before she took on too much water. But more than one sailor cast murderous glances at Nora, while muttering curses to his shipmates.

"Do they blame me?" Nora whispered to Fionn.

His face was grim. "I'll protect you. I'll bribe every sailor on this ship if I have to." He was leading her down to their cabin when a sailor panted over to her. "Mistress O'Hanlon, we need your help in the captain's quarters," he said, looking anywhere but directly at her.

"What's the matter?"

"Capt'n's injured," he said, leading the way down a narrow corridor. Fionn followed her, his hand on the small of her back. "And your husband said earlier you've some skill in healing."

"Jesus," Nora breathed, wondering what she would find. Possible scenarios ran through her mind: a gunshot wound, a sword in the gut, a cracked skull. But without sanitized instruments or any medical supplies whatsoever, she doubted she could be of any help. "What will happen with the ship?" she asked the harried sailor. "Can it be fixed?"

"We're putting in at Cork," he told her. "If we make it that far." He muttered something under his breath, but Nora only caught the words "trouble" and "woman" before he pushed open the door of the captain's quarters and motioned for Nora to step inside. "I found her, Capt'n."

Captain Deane's bed was set into the wall. The room was larger and better appointed than the one Nora and Fionn shared. But it was apparent that Deane was a merchant captain, not an English lord accustomed to all the finery Irish gold could buy. The table was covered in maps and nautical instruments, and a single lantern glowed from its protective sandbox. The high-backed chair in the corner looked well worn, a deep gully in the leather seat. MacSweeney, covered in blood and visibly beaten, stood by the captain's bed. A dog's bark broke the silence, and Bran came bounding out of the shadows of the room.

"There you are," Nora said when Bran came up to her, tail wagging. "I'm glad you're okay." Captain Deane was lying on the bed. The sheets beneath him were crimson, a marked contrast to the shining pallor of his skin.

"What happened?" Fionn asked.

"Shot him in the belly," the quartermaster said darkly. "He promised them no trouble if they spared the life of his crew, and then they did this." He cast a condescending look at Fionn. "What are you doing here? You should be helping the men, unless you're keen on drowning."

"My place is by her side," Fionn said, moving closer to Nora. "And I don't see you out there."

"My place is by my captain's side, to make sure this woman doesn't bring us even more ill luck." MacSweeney stepped between Fionn and Captain Deane.

"For Christ's sake, it's grand, Fionn. Go on and help the men. Mr. MacSweeney knows that if he lifts a finger against me, it's his beloved captain who will suffer."

"And Bran will rip out his throat for good measure," Fionn added. The wolfhound grunted, as if in agreement. "Are you certain?" he asked Nora in an undertone.

She nodded. "Go on. I've got this." *I hope.*

After giving MacSweeney one more threatening glare, Fionn left the room. Gently, Nora lifted the sheet that covered Deane's torso. *Jesus, Mary, and Joseph.* She tried to keep her face impassive, knowing the captain's eyes were on it. "Bring me alcohol and clean sheets, if there are any. But first, can you lift him up a bit? I need to have a look at his back."

The captain screamed as MacSweeney grabbed him under the arms and lifted. Nora quickly slid her hands over the captain's back, then nodded at MacSweeney to lay him down. "It's not gone through," she said. "D'you have any medical supplies?"

"Robson was our surgeon," he said. "The barber. But he's dead."

"Can you get his things?" she asked. "There might be something in there I can use."

MacSweeney looked first at Captain Deane, who grunted, "Go."

The quartermaster left, and Nora looked frantically about for some kind of sterile cloth, anything she could use to try to stop the bleeding. But there was nothing in sight. Not willing to let the man bleed to death for the sake of propriety, she took off her léine. The handbag containing the relic had been shoved down her bra, and she set it on the table beside them. Then she folded the léine and pressed it firmly over the wound. Even if she managed to stop the bleeding, there was nothing she could do to treat the inevitable infection. In 2005, she'd never been without some kind of disinfectant, even in the most remote hellholes of Earth.

"Damned pirates," Deane moaned. "Could have at least shot me in the leg. I've two of 'em."

"You're going to be grand, so you are," she said, keeping the pressure firm. Her mind was reeling. What could she possibly use? She'd heard of maggots being added to a wound in extreme circumstances to eat away the infected flesh, but first she had to get the bullet out and stop the bleeding.

MacSweeney burst into the room and stopped short at the sight of her, standing in her underwear and pressing the now-bloody léine to his captain's stomach.

"What the devil are you doing, woman?" he demanded, tossing a bottle of alcohol and the barber's leather kit onto the table. Nora craned her neck to see the contents without lifting the pressure from Deane's abdomen. A razor and a set of pliers were the only things she quickly identified.

"I needed a clean cloth, and this was the closest thing I could find," she said, well aware that her cheeks were flaming. "How far are we to Cork?"

"Nearly there. The shipmaster thinks we'll make it, praise be to God." He stared openly at her bra.

"Pay attention," she snapped. "I need to take the bullet out. Hold him down."

She grabbed the pliers from the barber-surgeon's kit and held them over the lantern flame for several seconds, hoping it would kill at least some of the germs. She waved them in the air to cool them off, then nodded at MacSweeney. Deane writhed in pain as she felt around inside the wound, but the quartermaster was able to hold him steady enough for Nora to grasp the bullet and pull it out. Deane went limp, his entire body beading with sweat.

"Is that it, then?" MacSweeney asked.

"No. I need to cauterize his wound to stop the bleeding. Is there a large fire somewhere on the ship? It should be extremely hot."

"Are you mad? Half the ship's taking water. O'course there's no fire."

"Ballix. Grand so, I'll use gunpowder and the lantern."

"Like hell you will!"

"I don't have time to argue with you," she shot back. "If I don't stop his bleeding, he will die before we can get him off this ship. And I doubt any doctor in Cork can save him at this rate." A flush of fear ran through her. What would happen to her if Deane died under her care? Would Fionn really be able to protect her from the rage of two dozen sailors?

"You've a lot of opinions, for a woman."

"Tell me something I don't already know. Are you going to help me, or not? Hold this tight over his wound. Did they take your gun?"

"Aye." He moved beside her and pressed his hands on the cloth.

"Is there one close by?" she asked in exasperation. "I just need a new bullet, or some gunpowder."

"In the chest," the captain wheezed. Nora hadn't realized he was still conscious. "False bottom."

She ran to the chest against the wall and dumped the contents onto the floor, frantically feeling for the trip to the false bottom. It popped open, and she pulled out a rusted musket. There was a small bag of black powder—mercifully dry—in a metal box beside it.

"All right, take it off," she instructed MacSweeney. He removed her now-sodden léine from the captain's wound, and she winced at the sight of all that blood. She felt for a pulse in the captain's wrist—it was just barely there. "Get him something to bite down on," she ordered.

MacSweeney found a rod in the barber's kit and put it between the captain's teeth. Then Nora splashed whiskey on the wound. Deane howled in pain, then fell silent, his entire body beading with sweat.

"Have you done this before?" MacSweeney asked, glaring at her. "Are you sure you're a healer?"

"I'm no doctor, and no, I haven't done this before," Nora said. "But I've read about it and know people who've done it, so . . ."

"If he dies, it will be your fault," MacSweeney growled.

Nora flinched but didn't respond. She sprinkled the gunpowder in a circle around the wound. Then she crossed herself and said a quick Hail Mary in her head.

"Are you a papist?" MacSweeney gaped. "You'll not be poisoning his soul with your papist ways!"

"Will you shut up?" she roared at him. "Or get the hell out. I'm trying to save this man's life." Bran, crouched at her heels, gave a low growl. MacSweeney fell silent. "Pass me the lantern. Then hold him down." He did.

She eased the candle from its holder in the glass cage. "Got him?"

MacSweeney grunted, pressing his hands down on the captain's shoulders.

Nora took a deep breath, praying she wouldn't be hastening the man's death—and perhaps her own. Then she held the candle to the gunpowder.

It went up in a ring of flame and a flash of intense heat. Deane's mouth opened, and his eyes rolled wildly in his head. MacSweeney's arms rippled with the effort of holding his captain still. "Just one more thing," Nora said, splashing more whiskey onto the now-blackened wound. Deane's weakened system couldn't handle it, and he collapsed back into the mattress, unconscious at last. Nora grabbed his wrist and then sighed in relief—he was still alive. For now. She found some thread and a needle in the barber's kit and stitched up the wound. Without modern antibiotics, Deane's life still hung in the balance, but at least he wouldn't bleed out before they reached Cork.

She dragged a chair over beside his bed and sank into it.

"I'll sit with him," she said, holding his limp wrist between her fingers. "Could I trouble you to find me something to wear? I don't fancy going out dressed in naught but my skivvies."

MacSweeney was almost as pale as Deane, but he jerked a nod in her direction and left the room, wiping his bloody hands on his trews.

Nora examined her own red hands. Had she done the right thing? Why hadn't she thought to bring medical supplies from the 1920s?

The door opened and Fionn came in, interrupting her morbid thoughts. "Are you all right?" he asked, alarmed. She was almost naked, smeared and splattered with Deane's blood.

"I'm grand," she said automatically. "I don't know about the captain, though. I stopped the bleeding, but—"

"MacSweeney told me," Fionn said. He handed her a dirty léine. "He also told the men that you saved the captain's life, and that anyone who said a word against you would be run through."

"That's a relief," she said, accepting the léine. She didn't ask where he'd gotten it, or from whom. She stuffed the bag containing the relic back into her bra, then shrugged the léine on over her head and shivered. Now that the warmth of exertion had worn off, a chill was seeping into her bones. Fionn took one look at her and pulled her into his arms. "You did all you could."

"I just feel so helpless," she muttered into his chest. "What's the point of being from the future if you can't help people?"

"You *did* help him," Fionn said. "But we've had this discussion before—you can't help everyone. Being from the future doesn't make you God."

"Well, he's in the hands of God now. With no antibiotics, that wound is sure to get infected, and—"

Fionn put a finger to her lips. "Shh. Stop blaming yourself. 'Twas the Spanish who shot him, not you. We're almost to Cork, where they're putting in for repairs."

"Will they go on to Galway?" she asked. "With all the cargo stolen?"

"I don't know. It could take weeks to repair the ship. We may have to find another one."

"Did the pirates take all your money?"

"I'm better at hiding things than they are at finding them," he said with a smile. "We'll be all right. And we'll buy you some proper clothes once we make land."

Another sailor came to watch over the captain, and Nora joined Fionn on the top deck. The men were somber and walked with heavy steps and stooped shoulders. "Were many killed?" Nora asked.

"Four," Fionn answered. "They've already been buried at sea."

Nora stayed by the rail as the *Barke Burre* limped to the harbor at Cork. The tiny city—a village, really—beckoned them, promising rest for the weary sailors in the arms of its taverns and brothels. Nora said a silent prayer as the men lowered Captain Deane into the waiting boat that would take him to shore.

"I need to say something," Fionn said quietly, looking out at the spires of the cathedral that rose above everything else on the horizon.

"Ach, aye?"

"About earlier today. Before the attack."

Nora's pulse quickened. She hadn't forgotten, despite her fear for her life and her worry over Captain Deane. There'd been no audience in their tiny cabin, no need to pretend they were a couple. It had just been the two of them, drawn together by an attraction she could no longer deny.

"It was a mistake," he said.

Her hands tightened on the rail, the sting of rejection whipping her in the face like a blast of salt water from the sea. She was no stranger to the feeling, but this time it had a stronger bite to it. They'd known each other for only a short while, but they'd already had a lifetime's worth of shared experiences. He was, she had to admit, one of the only people who truly knew her. Maybe the only person.

"How do you mean?" she asked, her tone cautious. Perhaps she'd misunderstood him. She'd felt his desire. What had happened in their cabin had been no mistake.

He turned to face her, his eyes imploring her to understand. "I told you about my past. I can't get close to people—it always ends badly for everyone. I *must* keep my distance. It's the only way I've learned to survive."

She squared her shoulders, still gripping the rail with one hand. "Then why—?"

"Because you're unlike anyone I've ever known," he blurted out, his tone hot. "And we've been thrown together in this mad endeavor, to try and change history, for Christ's sake! And I keep trying to protect you, but you always end up protecting me instead, and . . ." His breath was labored, and he dropped his eyes, as though ashamed of his outburst. "I'm very fond of you, Nora," he said, more calmly this time. "And I'm glad you're here with me. But please understand that I just . . . *can't*."

She nodded slowly, digesting this. She still had so many confusing thoughts and feelings around Fionn. It seemed ludicrous that she could have a relationship with Fionn mac Cumhaill. Yet each day they spent together, eating and drinking and bantering and trying to change the world, he seemed less and less like some mythological giant. Just like everyone, he had his good traits and bad traits, his weaknesses and strengths. Which was why she had thought maybe—just maybe—it could work between them.

But she also knew a thing or two about losing those you loved and didn't blame him for not wanting to relive that experience every time a pretty girl walked into his life.

"I *do* understand," she said, forcing her lips into a smile. "It's grand, so it is."

"Are you certain?" he asked. "I don't mean to hurt you."

She cocked an eyebrow at him. "Ach, Fionn, it'll take more than a case of blue balls to hurt me. Besides, we've a tough job ahead of us. Best not to get distracted."

It was their turn to be taken to shore. Nora climbed carefully down the wet rope ladder, past the holes the Spanish cannons had blasted into the hull of their ship. The sailor who helped her into the boat had an angry red slash across his cheek. "How long will repairs take?" Fionn asked as a couple of men lowered Bran in a fishing net.

One of them shook his head. "They'll not be doing repairs any time soon, especially not with the captain on his deathbed."

"Why not?" Nora asked, moving over so that Bran could settle herself by her feet.

"Because every able-bodied man will be on the next ship out of here, no matter where it's headed. Haven't you heard? Cork is overrun with the plague. The only people waiting around will be those with a death wish."

Chapter Seven

"The . . . the plague?" Nora sputtered. "As in, the Black Death?"

"'Tis the one," Fionn said. "I don't suppose you've one of your fancy vaccinations for that?"

She shook her head. She'd worked in West Africa for a few months during an Ebola outbreak. As a member of the logistics team, she'd had no direct contact with the infected patients, but she remembered the long, arduous procedure the doctors and nurses, all of whom wore full-body hazmat suits, went through each morning and night to protect themselves from the contagion. Even the support personnel had been subject to daily temperature readings and strict rules about every movement and contact.

The plague was just as infectious, and just as deadly. And they'd no hazmat suits, no hand-washing stations, no quarantine tents. They were as vulnerable as anyone else.

"How bad is it?" she asked the sailor as he rowed them closer and closer to the infested city.

"Well, they say the churchyard's overflowing, so they've dug some more pits just outside the gates. One in five, they're saying. Divine punishment for the rebellion."

Nora fought off the panic that clawed at her nerves. "What if we can't find another ship? Can we at least find horses? Ride to Galway?"

The muscles around Fionn's mouth tightened. "It's not a journey I'd take you on willingly. It's at least four days of hard riding, and the roads in this part of the country are near impassable. Then there's the risk of tories—highwaymen—and—"

"Aye, but if people are fleeing the city on ships, they'll likely bring the plague with them. Riding would be less risky. And we have to keep moving. *We have to get to Granuaile.*"

"Can you handle a four-day ride?" he said doubtfully.

Nora's legs still ached from their ride to Dublin. "I'm not looking forward to it," she admitted. "But I'll do whatever it takes."

An hour later, Fionn had bribed a city official to sell them two of the guards' horses. They were debating a quick trip into Cork for food and fresh clothing when a cart trundled past the city gates. It was loaded with so many bodies that a jolt from an inopportune pothole sent several of them tumbling over the wooden sides and onto the street. Bran's ears flattened, and she emitted a soft whine.

"Jesus, Mary, and Joseph," Nora breathed, crossing herself. Some of the bodies had been wrapped in sheets, but others lay sprawled and uncovered, the skin blackened. A head hung grotesquely off the back of the cart, bouncing with every turn of the wheels on the dirt road.

Fionn set his jaw. "We can't risk it," he said. "I could go myself, knowing I can't die of it. But I can still contract the disease and spread it to you. We must leave at once."

Nora's body gave a great shudder. Her borrowed léine hung on her loosely, and the biting wind attacked her uncovered skin. Her feet were bare; her legs were splattered with mud up to her knees. Fionn shrugged out of his heavy wool cloak and passed it to her wordlessly, the concern clear in his eyes. She clutched the cloak tightly around her chest, trying to transfer Fionn's warmth to her own frigid body as they rode away from the cart, away from the city guards, who were helpless in the face of this invisible, mortal enemy.

Nora's rosary still hung around her neck—above the purse she'd hidden against her chest—and she touched the beads with her fingertips. She didn't care if it branded her a papist; it was her one tie to her old life. Lifting it to her lips, she said a prayer for the poor souls whose bodies had been piled in that cart. Soon they would be dumped unceremoniously into a pit on the outskirts of the city. There they would lie until some modern developer dug them up. Teams of archeologists would marvel that Cork had suffered such a huge outbreak of the plague while the rest of Ireland had gone mostly untouched.

And Nora could see why. The road from Kildare to Dublin in the English-settled Pale had been bordered with lush fields, full of white sheep and black cattle, and sturdy homesteads with neat stone fences and fertile gardens. Here, just outside of Cork, the fields were bare. No, more than bare—they were as blackened as the corpses in that cart. There was no bellowing of sheep, no soft lowing of cattle, no sign of any living thing at all. There were no foxes for Bran to hunt, no rabbits. Even the birds had deserted the area. They rode by a shell of a house. Mud-and-wattle walls still standing in an empty field, roof missing, door open. A faint stench wafted toward them on the road, and Nora slowed her horse. But Fionn took hold of the reins and tugged them both forward.

"What happened here?" she asked.

"This is what happens when the people fight back," he said, anger evident in the tightness of his muscles, the straight line of his back. She waited, knowing there would be more. After he'd regained control, he added, "Elizabeth sent Lord Grey and several thousand English soldiers to quell the Desmond Rebellion. To say they lost is an understatement. They were decimated. Grey showed no mercy. The leaders and any known sympathizers were hung, drawn, and quartered. Many of the regular people, who'd had no part in the rising, were slain as well, because their chieftain or lord had dared fight. Then the English armies set about slaughtering the cattle and burning the fields."

"Slash-and-burn tactics," Nora said, her eyes on the desolation around them. "I've seen them used before by rebels fighting the government. But the people it really hurts are the innocents."

Fionn's jaw was so tight she wondered how he could speak. "They say one out of every three Munstermen died. No one was spared—men, women, children, and the elderly. Those who weren't slaughtered or executed starved to death. Those who had the strength crawled their way to Cork, just in time for the plague." Bitterness dripped from his words. His nostrils flared, and his lips curled back over his teeth. "Grey thinks the Irish are nothing but barbarians. Animals to be destroyed, so he can repopulate our country with the 'genteel English.' They've already started bringing over settlers, giving them Irish estates. The few proud souls who survived this massacre will become servants and slaves on their ancestral lands."

There was nothing Nora could say to this. It seemed she had arrived in Ireland's darkest night, when the last vestiges of the old Gaelic world were being cruelly stamped out, when the stage was being set for the struggle that would consume her country for the next four hundred years. Munster would be free again one day, although centuries of English rule would have an indelible influence on the people and culture. But Ulster . . . Ulster still suffered under the English thumb. And all she could do for the time being was ride through the ruined countryside toward a woman whom Brigid believed could help them.

It started to rain after several hours, not the usual mild drizzle that came and went on any given day, but a hard, steady rain that forced them to bow their heads and curl into themselves. Fionn's cloak repelled a great deal of the water from Nora's chilled skin, but he was soaked through, his gray hair flat against his forehead, water streaming off the end of his nose. Up ahead was a small copse of trees in the middle of a barren field, and he turned his horse toward it. The horses picked their way toward the middling shelter, maneuvering around stones and the barren stalks of destroyed crops.

Nora slid off her horse gratefully, her legs happy for the change in position. The trees above them caught most of the rain. Bran shook herself hard, soaking the trunks around them. Nora shrugged off the cloak and shook it, following Bran's lead, then offered it to Fionn.

"Your turn to be warm," she said, holding it out to him. He looked as though she had handed him her horse's droppings.

"Never in over a thousand years have I allowed a lady to ride cold and wet beside me while I stayed warm and dry under a cloak."

"Well, it's actually a bit damp and not very warm," Nora said, still thrusting it toward him. "Really, you'd be doing me a favor, so you would."

"Nice try," he said. "How are your legs?"

"Grand," she lied. "I could do with a shower, though. Or a hot tub."

A rustling in the trees made Nora stop and listen.

"It's just Bran," Fionn said, noting her worry.

"It's not," Nora said. Bran was beside her, and the sound had come from the other direction. "I lost my weapon on the ship," she said, moving toward the horses. "Are you armed?"

Fionn slid a small dagger from his waistband, but there was no sign of his revolver. The rustle came again, and something emerged out of the bushes behind them.

At first Nora thought it was an animal, some sort of dog, crouching low to the ground. Then her fingers flew to her mouth. It was a person, crawling toward them on hands and knees. A woman, judging by the shriveled sacks that hung from her chest. She was naked, every bone visible under the pale skin that stretched over her skeleton. Her eyes were hidden under the matted hair that hung over her face.

Nora rushed toward her with a cry. The woman flinched back, then raised one bony hand in supplication. A moan escaped from dry, cracked lips. "Sweet Jesus," Nora said, falling to her knees. The woman was still on all fours, and when Nora gently laid Fionn's cloak on her back, she collapsed under its weight. As gently as she could, Nora gathered the woman in the cloak like she would a child in a swaddling cloth. Then she rolled her over so that her head rested on Nora's lap. The woman closed her eyes, dark hollows in her sunken face. The skin around her mouth was stained green.

"She's been eating nettles," Fionn said, crouching beside her. His jaw was set.

"What can we do? We don't have any food," Nora asked.

He shook his head. "There's naught we can do at this point. She's moments away from death."

"We could take her with us," Nora insisted. "We'll pass through Limerick tomorrow. Surely someone there can help her. At least we could buy some food and find her some shelter."

"She would never survive the journey," he said.

"How will we know unless we try?" Nora said, the blood rushing to her cheeks. "We can't just leave her here to die!"

"She's going to die whatever we do," he said gently. "I know you want to help her, but it's too late."

She knew he was right. This was not the first time she'd seen the effects of famine close-up. Even if they had a modern hospital at their disposal, complete with IV drips and monitors and feeding tubes, this woman's body was too far gone. Several of her internal organs had probably already shut down. It was too late to reverse the process. Hot, angry tears splashed down Nora's face.

"What's this woman ever done to them, except try to survive?" she said, clutching the emaciated body to her. "And the queen of England decides to starve her to death so that she can steal her land and give it to some motherfucker who doesn't deserve it, who has no idea whose land he stands on."

"Nora," Fionn said, his hand tight on her arm. "Nora." His use of her name made her look up. His eyes were wet as well. "We need to keep going."

"I'm not just leaving her here," she said through gritted teeth.

"She's dead. It's over." Nora looked down at the face in her lap. The green mouth hung slackly open, but no breath came from it. "There are more like her," he said. "And they are all starving, and we have two healthy horses. If we stay in one place for too long, they'll find us, and if their numbers are great enough, they will overwhelm us." He looked down sadly at the dead woman wrapped in his cloak. "I don't know if it's true—I wasn't here to see it for myself—but they said some even resorted to cannibalism."

"I'm not afraid of them," Nora said, but she slid the woman gently from her lap and started to unwrap the cloak. "Look at her. She could barely crawl."

"They're not all as weak," Fionn said. "But they are as desperate as a people can get. We have to keep moving."

"Can't we at least bury her?"

Fionn shook his head. "With what? It's a four-day ride to Galway, and we've no food of our own. The longer we go, the weaker we'll get. We'll find food and shelter in Limerick, but between here and there this is all we'll see. Burned-out fields and starving people."

Nora walked numbly back to her horse and allowed Fionn to help her into the saddle. She glanced behind her as they left the shelter of the trees. The woman's body was so frail, so thin, it seemed to melt into the earth. Perhaps the fairies would take her to the Otherworld, where she would spend her days and nights dancing and feasting and being merry with her fellow countrymen. A few months ago, the idea would have seemed ludicrous to Nora. But now that she was riding through the past beside Fionn mac Cumhaill, anything seemed possible. She fingered her rosary and said a prayer, asking God to send the Little

People to this abandoned grove. She didn't care who took possession of the woman's soul—God or the *sidhe*—as long as someone stepped in where Nora herself had failed.

They slept that night in an abandoned cottage near the River Blackwater. The water was freezing, but Nora plunged in, desperate to wash away the mud and despair that caked her body. She'd taken off her léine and laid it on the bank of the river. Fionn and Bran were there, too, all of them silent and sober. Nora didn't even care that she was naked in front of them. Sex and romance seemed unimportant in light of the tragedy unfolding around them. They brought the horses inside for the night. Fionn found a flint box and a few crumbling sods of turf and made a fire in the hearth of the empty cottage. They huddled together for warmth under his wool cloak on the mat of stale rushes that had once held a family. Bran stretched out beside them.

There were no signs of what had happened to those who had lived in the cottage. No bodies. Nora told herself that maybe they had gone to stay with relatives in another county, one the English had yet to turn into hell on Earth. But did such a place even exist in Ireland anymore?

She turned the box containing the relic over in her hands. She needed a better way to keep it safe. To keep it close to her. She lifted the lid and brought the bone out, examining it in the firelight.

"Going somewhere? Or . . . sometime?" Fionn asked, a nervous twitch in his voice.

"I'm just afraid I'll lose it. I can't keep carrying it in my purse; what if it's stolen?"

"How does it work? Obviously not from just touching it."

"I don't know," she admitted. "I think Brigid has to be there as well. The first time I used it, I was with a woman named Mary, but I think she was Brigid in disguise, like how she posed as a Brigidine Sister in 1923. And both times I had to squeeze the relic and concentrate really hard on where I wanted to go."

Fionn held out his palm, and she dropped the relic into it, pushing away the sudden fear that he might vanish from beside her. He held it up in front of his face, squinting at it. "Let me see your rosary."

"My rosary?"

"Aye. Give it here."

She lifted the beads from around her neck and coiled them into his outstretched hand. "What are you doing?"

"You wear this on you all the time?"

"Aye. For safekeeping."

"And would it be sacrilegious to add to it?"

Without thinking, she snatched the beads back and pressed them to her chest. "My brother made these for me."

"I know," he said gently. "And I know how much you treasure them. That's why it's the safest place for this." He rolled the relic between his finger and thumb. "I could just rework the wire a bit. There's a groove here on the bone that would make a good hold."

Nora still clutched the wooden beads in her hand. She wanted them to stay exactly as they had been on the day Eamon had given them to her. After she succeeded in saving him, she'd be able to show him that she'd kept them all these years. But losing the relic would mean losing her last chance to see Eamon again. She pressed the warm beads to her lips, then held them out to Fionn.

"Just try not to mess them up too much."

He used a sharp stone as a tool to worry the wire loose. The fire glinted off his silver hair as his fingers danced nimbly among the beads and the tiny cross. Then he straightened and handed it to her.

"I suppose it's symbolic, isn't it?" Nora said, inspecting his handiwork. The smooth white bone now dangled next to the cross. "Jesus and Brigid. Catholicism and paganism. Both parts of my life now." She lifted the rosary over her head and tucked it inside her léine, feeling the unfamiliar shape against her chest.

"You keep those safe, and I'll keep you safe," he said, pulling the cloak tighter around her shoulders.

She relaxed against him, aware of his heat beside her—and of his words on the ship. She would respect his wishes. "I feel like we should be telling stories around the campfire."

His chest moved with quiet laughter. "Shall I tell you one?"

"Aye. Tell me a story of your people. Never thought I'd get it straight from the horse's bake."

"Very well." He stared into the flames, thinking. "I'll tell you about my son, Oisín."

"Is it a sad story?" She was beginning to feel sleepy now that her body was warming.

"I suppose it is," he said. "Though there's plenty of joy in it as well." He shifted position slightly. "Bran remembers this, don't you?" He ruffled her fur, and she yawned and stretched. "In fact, it was she who found Oisín's mother, Sadbh."

"Oh, aye? Was she hunting?"

"As a matter of fact, she was, with her sister Sceolan. Only when she caught up to the doe that they were tracking, they could tell something was different. They had a knack for that. Instead of bringing her down, the hounds started to play with her. Not the expected behavior from Ireland's greatest hunters, to be sure."

"Let me guess. The doe was Sadbh?"

He smiled warmly. "Ah, I knew you were getting the hang of this. Aye, Sadbh led us to the Hill of Allen, where we spent the night. When I awoke, she was in the form of a beautiful woman—"

"O'course she was."

He seemed flustered by her interruption. "Anyway, I offered her my protection, and . . . well, she became my wife, after a fashion. We were happy. But I had to leave for a time to fight a group that was invading from the east. When I returned, Sadbh was gone."

"She left you?"

"Not of her own volition. She'd been cursed by one of the sidhe. As long as she was under my roof, my protection, she could retain her human form. But the sidhe lured her away while I was gone." He turned his head slightly so she couldn't see his eyes. "The last my men saw of her, she had turned back into a doe and was running toward the forest, following a hooded figure. We never found her again."

Nora placed her hand on his arm. "I'm sorry."

"We did, however, find a little boy. It was years later, o'course. Bran and Sceolan found him under a rowan tree. They protected him from the other hounds. When I arrived, I recognized his mother's eyes. He'd been raised by a doe, so he told us, but she'd been forced to leave him by a dark figure."

"And the boy was your son?"

"Aye. I named him Oisín, little fawn. And he was a wonderful child, full of life and passion and bravery. He became a great poet. And my best friend, once he was grown."

"I've heard stories about him. About how he went to Tír na nÓg and—" She cut herself off, realizing this was the sad part of Fionn's story.

"Yes," Fionn said, nodding. "He fell in love with one of the sidhe, Niamh of the Golden Hair, she was called. She took him to Tír na nÓg, knowing he could never return. He was happy there, or so I believe. But he longed to come back and see me. She granted his wish on one condition: he must remain on his horse while in our world. What he did not know was that hundreds of years had passed on Earth for the few years he had spent in Tír na nÓg. My people, the Fianna, were no more. Everyone he had known was long dead."

"But you were still alive."

"Aye, but I was in a different part of the country. By the time the news reached me, Oisín was dead. Do you know what happened?"

She kept her eyes on the ground. "Aye. He got off his horse—to help someone, wasn't it?—and turned into an old man. He died soon after, but not before he told the stories of the Fianna. That's how we know of them today."

Something like pride flickered across Fionn's face. "He was a master storyteller. The best of us all. I only wish I'd been there."

"He'd been gone hundreds of years. You couldn't possibly have known he'd come back."

"I know," he said. "But it taught me one thing: sometimes second chances are just that—chances."

Chapter Eight

When she awoke the next morning, Nora could barely move her legs, so sore were they from the day's ride. She walked for the first couple of hours, allowing her muscles to limber up and work out some of the discomfort. Bran ran alongside them, occasionally disappearing to follow some interesting scent. Nora's stomach burned with hunger, but she refused to complain, even to herself. The hunger pangs made her think of Pidge Gillies and her desperate hunger strike. They'd known each other for such a short period of time, but she missed her friend greatly. What would Pidge have thought of all this? *Perhaps I can go see her again sometime.*

They walked and rode in silence for most of the day, stopping at the rare patches of green grass so their horses could graze and drinking their fill at each river or stream they encountered.

"I've been thinking more about the Battle of Kinsale," Nora said as they remounted after one such break.

"Oh?" Fionn's voice was cautious.

"We can win it. I know it's several years away, but maybe it's what Brigid wants us to work with Granuaile to change. We both know the battle was lost mostly because of bad luck and miscommunication, but we can change that." When he didn't say anything, she took it as an invitation to continue. "My history is a bit shite, but Eamon always said that Hugh O'Neill was the closest thing to a savior that Ireland had. He routed the English at the Battle of the Yellow Ford and built a unified Irish army, something that hadn't been done since Brian Boru." Her voice lifted in a glimmer of hope. "Maybe we—and Granuaile—can help him win Kinsale."

Fionn raised an eyebrow but otherwise stayed quite still on his horse. "And how do you propose we do that?"

"Think about it!" Nora was excited now, the hunger and discomfort driven from her mind by the possibility of victory. "We're both soldiers from the future, so we've loads of military knowledge they don't. I could teach the Irish to make explosives. I mean, I wasn't the explosives expert for our division, but I'm sure we can figure out how to work with the materials on hand. You trained with Liam Lynch; you must be an expert in guerrilla warfare. *And* we know all the reasons why they lost. We just need to convince Granuaile to believe us. If she's not involved herself, maybe she can help us convince O'Neill."

Fionn raised a finger. "Aye, there's the rub. What makes you think he'll cooperate?"

Why was he being so obstinate? "Why wouldn't he? He's a *great* leader. If we give him the tools he needs to achieve certain victory, why wouldn't he do what we say? We've giving him an advantage the English could only dream of!"

"What do you know about O'Neill?" He kept his tone measured and calm, but she sensed a growing frustration underlying his words.

"I know enough. He's the closest thing we have to a king of Ireland, the only one who can unite the clans! Actually, why wait for the Battle of Kinsale? We could help O'Neill rally the chiefs together to challenge the English *now*."

"Nora," he said, and his voice was slow and kind, as though speaking to a child. "It's more complicated than that. Much more."

"Why?" she demanded. "Why wouldn't it work?"

"Because sometime soon, perhaps as we speak, O'Neill receives the earldom of Tyrone from Queen Elizabeth I as a reward for his services to the Crown in suppressing the Desmond Rebellion."

Nora stared at him uncomprehendingly. "He . . . what?"

"You must know he was the Earl of Tyrone."

"Well, aye, but I assumed it was just an honorary title, one he used to appease the English. He was also *The* O'Neill. That's the banner he fought under, wasn't it?"

"Not yet. Turlough Luineach O'Neill is The O'Neill."

Nora brushed this off. "He *becomes* The O'Neill—that's what's important."

Fionn grabbed the reins of Nora's horse and brought them both to a halt. "Did you not hear a word I said? Your great hero Hugh O'Neill did this." He spread out his arm, indicating the scorched earth all around them. "He fought *for* Lord Grey, not against him. *He* starved that woman to death. *He* burned his own countrymen out of their homes. *He* rounded up the leaders of the rebellion and had them executed."

"But . . . no . . . ," Nora said weakly. "That's impossible. He wouldn't have."

"You're right: your history *is* shite. But it's not your fault; history books have always been selective. Yes, O'Neill eventually turned his back on the English. Yes, he was the military commander who won the Battle of the Yellow Ford. He did all those things you love him for. But he didn't do it for love of Ireland. And his army was far from unified. Everything that man ever did was for his own ambition. When it suited him to serve the Crown, he willingly spilled the blood of his own people. And when he saw the tides turning, he switched coats. Again and again and again. He was as divisive as the rest of the chiefs, and the only rebellion he would support was his own. So you can try and talk to him if you'd like, but right now he's probably licking Elizabeth's boots and paving the way for English settlers in Munster. I doubt he'd be interested in knowing how to make a land mine. Even if he was, he'd be just as likely to use it against the Irish as for them."

Nora sat stock still on the back of her horse, stunned. Whenever she'd heard the name Hugh O'Neill, it had been uttered with pride and sorrow—pride that he'd brought the Irish to the brink of victory, and sorrow that it hadn't been enough. Many considered him one of Ireland's greatest heroes, up there with Brian Boru and Jim Larkin and Liam Lynch. Now she didn't know what to think.

"I'm sorry," Fionn said. "I didn't mean to sound so harsh. Your idea is sound, in principle. But I don't trust O'Neill. Any information we give him now he might share with his English overlords to curry favor. We'd do best to wait until he's decided to switch sides on his own. Then perhaps we can change the outcome."

"What else am I wrong about?" Nora asked, recovering her voice. "We *did* almost win, did we not?"

"Aye," Fionn said, tapping his horse and moving forward again. "O'Neill and Red Hugh O'Donnell did assemble an army from all over Ireland, and they trained them well. O'Neill received shipments of weapons from the Spanish—with help from Granuaile's fleet—and tricked the English into sending him building supplies. He was a king of deception, if nothing else. And the English made the mistake of filling their ranks with Irishmen, who turned on them as soon as O'Neill started gaining traction." A wistful expression settled on his features. "It did seem, for a while, that we might win." He gave her a forced smile. "And perhaps we will, this time. Forget O'Neill. Granuaile is the one who will be able to help us. We have to trust in that."

They reached Limerick that day and spent the night in a tiny hovel of an inn. But there was food and ale, and they were able to purchase a proper set of clothes for Nora off a local tailor. The horrid linen-roll hat had been lost at sea, thankfully. In its place Nora chose the warmest option—a black felt contraption that, as Fionn had warned her, looked rather like a chimney stack. They also bought enough food and drink for the rest of the journey to Galway, which Fionn estimated to be another two days.

Nora's legs were starting to harden, though she found herself daydreaming about the ease of modern travel—cushy car seats and train compartments—especially when the rain soaked through her heavy traveling cloak or they had to lead their horses through ice-cold streams.

They didn't speak any more about O'Neill over the next couple of days, though Nora couldn't help but stew about what information would be most useful to the Irish rebels. Now that she really thought about it, she wasn't sure she could manufacture explosives without C-4 and Semtex. Why hadn't she'd paid more attention when Paddy was making bombs in Mick's kitchen? Automatic weapons would make an enormous difference, too, but she'd no idea how to build one. A chemist or a weapons expert would have had a much easier time of changing the history of warfare.

As they grew closer to Galway, the world didn't seem so desperate.

"Connacht has had it easy, relatively speaking," Fionn said. "The chieftains here have enjoyed the kind of independence the others haven't had in decades. But it won't last." His voice was haunted. Nora wondered again what it must have been like for him to suffer failure after failure, standing by helplessly as his country suffered. What if they failed this time? What if he had come back in time with her only to relive his pain? *We can't fail*, she told herself bracingly.

They reached the top of a ridge and finally saw the ocean stretching away from them to the west. "Are those the Aran Islands?" she asked, relieved. That meant they were close to Galway.

Fionn nodded. "Aye. We're almost there." The islands rose out of the sea like lands from another time, another world. In Nora's present, they were one of Ireland's greatest tourist attractions. But that was hundreds of years from now. The ships in the harbor now were working ships like the *Barke Burre*, not ferries filled with tourists. She urged her horse onward. Bran ran ahead, feeling their urgency.

"D'you know exactly where to find Granuaile?" she asked. "You said she's in Clew Bay, up in County Mayo?"

"That's where the O'Malley clan lives," Fionn said slowly. "But as for Granuaile herself? Well, that's another question altogether. She could be at one of her castles, or with one of her children, or out on the sea somewhere. Galway is a trading town, and that means gossip is traded as much as anything else. Someone is bound to have heard something." He frowned. "She was in and out of English prisons, so we shouldn't rule that out, either."

"Lovely." What kind of wild-goose chase had Brigid sent them on?

The gray walls of Galway were soon visible. Nora wanted to start asking around for Granuaile's whereabouts right away, but Fionn urged caution. "She's a notorious pirate, an enemy of the English, and this is an English town. We have to find the *right* people to ask."

Exhaustion and hunger won the argument, and they found a decent-enough inn for the night. Still posing as husband and wife, they retired to the same bed after a light meal of soup and bread. Beside her, Fionn fell asleep almost instantly, his cloak wrapped tightly around him. Bran lay at their feet. Nora was beyond shattered, but sleep refused to come. She stared into the darkness, listening to the roll of wheels on the cobblestones outside and the clatter of dishes in the kitchen through the thin wall. The shock of what she'd seen in the Munster countryside was starting to wear off, and Fionn's warmth was both welcome and distracting.

Leave it, she told herself, rolling over to face the wall. But she couldn't stop thinking about the way he'd kissed her on the *Barke Burre*, the way he'd looked at her in 1923 when she'd been lying in a hospital bed with a bullet in her leg. Whatever he said, however he felt he had to protect himself, they were bound together by more than just their mutual mission.

"Let's get going," she told him over the rim of her mug of warm ale the next morning. "The people who are most likely to know Granuaile's whereabouts are other sailors. We should go down to the docks, keep an ear out for anyone speaking Irish instead of English. Ask some questions. We can say we have goods that need transporting or something."

"A sound plan. Only . . ."

"Only what?"

"Women don't normally go down to the docks. It might be easier if I went alone. Not to mention safer."

Nora let out a long, slow breath. He was right, but she hated the idea of being left behind. "Where *do* women go?" she asked. "What about the shops? Surely it would be safe enough for me to go there and ask a few questions. If the merchants are trading with the ships that come in, there's a good chance they'll have heard something. I'll pose as a merchant's wife from Dublin, curious about the tales of Granuaile."

Fionn looked doubtful. "Aye, I suppose. No one should bother you if they think you're just a merchant's wife. But be careful."

"O'course I'll be careful. As will you," she said pointedly.

"And you'll take Bran with you."

She didn't argue with this. While she didn't want to sit in this inn while Fionn made himself useful, she had to admit the idea of setting out into sixteenth-century Galway on her own was a wee bit daunting—and exciting.

"I'll come find you if I learn anything," he said. "Either way, let's meet back here at noon. And remember to stick to the shops."

Fionn walked her one block over, to the curving street where most of the shops were located. Nora had never been to Galway, but she knew the medieval section of the city still existed in modern times. She wondered which of these stone buildings still stood, perhaps now the home of a Baby Gap or something equally depressing.

"Tailor, bakery, and—if our innkeeper is right—the best pie shop in town," Fionn said, pointing down the narrow lane. He handed her a leather purse of coins. "Are you sure about this?"

"I'll be grand," she said. "Good luck at the docks."

He gave her a nod, stooped to ruffle Bran's fur, and headed off toward the water. Nora took a deep breath, then wished she hadn't. Galway smelled only slightly better than Dublin.

The sky was overcast, but the rain was holding off for now. Nora went first to the baker, lured in by the smell of fresh bread. A bearded man collided with her as she entered the shop, and she made a hasty apology. He said nothing to her, only stared at Bran before heading into the street.

"Hello," she said to the shop assistant, trying her best to affect an English accent. The assistant bobbed his head and asked, "What can I get for you, mum?"

"Um, a loaf of bread, please," Nora said, fumbling with the small bag of coins Fionn had left her. She handed one to him, hoping it was enough. He glanced at it, then handed her back several smaller coins. "You know," she said brightly. "I'm just visiting from Dublin. My husband is doing some business here. And I've heard so much about some pirate woman. I find the idea ridiculous, myself. I mean, really, a female pirate? It's not true, is it?"

"'Tis," the shop assistant said, looking at the floor. "They call her Granuaile. She's a right terror, so they say."

"You're not serious. Does she live here in Galway?"

He busied himself with wrapping her loaf. "No," he said. "Her people are up by Clew Bay, from what I've heard."

"Aye, I see. How strange to think she actually exists. Does she come through here often?"

He shrugged and handed her the wrapped loaf. "She doesn't come into the shop, if that's what you're asking. But last I heard,

Bingham—that's the governor here—had arrested her. Mebbe she's busted out, I dunno. I'd be on the run if I were her."

Nora's hopes sank. "Ta," she said, tucking the loaf under her arm and leaving the shop. She went to three other shops, but no one knew anything more than the shop boy. Or they were unwilling to talk about it. If Granuaile had truly been arrested, how would they get to her? Her gut told her she was looking in the wrong places. These were all English settlers and merchants living in England's stronghold in the west of Ireland. They wouldn't admit to knowing anything about the activities of a known enemy of the state, no matter how clueless she acted.

The brothel. Why not? Surely the sailors gossiped as they drank, and surely a woman pirate would be a popular subject of conversation. If Fionn couldn't get anything out of the sailors themselves, perhaps the women who worked there would be willing to talk—for a price, of course. But she couldn't go herself; that much was obvious. They'd assume she was an angry wife come to find information about her husband. She was less than enthusiastic about the idea of Fionn prying information out of a bunch of prostitutes, but surely she could trust him.

Trust him to do what? she chided herself. *He's not yours. He can do whatever he pleases.*

She gave the bread to a beggar sitting by the side of the road. He mumbled a blessing that sounded Irish, though he had lost so many teeth it was a struggle to make out his words. She squatted down beside him. "I'm looking for Granuaile," she said in her rusty Irish. "D'you know where she is?" The man's eyes widened, and he backed away from her. Nora leaned in. "Or the . . ." She didn't know the Irish word for *brothel.* "The place where there are many women." A schoolyard taunt came back to her, and she remembered the word for *hooker.* "A house with whores."

The toothless man grinned and pointed down the road. "Dunton's Tavern."

She grinned back. "God be with you."

She continued in the direction of the tavern, Bran at her heels. If she found its exact location, she'd be able to bring Fionn there later. With any luck, someone on the docks would tell him where to find their quarry and the brothel would not be necessary.

The fall of rapid footsteps behind her made her stop and look over her shoulder. Bran did the same, then moved behind her, hackles raised. Three armed soldiers were hurrying toward them.

"You there!" one called out. Nora looked around, but no one else was nearby. *Shite.* What had she done wrong?

"Go," she whispered to Bran. "Get Fionn." He'd be better suited to sort out whatever misunderstanding had arisen. Bran growled at her as the men grew closer, then slipped down the nearest laneway.

Nora considered running, but where would she go? Besides, she'd done nothing wrong; they'd no reason to bother her. "What is it?" she asked in her most proper English accent. The men encircled her.

"Who are you?" one of them asked.

"Nora O'Reilly," she said automatically before remembering that Fionn was pretending to be an O'Hanlon. She plunged forward. "I'm a merchant's wife. My husband is doing business in town. May I ask what the problem is?"

"You're under arrest for association with an enemy of the Crown, the pirate O'Malley."

Chapter Nine

Several panic-stricken minutes later, Nora was standing in the courtyard of the city jail, her wrists secured in cold iron cuffs. Where was Fionn? He knew the political and legal landscape; surely he could sort this out.

"I told you, I didn't even know O'Malley was a real person until today!" she insisted again, but the soldier only gave her another shove forward.

A thin, pale man with a long, narrow nose stalked toward them. He wore a ridiculously large ruff and a bright-blue doublet over black and silver hose. "What's the meaning of this? Who is this woman?" he barked, looking down his red-tipped nose at Nora.

"She was asking around for the pirate whore O'Malley," one of the men said.

She took a deep breath to calm her voice, but panic was taking over. Kilmainham had been bad enough; she couldn't imagine the horrors of a sixteenth-century prison. "This is all a misunderstanding. I insist you let me go at once."

The man in the ruff drew closer. "Why were you looking for O'Malley?"

"I wasn't looking for her; I was only curious about her." She could hardly deny that she *had* been asking about Granuaile.

The man slapped her hard across the face. She grunted, her cheek feeling twice its normal size. He folded his arms, acting almost bored. "Do you know who I am?"

She didn't give him the satisfaction of an answer.

"Sir Richard Bingham. Governor of Connacht."

Nora's stomach tightened. "I was only curious, I swear. I'd never heard of a female pirate."

Bingham drew closer. "I highly doubt that. Who are you really? By your dress and speech you're an Englishwoman, but your name betrays you."

Nora kept her lips tightly closed. She needed time to think, but Bingham wasn't about to afford her that luxury. "Lock her up," he said. "She'll talk soon enough." He turned and started walking back toward the barracks.

"On what grounds can you possibly arrest an Englishwoman for asking a few questions?" Nora blurted out. "I'm telling the truth. I had no motive; I didn't even want to meet her! I thought it more likely that she was a legend than a real person. You can't arrest me for that!"

Bingham stopped, a smile playing on the corner of his thin lips. "I can arrest you for whatever I want," he said smoothly. "And I'll arrest your husband if he comes to find you. Trading in Galway with a name beginning in 'Mac' or 'O' is illegal."

The guards grabbed her arms and dragged her into the stone building. They half-carried her down a spiral of steep stairs, dimly lit by torches in brackets every few feet. The deeper they went, the colder the chill in Nora's bones. Something large and black rustled out of their way as they reached the bottom step. A series of cell doors lined the walls, and each had a small barred window.

"You get someone to keep me company, boys?" a woman's voice called out from one of the cells. Nora swiveled around but couldn't make out the features of the dirty face pressed against the bars.

"Shut up, O'Malley!" one of the guards yelled before spitting in the woman's direction.

O'Malley. Was it possible?

"Granuaile?" Nora called as they dragged her past the cell.

"You shut it, too," the guard said, punctuating his command with a jerk of the chains around her wrist.

"Hang in there, love!" the woman called after her. "You're not alone!"

They tossed her into a tiny cell, even smaller than the one she'd had in Kilmainham. There was no mattress, no pillow, no candle for warmth and light. Only stone walls and that small barred window in the door. "Wait!" she called out, panic setting in as they closed and locked the door. She ran to the window. But the guards didn't even look back as they walked off and ascended the stone steps back to the land of the living.

Nora slammed her hand against the door. "Ballix!" she screamed. She peered between the bars. Was Granuaile truly only a few cells away from her? Had her foolish questions led her directly to the woman they'd been seeking?

But for what? They were hardly of any use to each other down here. "Granuaile?" she called, but there was no answer.

She paced the cold, damp cell—a couple of steps in one direction, then a couple of steps in the other. A scurry in the corner told her she was not alone. She took a deep breath and reminded herself of the courage of her fellow inmates in Kilmainham in 1923, of the hundreds of Irish patriots who had languished and died in British prisons during the Troubles. There was no victory without sacrifice. They couldn't keep her here forever on such weak charges. Her detainment would only make her a more formidable enemy in the end.

By nightfall, some of her patriotic fervor had died down. A bowl of watery gruel had been shoved toward her an hour ago. Her stomach had ached with hunger, so she'd forced it down. But her bowels had rebelled, and there'd been no choice but to squat in a corner of the cell. The stench of her own waste now filled the small space, and she huddled in the opposite corner, trying to retain whatever warmth was left in her body. To console herself, she thought of the "dirty protests" the boys in Long Kesh prison had held before going on the hunger strike that would kill ten of them. They'd covered their cells and their bodies with their own shit and had flooded the hallways with their piss. They'd refused to shave or wash. *What a sight that must have been.* She leaned her head against the stone wall. *Perhaps I can give the guards facefuls of shit until they let me go.* With that happy thought, she leaned her head to the side and managed a few hours of uncomfortable sleep.

Eventually she heard the troops moving about above and assumed it was morning. If only she had a window to the outside . . .

Had Fionn been captured, too? No, he'd probably been far too careful. What had she been thinking? She shook her head. Dwelling on her own stupidity wouldn't help. She needed a plan of action.

A commotion from outside her cell drew her to the barred window. The guards were dragging someone from another cell—it was the woman who had called out to her. Tall and big-boned, the woman had a wild mane of black hair that spilled over her shoulders. One of her eyes had been blackened, and a gash was healing along one cheekbone.

"Where are you taking me?" the woman demanded, struggling against their rough grasp.

"We've a surprise for you, O'Malley," one of them said.

The other bellowed a nasty laugh. "I'll give you a hint," he said. "It rhymes with *hallows*."

"No," Nora breathed. She pressed her face to the bars on her tiny window. "Stop! Leave her alone!" Her blood rushed and pounded in her ears. If this truly was the woman they'd been seeking for so long, she *had* to survive.

"Bingham promised me a truce!" the woman said, struggling in earnest now.

"Wait!" Nora called again. "Are you Granuaile?" The guards shot her looks of shut-the-hell-up, but the woman didn't react at all. "I'm a friend of Brigid's," she tried again. "She sent me to find you."

At this, the woman stopped struggling and looked back at Nora. "Brigid?"

"Aye," Nora said. "*The* Brigid. She said she was your friend."

The woman spat on the ground, barely missing the shoe of one of her jailers. "Then this would be the time for her to prove it."

"Enough!" the guard said, dragging her toward the stairs.

"No!" Nora screamed. "Let her go!" But her pleas echoed off stark stone.

As the sounds of struggle receded, Nora slid to the filthy ground inside her cell, her face in her hands. She was sure the woman was Granuaile. Would they really hang her? They couldn't; that wasn't how it was supposed to happen. The pirate queen had died an old woman, hadn't she? Or had Nora and Fionn's arrival in Galway somehow changed things?

Hours later, the cell door banged open and a guard stepped in. "Come with me," he said.

Nora got to her feet, her muscles stiff. "Where?"

"Doesn't matter."

Nora stayed where she was, a trickle of fear running down her back.

The guard jerked her forward by the arm, then slapped chains around her wrists. "Where are you taking me?" she asked again. He marched her up the narrow stone steps and into the bright light of the courtyard. "Where's O'Malley? What happened to her?" Another soldier sat in the front seat of a small black carriage hooked to a single horse. The guard shoved her in the back and climbed in after her. He gave a quick tap to the front of the carriage, and the contraption jerked forward.

"What's going on?" Nora asked as they began to move. "Am I being released? Where's Bingham?"

"Sir Bingham is a very important man," the guard said stiffly. "He has a whole country of barbarians to subdue. He has better things to do than deal with some Irish wench masquerading as an Englishwoman—or, worse, an Englishwoman who married an Irishman. He doesn't know who you are and, frankly, doesn't care. So he's relinquishing you to the custody of the Earl of Thomond. Let *him* figure it out, or dispose of you as he wishes."

"Who the hell is the Earl of Thomond? What does he mean by 'custody?'" *What does he mean by "dispose"?*

"You *are* a strange one, aren't you? Donough O'Brien is the Earl of Thomond."

"And where is this earl?"

"Doonbeg Castle. It will be up to him to decide where to keep you. I hear the dungeons are quite desolate there."

Nora didn't recall anything about Doonbeg Castle. Wherever it was, the chances of Fionn and Bran finding her there were next to none. They'd be searching in Galway, not some far-off castle. She pulled open the curtain on the carriage window, an awkward maneuver with her bound hands. They were traveling through the city, toward the sea. Possible escape scenarios flooded her mind, but she was useless at unarmed combat.

"What happened to Granuaile?" she asked again. "Was she hanged?"

"That's not your concern," the guard said. The carriage stopped, and she was dragged out. They were at the docks. Nearly a dozen ships were anchored in the harbor. She craned her head around, looking for Fionn or Bran, but there were no familiar faces, only curious stares at the well-dressed woman in chains. The guard helped her into a small boat filled with sailors and then had a private word with the man in charge. She couldn't hear what they were saying, but it was obvious the man was angry. He was displeased to have a woman on board his ship, no doubt. Money exchanged hands, and the disgruntled sailor got into the boat and commanded his men to start rowing. When they reached one of the ships in the harbor, the sailors climbed the ladder one by one. Finally it was just Nora and the man who had accepted the guard's bribe. "How the hell am I supposed to climb this ladder with my hands tied?" she said. His response was to pick her up and throw her over his shoulder. She kicked in protest, but he stopped her with a snarl.

"You want I should throw you into the sea?" he asked. "I made no promises about getting you to Doonbeg alive." Nora stopped kicking and hung limply over his shoulder, trying to grip his belt with her hands to steady herself. He heaved them both up the ladder one rung at a time, breathing heavily. At the top, a sailor hoisted her over the rail by her waist and then dumped her onto the deck, leering licentiously.

"Lock her below," her captor said.

The sailor growled, clearly displeased with his orders, and pushed Nora below deck more firmly than necessary. He shut her into a bare cell that reeked of urine.

Nora sank into a corner and rested her head on her arms. No one else was in the cell or anywhere nearby, from what she could tell. The sailors were all above, getting the ship ready. Once alone, Nora allowed herself the luxury of tears.

Chapter Ten

It seemed as though they'd only been sailing for minutes when a man unlocked Nora's cell. They looked at each other warily. "We're putting you off here," he said, jerking his head to the upper deck.

"Where is 'here'?"

"Doonbeg, o'course." So it wasn't too remote, after all. They couldn't be too far from County Galway. A small spark of hope flared in her chest. If she managed to escape, she could still find her way back to Fionn.

She left the ship in the same manner as she'd arrived, only in the opposite order: slung unceremoniously over the shoulder of a brawny sailor, dumped in a small boat, and then rowed to shore. They had sailed into a bay and then continued partway down a narrow river. A gleaming white tower house five stories high rose to the south, beside a thick stone bridge that crossed the river. An outer wall wrapped around the tower on three sides, the river on the other. It was a breathtaking sight, one that could never be properly recreated with restored ruins and actors in costume. Her momentary surge of awe was quickly replaced by annoyance at herself. She wasn't here as a tourist. She was here as a prisoner.

The sailors rowed into a small man-made inlet in the wall, just large enough for a boat their size. A guard was waiting to meet them, no doubt having watched their progress from the many turrets at the top of the tower. One of the sailors handed the guard a sealed letter before helping Nora, still bound, out of the boat. The two men spoke in hushed voices. Then the sailor climbed into the boat and began to row back to the main ship, leaving Nora on the shore with a new captor.

She didn't bother to argue or insist on her innocence. No doubt the letter clutched in the guard's hands was an account of her crimes as seen by Sir Bingham. She would make her case directly to the earl rather than one of his powerless foot soldiers.

The guard marched her up to a narrow gate in the castle's outer wall. Another soldier nodded him through, though he gave Nora a quizzical look as they passed. Then they entered the castle itself through a massive iron door that swung open with a scream. Nora glanced upward and saw the murder hole above them, ready to pour boiling oil or burning-hot sand on any unwanted intruders. The entrance hall was small and dark, lit only by two torches glowing against the stone walls. More murder holes were set into the low ceiling above them. Cheery. A side door in the hall opened, and a thin, stooped man approached, regarding Nora with a sharp expression. He was bald except for a strip of hair around the back of his head, which hung to his shoulders. He was dressed in the English style: ruff, doublet, and hose, though his were in subdued colors rather than the garish hues paraded by Bingham.

"Are you Donough O'Brien?" she asked, not waiting for an introduction. The man stopped short, wispy eyebrows raised.

"His Lordship the earl is not at home," he said. "I am Gerald, his porter. Who is this?" He spoke now to the guard, turning away from Nora.

"A prisoner sent from Sir Bingham," the guard said, handing the porter the sealed letter.

"A female?" the porter asked in disbelief. "First he asks us to foster sons for the chiefs; now he is sending us their daughters?"

"She is an Englishwoman. A traitor," the guard said.

"I'm not!" Nora spat at him. "This has all been a mistake!"

"Curious," the porter said. "But it's not unlike Bingham to send us his burdens. What is your name, woman?"

"Nora O'Reilly."

"An O'Reilly with impeccable English. Interesting. I didn't realize civilization had reached Breifne."

Nora bit back the curses she wanted to spew at this man. Her mouth had already landed her in enough trouble.

"Want I should take her to the dungeon?" the guard asked.

"I think that's the perfect place for her," Gerald said.

Nora spent the next day and a half chained to a stone wall on a dirty, straw-covered floor. She'd screamed all sorts of abuses at Gerald, collapsed into tears a time or two, and then resigned herself to wait it out. The feel of her rosary around her neck gave her comfort, and though she could not touch the beads, she said every prayer she knew, beseeching help from God, Saint Brigid, the goddess Brigid, the sidhe, and anyone else who might be listening.

She was in a painful half doze when she heard footsteps. She straightened up as much as she could, alert at once. It could be Gerald or one of the servants, bringing her some gruel. She'd lost track of what time it was. Or maybe it was Fionn, here to rescue her as she had rescued him from Kilmainham. No, there were two sets of footsteps descending the stairs.

She didn't recognize the man who stood gaping at her through the bars of the dungeon door. He was young—younger than her thirty years, at any rate. His espresso-colored hair was swept back off his high forehead, and his tight-fitting doublet showed a strong chest and narrow waist. He wasn't handsome, exactly—his eyes were too narrow, his nose too large and hawkish—but he exuded enough power and confidence to give him a certain magnetism. He stared at her; she stared back.

"Good God, man! What were you thinking!" The stranger spun around to face Gerald, who had come down the steps after him.

"She's a prisoner! The message said so!" Gerald protested.

"You haven't even read the letter Bingham wrote to me. It was sealed. If you had read it, you wouldn't have thrown this woman into the dungeon like some common thief!"

Gerald quailed under his master's furious glare.

"Why are you standing there? Unlock it!"

Gerald fumbled at his waist for a set of keys and placed one in the keyhole with shaking hands. Nora waited calmly while he opened the door and then unshackled her wrists. She rubbed them gently, trying to ease some circulation back into her hands.

"I take it you're the Earl of Thomond," she said to the young man.

"I am. And I'm to find out exactly who *you* are."

Nora got shakily to her feet and stepped out of the cell, not waiting for an invitation. She walked past both men and proceeded up the stairs, one hand on the wall to steady herself.

"Where are you going?" the earl called, starting up the stairs after her.

"Away from here."

"Wait!" he caught her arm just as she reached the landing. "I may have released you from the dungeon, but you cannot leave. Bingham has instructed me to keep you here."

Bingham can go fuck himself, she thought, but spoke more diplomatically. "I thought you were an earl. Surely you're the one who makes the decisions around here?" She actually had no notion of the pecking order in Elizabeth's Ireland.

"I serve Her Majesty," he said, affronted. "And Bingham is her representative. You cannot leave."

Nora sighed, sagging from the exhaustion weighing her down. "Grand so. If I can't have my freedom, I'll settle for a hot bath and a change of clothes. And some whiskey. Please tell me you have whiskey."

To her surprise, the earl smiled. "Ah, yes. We have whiskey."

Thomond himself led Nora to a plain chamber on the fourth story of the tower house. The floor was covered in rushes, and the only furniture was a thin straw mattress against the far wall. A small window let in a dusty ray of light.

Nora nervously stepped into the room, a vast improvement over the dungeons. Were the earl and his manservant playing some sort of good cop, bad cop routine? She crossed to the window and looked out. The bay they had sailed into spread out in front of her, opening to the wide sea. The green land below shimmered with life, reflecting the sun almost as much as the water did. A herd of black cattle grazed by the river, unconcerned with anything except the food in their mouths.

"Ireland has a certain rustic beauty, I must admit," the earl said from behind her. "I find myself almost getting used to it."

She turned at this. "Getting used to it? Don't you live here?"

He shook his head. "Only recently. I was brought up in Her Majesty's court. I only returned five years ago, upon my father's death. Doonbeg is not my primary residence."

Raised in Her Majesty's court. She turned her attention back to the window.

He cleared his throat. "I'll send a servant up to tell you when the bath is ready." She could feel him waiting for a response, but that didn't mean she was about to give him one. She needed to wrap her head around these new circumstances before she could plan her escape. The door closed, and a loud turn of an outer key announced that she was still a prisoner.

She collapsed onto the thin mattress, running scenarios through her mind and discarding them one by one. She needed more information—the exact location and layout of the castle, the movements of the guards, and the quickest route to Galway. Could she turn Thomond's sympathies toward her, persuade him to let her go?

Several minutes later a knock came at the door, and a pale servant girl unlocked it and stuck her head in. "Your bath is ready, Mistress O'Reilly. If you'll come with me."

Nora followed the slight girl down the tightly curved staircase. At first it seemed they were headed in the direction of the dungeons. Fear pricked at her. Had the earl's kind treatment been a cruel game? The girl saw her confusion and said, "The bath's just off the kitchen; we're nearly there."

The "bath" was a large copper tub shaped more like a cooking pot than anything Nora would normally associate with bathing. A set of wooden steps was propped against it. Nora looked expectantly at the girl, waiting for her to leave.

"Shall I help you undress?" the servant asked, looking nervous under Nora's gaze.

"No! I mean, I can manage, ta. But some privacy would be nice, so it would."

The girl looked confused. "Don't you want me to help you?"

Nora took the girl's elbow and led her to the door. "Where I come from, we bathe ourselves. I'm quite used to it, I promise. Is there soap?"

The girl nodded and pointed to a dish on the side of the copper pot, then left the small room and closed the door. Nora undressed, climbed into the lukewarm water, and crouched down, submerging as much of her body as she could. Her wrists stung where the restraints had chafed the skin. She stayed until the water became uncomfortably cool, then scrubbed herself all over with the chunk of soap. She spotted a towel of sorts slung over the back of a chair and used it to dry herself, shivering. She was loath to put on her old clothes, which were in sore need of a wash, but neither did she fancy making her way back through the castle wrapped in a towel. She was relieved when the servant girl returned.

"I've brought you one of Lady O'Brien's gowns by His Lordship's request, and I'll launder your old garments for you," the girl said. She entered the room, keeping her eyes on the floor, and laid a heavy pile of clothes on the chair where the towel had been.

"Ta," Nora said. "What's your name?"

"June," the girl whispered.

"Thank you, June."

"I'm to help you dress, then take you to dinner."

"To dinner?" Nora asked with an arched eyebrow.

"With His Lordship."

Let the games begin.

Chapter Eleven

It took Nora and June the better part of half an hour to dress her. The ensemble had to be donned in several steps: first a linen shift, followed by a kirtle and a stiff piece wrapped around her torso, then a farthingale, which spread her skirts so wide Nora wondered if she'd fit through the door, then a petticoat. When finally Nora's waist had been narrowed and her breasts flattened, June fastened the heavy outer gown over it all. It was a beautiful deep-blue color, like the sky at twilight. Tiny pearls glittered like stars over the bodice. The sleeves were added separately, slashed to reveal the white cloth underneath. Finally, June fastened a stiff ruff around Nora's neck, tucking it into the collar of the gown. "So people actually did dress like this," Nora muttered, looking down at the magnificent skirt and the rich embroidery on her sleeves.

While dressing, she played her cover story over in her mind. She'd had plenty of time to concoct it while shackled in the dungeon, but she had to be convincing. If she could prove to the earl that she was harmless, he would surely let her go. Maybe he would even help her return to the city. She followed June through the kitchen, where a sour-faced woman was pounding dough into submission on a long wooden counter. "Is that the cook?" Nora asked June, keen to know as many of the castle inhabitants as possible in case she needed a plan B.

June jumped as though Nora had pinched her, then nodded in a frightened sort of way. "Aye, that's Aoife."

An Irishwoman, Nora noted, filing that bit of information away.

The kitchen level was in the basement, so they headed for the spiral stone stairs that twisted up the entire height of the tower. "What's on this floor?" Nora asked as they passed the door to the main level.

"That's the entry, o'course, and the hall, for entertaining and the like."

"Where does the earl eat?"

"On the third floor, above the sitting rooms."

"So the top two floors are all bedrooms?"

"Yes."

Nora trailed her hand on the wall in the absence of a handrail. There were no windows on the bottom three levels, only slits large enough to shoot an arrow through from the inside, but an impossibly narrow target for anyone on the outside.

"Where exactly are we?" Nora asked June, pausing on the stairs.

June turned and looked back at her incredulously. "Why, Doonbeg, o'course."

"Yes, but I don't know where that is. I'm not from around here. Which shire are we in?"

"Clare, the parish of Killard, mistress."

"Are we far from Galway?"

From the expression on June's face, she might as well have asked if they were far from the moon. "At least three days' ride, more if the roads are bad."

Nora smiled. So about an hour and a half drive. How small the world had grown. June would likely never stray out of her own parish.

"D'you know why he's keeping me here?" Nora wondered how far she could push the timid maid. They reached the third story and came to a stop by a heavy wooden door. June stared at the floor and shook her head vigorously. Then she leaned in and whispered, "He's a good man, His Lordship is. I shouldn't think you need to be afraid."

Nora hadn't been afraid, but she thanked the girl and gave her a warm smile. Then she pushed the door open and prepared to dine with her captor.

Thomond was leaning on the wall beside a roaring fireplace, reading a book. "Mistress O'Reilly," he said, looking up and placing his book on the mantel. "Are you refreshed?"

"I am, thank you," she said, keeping her chin up. His eyes flicked to her hair, which at least resembled more of a pixie cut than a buzz cut these days. A table lined with several covered dishes sat between them. He gestured that she should sit down. She moved toward a chair and, with much difficulty, shifted the farthingale out of the way so she could sit.

"Wine?" he asked. "I haven't forgotten about the whiskey. But perhaps we'll save that for later," he said with a roguish wink. Was he flirting with her while she wore his wife's dress?

Nora hesitated before accepting his offer, but he'd not get any information out of her if he poisoned her. "Wine would be grand, ta."

He poured a glass of red and waited for her to sip it. It was exquisite, and she told him so.

"I'm glad it meets with your approval." He poured for himself, and then a man who'd been standing sentinel at the side of the room served them both from the dishes on the table. She chewed slowly, waiting for him to speak. What did Bingham want him to do with her? What instructions had been in that letter?

"Sir Bingham is quite interested in you," the earl said, sitting back in his chair.

"Ach, aye?"

"He says he suspects you are a spy, but is not sure which side you are on."

"And I suppose he wants you to figure it out."

Thomond dipped his chin in agreement. Nora continued eating—partly so Thomond would continue speaking, partly because she was famished.

He leaned forward, his green eyes glittering. "All right. Let's play a game. I'll ask you a question, and you'll give me an answer. Sound fair?"

Nora helped herself to a slice of bread and nodded.

"Are you a spy?"

"No."

He smiled. "But of course you'd say that. What kind of a spy would you be if you admitted it so readily?"

"If I were a spy for the English, I'd tell you, wouldn't I? Then your boss could verify my story, and you'd have to let me go. And if I were a spy for the Irish, then I'd be a sorry one. No threat to anyone."

"So, if you're not a spy, who are you?"

With a mental nod of gratitude to the film *Shakespeare in Love*, she sat back in her chair, took a sip of wine, and looked the Earl of Thomond in the eyes.

"I'm an actor."

He looked positively nonplussed. "A what?"

"An actor. And a playwright. Like Shakespeare and Marlowe." When he continued to stare uncomprehendingly at her, she sighed dramatically and refilled both of their wineglasses. "Here's how it is. I was born in Carlisle." She had chosen Carlisle because of its proximity to the Scottish border, which she hoped would help explain her unfamiliar accent. "My da used to read poetry and plays to us when we were wains. Ever since I was a wee girl, I wanted to write and act. O'course, when I got older I learned that it wasn't a fit profession for a woman, that

I was to stay at home and bear children, no matter how many stories the Lord had put inside me. But people also said a woman couldn't be queen, and look at Queen Elizabeth!"

She raised her glass in a toast, and Thomond followed suit. Once they had drunk to the queen's health, she continued her tale. "My parents died, and my siblings and I were sent to live with relatives. I went to an aunt in London. Sometimes she would take me to the theater." She purposefully did not name any plays in particular. Though she'd read the obligatory Shakespeare in school, she'd no idea which plays had been produced in which years.

She took a deep breath, as if preparing to divulge a terrible secret. "Anyway, I fell in love. Not with a man." She laughed at the curious expression on Thomond's face. "With the theater. And I thought, why shouldn't I do what I was born to do? God had made me a woman, aye, but he had also put this gift inside me. So I cut my hair and bound my breasts and pretended to be a man." She closed her eyes. "And it was the most amazing experience of my life, being on that stage. No one knew, not the playwright or the director, none of the other actors. To them I was Thomas Kent, a shop assistant. But when I was on that stage, I knew I was who God had intended me to be."

She dipped her chin. "And I should have left it at that. But I was greedy. I see that now. I was so inspired by our queen's greatness, I wanted to write a play to honor her—something about a woman in a man's world. It couldn't be about the queen directly, though. I wouldn't dare presume to put words in Her Majesty's mouth.

"Then I heard the story of the pirate Grace O'Malley. I knew instantly it was the story I wanted to tell. Everyone loves a villain, don't they? The tale has everything—adventure, drama, scandal. I was desperate to write it and see it performed. So I came to Ireland, hoping to hear the story from Grace O'Malley's own lips. Obviously, I didn't find her. And here I am, at your mercy."

She steadied her breathing and watched the earl closely. Had she convinced him?

"Fascinating," he said, his eyes slightly narrowed over the rim of his wineglass. "And most shocking, of course." Only he didn't look shocked. Amused, rather.

"It is, I'm sure, but hardly worth keeping me as a prisoner. I'm sure you've much better things to do with your time. I've explained myself, and now I must insist you let me go. I'll have to be making my way back to London."

"Which plays did you see?"

"I'm sorry?"

"You said you fell in love with the theater. Which play was your favorite?"

Shite.

"Impossible to say," she hedged. "Anything by Shakespeare, naturally; they're all brilliant. Which is *your* favorite?"

"Hmm. Yes, that's a difficult question. *The Delivery of the Lady of the Lake* was particularly moving. Have you seen it?"

A trick question? "I haven't had the pleasure, no."

"Of course not, as it was only delivered for Her Majesty while on progress at Kenilworth."

She huffed and gave him a dark look. "Are you trying to trap me?"

"What I'm trying to do is discover the truth. Your story is bold, but I sense it is not the whole truth. Or even part of the truth, for that matter. Let us be honest with each other. For starters, what is your real name? Why give your name as Nora O'Reilly?"

"I adopted it when I came to Ireland in the hopes the Irish people would speak to me more openly if they believed me to be one of their own. I didn't know how much trouble it would cause."

"And your real name? I assume it's not Thomas Kent." His lips quirked, and Nora bristled. He was laughing at her.

"Nora . . . Kent."

"So, Nora Kent, you would have me believe that you traveled to Ireland on your own for the sole purpose of meeting a notorious pirate and writing a play about her?"

"Aye, that's the truth, so it is. I know you probably think it outrageous for a woman to go off on her own, but I'm doing what God called me to do, so I am." Was she pushing the God angle too far?

"And why did you not tell Bingham all of this?"

Nora had anticipated he'd press her on that. "I was afeared," she said simply. "I'd heard of Bingham. People say he is brutal and unforgiving. I know . . ." She paused, pretending to think. "I know what I did was wrong—playacting as a man. Bingham didn't seem the type to understand that a woman might have her own dreams and desires."

"Then why tell *me* the truth?"

"Because you seem like a far more reasonable man. And because I want to go home."

Thomond leaned back in his chair, studying her. "There's no question you are an accomplished actor," he said. "You tell a convincing tale. I'm almost inclined to feel sorry for you, and find inspiration from your passionate pursuit of happiness. But I'm afraid there is just one problem."

Nora's stomach tightened. "What is that?"

"You said you love the plays of Shakespeare. I assume you speak of William Shakespeare?"

"Aye," she said tentatively, her fingers wrapped tightly around the stem of her wineglass.

"You see, I know Will Shakespeare. Met him through some mutual friends at court. And while I admit he is one of London's most talented actors, he is no playwright. So your moving tale of disguise and ambition begins to unravel."

"I meant the plays he has acted in," she said quickly, trying to remember her exact words. *Ballix.*

"Mmm," he said dismissively. His hand closed tightly around her wrist. "Who are you, really? Why were you asking about the pirate O'Malley? Did you have a message for her? From one of the chiefs, perhaps? Is another rebellion in the making? You know it will be suppressed as quickly as Desmond was. Only this time I do not think the lord deputy will be so gentle."

She snatched her arm away, nostrils flaring. "Gentle? Have you *seen* what he's done? The women and children he's killed? He's a butcher and a monster. You're an O'Brien, for Christ's sake, a descendant of Brian Boru! How can you stand by while your countrymen are slaughtered? Have you no pride at all? Or are you content to be the lapdog of some foreign queen?"

She didn't remember standing, but here she was, on her feet, shaking with rage.

Thomond looked as though he had been slapped, but didn't react with the anger she expected from him. Instead, he sat there gaping at her, his mouth half-open and his hands gripping the arms of his chair. "Fascinating," he said. He then pushed his chair back and stood up, rubbing his hands together. "Very well, Mistress O'Reilly—for I now suspect that is your true name—we shall continue this game tomorrow."

"Escort our guest back to her room," Thomond said to his servant, not taking his eyes off Nora. "Lock the door behind her; then send Gerald to me in my study."

Without further ado, the man took Nora's upper arm and steered her out of the dining room and up the curving staircase. He neither spoke to her nor released her arm until she was inside the room. Then he left her and, following his master's instructions, locked the door.

Nora paced furiously, her thoughts thick with wine. She silently berated herself. Why hadn't she thought of a better cover story? Something less elaborate, with fewer opportunities for error. Why had she based her story on a Hollywood film, of all things? This was not a movie—she was playing with her life.

Her hands raked through her hair. The problem was that there were flaws in each of the possible excuses she'd considered—parts of the story that didn't line up with how she had been dressed and how she spoke. How had Fionn pretended to be someone else for hundreds of years? It had been only a matter of weeks for her, and she couldn't seem to stop making mistakes.

She threw herself down on the mattress, arms and legs outstretched like a starfish, furious with herself and worried about Fionn. If they arrested him, she doubted he would be swept off to the house of a local lord, treated like a mystery to be unraveled. He'd more likely be marched to the gallows. Of course, according to him, he couldn't die. Something would intervene, and the hanging would never take place. But that wouldn't stop them from throwing him in a cell, or torturing him into madness.

A timid knock interrupted this disturbing thought. She ran to answer it, hoping she'd have another chance to convince Thomond to release her. "Hello?" she called.

A key clicked, and the door swung open. But it was only June, holding a glass of whiskey on a silver tray in her small white hands. "From His Lordship," June said. Nora would have laughed if her situation hadn't been so dire. At least the earl was a man of his word.

"Ta," Nora said, taking the tray. She chanced a peek out the door. The sitting room outside her chamber was empty. Should she make a run for it? No. She'd done enough damage by acting and speaking irrationally. Her escape required a better plan.

She made to close the door, but June blushed and said, "His Lordship said I should help you undress."

"Undress?" Nora asked, immediately suspecting the worst. Then she realized the simple practicality of his request. She had no idea how to get out of this dress on her own, or if it was even possible. "Ach, o'course. That would be grand."

She stood still in the center of the room while June unlaced and unbuttoned with practiced hands. Finally, after what seemed an eternity, Nora was left wearing only the soft white shift. She stretched, reveling in the freedom of movement.

June left and locked the door behind her. Nora examined the glass of whiskey, which she'd placed on the windowsill. A peace offering, perhaps? Or a slow, agonizing death? But as with the wine, why would he poison her? Granted, she did not know the earl very well, but she did not think he would delight in her painful death. Besides, there were other, far more efficient ways for him to rid himself of her. He could just shoot her, or hang her, or lock her away in the dungeon. She was, for now, his to do with as he wished. Poison seemed overly theatrical. She smiled at the irony, then took a sip. It seared its way down her throat and warmed her stomach, bringing with it a renewed glimmer of hope that she would recover from this misstep, after all.

Chapter Twelve

Nora spent the rest of the day alone in her room, with naught to do but pace, fret, and throw out one scheme after another. Finally, she fell into a restless sleep.

The next morning, she found her door unlocked.

Curious.

She peered out into the sitting room. Empty. She went back inside and closed the door, then made use of the privy, a tiny chamber set into the castle's outer wall with a wooden seat over a grate in the floor. She tried dressing herself but could not do up the elaborate ties and fasteners in the back of the gown. Finally, arms aching from twisting behind her, she gave up and left the room, intent on finding June or some other serving woman who could help her.

But the sitting room outside her chamber was no longer empty. A peat fire burned in the hearth, and the Earl of Thomond sat in a chair, staring into it. He turned when he heard her door open.

"Ah, Mistress O'Reilly," he said, standing. "I trust you slept well?"

"Grand, ta," she said, determined to keep her temper in check and her voice civil. "And you?"

He smiled. "Very well, thank you." His gaze roamed over her gown, which was hanging askew and missing the ruff and farthingale. "May I . . . assist you?"

Nora turned around wordlessly and allowed him to finish the process of lacing her up. "I want to apologize for my outburst last night," she said, grateful she did not have to look him in the eye. "I'd had too much wine and didn't know what I was saying."

"Then I should give you more wine," he said. "You have many interesting opinions." Nora unclenched her stomach slightly. She'd called him a lapdog and a traitor to his people, but if he wanted to overlook her outburst, that was grand with her.

"I insulted you," she said. "And that was improper." *And unwise.*

"It was," he said nonchalantly. "But we will speak no more of it, so long as such accusations are not renewed. Now that that's done, I had hoped you might join me for a morning ride."

She turned around to face him. "As in . . . on horseback?"

"Would you prefer another kind?" he asked, his eyes twinkling.

Nora flushed furiously at the insinuation. "A horseback ride would be perfect." Perhaps this would be her means of escape. "But June said this was Lady O'Brien's dress. Will she not mind?"

Thomond colored slightly. "Ah. The lady is not here. She prefers our home in London. Her family is all there, you see."

She had wondered about the missing Lady O'Brien. "Aye. Grand so. Lead on."

She followed the earl out of the castle and to the small stable, a wooden building inside the outer wall. His groom already had two horses saddled, a black charger and a smaller dappled steed for her. The groom helped her mount, and she followed the earl out of the gate and into the emerald countryside.

"Shall we ride by the ocean?" he asked, pulling his horse alongside hers.

"If you'd like," she said. Her mind was mapping the terrain, scanning the fields to the east for a church where she might claim sanctuary, and the sea to the west for a ship on which she might gain passage should she be able to nick something of sufficient value. She marked the gates of the castle wall in her mental map, straining to see which ones were guarded and which were merely closed doors.

"She's a suitable castle, for Ireland," Thomond said after they had been riding for several minutes. "I've several more, of course, much grander. But I do enjoy being by the ocean."

Nora inwardly rolled her eyes but outwardly gave him a bland smile.

"Why don't we try again," he said. "I'd like very much to know who you are, and what your purpose is here in Ireland."

"I told you," she parried. "I'd rather find out more about you."

He glanced over at her, amused. "Very well. What would you like to know?"

"Well, all I know is that your name is Donough O'Brien, you're the Earl of Thomond, and you were raised in Queen Elizabeth's court. How does that work, exactly?"

"It's quite customary for the sons of nobles. I was educated, disciplined, and taught what was expected of a man of my rank."

Nora bit back a sarcastic reply, forcing her features into an interested expression. "How d'you mean?"

"Court manners, international diplomacy, how to manage a large estate, that sort of thing."

"And you say you only came back to Ireland a few years ago?"

"Five years ago, yes. It's been a bit of a shock, to be sure."

"Aye?" Again she bit her tongue.

"Have you ever been to court?" he asked with a sidelong glance.

She shook her head.

"It's a wonderful maelstrom of activity—pageants and balls, jousting, business deals being made around every corner, favors being traded.

The never-ending game of politics. I had only just begun to play, and to play well, I might add, when my father died and I was forced to return here." He drew a hand out around him, indicating the countryside. The waves were foaming as they reached the shore, and the wind was sending up a light spray of sea mist onto their faces. The sky above them was dotted with heavy white clouds, rolling and tumbling through the blue sky.

"And is this place so bad?" she asked.

"You're an Englishwoman, so you say. I'd love to hear your thoughts on the Irish people."

Nora bristled before she managed to calm herself. "I think quite highly of them."

"Do you indeed?" His face had once again lightened in amusement.

"I have experienced nothing but kindness since my arrival here—until I met Bingham, o'course. Funny, isn't it? The only man who has mistreated me here is an Englishman."

"We are *all* subjects of Her Majesty," Thomond pointed out. "Unwilling though some may be."

Nora was tempted to press her heels into her horse's side and speed away. But she knew she'd never outride him, and the more she tried to escape, the guiltier she would appear.

"God save the queen," Nora said, choking slightly on the words. "But I'm curious. You come from a long history of proud Irishmen. Why bend the knee to a foreign sovereign? Is it just because that's how you were raised? Because your father and his father did the same?"

"Ah. Is this what you were trying to ask me last night?"

"Aye. Just with less shouting this time."

A grin softened his features. "I suppose I've never known life as anything but a loyal subject of Her Majesty. And why wouldn't I serve her? I had the best education a man can get, and my sons will receive the same. I own lands and castles and have influence with the privy council in Dublin and the court in London. I am proud to be an O'Brien, to be sure, but I've seen how some of my fellow chieftains live in mud-and-wattle huts, barely higher than their own subjects. They spend all their time raiding one another and engaging in drunken brawls. Would you have me go back to that?"

Nora scowled. She hated this stereotype of Irishmen but had little experience from this century with which she could counter it. "Believe me, I'm all for progress," she said, thinking of flush toilets and antibiotics. "But you take what you learned in England and use it against your people. Why not use it to help them instead?"

"And by 'help them,' you mean 'help them resist'?" His voice was measured, but she heard the danger in it.

"I knew another man called Donough once," she said. She didn't have to fake the wistfulness in her voice. "He sold bread out of the back of a van."

"A what?" he asked, apparently taken aback by the sudden change in conversation.

"A cart," she corrected. "He was always very kind to me." She smiled. "If I ever see him again, I'll have to tell him about you. He'd be tickled to share a name with an earl, so he would." Thomond's eyes were fixed on her, so she met them with a clear gaze and a bright smile. "He was a true Irishman—a hard worker, a fine storyteller, a man with sharp wit and a keen mind. There was a family living next to us; the da had left, and the ma was struggling to keep food on the table for her five wains. Whenever Donough came by with his bread cart, he'd leave half a dozen loaves outside their door. They never asked for it, and he never made a penny off them, though he barely had two to rub together himself. But he's all that stood between them and starvation."

"He sounds like a very noble man," Thomond said.

"What if the Irish win?" Nora asked. "What if there is another rebellion, and another, and another? You'll be on the losing side."

"Be careful, Mistress O'Reilly," he said, his voice deepening. "You're sounding less and less like an English playwright."

"I'm just stating what I see," she said clearly. "Think of me as a neutral observer."

He actually snorted at this. "The only way the Irish could ever defeat the English would be as a united country, and that will never happen. And there is nothing neutral about you, except, perhaps, the way you ride." At this he put his heels to his horse and sprinted ahead, his horse's hooves sending up a spray of salt and mud. Nora leaned forward in her saddle and urged her horse on. It obeyed with surprising speed, and she clung tight to the reins, adrenaline pulsing through her. After racing for more than a mile, Thomond reined his horse in to a walk. "Well done," he said. "I didn't think you could keep up."

"My ma used to say I'd do anything on a dare, even if it meant breaking my neck."

He laughed, and the sound was annoyingly pleasant. "Then I dare you to play a game of primero with me after dinner. You must be a fair gambler."

"One who takes stupid risks, you mean." She smiled back at him. "You're just trying to take advantage of me. Besides, I've no money with which to gamble."

"Then I shall loan you some."

Primero, she discovered, was similar to poker. Thomond was patient and explained the rules of the game after she admitted her ignorance. But she'd played many winning hands of poker in her day, huddled in a canvas tent or under a corrugated tin roof, her spirits buoyed by brown glass bottles of local beer and the camaraderie of her colleagues. And so she was able to take him by surprise, winning two of their three games.

A rematch was demanded for the following day, and Nora found herself quite looking forward to it. *He is the enemy. Keep your goddamn head on straight*, she reminded herself as she lay in bed, replaying the day's conversations. She hadn't forgotten her plan to escape, but now another idea was blossoming in her mind. What if she could turn the earl to her cause? He was an arrogant bastard, to be sure, and an exemplary servant of the English queen. But he had money and men—two things sorely needed in the Irish rebellion. True, he hadn't seemed very keen on the idea when she'd hinted he use his knowledge to help the Irish, but what if she could convince him that he was fighting on the wrong side? Perhaps it wasn't an accident that she had been brought here. Was Brigid directing her path, even now?

They continued on like this for another week—riding in the morning, cards in the evening after supper. In the afternoons, Thomond would either work in his study or visit his tenants, taking his porter, Gerald, with him. Nora was allowed the freedom of the castle, but the guards were under strict orders not to let her leave it. Despite this, she knew she would have to escape soon. Fionn had to be worried sick about her. She hoped he wasn't putting himself in danger to find her. Or had he already given her up for dead?

Thankfully, Thomond had stopped badgering Nora about her identity and her purpose in Ireland, quite possibly because she had stopped answering, always parrying his questions with ones of her own, always turning the conversation to her theory that he could be of great help to his people. Or perhaps he simply no longer wanted to suspect her of something underhanded. She saw the way he looked at her, the way his whole countenance brightened when she entered the room. And she could even admit to herself that she enjoyed his company and the banter they shared.

But he was, she kept reminding herself, the worst sort of Irishman—one who had rolled over and shown his belly to the invaders, all for a few drafty castles and an English title. A sharp contrast to Fionn, who had fought his entire life for Ireland's freedom, never wavering in his resolve, never tempted to join the winning side. Her stomach ached when she thought of Fionn. She wanted to ask Thomond if anyone else had been arrested in Galway that day, but the last thing she desired was for Fionn to become a wanted man. So she prayed to whichever gods were listening that he was safe—and that she would be able to find him again.

She decided to devote one more week to her effort to sway Thomond to the rebellion. If that did not work, she would make her escape. They'd been riding farther and farther in the mornings. She'd already confiscated a knife from the dining room and hidden it in her room. She just needed to wait for the right time, while they were watering their horses, perhaps, while he was bending low over the stream to cup his hands in the cool water. She wouldn't kill him, only injure him enough that he'd be unable to follow her. She was a fair-enough rider now, and her horse was fast. If she headed north, she would be far ahead of him before he could return to the castle and muster help. She could trade the horse for another in some village on the way to Galway, then disappear into the city. She'd search for Fionn, and if she failed to find him, well, she'd made enough in her gambling sessions with Thomond to buy passage from even the most superstitious captain. Fionn may have gone on to their original destination of Mayo to look for Granuaile. He didn't know that the pirate queen had been in a Galway jail cell, nor that she was quite possibly dead.

"What news of the outside world?" she asked as they sat down to supper, a creamy leek soup and a wheel of sharp cheese.

Thomond looked up from his soup, immediately suspicious.

"Ach, settle down, I'm not trying to weasel state secrets from you," she said with a roll of her eyes. "I'm just making polite conversation, is all."

He snorted. "Well, I did receive a letter from your friend Bingham today. He asked how I was getting along with my prisoner."

Nora's stomach fluttered, but she managed a casual shrug and cut a slice of cheese. "Ach, aye? And what d'you tell him? That I can beat you at primero nine times out of ten?"

He laughed. "Hardly. I think three out of five is a better assessment." He hesitated, then said, "I haven't answered him yet. What do *you* think I should tell him?"

"The truth, o'course," she said innocently. "Tell him you have determined that I am a wayward Englishwoman, trying vainly to make my literary mark in a man's world. I have seen the error of my ways and henceforth will be quite proper." Then she winked and added, "Maybe."

"Nora," he said softly. He had never called her by her first name before. "Haven't I been kind to you? Aren't we friends? I can protect you from Bingham. But please, I beg of you. Tell me the truth."

She was tempted. What would he say if she told him she was from the future? Fionn had accepted the truth readily, but he had already known magic to be real and believed in Brigid's power. Time travel had been a small step for him. But Thomond, whose life had been so tightly regimented, whose worldview was so narrow, so . . . well, medieval . . .

Would he have pity on her if he thought she was mad? Would he let her go? No, she had shown herself to be perfectly sane. He would merely think she was constructing another outlandish tale to deceive him. She would stick to her story. But this confrontation meant it was time to escape. She would have to leave tomorrow.

"I *have* told you the truth," she said earnestly. "So what if I thought Shakespeare was a playwright instead of an actor? I didn't profess to be an expert in the matter. And aye, what I did was reckless, but I think you know me well enough by now to know I'm quite innocent, so I am. Didn't you say just yesterday that my strong-headedness was part of my charm?" She took his hand, which had been resting on the table. The muscles tightened in his face as he held his breath. She smiled, then squeezed his fingers. "Donough, I must confess something."

"What is it?" He looked cautious but didn't withdraw his hand.

"I would like to stay . . . but as your guest, not as your prisoner." A stab of guilt pierced her as he squeezed her hand in return. For a long moment they just looked at each other, weighing the possibilities.

Mick O'Connor had tried to pimp her out once. They'd heard rumors of an impending attack on a leading PIRA member. Nora had been dispatched to a bar in East Belfast to nick the cell phone of an Ulster Defense Association member who was in on the plot. She was to use "whatever means necessary," Mick had said, his meaning plain. And she'd have done it, too. She'd have done anything to take a shot at the paramilitary gang that had murdered her brother, even if it had meant holding her nose and fucking one of them. But she hadn't needed to stoop so low. Her PIRA crew had staged an ambush as she and the UDA bloke stumbled back to his flat together. Mick had pulled her into a laneway while the others stole the man's cell phone and administered a hell of a beating.

I decided I didn't want to share, he'd said. Then he'd kissed her against the hard brick wall.

Would it come to that? If her escape attempt failed, would she become this young earl's mistress—learn his secrets, read his letters, be the spy he feared her to be? Perhaps she could find out information about English troop movements and political plays and smuggle the information out somehow.

But how? She had no contacts here. She didn't know how to distinguish between the lords who were loyal to England and the ones who were just playing the part.

There was another problem with that approach. She was pained to admit it, even to herself, but she missed Fionn with an intensity that shocked her. She couldn't remember the last time she had missed someone. She wasn't sure she enjoyed the sensation. It felt . . . vulnerable.

You fancy him. It was Pidge's voice, and she could easily envision her friend's saucy grin.

I don't, she insisted to herself. *He's right: it makes no sense for us to be together.* Then why did she feel so guilty for even considering a strategic liaison with Donough O'Brien? Fionn had made it clear that they were nothing more than partners on the same mission. Aye, there had been that moment on the merchant ship, but that had been the result of exhaustion and nerves and the intensity of their situation. She tightened her grip on Donough's hand. "What do you say?" she prompted. "Tell me you believe me."

"I have never known a woman like you, Nora O'Reilly." He wrapped both of his hands around hers. "To be honest, I still think there is more to you than you are saying. But I must admit that I look forward to figuring it out."

He snapped his fingers for more wine, and when it had been poured, he said, "I shall inform Bingham that I am convinced of your innocence, and that I have invited you to stay as my guest until transport back to England can be arranged. And if that happens to take a fairly long time, well then, how fortunate for me."

She grinned back at him. "And for me. Now, shall I beat you at primero again?"

"Actually, I've arranged something different for our entertainment," he said, looking quite pleased with himself.

"Oh, aye? And what's that?"

"A traveling bard," he said, sitting back proudly.

Nora's spirits lifted. Now *here* was a true medieval experience. "Really? Like, a singer?"

"A poet. I had Gerald audition him when he came to the door. My man assures me we'll find him quite pleasing."

"Sounds fabulous. And I would feel bad taking any more of your money, anyway," Nora said, laughing.

"Bring in the whiskey, and send in the bard," Thomond said to a servant. The desserts came first, a tray of marzipan and tiny pastries. They were just pouring the whiskey when a servant opened the door and said, "The bard Eoin O'Dugan, Your Lordship."

Nora had just taken a mouthful of whiskey when the bard entered, and she choked in her surprise.

"Are you all right?" Thomond asked, leaning toward her in concern.

"Grand." She waved him away with watering eyes, her hand clutching her chest. "Just choked a bit, that's all."

"We make it strong here," he said, leaning back with a grin.

Nora nodded and tried to smile, turning her attention back to the bard, who was straightening his brat and waiting for the earl's permission to speak.

It was Fionn.

Chapter Thirteen

Fionn's large, floppy hat partially obscured his face, but Nora would have known him from a hundred paces away. She took another large gulp of whiskey, willing it to calm her blazing nerves. Her mind bounced erratically from one thought to the next. How had he found her? Why was he here? To rescue her, of course. But how? What was she to do? And what must he think of her? Prisoner or not, she was dressed in one of the earl's wife's gowns, eating and drinking with him like an old friend. Or a lover.

Donough nodded at Fionn, who then bowed, first to the earl and then to Nora, as though he'd done this a thousand times. Of course, she remembered, he *had* played the part of a bard before, passing through his túath to catch glimpses of his grandchildren. Nora tried to relax, to not give herself away and land them both in the dungeon. But then Fionn began to recite, and all other thoughts were forgotten. The pastries and whiskey went untouched as he wrapped them in the soft, silky cocoon of his voice. She flicked her eyes to the earl. He, too, seemed transfixed by Fionn's poetry.

When it ended, it seemed too rude, too uncouth to applaud. The rough slapping of palms would break the delicate spell hanging in the air. Nora was half out of her seat, leaning toward Fionn. Their eyes met, but he still betrayed no trace of recognition. "That was amazing," she breathed. Despite the precarious danger of the situation, her body craved him.

"I thank you," he said with a nod of his head. "And now, if it please Your Lordship, I shall deliver a poem of the clan O'Brien."

As Fionn began to recite his ballad of the brave deeds of O'Brien men through the centuries, Thomond settled back into his chair and took Nora's hand, holding it in his lap. Fionn's crystalline voice wobbled for a moment, but he quickly recovered. Nora did not attempt to wrest her hand away; she must give Thomond no reason to suspect her tonight. She forced her attention away from Fionn's poem and started to consider their options for escape. The castle was heavily guarded, and the walls were high—she didn't see how the two of them could escape any easier than she could have managed on her own.

He wouldn't come here without a plan to get out. But what was it? How could she possibly get him alone without arousing suspicion?

Her strain must have shown on her face, because Thomond leaned in and whispered, "Are you all right, Nora? Don't you like the bard?"

"Ach, aye, I do," she assured him. "I'm just so moved by the stories, that's all."

He squeezed her hand and turned back to the bard. Fionn's poem was magnificent. Verse after verse extolled the virtues of dozens of O'Brien men—their victories in battle, their exploits on the sea, their own poets and bards of old, the beauty of their wives and daughters. He told tales of the ancient kings of Munster, and of their proudest son, Brian Boru, who became High King of all Ireland and defeated the Northmen at Clontarf. He spoke of the twelfth-century king Donal O'Brien, who defended against the Normans time and time again. Thomond laughed out loud in some places, and looked close to tears in others, all the while nodding his head to the rhythm of Fionn's voice. Finally, Thomond's own father was mentioned, though by his Irish name and not his English title.

Connor mac Donough, the long-nailed, the wily
Who rose against the invaders only
And defended the honor of the Dal Cais
'Til at last he grew weary to fight
The battle that was lost.

After Fionn finished with a verse wishing long life and good health on Donough O'Brien, Thomond got to his feet and applauded enthusiastically. Fionn smiled and bowed. His arms glistened with sweat, and a string had broken on his lute. But he looked very pleased with himself as he said, "Did Your Lordship enjoy my humble offerings?"

"Tremendously," Thomond said. "Didn't we, Nora?"

Nora stood as well and smoothed the front of her skirt self-consciously, her eyes shining. "It was the most beautiful poetry I've ever heard. You are very, very welcome here, sir."

She realized belatedly that she had spoken like the lady of the house, not as a captive. Thomond grinned down at her. "I see you are making yourself quite at home," he said. Then he leaned forward and whispered in her ear, "I like it."

She blushed and looked away, conscious of Fionn's gaze on them. Then an idea came to her—she just hoped it played into whatever plan Fionn had for their escape. "I'd like to hear him again, so I would," she said to Thomond, giving him an endearing smile. "Can we ask him to stay the night, so he can entertain us again tomorrow?"

"An excellent suggestion," Thomond said. "Bard! My man will take you to my porter. He'll see to your payment, and you may stay in the stables tonight."

"The stables!" Nora exclaimed. "After what we've just heard? I thought bards were treated with great respect."

Thomond's face darkened. Had she pressed her luck too far? She slipped her small white hand into his. "If it pleases you," he finally said. Turning to a serving man standing by the door, he said, "Tell Gerald that the bard is to sleep in the castle tonight." He glanced at Fionn, almost as an afterthought.

"It would be my honor to perform for you on the morrow," Fionn said with a dip of his chin. Then he walked past them, his back very straight.

Nora exhaled. He would be inside the castle, at least. If they had any luck at all, they would be able to find each other after the castle's inhabitants were asleep. If nothing else, she could at least get a message to him.

"Join me for a last drink before we retire," Thomond said. He poured them each a fresh glass of whiskey, then sauntered over to the fireplace. Nora didn't hide a wide yawn. The sooner they all went to bed, the sooner she could find Fionn.

Thomond stared into the flames, his thick eyebrows knit together. Nora needed to be alert, so she only pretended to drink her whiskey.

"The bard's song stirred something in me," he said at last. "It's been many years since I heard the heroic tales of my forefathers."

Nora drew up alongside him.

He smiled down at her. "Or maybe it is you who has put me under a spell," he said. "You see the Irish people differently than I do—or than I did."

"But you're the Irishman, not me," she said gently.

"I am." He looked away, his eyes troubled. "But what kind of Irishman am I? What would my forefathers say if they could see me now?"

Nora almost wished that Fionn had not come tonight. If she'd had more time, she was confident she could have convinced the earl to turn his loyalty toward his own people. But the seed had at least been planted. "You've a long and noble lineage worthy of your pride. It's never too late for your own heroic deeds."

He kissed her then, his lips confident and hungry, those of a man accustomed to taking whichever woman he pleased.

"Let me come to you tonight," he whispered, one hand on the back of her neck, the other clutching her hand to his chest.

Hell no. Not tonight. "I'd like that very much, so I would. But it's my, you know . . . time of the month." She tried to look embarrassed. "Will you wait a few days?"

He raised her hand to his lips and kissed it. "If I must."

He walked with her back to her room, and kissed her again before she laughed and pushed him away. She slid inside the room and closed the door, then bolted it. *Ballix!* Without June, she could hardly undress on her own. When she opened the door again, Thomond was still there. He grabbed her around the waist and pulled her close, kissing her neck. "I knew you'd come back," he mumbled against her collarbone.

She pushed him gently away. "It's *still* my time of the month. Believe me, it's a mess down there. I came out to see if June would help me with my dress."

"Shall I help you?" he asked roguishly.

"No, not this time," she said, allowing a hint of impatience to creep into her voice. "Send June." Then she ducked back inside and closed the door. A few minutes later, there was a timid knock. "Who is it?" Nora called, bracing herself against the earl and his advances again.

"It's June, m'lady," the serving girl said. Nora let her in, and June began unlacing and unbuttoning the gown.

"Where is the bard sleeping?" Nora asked.

"In the servants' quarters, down by the kitchens," June answered.

"Did you meet him?"

"No, but I saw him. He's very handsome."

"Aye, he is. Can you fetch me something to write with? I'd like to send him my thanks for his performance tonight."

June looked confused but nodded and left the room. A few minutes later, she returned with a roll of parchment, a feather quill, and a bottle of ink. Nora took the writing instruments from her and settled down at the table. "Wait here and you can deliver it to him." She experimentally dipped the end of the quill in the ink bottle, then set it on the parchment. A great blob of ink spread out onto the page. She tried again, this time tapping the excess ink back into the bottle.

I've a plan. Meet me on the road to Galway tomorrow at noon.

That was it, really. Fionn could leave freely—for now. She would go through with her plan of escaping on horseback. She read the short missive again, then crossed it out and wrote, *Meet me on the stairs at midnight.* It would be better to tell him in person, lest the message be discovered. But what if *this* message was discovered? She crumpled up the paper and tossed it in the fire. It was too dangerous to put anything at all in writing.

"I've changed my mind," Nora said. "I can't think of the right words. I'll have to try again tomorrow."

June left, and Nora started pacing. Perhaps it would be wise to delay her plan by a day. She might find another opportunity to sway the earl to the Irish side. And perhaps she would find an opportunity to speak with Fionn alone, on the pretense of asking him about his poetry.

Patience, she told herself as she climbed into bed. *Everything moves slower now.*

And then the sky outside her window exploded.

Chapter Fourteen

Nora ran to the window, which was dark once again. Had she imagined the flash of light, the burst of sound? Thunder and lightning, she told herself, looking out at the black sky. There were no streetlights, no glimmer of life from the windows of houses, no cars streaming red and white along motorways. Even the stars were concealed by cloud, making the darkness absolute. The only light was the low fire flickering behind her. And then it happened again—a flash of light, an eruption of sound. This time, she was staring right at it, and in the milliseconds that the sky was illuminated, a ship in the harbor glowed like a specter, cannon fire blazing from its hull. But why fire the cannons? They were too far out to reach the castle. What were they—*ah.* She hurriedly pulled on a cloak over her léine and stuffed her feet into small black boots. The knife she had spirited away from the table was under her mattress; she retrieved it and tucked it into a pocket of her cloak.

The castle was alive now, shouts echoing from floor to floor. Nora started down the curved staircase and was nearly run over by Thomond, who was sprinting down the steps behind her, his sword in hand. He caught her around the waist before she could careen down the rest of the stairs.

"What's going on?" she asked. "I heard a noise."

"Pirates!" he said. "They're firing cannons from their ship. They can't reach us, but there may be boatloads of them coming to shore. Damn fools!" He grabbed her arms. "Don't worry, there is no way they can penetrate our defenses. They'll all be dead by morning. But go, stay in your room. You'll be safest there."

He kissed her hard, then continued running down the stairs. Nora waited until he was out of sight before creeping down after him. The castle was in chaos, servants running about, guards taking places at the arrow slits. She ran down to the kitchens, where the servants were putting pots of sand on the fire. Then someone grabbed her arm.

"Fionn," she breathed. She had the crazy impulse to throw her arms around him, to wash away the memory of the earl's kiss with the taste of Fionn's lips.

But then he tightened his grip on her arm and asked, "Do you *want* to escape?" His jaw was clenched, and there were tight lines around his eyes.

"I . . . o'course I do," she said, staggered. "It's what I've been planning! But what is this?" she said, and indicated the pandemonium around them.

"It's a distraction," he said. "Let's go."

They darted away from the kitchen, making for the door that opened onto the main hall. Fionn eased it open a crack.

"What do you see?" Nora asked.

"Guards. I'm unarmed," he said. "I could take a few of them, but not all. Not without a sword."

"I've this," she whispered, handing him her kitchen knife.

He looked at it, eyebrows raised, then took it and peered out the door again. "Your earl is there. If you can lure him away from his guards, I can kill him. We'll make our escape once I have his sword."

Her stomach clenched in horror. "Are you mad?"

"Lost your nerve, Nora? You looked quite cozy, playing the part of the Lady Thomond."

She snatched the knife back from him. "You don't know what the fuck you're talking about. But you can't kill him. He's not our enemy."

"He *is* our enemy," Fionn snarled. "Thomond sides with the English every time. He's killed thousands of Irishmen—or he will, if we let him live."

Nora struggled with this, but she couldn't kill in cold blood a man who had been kind to her—one who had appeared open to change. "If you kill him, it will bring down the wrath of England on all the innocent people in Clare. It will be the Desmond Rebellion all over again. And you're daft if you think we're getting out the front door."

She turned and headed back through the kitchen, leaving him no choice but to follow her.

"Where the devil are you going?" he asked, catching her by the arm.

"We'll go through the laundry."

"The what?" he snapped impatiently.

"June showed it to me. C'mon." None of the servants were paying them any heed, busy at their tasks. She grabbed a lit torch from its bracket on the wall and then led the way around a corner, through a wooden doorway, and down a half flight of stairs. A pungent smell wafted up toward them. Pressing her sleeve to her nose, Nora continued onward. The smell intensified as they barged through another doorway. "Look," she said through her sleeve. She pointed at a large wooden barrel in which the excrement of all the castle's inhabitants was gathered by means of a long chute inside the walls. "It's a bucket of shit." She grinned despite her nerves. "They hang their clothes over it. Then a man stirs it, and the gas it releases kills the bugs in the clothes. Isn't that disgusting?"

"Are you twelve?" Fionn said. "Besides, I used to own one of these; I know how it works."

"Ach, grand so, the door is over here, but it opens into the sea. That's where they dump it all. So be careful."

She extinguished the torch and then eased open the small door, relishing the blast of fresh air. A narrow stone ledge was all that stood between them and the dark sea. In the distance, the ship's cannons fired again—a burst of light that froze Nora in place. The castle's torches had been lit to allow the guards to better see their attackers. It appeared the pirates, or whoever they were, had yet to make landfall. Nora crept slowly along the ledge on her hands and knees, moving away from the front of the tower, where most of the guards were gathered.

"Stop," Fionn whispered from behind her. "Climb down here."

She craned her neck to look at him. "Climb down?"

"There's an embankment here. We'll go west along the shore. I've a boat hidden. Follow me." He swung his body over the ledge, gripping it with his fingers. Then he let go. There was enough faint light for Nora to watch him slide down the embankment, but she couldn't see where he landed.

"Here we go," she muttered, then eased herself over the edge. She clung to the wall for a few seconds, then closed her eyes and let go. The slide was rough, sand and grass and twigs whipping her in the face. The landing caught her by surprise, and she crumpled onto the rocky beach, a space just big enough for the two of them. "How'd you know this was here?" she asked Fionn as she got to her feet.

"Reconnaissance," he said. "I've been watching this place for days, figuring out the best way in."

"I'd a plan to escape, you know," Nora said, wondering what exactly Fionn had seen. Had he watched her ride out with Thomond day after day? Had he seen firelight glowing in the window of the dining room late into the night, heard their buoyant voices travel on the air as they played round after round of cards?

He didn't respond, just moved swiftly into the water. She followed, wincing as the icy waves slapped at her legs. It grew darker as they crept along the coast, and Nora was forced to put a hand forward and clutch Fionn's shirt like a child. Her legs were numb, but she pushed herself forward. They finally came to a small boat, drawn up on a bed of black rocks. Together they heaved it into the water and then climbed aboard. Fionn took hold of the single set of oars and rowed out into the dark sea with several strong strokes. Then he put his hands to his mouth and made an echoing hooting sound—the cry of an owl on the hunt.

"That's the signal for them to move," Fionn said. "We'll intercept them . . . if we can find them."

"Will the earl's men give chase?"

"Not while they're safe behind their walls. They won't risk it. They'll just assume the pirates lost their nerve. That is, until they discover the two of us missing. But I reckon that will take a while."

Nora stayed quiet, thinking of Donough. Would he believe she'd been kidnapped? No, he was too clever for that. He would know she had betrayed him. Had she just destroyed what little progress she had made in persuading him to support the Irish cause?

"How'd you find me?" she asked.

"Bran. Plus, soldiers talk, and the news of the arrest of a beautiful woman with shorn-off hair made the rounds soon enough. Bran did some snooping around the barracks and found you'd been moved to Doonbeg. I'll admit I expected to find you in the dungeon."

She bristled at the unspoken accusation. "Would you have preferred that? If it makes you feel better, I *was* in the dungeon, chained to the bloody wall, both in Galway and at Doonbeg. Did it ever occur to you that I had the brains to convince the earl I was innocent? In fact, I'd very nearly persuaded him to throw his lot in with the rebel chiefs." She paused, softening her tone. "Your poetry also helped. It was spectacular, so it was. I'd no idea you could perform like that."

"I had great teachers," he said, pulling on the oars. "Two women—one a great warrior, the other a great druid. They raised me and taught me almost everything I know. And no, o'course I wouldn't have preferred to find you in chains. I was just surprised. Confused."

They rowed in silence for a minute. It was unnerving, being out on the open sea in a mere rowboat. She felt raw, exposed.

"The earl fancies me," she admitted. "O'course, he probably fancies every woman that crosses his path. His wife's in London."

"Did he . . . mistreat you?" Fionn asked, his voice wobbling slightly.

"Not at all," Nora said quickly. "He was a perfect gentleman, as they say. And I let him fancy me. I suppose I even encouraged it. But it was all to lull him into a false sense of security, so it would be easier for me to get away. And if it helped me convince him to support the rebels, then all the better."

"How'd you convince him you were innocent?"

Nora was glad it was too dark for him to see her cheeks flare. "It was a bit of a mess, actually." Haltingly, she told him the pack of lies she'd unloaded on the earl.

"Where the devil did you get that daft idea?"

"It was from a film—you know, a moving picture. *Shakespeare in Love*. There's a woman in it who pretends to be a man so she can act, and Shakespeare is in it, obviously. I assumed Shakespeare had started writing plays by now, but apparently he's still just an actor. That's what Donough said, anyway."

"Donough." He managed to relay a world of insinuation in the single word.

"Yes, *Donough*," she snapped. "*Now* who's acting twelve?"

Fionn stopped rowing. The sky had cleared, and the stars and moon gave enough light to reveal the outline of his body. A faint halo of moonlight reflected off his silver hair.

"You're right," he said, holding out a hand to her from across the boat. "I'm sorry. Truce?"

Though she was soaking wet and chilled to the bone, she warmed slightly. "I'm sorry, too. I hate fighting with you. I just can't seem to help myself." She accepted his hand. "Truce. And thank you for coming to get me."

"I wouldn't leave you behind, Nora." There was a pause; then he laughed softly. "I was going to say you wouldn't last a day without me in this century, but apparently you'd do quite well for yourself. Tell me about this escape plan of yours." He started rowing again, and Nora thought she could make out the ghostly shape of a ship on the horizon.

"Ach, it was simple enough. Ride out with the earl, catch him unawares, stab him, then ride off."

Fionn snorted. "No, truly, what was your plan?"

"That *was* my plan," she retorted. "It would have worked just fine."

"I thought you didn't want to kill him? What about bringing the wrath of England down on the innocents of Clare?"

"I wouldn't have killed him, just wounded him enough so he couldn't follow me."

"Have you ever stabbed a man?"

"No. It's not really necessary when you've a gun. But it's not like there's a real technique to it." As she spoke, the flaws in her escape plan became more and more apparent. "Look, I know it wasn't perfect, but I need you to know I wasn't just sitting there drinking his wine and acting the maggot. I would have figured a way out, sooner rather than later."

"I'm sure you would have. Still, I won't let this happen again. No more splitting up. Bran was furious."

"It was my idea," she reminded him. "Not one of my better ones, apparently. But don't beat yourself up. It's not your fault my tongue is faster than my brain."

They drifted in silence for a moment; then he asked, "Have you ever killed anyone?" His voice was curious but nonjudgmental, as though he were asking what kind of books she liked.

"Aye." She didn't elaborate.

"There is much I don't know about you, Nora O'Reilly from the twenty-first century."

"Aye, well, there's plenty I don't know about you, either, Fionn mac Cumhaill from all centuries. Tell me more about these women who raised you. Where were your parents?"

Before he could answer, the low hoot of an owl drifted through the air. Nora turned and saw that the ship was almost upon them.

"That story will have to wait," Fionn said. He hooted back as he rowed their small boat closer to the ship.

"How'd you convince the captain of this ship to help you?" Nora asked.

"You'll see," he said as they drew up to the side and a rope ladder was lowered toward them. "You go first," he said, tying the boat to another rope that had been tossed down.

Nora stood shakily and grasped the rough ladder, then hauled herself and her soaking skirts up one step at a time, feeling her way in the darkness. Hands helped her over the ship's rail, and then a glowing lantern was swinging in her face, blinding her.

"Welcome aboard the *Queen Medb*, Mistress O'Reilly," a deep but unmistakably female voice said. "You'd better be worth the trouble."

The lantern withdrew, giving Nora a better look at the speaker. She was dressed as a man, with a leather vest and trews, and a heavy fur mantle draped around her. A wide-brimmed hat was perched on top of her coal-colored hair. A long silver sword glittered from one hip, a pistol from the other. But despite her change of clothing, she was unmistakable.

"Jesus Christ," Nora said. "Granuaile."

Chapter Fifteen

"How'd you escape?" Nora asked, gawking at the woman in front of her. "Last I saw you, they were taking you to the gallows." Granuaile looked the part of the quintessential pirate captain from the storybooks of Nora's youth. She only lacked an eye patch and a parrot on her shoulder. But despite the man's clothing, she had an unambiguous femininity. Her cheekbones were high and sculpted, though one was marred by a faint white line. Her ample chest was clearly visible under her leather vest, and her trews clung to the curves of her legs. Her thick hair, scattered lightly with silver, belied her nickname. Legend had it that she had been so desperate to join her father, the great Owen Dubhdara O'Malley, at sea that she'd chopped off her own hair and disguised herself as a boy, earning the nickname Gráinne Mhaol—Grace the Bald. Now her hair flowed free underneath a sweeping captain's hat tilted to one side.

"I didn't escape," Granuaile said brusquely, moving to the rail to help Fionn. "The Devil's Hook took my place."

"What?" Nora asked blankly.

"Her son-in-law, Richard Burke," Fionn answered, rubbing his hands together to warm them. "He agreed to be hostage in her place."

"It should have been me." A young man strode toward them, looking anxious. "But Richard got there first."

"And I'm glad for it," Granuaile said, smiling affectionately at him. She was missing two teeth. "This is my son, Tibbot."

Tibbot dipped his chin graciously to Nora. "Your escape was uneventful, I assume?"

"Aye, 'twas," she said, still unsure of the situation.

"Enough chatter," Granuaile said, moving swiftly between them and toward the forecastle of the ship. The eyes of her men were drawn to her like magnets. "Turn her around, boys. Let's go get us some redshanks. To Scotland!"

There was a cheer from the crew, followed by an outbreak of activity.

"Come on," Fionn said. "We've some dry clothes below, and Bran is eager to see you."

She followed him to a tiny cabin. When they opened the door, the hound barked in excitement and thumped her tail against the floor. Nora sank to her knees and wrapped her arms around the wolfhound. "I'm glad to see you, too," she said. Brán turned her soulful eyes on Nora and then nuzzled her face.

Fionn was already changing. He had stripped down to his sodden trews, and the light of the lantern bounced off his bare chest. Nora caught herself staring and turned around swiftly.

"Sorry," he muttered, and she could hear him pulling on a dry léine.

"It's grand," she said lightly. "I've seen men shirtless before, so I have." She shook off the loose robe she'd pulled on over her own léine and let it fall to the floor in a sodden heap. Then she grabbed the hem of her léine and lifted it over her head, leaving herself in her bra and panties. These, too, had been soaked with seawater, so she removed them, keeping her back to Fionn. A dry léine had been laid out on the single bed, and she pulled it on. Exhaustion suddenly overcame her, mingled with the relief of having escaped, the adrenaline of their flight through the castle, and the shock of Granuaile's role in her rescue.

"Are you all right?" he asked, but he didn't move toward her. He was standing in the exact same place, still wearing nothing but a léine and wet trews, struggle written across his face. Perhaps stripping naked in front of him had not been the wise thing to do.

"I'm shattered. And I can't believe it. Granuaile, here." She gave him a tired smile. "We found her. Well, *you* found her. How? What'd you tell her? Is she going to help us?"

"That can all wait. You should rest," Fionn said. Then he hastily left the room, leaving a trail of wet footprints behind him.

Nora stared after him. Had she thrown him off by undressing in front of him? Or was he still upset that she hadn't been locked in the dungeon? "D'you think he's as confused as I am?" she whispered to Bran, who'd padded over. Bran huffed, then jumped up on the bed. Nora curled around her, grateful for the warmth, and drifted into an uneasy sleep.

Fionn woke her in the morning with a gentle shake of the shoulder. She rubbed her face blearily. He was fully dressed. Where had he slept? She had tossed and turned most of the night, and only Bran had shared her bed.

"The captain would like to see us in her cabin," he said.

Nora dressed hurriedly, anxious to finally discover why Brigid had sent them to Granuaile. The clothes the captain had sent for her were simple, a sharp contrast to the elaborate gowns of Lady O'Brien. Over the léine, she wore a simple outer robe that tied under her breasts. A straw hat had been placed out for her, but she left it on the table. Surely she didn't need to stand on ceremony among a crew of pirates.

"Grand so. Let's be off," she said. "Where's Bran?"

"Hunting for rats," he said. "I should warn you that I told Granuaile my name is Fionn O'Hanlon."

Nora nodded, glad Fionn had not yet told her his true identity.

Granuaile and Tibbot were waiting for them in the captain's cabin—a larger, better furnished version of the one where Nora had slept. The single bed was neatly made in the corner, a curtain drawn partially around it. Several shelves and cases filled with books and artifacts were fastened to the walls. An elephant tusk was proudly displayed on the wall above a rectangular wooden desk littered with maps and papers and strange metal instruments.

"You are rested?" Granuaile asked, handing Nora a pewter mug of ale.

Nora was suddenly nervous, standing in the presence of this woman of legend. Granuaile might not be a goddess like Brigid, but she had the same bearing of a woman with unfaltering confidence in herself. Nora lifted her chin, trying to instill a confidence she did not feel. "I am, ta. And thank you for coming to get me."

Granuaile gestured for her and Fionn to take the seats across from her desk. "'Twas one of the more foolhardy things I've done, breaking out an English prisoner only days after I was released myself," Granuaile said once they were seated. Then she laughed, a deep rolling sound filled with pleasure.

"I don't know, Mother," Tibbot said. "Seems like exactly the sort of thing you would do." He shot Nora a rakish grin. "Once the Earl of Howth refused to offer my mother hospitality, so she kidnapped his heir and held him captive. And d'you know what she demanded as the ransom?"

Granuaile's lips twitched. Nora looked between them nervously. "Gold?" she guessed.

Tibbot slapped his knee and laughed. "One would think! No, she made him promise that the gates of Howth Castle would never again be closed to those seeking hospitality. I hear he still sets an extra place at his table to show his sincere repentance."

Granuaile grinned broadly. "As he should." Then she sobered. "The English keep trying to teach me a lesson, but they killed my boy. They're the ones who will be taught a lesson."

"They killed your son?" Nora asked, glancing at Tibbot.

"Aye. Gentle Owen, my second son. Bingham's brother murdered him two years ago." Granuaile's jaw tightened. "Stabbed him twelve times before leaving him for carrion. Richard Bingham thought I was a nuisance in the past, but now it's personal."

Tibbot rubbed the back of his neck. "Bingham has taken a special interest in our family. I was his hostage for two years. I was only released last year."

"That must have been awful," Nora sympathized.

Granuaile snorted. "'Twasn't so bad. He met and married the daughter of Donal O'Connor Sligo, one of Bingham's lackeys. And Bingham only released Tibbot in the hopes my son would be able to subdue the clans through reason where he himself had failed by force."

Tibbot lifted his chin. He couldn't have been more than twenty. What must it have been like to grow up under the shadow of such a formidable and notorious woman?

"Have you not had enough war, Mother? Would a little peace be so bad?"

"You have your peace. I'll have revenge."

"Did you meet Bingham himself, or just his subordinates?" Fionn asked Nora in a blatant attempt to redirect the conversation.

"Ach, I met him. Seems like a nasty piece of work."

Granuaile offered Nora a piece of dried fish from a tray, which she declined. "We need more men," Granuaile said, chewing on the tough meat. "There aren't enough of us to fight him, and the English are too well armed. I was on my way to get the redshanks when Bingham had me arrested. So now we'll try again."

"Redshanks?" Nora asked.

"Scottish mercenaries," Fionn explained. "The Irish have used them for years in their battles with each other, and now we're using them against the English."

Granuaile leaned forward, her hair falling over one shoulder, her eyes bright. "There is much to discuss. But first, tell me, did you learn anything of use during your time with Thomond? The O'Briens are pathetic little shits, aren't they? Elizabeth could tell Thomond to slit his own throat and he'd do it if the price were right."

"I don't think that's completely true," Nora said, hoping it wasn't just wishful thinking on her part. "He's outwardly loyal to England, aye. But that's because he loves power and progress. He sees the English ways as being more advanced than the Irish. But he was very moved by your poem of his ancestors, Fionn. I'd not seen him like that before. He appeared to be second-guessing himself. I tried to persuade him without giving myself away."

"Persuade him to what?" Tibbot asked.

"To support the rebel chiefs. To become one. I told him he could only bring progress to Ireland as a leader, not as a subject to a foreign queen. He didn't like that very much, but I think the idea stuck."

"Did he say anything about their plans against us?" Granuaile's gaze was intent on Nora.

"Nothing specific. But their strategy in general is pretty simple. And effective, apparently," she added bitterly. "Divide and conquer. They're actively fostering conflict between the clans to keep the chiefs from uniting against them."

Granuaile sat back in her chair, her fingertips steepled under her chin. "I know we're a quarrelsome lot," she said. "It's the Irish bailiwick, so people say."

Nora leaned forward. "Donough let it slip that if the clans were united, the English wouldn't stand a chance. Is that your plan? To unite the clans under one leader? It almost worked, with—" She stopped herself short and shot a hasty glance at Fionn.

"Tibbot, go find the quartermaster, and tell him I want to see him in my cabin in half an hour," Granuaile said. Tibbot looked displeased by the lowly task but obediently kissed his mother on the cheek and slipped from the room.

Granuaile turned back to Nora. "Don't worry yourself, child. Fionn has told me. You're from the future."

Nora twisted to face Fionn. "You *told* her? Without speaking to me about it?"

"I admit, I thought he was mad at first. But then again, it's quite possible we're all mad," Granuaile said sardonically. "Apparently we have an acquaintance in common, so perhaps we've her to blame."

"Brigid," Nora said. "So you understood what I said at the jail."

"Aye, Brigid. Where is that troublemaker, anyway?"

Nora shook her head. "We've no idea. All we know is that she sent us here to find you."

"Well, I'm not sure of the reason for that, but it will make itself plain soon enough," Granuaile said. She took a pipe out of a drawer and started stuffing it with leaves.

"You mean you don't have any idea of what we're supposed to change?" Her mouth hung open. She'd been sure that everything would become clear if only they managed to find Granuaile.

Granuaile looked up sharply. "Change?"

"Well, that's why we're here—to change the future." She turned to Fionn. "How much did you tell her?"

"Only that we're from the twentieth century, and Brigid sent us back in time to save Ireland."

She swiveled back to Granuaile. "And you believe us."

"I've seen many strange things in my long life. And the Brigid your friend described to me is the Brigid I know and, begrudgingly, love."

"Why begrudgingly?"

"You'll understand soon enough, if you're caught up in her plans. She makes you think you can rely on her, and then one day you find out you can't. You're on your own. It's a lesson, see, and a hard one, to learn one can only rely on oneself."

Nora digested this. She'd learned that lesson a long time ago. How had Brigid failed Granuaile? It wasn't her place to ask. "And has Fionn told you what is going to happen?" Nora asked cautiously.

"No, because I asked him not to. It's not natural to know the future. Even Brigid should mind that. Time is meant to be lived forward, not backward. She's messing with things bigger than herself, and that's saying something."

"Even if it can help us win?"

"Win what? My only concern is to protect my clan and my territory. Besides, knowing what will happen won't necessarily stop it from happening, now, will it?" Granuaile said decisively, taking a long pull on her pipe. "It'll just make it harder to watch. But you *have* given me interesting information from Thomond." She blew out a cloud of sweet-smelling smoke. "Unite the clans, you say?" She shook her head. "Each is fiercely loyal and protective of its own people and land, but none pay heed to anything greater. You'd be as apt to unite the stars."

"Would they follow *you*? Could *you* unite the clans?" Nora asked, leaning forward in her chair.

"O'course not," Granuaile said dismissively, waving a hand. "I'm a woman, and besides, I'm no chief. Some say *I* rule the O'Malley clan, with Tibbot as my *tánaiste*, but I don't. Would the other chiefs unite behind me and follow me into battle?" She shook her head.

"What about Tibbot?"

Granuaile pursed her lips. "I love my son. He is the pride and joy of my life. But you heard him yourself—he longs for peace, not war. He's still young, and as much as it pains me to admit it, I think he is torn. He does not yet know which side he will stake his claim on."

Fionn stood and started pacing the small cabin. "What is your plan once we have the redshanks?"

"Wreak havoc on Bingham, o'course," Granuaile said. "Make him pay for the death of my Owen, and my nephews. They were arrested with me, but the Devil's Hook was too late to bargain for their lives."

She set her pipe down and stretched. "Now, if you'll both excuse me. I've been up all night making sure we didn't get intercepted by Bingham's ships off Connacht. I've taken you in as friends of Brigid, but I've a rebellion to stir up. And for that, I'll need at least a few hours of sleep."

"Thank you for the drink," Nora said as she and Fionn slipped out the door. Once it had closed behind them, she said, "Let's go up top. I need some fresh air."

They climbed the companionway to the main deck. The wind was strong, and the craft was moving swiftly; the west coast of Ireland was already a dark smudge on the horizon. The sky was punched with clouds, white and gray swirled together. The cold wind blew the remaining cobwebs from Nora's mind. Now that it was light, she could see that they weren't alone. A fleet of six other ships sailed with them. "I'm still amazed she believed you."

"She wouldn't have if you and I hadn't both told her about Brigid. She still didn't want to help, but she says she owes Brigid. For what, I don't know."

They stood by the rail, the wind blowing Fionn's hair in his eyes and making Nora's stick up on end.

"Do *you* think she could do it? Unite the clans?" she asked.

He shook his head. "She's a fine captain on sea—the best there is, probably. But this will be a land war. She has little military experience on land."

"Maybe she could ally with one of the chiefs? What if she leads the attack by sea and someone else leads the land campaign?"

"Bingham destroyed most of her fleet," Fionn said. "This is almost all that's left. Hardly enough to wage war against the English navy."

"It would be nice if *you* came up with some ideas, y'know," Nora said pointedly, "instead of just shooting mine down."

"I've been trying, but like I said before, it's not as easy as you think. There are so many players, so many moving parts. The concept of a united Ireland is as foreign to these people as this Internet you spoke of.

To you and me, it seems natural, inevitable. But the only thing they are united in is their misery. Besides, we can't be sure changing one thing won't make another worse."

The thought troubled her. What if their actions brought even more suffering to the Irish people? But if they did nothing . . .

"So what *have* you been thinking?" she prompted.

"Brigid sent us to Granuaile for a reason. Obviously Granuaile herself doesn't even know what that reason is. We just have to wait until it presents itself."

"Patience isn't my strong suit."

"I know."

Chapter Sixteen

Tibbot wanted to reunite with his wife, Maeve, and continue his diplomatic work among the chiefs of Mayo, so he parted from the group near Clew Bay. Nora stood beside Granuaile as the ship carrying her son and some of the crew broke off toward land. "I'd have him by my side at all times if I could," Granuaile said, a sudden wistfulness in her voice. "But he wants to be his own man, and so he should be."

"He seems like a very thoughtful young man," Nora offered.

"Aye, that he is, though I don't know where he got it. His father was all piss and vinegar, and I'm not known for my even temper."

As quickly as it had arrived, the moment of intimacy between the two women disappeared. Granuaile gave a great sniff, then stalked off across the deck, shouting orders at lounging sailors.

A week of hard sailing passed, and no one spoke any more of Tibbot. The talk had turned to the number of redshanks they would hire, how long it would take to ferry them back to Mayo, and what kind of results they could expect this time from their rented army.

Nora found Fionn on deck, adjusting the cordage attached to the foremast. He'd thrown himself into the work of a sailor, but Granuaile had insisted Nora "recover from her ordeal" and tried to keep her below deck and away from the sailors whenever possible. Obviously, Granuaile didn't believe in the superstitious nonsense about having a woman on board, but she also didn't want her sailors distracted, or so she said. Fionn had been sleeping on the deck with the other sailors, and Nora had hardly seen him.

Just as Nora approached Fionn, a voice cried out from high above them, up among the spars and sails. She didn't understand the words, but Fionn's face darkened. "Storm ahead," he told her. "And a bad one. Can you swim?" He grabbed both her arms as the ship began to sway and an icy wind made the sails crack and billow.

"Yes, but—"

"If the ship goes down, grab on to anything that floats. *I'll find you.*" Then he shoved her toward the trapdoor that led to the lower decks. "Go! Stay in your cabin. Stay with Bran."

"If the ship goes *down*? What about you? What about sticking together?" she cried. The wind whipped around them, and men ran past her, hauling ropes and shouting at one another in Gaelic.

"I can help!" he called. "Go! And wake Granuaile!"

She wanted to argue that she could help, but in this particular situation, it wasn't true. So she lifted the trapdoor and climbed down. Granuaile was not one to sleep through a storm, and she nearly collided with Nora in the darkness of the lower deck. "What are you doing here? Get into your cabin!" Granuaile commanded, and Nora, having nothing else to do, obeyed. Bran was pressed against the floor, her ears back and eyes wide.

"Come on," Nora said, climbing onto the bed and patting the mattress beside her. Bran leapt up, and Nora wrapped her arms around the great hound. "It's just a storm," she told her. "It will blow over." Her stomach heaved as the ship lurched sideways. Bran whined and cowered closer, shoving her snout under Nora's arm. "Ach, are you afeared, you big puppy?" she asked, stroking Bran's head. "We'll be grand, so we will."

She could hear nothing of the upper decks over the roar of the wind and the hammering of the rain. A part of her longed to see what was happening, but a moment's distraction could cost a sailor his life. Instead, she lifted her worn rosary out of her dress, kissed the tiny cross that hung beside the saint's finger bone, and prayed.

The *Queen Medb* was tossed about like a toy boat in a child's bath for what seemed an eternity. Nora and Bran were both thrown out of the bed more than once, landing hard on the floor and sliding halfway across the room. She threw up her ale in the chamber pot, the acid burning her esophagus. Then she looked around for something that would float. A small square table was nailed to the floor, but she hadn't the strength to pull it free. She went to the door and wrenched it open to examine the hinges. If the ship went down, she and Bran could both fit on the door, if she could manage to hang on to it. Then someone on the deck above screamed in terror. "*Tine*!"

Nora's head jerked up. She knew that word.

Fire.

She ran toward the sound, bolting up a small companionway. A single shirtless sailor was on the gun deck, which was between her cabin and the upper deck. The six brass cannons were straining against the heavy ropes that held them in place as the ship pitched and swayed. Round shot was everywhere, having broken through the wooden barriers intended to keep them in place. The fire was in the center of the floor, and a sailor was trying to smother it with his léine, which was now engulfed in flames. He was screaming over and over again, "Tine! Tine!" as he whipped the flames with the burning léine. Nora grabbed his arm and pulled him away from the fire.

"Stop!" she said. "You're making it worse!" Glass crunched beneath her feet. The remnants of a lantern. The man pointed at the other side of the flames. Nora followed his terrified gaze to a single squat wooden barrel, just over a foot and a half high and a foot in diameter. The sailor grabbed her arm to get her attention, then mimed an explosion, his hands shooting out to his sides, fingers splayed. His eyes were frenzied.

Oh, sweet Jesus. That barrel was full of enough gunpowder to blow a hole in the bottom of the ship.

Nora ripped off her brat and started beating at the flames, but they were too hot, too hungry to be subdued in this way. "Go!" she shouted, pointing at the companionway. "Get help!" The man sprinted toward the upper deck, bellowing the whole way.

Bran was behind her, barking frantically, running between her and the stairs. And then Fionn appeared in the doorway. His face was ashen as he jumped down and took in the scene.

"Get away!" he shouted at her, taking her arm and yanking her roughly toward the stairs.

"I think there's gunpowder over there!" Nora yelled over the roar of the flames, pointing at the wooden barrel in the corner. "We have to get it out!" The ship lurched again, and she stumbled, sprawling down on the floor. Other sailors had formed a line and were passing buckets of seawater down the stairs, but the flames refused to be doused.

"I can reach it!" Fionn shouted. He made for a gap in the flames, where they had not yet formed a solid wall between the sailors and the gunpowder. With one massive, outstretched leap, he reached the other side. Nora watched his figure waver and flicker as he raced toward the barrel. But the ship rocked just as he hoisted it into in his arms. He stumbled, and the flames roared, joining together and cutting off his escape.

"Fionn!" Nora screamed, the smoke tearing at her throat. He dodged from side to side behind the wall of flame, trying to figure a way out. But they were too high now, too hot. The sailors started retreating, scrabbling their way to the upper decks, where at least they'd stand a chance at survival. "Fionn!" she screamed again. Bran ran back and forth in front of the wall of flame, barking frantically, desperate to reach her master. Nora grabbed handfuls of Bran's fur and pulled the hound back from the flames.

And then Fionn burst through, the barrel clutched under his arm. The flames would not surrender their prey so easily. They reached out and caught their target as he passed through, burning both flesh and wood. "Move!" Fionn bellowed, and Nora jumped out of the way, her eyes wide and red. He cast a quick glance at the gun ports—too small for the barrel to be shoved through—then sprinted up the stairs, flames licking at his clothes, his hair as he clutched the burning barrel under his arm. She ran up the steps after him, the wolfhound on her heels. Sailors skittered away as he reached the top deck. Nora arrived just in time to see him heave the barrel over the side. The *Queen Medb* shifted suddenly at that exact moment, sending Fionn tumbling over the rail.

Nora's heart stopped. A sailor caught her around the waist and dragged her back just before the explosion rocked the ship and they all fell to the deck. Nora pushed him off and ran to the side. Ragged strips of wood floated in the water, but there was no sign of Fionn.

He was gone.

Chapter Seventeen

The storm scarpered as quickly as it had arrived. The sea, having received its offering, was still. But the frenzy continued on deck as though Fionn had not gone over at all. Granuaile was in the middle of it, one eye on the *Queen Medb* and the other on the ships bobbing around them in the calming sea. Bran stood beside Nora, her front legs up on the rail, still barking. A team of storm-soaked men rolled huge barrels of drinking water toward the lower decks, from which the smell of burning wood was wafting.

The fire, she thought numbly, still searching the waters below for any sign of Fionn.

Granuaile appeared beside her, her lips tight. "I'm sorry, Nora. He was a brave man. He saved us all."

"He's not dead," Nora said, not taking her eyes off the sea.

"He couldn't have survived—"

Nora swiveled until their faces were only inches apart. "*He's not dead.* But he's hurt. We have to find him." She grabbed a rope from the deck, wound it around a bracket on the side of the rail, and then tied the other end around her waist.

"What the devil do you think you're doing?" Granuaile asked, grabbing Nora's arm. Nora wrenched it away, then climbed over the rail and started lowering herself down. "I have to find him!"

She splashed into the water, gasping from the shock of the cold. She floundered a bit before finding a steady rhythm with her legs. Screaming Fionn's name, she twisted about and looked for him, ignoring the sailors who watched her from above. She filled her lungs with air and then dove under the surface as far as the rope tethering her to the ship would allow. Again and again she dove—arms reaching, legs kicking, eyes opening to the sting of salt water. She breached the surface again and opened her mouth to gasp for air, but a wave smacked her in the face, filling her lungs with water. She choked and coughed, and then she was going down, and she couldn't tell which way was up, and her legs were so tired, and Fionn was gone.

Something grabbed hold of her around the waist—the rope. She was being pulled to the surface, then through the air, the thick cord almost cutting her in half. She landed hard on something solid, and the next thing she knew, someone pushed her chest and rolled her over. Then air, sweet air, filled her lungs, and she thought she threw up, but couldn't be sure. Gradually, the world became clearer. An eye in the wooden floor stared back at her. Something rough rubbed against her skin.

"Nora?" a voice was saying. Granuaile. The pirate queen had plucked her from the sea.

"Did you get him?" she asked, wincing at the burn in her throat. She pushed Bran, who had been licking her face, to the side so she could sit up.

Granuaile shook her head. "I'm sorry, dear. But he's gone."

"No." Nora got to her feet, her legs wobbling. "He can't die," she croaked.

"Everyone can die," Granuaile said, not unkindly. She shrugged out of her brat, which was soaking wet, and slung it around Nora's shoulders.

"He's not dead," Nora muttered again. Granuaile barked some orders to the men, then took Nora downstairs. Like a mother, she stripped Nora out of her wet garments, gave her a dry léine, and tucked her into bed. "I must see to my ships," she said. "Stay here."

"The fire . . . ," Nora started to ask.

"It's out," Granuaile said. "I meant what I said. He saved the *Queen Medb* and everyone on it." Then she left Nora alone.

Nora stayed under the covers until the shakes subsided. Bran had followed, of course, and had lain practically on top of her.

This is ballix. She wasn't going to stay in bed while Fionn was suffering. She didn't want to think about his condition, but the image of him pushing past her, flames eating at his clothes and skin, wouldn't leave her mind. The explosion had ripped that barrel to shreds. How could he have possibly survived?

When she reached the upper deck, the shore was in sight. But the shore of what? Had they sailed as far as Scotland? The land that lay before them was all green hills and rocky outcroppings. They could be almost anywhere. Granuaile, standing in her station on the forecastle, caught her eye from across the deck. Nora looked away. She wouldn't allow herself to be sent to bed like a child. She searched again for Fionn, hoping he might have been rescued and brought onto the ship, but there was no sign of him. She caught a passing sailor. "Where is this?" she asked as they limped toward the shore.

"Ulster," he answered, brushing past her. She let him go. So they'd put in at Ulster for repairs.

She was nearly certain that Fionn was alive. Surely he must have faced almost every kind of death in the many centuries he'd lived. Surely he could survive an explosion, a drowning?

But how? A sliver of doubt needled into her. How could he have survived that? And if he had, where was he now?

She stepped out of the way as a sailor slipped behind her, pulling one of the ropes attached to what was left of the sails. As they drew closer, a stone tower house rose above the cliff. Men were coming down a winding path to the shore. Were they friend or foe? By the mood of the crew—subdued but not afraid—these must be friends.

"Donegal Castle," Granuaile said over her shoulder. "So this is where fate has blown us."

"Who lives here?"

"Sir Hugh O'Donnell, Lord of Tyrconnell."

"Hugh O'Donnell? Do you mean Red Hugh O'Donnell?" Nora asked, her interest piqued.

"His father," Granuaile said. "But how do you know of Red Hugh?"

"You said you didn't want to know the future," Nora answered.

Granuaile left it at that.

Nora was one of the first sent ashore, rowed in one of the small wooden boats that had not been smashed to pieces by the wind. The others in her boat, mainly sailors who had been wounded, limped up the steep path that led to the castle. Those who could not walk were carried. But Nora, Bran at her side, did not follow them. Ignoring the calls behind her, she walked along the shoreline, looking for a broken body. She didn't care if this was enemy territory, or if she was trespassing, or if she was breaching some sixteenth-century protocol.

But there was no body, dead or alive. Vowing to come back to look for him, Nora reluctantly trailed Granuaile and her bedraggled crew through the gate in the high wall surrounding the castle. Bran followed her, keening softly. This was more than a tower house; it was a medieval castle in all its glory, a warning to those who would attack Ulster from the northern sea. The survivors clustered in the yard, brothers searching for brothers, sons for fathers. Low curses rent the air as news spread of those who had been injured or lost. The men parted to let their captain through. Granuaile strode forward, head held high, as an elderly man descended the castle steps to greet her. His slumped posture only accentuated his lack of height. Two puffs of gray whiskers protruded from under his nose, which was long and crooked, as though it had been broken multiple times. His thin chest heaved as he shuffled down the stairs. Behind him, a striking woman many years his junior surveyed the rugged gathering in the yard before them. Her scarlet hair was pulled back by two jeweled combs that caught the sunlight, and her high cheekbones and large almond eyes gave her an otherworldly look.

The couple embraced Granuaile, and the three of them spoke in voices too low for anyone to overhear. Granuaile gestured to the yard full of men, and the man to whom she was speaking summoned a servant closer. Then Granuaile turned to address her sailors.

"The O'Donnell, Earl of Tyrconnell, and his wife, Lady Tyrconnell, have long been friends of clan O'Malley and have offered us shelter while we repair our boats and tend to our wounded. Ship captains and quartermasters, you will have the hospitality of the castle. For our brave sailors, the O'Donnells will pitch tents for you on the grounds. Food and ale will be brought shortly." There was a general cheer at this news.

The yard swarmed with activity as sailors transported supplies out of the ruined boats. Nora followed Granuaile into the castle, intending to ask her to send some men to assist with the search for Fionn. As she passed through the imposing iron doors, she cast her eyes about for anyone who might be Red Hugh, the O'Donnell son who would join forces with Hugh O'Neill to challenge the English in the Nine Years' War and the Battle of Kinsale. Granuaile stood near the fire at the back of the hall, deep in discussion with Lady Tyrconnell and her husband. Nora waited impatiently, one hand on Bran's back. Lady Tyrconnell saw Nora staring, and bent her head closer to Granuaile. Then the two women broke off from O'Donnell and approached her.

Nora didn't know if she was supposed to curtsey in the presence of a chieftain's wife, so she gave an awkward half bow. "Welcome," the woman said. "I am Fionnuala Nic Dhomhnaill. Here, they call me the Iníon Dubh," the woman said. "My friend Gráinne Ní Mháille tells me you are an adventurer, recently returned from the Continent. I was saddened to hear of your companion's death. He saved a lot of souls today."

"Aye," Nora said simply. She turned to Granuaile. "I'm going back to the beach to search for him. Can you spare a couple of men to help me?"

"Nora . . . ," Granuaile said, giving her a look of deep pity.

"He's alive, I know it," Nora said. "And even if he wasn't, I'd still want to recover the . . . the body."

Granuaile's expression turned to annoyance. "You have a lot to learn about life at sea. I am sorry for your loss, but we need to tend to the living and repair our fleet. I can spare no one."

Nora's grip tightened in Bran's fur, and the wolfhound whined. "Grand so. I'll look for him myself."

But hours later, her skin raw from the biting Atlantic wind and her feet numb from the icy water, Nora was forced to retreat to the castle for the night. The men had set up tents in the castle yard, and straw mattresses had been laid out on the floor of the great hall for the wounded, but Nora was given a room and bed in the east tower. It was meager comfort. She and Bran huddled together on the bed while Nora tried to block out images of Fionn, his body burned and bloated, drifting away from her on the tide. What little sleep she managed was restless and haunted.

The next day, after scouring the coastline once more, Nora pitched in as best she could, helping to treat the wounded men. The servants thought her mad for her obsession with washing hands and boiling strips of cloth, but they did as she bade them on the Iníon Dubh's orders—encouraged by Granuaile, no doubt. As much as Nora wanted to help these sailors, her heart and mind were fixed on Fionn. Was he in pain? Was he truly still alive? And if so, where was he?

Granuaile interrupted her anxious thoughts. "The O'Donnell has invited us to dine with him."

"Us?"

"Yes. The invitation was extended to the captains of my fleet and my 'lady adventurer friend.' So you'd better come up with some entertaining stories about your time abroad."

"Right."

Granuaile looked appraisingly at Nora. "I've had my chests brought up from the ship. I've a spare dress that might fit you. You can't dine with the chief dressed in only a léine."

The Chief. It was the nickname that would be given to IRA chief of staff Liam Lynch hundreds of years in the future. A swarm of memories came back to Nora: Lynch's willingness to believe her information about the coming skirmish, his refusal to stop fighting for the Republic, and his glassy eyes staring at her from a pool of blood on the floor. She closed her eyes and tried to clear her mind. This time would be different. It had to be.

"Are you well, Nora?" Granuaile asked.

"Aye, I'm grand," Nora said. "When is supper?"

"They'll ring a bell. I'll send the dress to your room, shall I?"

"Aye." How the hell was she supposed to dine with The O'Donnell without sounding like an eejit? She wasn't an adventurer.

But then again, she supposed she was. She could talk about the animals she'd seen on safari in Africa. She could talk about the ruins of Greece and Italy, the great cathedrals of Europe. Of course, for all she knew, the ruins were not yet ruins and the cathedrals had not yet been built, but her dining companions would not know enough to correct her.

If Fionn had been with her, they would have enjoyed spinning an elaborate backstory together. But just when Nora had started depending on him, he had been taken from her. And now she was truly alone in this wide, unknown world.

Chapter Eighteen

An hour later, dressed in a simple borrowed gown the color of violets, Nora followed a servant into a cavernous room that was chilly despite the twin fires burning at either end of it. A long wooden table ran through the center, above which hung elaborate candelabras made from antlers and carved wood. Brightly colored tapestries adorned each wall. Nora was tempted to run over to the tapestries and gape at them like an awestruck tourist, but she managed to feign an expression of detached interest. The servant led her to the long table, where Granuaile was seated at O'Donnell's right hand. A seat had been saved for her next to Granuaile, much to the disgruntlement of the men seated farther along the table. The Iníon Dubh sat at O'Donnell's left.

"Welcome, Mistress O'Reilly," Hugh O'Donnell said in surprisingly good English. "I understand you've already met my wife, Lady Tyrconnell." In Gaelic, he said to those around them, "This is one half of the adventuring couple Granuaile picked up on her travels. Tragically, her male companion was drowned while saving the *Queen Medb* from fire."

He's not dead. I mustn't listen to them. He's not dead.

"Lovely to meet you," she said. "And thank you for your hospitality."

"Hospitality?" O'Donnell said, looking at her blankly. "Whatever do you mean, child?"

Nora opened her mouth to respond but didn't quite know what to say. Had she breached some formal protocol? Caused offense to their hosts?

"It's all right, dear," the Iníon Dubh said, leaning in and taking her husband's hand. "You have offered Granuaile and her friends the hospitality of Donegal Castle."

"Have I? My apologies. Sometimes I get . . . confused." His cheeks flushed red.

The Iníon Dubh shot Granuaile an apologetic look, then leaned in to whisper, "My husband's mind is not as strong as it once was. His memory is slipping, I'm afraid."

Granuaile nodded slowly, keeping her eyes on Lady Tyrconnell, who smiled brightly at Nora and asked, "Gaelic is not your first language, is it?"

"I'm afraid not. I was raised by an English family after my parents died when I was young. We were traveling in England at the time."

"And were they adventurers, too?"

"Wine merchants, mostly," Nora fabricated. "Though they did like to travel as far as possible. Sometimes I think the business was just an excuse for the travel."

Granuaile and the O'Donnells laughed heartily. Nora accepted a glass of wine and took a large gulp.

O'Donnell leaned toward Granuaile. "I am sorry for your trouble, but I think your arrival must be a sign from God. He has brought you to us whether you wanted it or not. Now you can give us your council."

"Oh?" Granuaile's eyes flicked to the Iníon Dubh.

"Indeed," she said. "You will not be the only visitors to Donegal Castle. Hugh O'Neill should arrive within a day or two."

"Hugh O'Neill? Your son-in-law?"

"The very same," the Iníon Dubh answered. "He and my stepdaughter Siobhán are on their way as we speak."

On the pretense of refilling her wineglass, Nora leaned closer to Granuaile, straining to hear what the two were discussing. *The* Hugh O'Neill who had fought with the English to suppress the Desmond Rebellion? The Hugh O'Neill who would fight with Red Hugh O'Donnell against the English at Kinsale? Nora hadn't known the two were related, but it made sense. Both were from Ulster; both would become the heads of their powerful, ancient families.

"We could use you here, Granuaile," the Iníon Dubh said. "Your fleet is strong, and you have excellent captains. Most fleets would have been completely destroyed during that storm, but you didn't lose a single ship. No one knows these waters better than you. And the presence of your fleet would encourage Lord Deputy Perrot to leave Ulster to our own affairs."

"And what would you have me do?" Granuaile replied, raising her hands to the sky. "I'm already ferrying redshanks from Scotland to Connacht—at great risk, I might add. I cannot fight both Perrot and Bingham. The devil himself lives in that man. I only just escaped his clutches. Again."

"No one expects it to come to a fight," the Iníon Dubh insisted. "Your mere presence would be enough to make Perrot think again about making incursions onto our land."

"Or it would draw him here," Granuaile countered. "I must continue north. I need more Scots."

"What you *need* is a united Ireland," Nora interjected, unable to stay quiet. "If all the fighting men of Ireland united behind one leader, you could defeat Perrot and Bingham and all the English."

The Iníon Dubh shot Nora a shrewd look. "A noble concept, to be sure, but the Irish have not united behind one leader since Brian of Bóruma. I can assure you Tyrconnell will not bow the knee to some chieftain of Munster or Leinster. Are the O'Malleys willing to submit to the Burkes of Clanricard?" She said this with a laugh in her voice.

"Most of the clans have already submitted to the English. Why not unite behind an Irishman and fight as one for your country?" Nora argued.

The Iníon Dubh stiffened. "Submission is a political necessity, but that's as far as it goes. You do not challenge our honor, newcomer?"

"O'course not," Nora said, her voice faltering.

O'Donnell cleared his voice and called for more wine, breaking the tense silence. Then he said, "Granuaile tells me you are a great adventurer, much like herself. Entertain us with some stories of your travels."

Nora forced her face into a smile. *Patience*, she urged herself once again. Then she launched into a retelling of her last safari in Kenya, modifying details to fit the sixteenth century.

"So they really exist, do they?" O'Donnell asked eagerly. "The great-tusked animals?"

"They're called elephants," Nora said. "And aye, I saw several of them. The babies themselves weigh about two hundred pounds, and they travel in herds for protection."

"I was there once," Granuaile said wistfully. "But only in the towns and markets where we could trade. I bought a great tusk—you saw it in my cabin on the *Queen Medb*. I longed to see the real thing, but my men got in too many brawls with the Moors. I could have stayed there for years. The heat was incredible."

"Aye," Nora agreed. "'Tis an amazing place, so it is. Have you ever experienced a sandstorm?"

Granuaile shook her head.

"Imagine the wildest rainstorm you've ever been in, with winds so strong they nearly knock you on your arse. Then replace the cold wind with scorching heat, and the rain with sand. Even if you cover up, it gets everywhere—and I mean *everywhere*. All you can do is wait it out, and then, when it's over, the land around you has completely changed. There are valleys where there were hills, and hills where there were valleys. It makes it difficult to navigate, so it does."

"I wish my son Hugh Roe could hear your stories. He dreams of such grand adventures," the Iníon Dubh said wistfully.

"Red Hugh? Is he here?" Nora asked, holding her breath.

"No, he's in Rathmullan. With MacSweeney of Fanad and his sons. He was fostered there, and has quite the bond with them. He will return to us in the spring, God willing."

Nora slumped with disappointment. She'd started to think that fate—or Brigid—had led them here, to a critical meeting of Red Hugh and Hugh O'Neill, future allies. But Rathmullan was on the other side of County Donegal, near the most northern point of Ireland. But at least O'Neill was on his way. Perhaps his time here at Donegal Castle would be the turning point. Perhaps this was where he would have the change of heart that would transform him into the revolutionary leader Nora remembered from her history books.

"Is the man you speak of, Hugh O'Neill, the Earl of Tyrone?"

"That he is," The O'Donnell boomed. "So now he has a title to equal my own."

"I have heard of the strength of the O'Donnell clan," Nora said tentatively, trying to get a feel for clan politics. "Perhaps Red Hugh's heart for adventure will lead him to great things someday."

"Perhaps," the Iníon Dubh said, her eyes flicking to her husband, who was wiping wine from his beard with the sleeve of his léine.

"Is Domhnall Dubh still the O'Donnell tánaiste?" Granuaile asked, giving Nora a warning glance.

"He is," Lady Tyrconnell said begrudgingly. "For now. And Niall Garve thinks he has the next best claim. But we must prepare our son regardless. These are dangerous, unpredictable times."

Nora's face tensed as she searched her memory. She knew Red Hugh eventually became The O'Donnell. So what happened to Domhnall and Niall? *Watch your step*, an inner voice warned her.

"We will have many discussions about the current state of affairs when O'Neill arrives," the Iníon Dubh said, still addressing Granuaile. "I do hope you will join our counsel."

Nora was surprised at the way The O'Donnell allowed his wife to speak for him, but it validated her early impression of the situation. The Iníon Dubh was the one truly in charge. Had it always been this way, or only since he'd started going senile? He didn't seem to mind at all. Instead, he smiled congenially at his wife and then at Granuaile. "Indeed, we would."

Granuaile inclined her head toward the old man. "My only wish is to continue my trade and ensure the safety of my remaining children and grandchildren. But while Bingham remains governor of Connacht, that wish will be continually thwarted. My fleet—what remains of it—and I will do what we can. I'll give you my advice on affairs in the north, for what it's worth. But I must look after my own."

Nora fought back a groan. *This is why the English never leave. Because it's every man—or woman—for themselves. Families and clans always come before country. It's so shortsighted. If only they knew what I know . . .*

How could she convince them that their only hope lay in coming together? Granuaile had made it quite clear that she didn't wish to know what the future held. Now that Nora was here, face to face with those in power, should she risk telling the truth? Or would she end her life tied to a burning stake?

Granuaile must have sensed what she was thinking, for she said, "You look unwell, Nora. Perhaps you should retire for the evening."

The two women waged war with their eyes. But Nora needed Granuaile as an ally, so she pushed her chair back and stood. "Aye. I'm quite tired, so I am." She curtseyed to the O'Donnells.

"You let us know if there's anything you need, child," O'Donnell said. The Iníon Dubh said nothing.

Nora went back to her room in the tower, but not to sleep. Bran was waiting expectantly by the door. After wrapping a thick cloak around her shoulders, Nora patted Bran's head and said, "Let's go." The wolfhound followed her silently down the curving stair and into the entrance hall. Nora lifted a torch from a bracket on the wall, ignoring a protest from one of the injured men on the floor, and headed out into the dark, chill evening. Keeping one hand on Bran's back for balance, she wound her way down the path that led to the rocky shore.

"Where are you?" she whispered into the night, but the only reply was the crash of waves coming in from the vast Atlantic Ocean.

Bran suddenly stiffened under her hand. Nora swung the torch around, a flush of fear spreading through her. Footsteps crunched toward them, but the torch's light did not reach the intruder.

Then Bran wrenched away from Nora and gave a joyful bark as she tore down the beach.

"Wait!" Nora cried, stumbling along behind her, tripping over stones slick with seaweed. There was a thump ahead of her, and then a long, high whine from the hound. Bran reappeared at her side and guided her to a man who lay crumpled on the beach.

"Fionn," she breathed. "Oh, thank God, you're alive, you're alive."

He moaned and rolled over, so that the light from her torch shone on his pale face. "Barely," he whispered, but his lips lifted in a shadow of a smile. "I told you I would find you."

She fought back the tears that pooled behind her eyes. "You did. But . . . how?"

He tried to stand, but his legs shook violently with the effort. Nora wrapped her cloak around him and then hoisted him to his feet, letting some of his weight rest on her shoulders. "Never mind," she said. "Let's just get you up to the castle."

Slowly, she half-supported, half-dragged him along the shoreline and up the path. Once she was in earshot of the castle, she yelled for someone to come and help. Two sailors ran toward her torch but stopped cold at the sight of Fionn. Their lips moved silently as they crossed themselves. Then they began to back away.

"What are you doing?" Nora shouted. "We need help!" But the men raced back to their tents in the castle yard. Nora let loose a stream of curses after them, then continued hauling Fionn toward the castle steps.

"They think I'm cursed," Fionn whispered, his voice so faint she could hardly hear him.

"You *are* cursed," she pointed out.

"The sea does not give up her victims willingly. They'll think I made a deal with the devil to survive."

"Well, they're nothing but superstitious eejits," she said, but her joy at finding Fionn was slightly dampened. If the others assumed the worst, what would they do to him? Surely Granuaile at least would be glad to see him alive.

Light spilled out of the castle door as they approached the steps. One of the guards shouted to someone on the inside. A few moments later, Granuaile was framed in the doorway, staring down at Nora and her burden. She gave a loud gasp, then rushed down the stairs toward them. Bran barked loudly at her, but the pirate queen hushed the hound and wrapped Fionn's other arm around her shoulder.

"He needs medical care," Nora grunted, "but not in the hall. We'll take him to my room."

"I can walk," Fionn said, unwrapping himself from Nora and Granuaile. But he stumbled and fell on the first step. Two servants stepped forward and helped him to his feet.

"Take him to the east tower," Nora told them, and they set off, Bran leading the way.

Nora put her hands on her knees, her breath labored. "I told you . . . he was alive," she panted.

"So you did," Granuaile said, her eyes wary. "But how? How did he survive?"

"I don't know," she said truthfully. "But it doesn't matter. He's alive." Then she turned her back on the other woman and followed Fionn and the servants up the stairs.

Chapter Nineteen

"Can I bring you anything, mistress?" one of the servants asked after they had laid Fionn on the bed in her room. Nora perched on the bed beside him.

"More fuel for the fire," she said. "Water, and a pot to boil it in. Food and ale. And some clean cloth I can tear up to use as bandages."

Once they had gone, Nora leaned over Fionn and brushed his hair off his forehead so she could inspect the red blotches on his cheeks. These burns were not too bad; she didn't think they would leave a scar—if he *did* scar. The burns on his torso and arms were worse, but the salt water had at least kept them clean. The pain must have been excruciating.

"What are you doing to me?" she whispered.

His eyes fluttered open. "Trying to keep you alive, for starters," he said, his voice raspy.

Nora exhaled, her shoulders relaxing. "You're a madman."

"You're the one who was trying to put out a fire with your brat," he said.

"I was going to say, 'You could have been killed,' but I suppose that's not true, is it?"

He shook his head, then winced. "I told you, I'm indestructible."

"Immortal, maybe. But your skin is plenty destroyed in places."

"It'll heal."

"What happened?"

"I was knocked unconscious by the blast. When I came to, I was floating on top of the water, but the ships were gone. And so I'd no choice but to swim for shore. It took me a couple of days. I could only hope Granuaile had put in at Ulster, and I was right."

"You've been swimming this entire time?"

He closed his eyes. "Swimming, floating, more swimming. It's rather exhausting. Where are we, exactly?"

"We're at Donegal Castle. The O'Donnell chieftain is here. He's letting us stay until they can fix the ships."

"Ah. Is the Iníon Dubh here as well?"

"Aye. She seems quite formidable. And here I thought Granuaile was one of a kind in this day and age."

"Ha!" Fionn wheezed. "You can't throw a stone without hitting a formidable Irishwoman, not that I'd recommend it. We're as far away from English power as you can get in this day and age. The Iníon Dubh—it means *Dark Daughter*—is the real O'Donnell in all but name, just as Granuaile should have the title of The O'Malley. A good woman, as long as you don't get in her way."

Dark Daughter indeed. Nora wanted to ask where the Iníon Dubh had earned this nickname. It certainly wasn't from her coloring. But that could wait. "The O'Donnells, you say," Fionn muttered. "And Red Hugh? Is the lad here?"

"No," Nora said. "But don't worry about that now. You need to sleep, and heal. Are you in a lot of pain? Is there something I can give you?"

"Mostly just knackered. Besides, I like to view pain as penance," he said, the corner of his lips twitching in a wry smile. "Sadly, proper painkillers haven't been invented yet. A shame we didn't bring any morphine."

"A shame we didn't bring any number of things," Nora said, thinking of antibiotics, toothpaste, a good history book, and portable artillery.

"It's a more authentic experience this way, I suppose," Fionn said with a lazy grin.

"Hush. Just get some rest."

Nora spent the next two hours tending to Fionn. The Iníon Dubh sent him a fresh léine, along with a bottle of whiskey and a jar of comfrey salve for his burns. He gladly claimed the bottle of spirits, and after he had taken several large swigs, Nora applied the salve to his burns and wrapped the boiled cloths around his arms and chest. Eventually he fell asleep. She put another sod of turf on the fire, then lay down beside him on the bed.

He stirred and opened one eye. "Thank you for taking such good care of me," he whispered.

"Thank you for keeping the ship from blowing up," she answered, her eyes fixed on the ceiling. "I really can't swim all that well."

"Maybe Brigid knew what she was doing, after all."

Nora didn't know what to say to that, so she closed her eyes and pretended to sleep. Fionn's breathing soon returned to a slow, steady pace. Nora rolled onto her side to watch him in the dim moonlight streaming through the tiny window. She fought the urge to run the back of her fingers along his cheek, fought the urge to take him in her arms like a child and weep for joy that he had not been killed.

The next evening they took a tentative walk through the castle grounds to test Fionn's strength. He moved gingerly, his upper body swathed in fresh bandages under his léine. But a long rest and a hearty breakfast had restored much of his strength. The story of his remarkable survival had obviously spread, and everywhere they went the O'Donnell men and Granuaile's sailors gave them dark looks, muttering curses under their breath. Nora tried not to notice, but the skin on the back of her neck prickled.

They sat on an outcropping of rock on the eastern side of the castle, away from the sailors' frantic activity and frightened glares. The woods near Donegal Castle were still intact, unlike many forests in the rest of Ireland, which had fallen under the English axe. The fields surrounding the castle brimmed with activity as men felled trees and shaped them into planks and masts, mended canvas, and wove thick ropes from hemp strands. Another crew hunted and cooked for the sailors, so as to not deprive the O'Donnells of all their stores. A small brewery had even been set up, though Nora declined to sample its wares, preferring to stick to the tried-and-tested burgundies and clarets the O'Donnells kept stocked in their cellar.

Nora gave Fionn a recap of the conversation at supper the night before.

"Hugh O'Neill is on his way here?" Fionn asked. "That's very interesting."

"What do you think it means?"

"I've been trying to remember the order of things. The Nine Years' War starts in 1594. That's when Red Hugh O'Donnell and Maguire of Fermanagh declare open rebellion against the English. Hugh O'Neill eventually joins them. But the chiefs of Munster would rather die than support O'Neill after what he did to their province. And Red Hugh raids Connacht—he gets the English out, but he's just as ruthless. So the rebels lose the support of Connacht as well. Most of their men come from Ulster, though some hail from the middle clans like your ancestors in Cavan. But it's not enough. They need Spain because they don't have the support of their own people. And when Spain balls up the Battle of Kinsale, we lose."

"So if O'Neill and O'Donnell weren't such arseholes, we might stand a better chance," Nora observed.

"Aye, but it's too late to do anything about O'Neill. He's already done his damage. O'Donnell, however, is still just a lad. He might be the one we could influence." He broke off, looking thoughtful. "He spends several years as a prisoner in Dublin Castle. I sometimes wondered if it was his treatment there that made him such a heartless bastard, or if he was just born that way."

"When does he go there?"

"I can't remember," Fionn said, frowning. "Obviously it hasn't happened yet."

"I'd give my right arm for Google right now," Nora said.

"For what?"

"Google. It's part of the Internet. We could type in 'When does Red Hugh O'Donnell get arrested?' and it would tell us the answer."

"Sounds like magic."

"It is." But there was no Internet here, no library, no historians to consult. Just the two of them, trying to piece together what they knew of the past and figure out how best to change it. It felt like a fool's errand. But it was *their* errand.

She picked at a dry cuticle on her finger. "That seems like a long shot. Find Red Hugh and convince him to not be an arsehole?"

"We can prevent him from being kidnapped and spirited away to Dublin Castle."

"But what if his stay in Dublin Castle is what gives him the will to stand up to the English? Or what if we can't reach him in time? What if we can't change who he is, and he burns Connacht anyway and loses the support of the chiefs?"

"What other plan do we have? I'm as disappointed as you that Granuaile seems so disinterested in helping us. Fate blew us here—to O'Donnell's home—just when Hugh O'Neill is due to arrive. Perhaps that is what we are meant to change." The undercurrent of desperation in Fionn's voice stabbed at Nora's chest.

"You know I dislike O'Neill," he continued. "And O'Donnell is not much better. Neither are kind men, but kind men don't make history. That much I've learned. I cannot see what else we can do. We must change *something*. We *know* O'Neill and O'Donnell come very close to unseating the English. Perhaps you are right. Perhaps all we need to do is change their approach, give them the information and support they didn't have last time."

"Wait until Kinsale, you mean?"

"No, it needs to start before then." The lines on his forehead deepened. "If we can prevent Red Hugh's capture, he'll have more years to build his following. Hopefully he'll learn a little more kindness and love for his countrymen. We can encourage him to build bridges with the other clans instead of destroying them. That alone might be enough to change the tide."

"And how do we do that? He's in Rathmullan, remember? We don't even know exactly when this capture takes place."

"We'll need to warn his father somehow. And MacSweeney, if that's where he's staying."

"Warn his mother, you mean. She's obviously the one who wears the trews, so to speak. It wouldn't surprise me if she's the reason her son becomes chieftain, even though he's not the tánaiste."

"The road to the *taoiseach* is a bloody one. That's why many of the chieftains favor the English way of primogeniture, the succession of the firstborn child. It's simpler that way. The Gaelic way, there's no guarantee that your son will succeed you as clan leader. Might be a nephew, or a cousin—whoever the clan elects as most worthy."

"But the English way also has its faults. What if the firstborn child is an eejit? Or a madman? And it's far from simple. Look at the War of the Roses!"

"The Irish aren't perfect, Nora, and the sooner you come to terms with that, the clearer your head will be. It's not as simple as 'The English are evil' and 'The Irish are good.' There's plenty good and evil to go around."

Nora plucked a tiny green leaf that had somehow grown on this outcropping of rock despite the lack of soil and the inhospitable weather. So small, so resilient. And yet with one careless action she had ended its brave life. "I wish it were that simple, but I know it's not. I know much of the world brands us the bad guys. Terrorists. The Provos—I mean, the IRA up in Northern Ireland. And maybe we are. I used to think we were the last Irish freedom fighters." She and Fionn had never really talked about her former life as a Provo, about the people she'd helped kill, about the buildings she'd destroyed.

"If I'd done what I was meant to do, none of this would have happened," he said. "You wouldn't have had to kill anyone."

Nora turned toward him, the leaf still in her hand. She gave him an incredulous look. "The entire history of Ireland is not on your shoulders, Fionn."

"Isn't it?" he said. "I was given one task: save Ireland from her enemies."

"An impossible task," she shot back. "Aengus Óg took away all your power, made you an ordinary man, and then asked you to do what entire armies have been unable to do over hundreds of years. He set you up to fail." Her voice was filled with unexpected venom.

"I don't doubt he is relishing my failure, wherever he is. But things have changed. I have something I didn't have before: the knowledge of what's going to happen next."

"You're right," Nora said, eager to fan his tiny spark of hope. "And we need to act on it." She paused, considering. "Let's start with O'Neill, since he's on his way here. We'll talk to him, then send word to Rathmullan that . . . what? That Red Hugh is going to be kidnapped?

It could be years from now. And they might think we're in on it. Unless . . ."

"What?" Fionn asked, his voice guarded.

"I can say I overheard Thomond talking about it, or saw a letter addressed to him. He's in tight with the English; maybe he knows about this plan in real life. Either way, I can use my time there as an excuse to tell the O'Donnells what the English are up to. Put them on their guard."

"I suppose that could work. And if it gets Thomond in trouble, all the better."

"Don't be a child," she said, but she smiled.

The sky was near dark. Nora helped Fionn to his feet, ready to help him back to the castle. Before they could get far, two men stepped out from behind another outcropping, blocking their path. Each man held a short sword, and the bottom half of each of their faces was covered with cloth.

Nora stepped in front of Fionn. He was in no condition to fight.

"Get out of the way, woman, and ye willna be harmed," one of them growled.

"She's prob'ly in on it," the other said to his mate.

"Leave now, both of you," Fionn said in a menacing voice, pulling Nora to the side.

"No one could have survived that blast, and two days at sea," one of the men said. "You done some dark magic. In league with the Evil One, mebbe." They crossed themselves with the hands not wielding their cutlasses. "It's not right."

"So you've come here to kill me, because I'm lucky?" Why was he so calm? "Nora, go back to the castle."

"Like hell." She took a step toward the men. "You don't need to be afraid of him," she said. "'Twas God who saved him from the sea, not the devil."

Fionn pulled her back once more. The men shook their heads, their eyes wide with fear and anger. "There's something strange about the two of you—speakin' funny, always whisperin' together, meetin' in secret with the capt'n. 'Tisn't natural. Nay, I'd say the devil 'imself is at work 'ere."

Then he lunged at Fionn, who shoved Nora out of the way and deftly sidestepped the blade that soared through the air toward his head. The other man made to follow, but Nora threw herself at him, knocking them both to the ground. He recovered with astonishing speed and raised his blade over Nora, but then a rumble split the air. Bran soared toward them, all teeth and raised fur as she launched herself at Nora's assailant. The cutlass landed with a clatter beside Nora's head as the man was pulled off her, screaming in agony.

"Don't kill him," Fionn said, as the hound looked poised to rip out the man's throat. Fionn had disarmed his assailant and was standing with a boot on the man's neck. "Nora?"

"I'm all right," she said, getting shakily to her feet. "You?"

"Aye. Let's get these two back to the castle."

Granuaile was most displeased. She had the men flogged in the courtyard of Donegal Castle and demanded that every one of her men be there to witness it. Then she gave them a scathing reminder that it was Fionn who saved the *Queen Medb* from going down, who saved her life and many of theirs. She told them in no uncertain terms that Fionn had been saved from the sea by God as a reward for his selfless act. And she warned them that the next person to raise a hand against Fionn, Nora, or any other member of her crew would be keelhauled the minute they set sail.

"What does that mean?" Nora whispered to Fionn.

"It means you'll be dragged under the ship while the barnacles slice away your skin."

Chapter Twenty

Granuaile was so busy overseeing the repair of her fleet Nora hardly saw her over the next few days. The pirate queen had to be nearing sixty, but she worked as hard as any of the men. Nora helped her whenever she could, trying to find a moment when the two of them could speak alone, but the only time Granuaile seemed inclined to speak to Nora was to give her a command that usually took her to another part of the castle or grounds.

"That's odd. She's been fine with me," Fionn said when Nora confided in him as she checked his injuries. The burns were healing well, and no infection had set in. "But . . . well . . ." To Nora's surprise, the fair skin of Fionn's cheeks turned a rosy pink.

"What?" she demanded.

"Granuaile and Queen Elizabeth have something in common—many things, actually. But they are both rather fond of, well, younger men."

Nora stared at him. "Are you saying she came on to you?" Sure, Granuaile was older, but she was an undeniably attractive woman with more sex appeal than Nora could ever hope to achieve. She was famous, powerful, and more than a match for Fionn mac Cumhaill.

"Not exactly," Fionn said, avoiding her gaze. "I mean, she may have been a bit suggestive, I suppose."

So that's how it is. And why not? They were a perfect match, these two larger-than-life figures. The Iníon Dubh had found Fionn a room of his own in the west tower, far from Nora. A favor to her friend Granuaile? She bent over the cloth strips in her lap so Fionn couldn't see her face. He'd said he didn't want to form any emotional ties. But maybe he'd meant that only about *her*.

"I'm glad she came to your defense, at any rate," Nora said. There were still whispers, still frightened and angry looks cast at them by the sailors, but at least no one had tried to attack them again.

He shrugged. "I'm used to people thinking I've made a deal with the devil, though usually it's because I don't age, not because I've survived being blown up and thrown into the sea. We'll leave here soon enough, and it will be behind us."

"Until next time." Her forehead crinkled. How would it feel to go through this time after time after time? To have everyone, even those you love, suspect you of devilry? It was no wonder he preferred to keep to himself.

It was another week before Hugh O'Neill and his party finally arrived, having been delayed by bad weather. Granuaile's captains and quartermasters moved into the yard to make room for O'Neill's contingent, and most of the sailors moved back onto the ships.

O'Neill's arrival was accompanied by great fanfare, even though, as Fionn had reminded Nora, he was not yet The O'Neill. But he *was* the Earl of Tyrone.

"So he comes straight from Elizabeth to plot against her?" Nora muttered as they stood at the tower window, watching the retinue ride toward the castle with banners flying.

"I don't think he's plotting rebellion just yet, at least not outright," Fionn said. "Like the O'Donnells, O'Neill is most concerned with keeping the English out of his affairs—and out of Ulster. Remember, we can't tell him anything that could help him until we know for sure he won't use it against us."

"I still can't believe he was part of the slaughter in Munster," Nora said. "Bastard. His own people!"

"He doesn't see the Munstermen as his own people. He's an Ulsterman. It's practically a different country. You're looking at this with modern eyes, but Ireland is still a very tribal place. Aye, he's a mean bastard, but perhaps that can be used to our advantage. Let's go down to the yard to meet them."

They stood a few paces behind Granuaile, who herself stood behind The O'Donnell and his wife. Nora's stomach twisted with apprehension. O'Neill was a seasoned military man, well traveled, and had been raised with an English family. He would not be easily swayed, especially if they were to suggest he abandon his clan-based aspirations and throw his support behind the leader of another clan, like young Red Hugh.

O'Neill leapt down from his horse with such confidence you would think he was the owner of this castle instead of his father-in-law. He had a swarthy complexion, thick black eyebrows, and a well-groomed black beard. His hairline was receding away from the widow's peak that dipped down onto his forehead, and both hair and beard were lightly seasoned with gray. His long straight nose and slightly protruding eyes gave the impression of an eagle. A bird of prey. Nora's stomach fluttered.

The O'Donnells strode forward to greet him. O'Neill clutched his father-in-law's arms in greeting, then kissed the Iníon Dubh on the cheek.

"Welcome," she said smoothly, though she could not hide the edge in her voice. "Where is Siobhán? Did she not make the journey with you?"

"She is further back, with her ladies," O'Neill said, throwing a careless hand behind him. The lines around the Iníon Dubh's mouth tightened a little, but her husband didn't seem to think anything was amiss with the arrangement.

"We have some additional guests," said O'Donnell, seeming quite lucid at the moment. "But I think you will be quite delighted to find out who they are." He stepped back and waved his arm for Granuaile to come forward.

"Bless my eyes!" O'Neill exclaimed. "If it isn't the pirate queen of Connacht!"

"For God's sake, don't call me that," Granuaile said, but she returned his embrace warmly and accepted kisses on both of her cheeks.

"I have heard talk of you in Her Majesty's court," O'Neill said. "Sir Richard Bingham has given you a new name: the nurse to all rebellions."

Granuaile's cheeks flared with pride. "A title surely just as undeserved. I only seek to protect that which is mine."

"I would that all of Ireland were yours, then!" O'Neill exclaimed. He clapped his hands and rubbed them together. "Ah, here is Siobhán." A groom helped Lady Tyrone down from her horse. She straightened her skirt and then went directly to the O'Donnells, ignoring O'Neill altogether. The women exchanged embraces, and O'Donnell beamed happily at his daughter. The two couples and Granuaile went into the castle, followed by several women Nora assumed were Lady Tyrone's servants. The men busied themselves with the horses and the unloading of carts.

Fionn looked sideways at Nora. "So what did you think of our great earl?"

"I think he'll be a hard nut to crack," she said. "He's older than I thought. I can't see him letting Red Hugh take the lead in the rebellion."

"Aye, O'Neill was always seen as the brains behind the operation. Red Hugh was the charisma—until he started raiding his own people, that is."

"Let's go back in," Nora said, but she stopped short on the steps to the castle door. "Wait. I thought you said you helped O'Donnell and

O'Neill with the Nine Years' War—supplying arms and all that. Why don't they recognize you?"

"Because I haven't offered them my help yet," Fionn said. He scowled. "I suppose that could be troublesome when my other self goes to meet with them and they already know me."

"When d'you meet with them?" Nora asked as they entered the castle.

Fionn exhaled loudly, thinking. "Fifteen ninety-five or so, I think. The former self we almost encountered at my estate should have returned to the Continent by now. As far as I can remember, I don't make the trip to Ireland again for quite some time."

"We don't have to worry about it just yet. Maybe we can make sure you don't return."

He raised an eyebrow at her. "You're not thinking of trying to kill me, are you?"

"O'course not, even if it were possible," Nora said, pinching the bridge of her nose. "Jesus, this is confusing. The you who's in Portugal right now is the one who will eventually become the you that I met in 1923, right? But *that* person is you, the one standing in front of me right now. How is it possible you both exist in the same year?"

"Maybe we don't," Fionn said thoughtfully. "Maybe the act of coming back in time erased the man I used to be. Neither of us actually saw the man at my estate, after all."

"This is mad. I'm going to Granuaile."

"To do what?"

"To ask her to introduce us to O'Neill."

Fionn followed Nora as she strode to Granuaile's chambers. They found her inside, polishing a long silver sword.

"If you're looking for O'Neill, he's not here," Granuaile said, not looking up as they entered.

"Aye, but can you introduce us?" Nora asked.

"You'll meet him soon enough, I reckon."

"I'm not so sure about that," Nora countered. "You've been ignoring me ever since our first night here, when I gave my opinion on uniting the clans. What's going on?"

Granuaile slid her stone to the edge of the sword, letting it glide off the pointed tip. She checked the edge with a thumbnail, then, satisfied, slid the sword back into the leather scabbard propped against her chair.

"Brigid said you would help us," Nora pressed.

"Us?" Granuaile asked, her eyes dancing toward Fionn. "Your man seems to be holding his tongue."

"Granuaile, you know why we've come," Fionn said, holding the older woman's gaze. "You know we need to speak with O'Neill."

"And say what? He knows nothing of Brigid, nothing of magic or journeys through time. He'll either run you through or think you a madman."

"But if you believe us, how can you not help us?" Nora asked. "I know it frightens you to think we're from the future, but it's true." She paused. "Brigid said—"

"Brigid speaks only for herself," Granuaile snapped. "She sent you here on a fool's mission. She toys with us all, and I want no part of it. Not this time."

"What are you so afraid of?" Nora burst out, taking a step forward.

In a split second, Granuaile was on her feet and a hairsbreadth from Nora's face. "I won't shed blood in my host's home. But insinuate that I am a coward again, and I will drag you outside and slit your throat. I have been fighting since before you were born, and I will continue to fight until my enemies succeed in killing me. But I don't pretend to think it's a fight we can win." She backed away from Nora, and her voice softened. "You think you have all the answers. But you haven't lived here. You don't understand our struggles." Her eyes drifted toward the window, which showed a fine view of the sea and her tiny fleet. "My first husband, Donal, was always fighting. 'Donal of the Battles,' they called him. I was fifteen when I was given to him. A great honor, I was told, to be married to the tánaiste of the O'Flahertys." She laughed in derision.

Nora couldn't laugh. Of course, women married much earlier in this age, but the thought of a fifteen-year-old girl being married off to someone she didn't even know—a much older man, mostly likely—horrified her. Nora hadn't been capable of taking care of herself at that age, let alone managing a household and raising several children.

"I'd like to say Donal was unique," Granuaile said. "But there are many other chieftains and tánaistes like him. They can't stand peace, even though it's what their wives and children and most of their men want. They need a fight, something to make the blood boil and the heart sing. They want to be the great warriors of old, but in reality they're just a group of quarrelsome old women, picking fights where there are none and dredging up old grudges when there's no cause to make new ones."

She fixed Nora with a steely glare. "*This* is what you're up against. You come here with all this high talk about mending fences and building bridges and uniting together. And maybe you're right. You say it ends badly, and I believe it. The writing's been on the wall for some time. But all the hindsight in the world can't change who we are as a people—how we think, how we feel, how we operate. Even if you told the whole island that you're from the future, that you know how we are to be defeated, even if they believed you, you can't change the heart of our people. And for better or for worse, the Irish love fighting with each other even more than they hate the English."

We can change, Nora thought. But the memory of the Civil War was still raw in her mind. Three hundred and thirty-six years from now, the Irish would still be fighting each other. Nora's hands twitched, and she had to stop herself from grabbing Granuaile by the collar and shaking her. That was the old future, and they were here to build a new one.

"What you say is true," Fionn said, coming forward. His face was very serious, and a hint of the torment that weighed on him fluttered across his features. He knelt down beside Granuaile and took her hands in his, lowering her into the chair by the window. "But the future we have seen is also true. We know our forests will burn and our people will be slaughtered. We know they will starve to death by the millions, while the English eat their fill of Irish grain. We know our people will be crushed under the English heel again and again. Brother will turn against brother. Sons against mothers."

Granuaile's face tightened, but she stayed silent, her bright eyes fixed on Fionn's sorrowful gaze.

"Nora comes from a time beyond when I have lived, and she tells me that we *do* eventually gain our freedom from England—nearly four hundred years from now. Except for Ulster, which is still, even at the turn of the millennium, ruled by England. We want to change the future for Ulster, but also for the millions of Irish men, women, and children who will suffer and die in the next four hundred years. Brigid has given us a second chance." His voice broke, and he let his head hang over Granuaile's lap. When he was able to speak again, he said thickly, "Knowledge of the future is a curse. But if you knew the horrors that lie ahead, you would raise an army that would strike so much fear into the English heart they would never set foot on Irish soil again."

Granuaile withdrew her hands from Fionn's and stroked his hair, her cheeks wet. "Come, come," she whispered. "I will help you."

Fionn stood, his face a mask of perfect misery. "Thank you," he said. "We must speak with The O'Donnell and the Iníon Dubh about their son. And with O'Neill."

"They won't believe you," Granuaile warned. "I only do because Brigid has taught me that anything is possible."

"I know," Fionn said. "We will have to frame our argument differently. But you will help us persuade them?"

Granuaile nodded, though her expression was uncertain. "I can only tell them that I agree. They may enjoy my company and the use of my fleet, but they still believe war is a matter for men. *You* will need to take the lead on this." She glanced sharply at Nora to make her point.

Nora stayed silent. Fionn had convinced the pirate queen to help them, and that was enough.

Chapter Twenty-One

Later that night, they all gathered in Donegal Castle's main hall to feast and toast the arrival of Hugh and Siobhán O'Neill. Nora wore the same gown she'd been given by Granuaile on their first night in the castle. It was still the only thing she owned besides her léine and a simple cloak sent by a servant from the Iníon Dubh. Fionn had fared much better. Apparently, he had purchased new clothing in Galway in preparation for their rendezvous with Granuaile. His new wardrobe had been stowed aboard her ship when they set out to find Nora. *At least one of us looks the part of the wealthy adventurer.* She admired the shape of his legs in his silk hose. A sword swung from his hips, its hilt decorated with hounds.

Musicians tuned their instruments in a corner, and Nora remembered fondly how Fionn had come disguised as a bard into Doonbeg Castle. But he was deep in conversation with Granuaile, so she could not ask him if he would perform for them that night.

The three of them were seated near the front of the table, across from Hugh and Siobhán O'Neill. The O'Donnell's voice boomed from the head of the table. "May I introduce you to the Earl and Lady of

Tyrone," he said to Fionn and Nora. "These are some new acquaintances of ours. Uh . . ." He trailed off, evidently at a loss for their names.

"Fionn O'Hanlon and Nora O'Reilly," the Iníon Dubh supplied. "Adventurer friends of Gráinne's."

Lady Tyrone looked at Fionn and Nora with interest, but the earl regarded them with a cold stare, as though they were not worthy of his attention. "And what brings you to Ulster?" Siobhán asked Fionn.

"Good fortune," Fionn answered smoothly. "We were guests on board the *Queen Medb* when we encountered a storm and were forced to make land here. The lord and lady of Tyrconnell have been more than gracious to us."

"Let me guess," the earl said to Granuaile with a small smile on his thin lips. "You were en route to Scotland for more of their fine fighters."

Granuaile did not deny it. "I need more fighting men to ward off Bingham and keep him away from my people. Care to help me, Hugh?"

His smile widened into a smirk. "After I have just been invested with the title of Earl of Tyrone? I daresay Her Majesty would not appreciate the gesture."

"Pffft. That old heretic hag," Granuaile said. Those within hearing visibly tensed at the traitorous words. "I don't care who hears me," she continued defiantly. "I'm already branded a traitor, am I not? Richard Bingham would see me hanged for worse than that. I may as well speak my mind, here among friends."

"Then as friends we must warn you that it is not wise to plot openly against the queen," O'Neill said, his voice low.

Granuaile locked him in her gaze. "You may wear the title of Earl of Tyrone, and lord knows you deserve all the titles they can give you. But I know your heart, Hugh O'Neill. You'll take what they give you; it's what they'll demand in return that will make your decision for you."

O'Neill took a bite of food and chewed it slowly. "And what decision is that?"

"Which side you'll be on when it comes down to it," Granuaile answered. "Don't tell me that's not the reason you've come here. This is no social visit between the heads of two great clans." Her head swiveled between O'Neill and The O'Donnell. "If the two of you have finally stopped fighting each other, it means you must have a mutual enemy. You've plans in your heads. And I mean to hear them."

"You may be right," O'Neill answered, with a glance down the long, full table. "But this is not the place to discuss them. We shall talk more later."

"We would be pleased to offer any assistance as well," Nora cut in. "And there is something I must tell you, something that cannot wait until later." Fionn tensed beside her, and Granuaile's mouth turned into a dark line.

"Well? Spit it out, girl!" O'Donnell said.

"I believe Red Hugh is in danger."

"Danger?" The O'Donnell boomed. "What kind of danger could our son be in, here in our own kingdom, with the full protection of The MacSweeney?"

"I was a . . . guest of the Earl of Thomond recently," Nora said carefully. "And I overheard a conversation. I didn't understand it at the time so thought naught of it. But the more I reflect on it, the more I realize who they were talking about. It was Red Hugh; I'm quite sure of it now. I believe the English plan to take him captive."

"Thomond dares to think he can capture our son?" the Iníon Dubh erupted. "Clare is not so far away that we cannot bring a hail of destruction down on him!"

Shite. "Thomond is innocent, I believe. It wasn't him I heard talking. I don't know who they were—two English gentlemen, that's all. He wasn't even in the room." Sweet Jesus. Had she now ignited a war between the O'Donnell and O'Brien clans?

"It will perhaps come to nothing," Fionn said in a calming voice. "I'm sure the English would love to have the sons of all the great chieftains in their custody. But perhaps a little extra caution is in order. A word sent to your son, urging him to be vigilant."

Granuaile eyed them beadily, trying to decipher the truth from their lies, no doubt. But then she turned to the O'Donnells and said, "The boy has shown himself to be a capable military strategist, from what you have told me. What we see in him, the English will see in him as well. Whether this plan has actually been hatched or not, it would be wise to urge your son to caution."

Nora shot her a look of gratitude, which the older woman ignored. The Iníon Dubh still looked murderous. She glared at O'Neill, who was noticeably quiet. Then she beckoned a servant closer. "Bring me a messenger," she snapped.

The meal continued, but the tension could be tasted with every bite. In the end, hospitality won out, but Lady Tyrconnell's remarks were stilted in the conversation that flowed between Granuaile, O'Neill, and O'Donnell, who kept asking the others to repeat themselves. The Iníon Dubh glanced repeatedly over her shoulder at the door to the hall. Finally, a panting young man was ushered in by a guard. He fell to one knee when he reached the head of the table.

"Finally!" the Iníon Dubh said, drawing his attention away from her husband, who was gazing blankly at the young man. "We have an urgent message for you to send to my son."

"Your son?" the messenger asked, echoing The O'Donnell's blank expression.

"Hugh Roe," she replied impatiently. "He is with MacSweeney of Fanad, and you must go to him at once."

"My-my lady, there is some mistake," he stammered. "I have just come from Fanad."

"You what?" she demanded, eyes narrowed.

"I have only just arrived. I have terrible news."

Nora paled. They were too late.

The Iníon Dubh stood up and grabbed the messenger by his collar, bringing the lad within inches of her face. "Where is my son?" She released him and took a step back.

"He was captured, my lady," the messenger said, rubbing his throat.

"Captured?" Hugh O'Donnell said from his seat at the table, a chunk of bread still in his hand. "What nonsense is this? We were just speaking of this! There was no time!"

"Who did this?" the Iníon Dubh hissed, ignoring her husband.

"The English, my lady. It was a trap. A ship arrived from Spain, or so they were led to believe, filled with fine wines. The MacSweeney, his sons, and Hugh Roe went on board to sample the wines. They were treated with all courtesy until men surged out of the bowels of the ship and overtook them. The others were ransomed and released, but your son . . ."

The Iníon Dubh trembled, her cheeks as flaming as her crimson hair. "Where is he?" she screeched.

"Those who were released said they heard their captors speak of Dublin Castle," the messenger said, quivering where he stood.

"Get out of my sight," the Iníon Dubh snapped. "But do not leave the castle. I will have a message for you to return to MacSweeney, if you can stomach it."

As the messenger ran with unseemly haste out of the hall, Nora was wrenched from her seat and thrown to the stone floor. The Iníon Dubh stood over her, pointing a silver dagger at Nora's throat. At once, Fionn was between them, palms raised. Granuaile, too, had risen from her seat, but remained on the other side of the table. The O'Neills and Hugh O'Donnell remained where they were, watching the scene with wary eyes.

"She had nothing to do with this," Fionn said. Nora scrambled to her feet and put her hand on his arm.

"It's grand," she said softly, stepping forward.

"You knew!" the Iníon Dubh said, still pointing the dagger toward her.

"They didn't mention him by name," Nora insisted, raising her hands. "I swear to you, I had nothing to do with this. I only just figured it out, and I told you as soon as I could."

With a swirl of her skirts, the Iníon Dubh grabbed Nora's raised arm and pulled her in with a twisting motion. Nora found herself firmly in the Dark Daughter's grasp, the silver blade pressed into the flesh of her neck. There was a scream of metal as swords were drawn throughout the hall, but Fionn was quickest. He kept his sword lowered, his hands trembling with the effort.

"Let her go," he said. "We are guests in your home, and you are dishonoring yourself."

Granuaile had drawn a short sword, which she held tensely by her side. One hand was stretched out toward her captains, who had been feasting at the other end of the table, seemingly holding them at bay. O'Donnell was unarmed but had risen to gape at his wife and the two adventurers. O'Neill had drawn his sword and was pointing it at Fionn, although the table still stood between them.

"Guests in my home," the Iníon Dubh spat. "Spies, more like it. Who are you, really? This one in particular," she said, giving Nora a firm shake that made her whimper as the blade dug into her skin. "With her strange speech and unlikely tales. I know Thomond, and he would never entertain a woman adventurer. Which are you, a spy or a whore? Did you come here so you could report back once the deed was done?"

"Fionnuala," Granuaile said, moving out from behind the table. "Nora is my guest. You have my word she is no spy. She was a captive at Doonbeg; I rescued her myself. Do you think *she* caused the storm that wrecked my ships and forced us to take refuge here? If you accuse her, you accuse me as well. Fionn, for God's sake, sheathe your sword." Despite her words, she did not relinquish her own weapon.

"Not until she lowers hers," Fionn said, his eyes never leaving the Iníon Dubh.

"And you!" the Iníon Dubh snarled at Fionn. "How *did* you survive those days at sea? Perhaps the rumors are true, after all. There's something not right about the two of you."

"The English killed my brother," Nora rasped, pressing her head back into the Iníon Dubh's shoulder to relieve the pressure on her neck. "I just want to avenge him." The woman's arm, already taut, tightened around her before slowly drawing away. Fionn reluctantly slid his sword back into its decorated sheath. Nora sank into her vacated chair, her hand on her stinging neck. When she brought it away, it was stained red.

"I know I'm an anomaly," Nora said, trying to smooth things over. "I don't blame you for suspecting me, but I swear, I only want to help you. All of you." She leaned against the oaken table as a rush of nausea swooped down on her, leaving her forehead clammy and dampening her upper lip. It was Liam Lynch all over again. They were too late. History would now unfold exactly the way it had the first time around. Red Hugh would languish in the bowels of Dublin Castle and escape a hard, angry man who would trample his own people along with any English foes who dared oppose him.

"I may have overreacted," the Iníon Dubh said stiffly, and Nora knew this was as much of an apology as she was going to get.

"Let's go talk to the messenger," Granuaile said in a conciliatory tone. "It's possible we can send a ship to intercept them before they reach Dublin." The Iníon Dubh was already marching toward the door, but her husband resumed his seat and put a dripping chunk of meat in his mouth.

"Stay with Lord Tyrconnell," Hugh O'Neill snapped at his wife before following Lady Tyrconnell out of the hall. Granuaile made to join them but then doubled back and pulled Nora aside none too gently.

"I have to be certain. Tell me you didn't have anything to do with that boy's capture."

"I didn't," Nora said, wresting her arm away. "I just knew it was going to happen, that's all. But I was too late; I should have warned them the first night we were here."

"I don't envy you," Granuaile said, her eyes clouded. "It must be a terrible curse, knowing the future. My sailors have a saying: you can't change the direction of the wind; you can only adjust your sails. What will be, will be."

Nora locked eyes with the pirate queen, hoping against hope that she wasn't right.

Chapter Twenty-Two

Darkness hung over Donegal for the next several days, as though the ocean fog had thickened and was trying to choke all hope from the castle's inhabitants. The messenger had been delayed by bad weather, and it had taken him over a week to reach Donegal Castle. It was too late to send out ships. Those who had kidnapped Red Hugh would be deep in English territory by now. The O'Donnell, the Iníon Dubh, and Hugh O'Neill had sequestered themselves in a chamber, armed with maps, parchment, and whiskey.

"It's not the end of the road," Fionn said, coming up behind Nora. She was standing on the battlements at the top of the castle, wrapped in a heavy fur cloak against the biting wind, staring out at the small fleet still undergoing repairs in the harbor.

"I know," she said simply. It had been a long shot anyway. Perhaps Red Hugh's personality was set, and he would have raided Connacht and alienated his fellow chieftains regardless. Could they have really had any influence on the young man, more so than his mother, clan, and the great Hugh O'Neill? She told Fionn as much, and he nodded soberly.

"Aye, you're right. It wasn't much of a plan, though if it had worked . . ." His voice trailed off. "I've been going over and over what I know of the Nine Years' War. We need more clans to stand with O'Neill and O'Donnell. I'm almost positive that would make the difference. But how?"

Nora grasped the stone edging, her face grim. "Maybe we wait until Red Hugh gets out and talk to him then. It might not be too late for him." But her lack of conviction was clear in her voice. She didn't fancy the idea of spending the next several years cooling her heels, waiting for Red Hugh.

"This isn't right," she said, raising her voice to be heard above the wind. "We need something bigger. Something more decisive." In a quieter voice she said, "Where the hell is Brigid?" She scanned the horizon, half expecting Brigid to ride toward them on the waves like the stories of the Tuatha Dé Danann. A skiff of cloud darkened the horizon in the distance, and she squinted to see it more clearly.

"Is Tír na nÓg real?" she asked Fionn. "Is there really a Land of Everlasting Youth across the water?"

Fionn, too, seemed captivated by the expanse of water that spread out before them. "The only thing across the water is America," he said with a sad smile. "I believe Tír na nÓg exists, but I know neither where it is nor how to get there."

"But that is where Oisín went, didn't he? Is that where you believe your friends are? And your family? Those who have died?"

"Aye. Is it so much different than your idea of heaven?"

Nora didn't know how to respond to that. Her fingers lifted to her rosary, moving from the cross to the relic. She was still struggling to reconcile her Catholicism with the pagan religion embodied by Fionn and Brigid. She'd always believed that to be Irish was to be Catholic. But she was no longer even sure what it meant to be Irish.

"I suppose not," she answered.

"Listen, I've been talking with Granuaile," Fionn said. "I was hoping that the capture of Red Hugh might spur his father—or mother,

I should say—and O'Neill to action. Move up the date of the revolt. But—"

Nora shook her head. "They won't revolt while Red Hugh is a hostage. There's no way the Iníon Dubh would allow it."

"She has great plans for their son; they won't risk angering the English while he's in their custody."

"I don't blame them. I'm just angry we didn't act sooner to protect him."

"We had no idea when this was going to happen. Don't beat yourself up over it." They stared out at the ocean in silence for a few moments; then Fionn spoke again, his eyes still fixed on the water. "Don't you find it odd that Brigid told us Granuaile could help us, yet Granuaile doesn't believe we should be messing with such things as the future?"

"Aye," Nora agreed. "I've spent a fair bit of time thinking about it. Maybe Granuaile has nothing to do with it, after all. Which pisses me off, to be honest. But there's nothing we can do about it."

The newly repaired sails of one of Granuaile's ships were being hoisted into the air, cracking and billowing in the brisk wind. The pirate queen had continued to intervene on behalf of Fionn and Nora. Maybe that's all Brigid meant for her to offer—her protection.

The shouts of the sailors drifted toward them on the wind. "We'll be ready to sail soon," Fionn said, following Nora's gaze.

"To Scotland?" Nora asked. "Or has the plan changed?"

"Aye, Granuaile is still set on bringing more mercenaries into Connacht."

"She'd be better off bringing them here to start building O'Neill's army," Nora muttered.

"I mentioned that to her. But she told me they can get their own damned redshanks. She's cut from the same cloth as the rest of them. They've spent their whole lives defending the interests of the wee bits of land they control, and they're not about to stop now."

Nora's eyes narrowed.

"You have to understand—" Fionn started, but Nora held up a hand to silence him. Her gaze was fixed on the *Queen Medb* bobbing in the water below.

"They found a ship," she said suddenly, lost in her thoughts. "Just before I left. In 2005. I saw it on the news."

"What?" Fionn said, looking thoroughly confused.

An idea started to roll around in Nora's mind. The details were elusive, but it might work.

"Give me some time," she said.

She wanted to be sure of her plan before she shared it. And she needed an ally. Over the next few days, Nora made herself as useful as possible to Granuaile, which was difficult considering she knew nothing about ships, and Granuaile was consumed with the repairs to her fleet. She spent most of her days inspecting the ships, her evenings drinking and gambling with The O'Donnell, the Iníon Dubh, and Hugh O'Neill. She refused to answer Nora's questions about what the O'Donnells were going to do about Red Hugh's capture, only saying it was "a clan matter" and had nothing to do with her.

Finally, four days after their conversation on the roof of the castle, Fionn and Nora were summoned. The O'Donnells, Hugh O'Neill, and Granuaile were gathered in an upstairs sitting room. The fire blazed hot in the hearth, and the chill was kept out by the heavy tapestries that hung against the whitewashed walls. A rug of woven rushes covered the floor. The four imposing figures sat in high-backed chairs in a semicircle facing the fire. Pewter goblets rested next to tankards on low tables beside them. A single servant stood inside the door when Nora and Fionn were admitted.

They were not offered seats, so they stood awkwardly inside the door. Nora shot a curious look at Granuaile, but her face was impassive. The Iníon Dubh watched Nora and Fionn with a suspicious gaze.

"You have traveled a great deal," O'Neill said. "And know many things that even our own spies and agents cannot tell us. And you have earned the confidence and trust of Gráinne Ní Mháille, which is no easy thing. She tells us you may be able to offer us counsel as we plan our next move."

Fionn bowed his head graciously. "Thank you," he said. "We will humbly offer all we know to help you."

"We cannot move against the English while they hold our son hostage," the Iníon Dubh warned, casting a severe glance at her husband. This was obviously a conversation they'd had before.

"My lord," Fionn said, addressing Hugh O'Neill. "You know the English and their ways. We must start training our men to fight them, and you are the best man for the job. You are a brilliant military commander. Only . . ."

O'Neill arched a thick eyebrow. "Only?"

"May I speak plainly, my lord?" Fionn asked.

"We have asked for your counsel," he said with a wave. The rings on his fingers sparkled in the firelight. "Speak."

"The chiefs of Munster will never support you—you must realize that. Whatever your reasons for supporting the Crown in the suppression of the Desmond Rebellion, the damage has been done. You will never be able to unite the chiefs, to build an army large enough to drive the English off our lands."

O'Neill's eyes narrowed, but he did not argue.

"With your military leadership, I believe we can defeat the English. They are spread too thin, and Elizabeth refuses to give the lord deputy the resources he needs to fully subdue us. But we need more men—all the fighting men of Ireland, riding together under one banner. We need to find someone who can rally all the clans behind him. I think Red Hugh might be that man."

We've been through this before, Nora thought. Fionn's plan hinged on their ability to tame Red Hugh's bloodthirstiness, his cruelty toward his own countrymen. It wasn't good enough.

O'Neill looked in surprise from O'Donnell to Fionn. "This is your idea?" he said to his brother-in-law. "You wish the O'Neills to bend the knee to your young whelp of a son, who is senseless enough to allow himself to be captured? He is not even your tánaiste!"

He rose from his seat and stared around the room defiantly. The Iníon Dubh rose as well. "How dare you insult my son?" she snarled.

"You insult me while I am a guest in your home. After all I have done to forge peace between our clans."

Granuaile moved between them. "My friends, no insult is being given here. You asked for an outsider's opinion, and that is what you were given. An *outsider*," she stressed. "The O'Donnells would not dream of making such a suggestion."

O'Neill glared at the Iníon Dubh, waiting for her to confirm this.

"What she says is true," the Iníon Dubh conceded. "We have never discussed or considered such a plan. Our clans are united by marriage, but we have no wish to usurp the power of the O'Neills."

"So you say," O'Neill retorted, looking thoroughly unconvinced.

"The fault is mine, my lord," Fionn broke in. "I meant no offense, and the O'Donnells had no prior knowledge of my suggestion."

O'Neill sat down, temporarily mollified. "Uniting the clans to fight the English is a preposterous idea. They have left Ulster alone. Why risk so much when they are of such little concern to me?"

Fionn's shoulders sagged.

"You're right," Nora said, taking a step forward. "The English may not be *your* enemies, but they are ours. We will deal with them in our own way."

Without waiting to be dismissed, she turned and left the room.

Fionn followed a few steps behind. "What are you doing?" he asked, his voice hushed and urgent.

She stopped so suddenly he had to grab her arm to keep from knocking her over. "I'm done with them. You said it: they don't care about anything other than their own families and clans. We can't do anything to change O'Neill or Red Hugh. We know they'll eventually join together to fight, but nothing we do or say now will speed that up or make them more effective. We're wasting our time here."

"And where d'you propose we go?"

"The only place we have a chance of changing things. Spain."

Chapter Twenty-Three

Nora's voice was hard, determined. "It's time we left Donegal anyway—the Iníon Dubh suspects we're not who we say we are. Remember a few days ago, when we were on the battlements? I said I might have a plan."

"Aye."

"I remembered that the archeologists in my time had recently found the remains of a ship from the Spanish Armada. It had been wrecked on the west coast of Ireland; dozens of them were. In the summer of 1588."

Fionn's mouth tightened.

"We know they lost, horribly," she continued. "It was a comedy of errors, everything going wrong that could."

"Yes . . . ," Fionn said cautiously.

"Think of how differently things will turn out if Spain succeeds in invading England. England won't have time for Ireland. Her troops will be recalled to fight the Spanish. It won't matter if the chiefs are united. Think about it!" she said, her voice excited and her cheeks flushed. "O'Donnell and O'Neill *almost* drove the English out, even with the clans divided. But if the English are distracted, weakened, and fighting a war with Spain, *that* could give them the edge they need. We don't need to change their minds or force them to rally the clans. We can change the outcome without changing *them*."

She paced the narrow corridor, brow furrowed and fists clenched, muttering under her breath as she considered all the possible scenarios.

"There's only one problem," Fionn said gently, as though afraid to break the bad news. Nora stopped.

"What?"

"Even in the past, Philip of Spain had several counselors telling him about the flaws in his plan. I know because I was—I *am*—one of them. He won't listen. He thinks it's God's will."

"Were you really one of his counselors?" Nora asked, eyes narrowing in thought.

"Not in an official capacity," he said. "But I'd been living in Spain and Portugal on and off for a number of years and I'd made some useful connections. It helps when you have access to a large amount of gold and the country has gone bankrupt several times," he added wryly. Then his face grew sober. "There was a call for private ships to join the armada, and I answered it. I knew the admiral: Don Alonso Pérez de Guzmán y de Zúñiga-Sotomayor, Duke of Medina Sidonia. It wasn't his fault—he didn't want the job in the first place, knew he wasn't qualified for it. He was only made admiral at the eleventh hour after Santa Cruz died. And he saw the problems with Philip's plan as clearly as we do today. But Philip forced him into it and then tied his hands behind his back, poor bastard."

Nora took this in. "You were part of the Spanish Armada," she said slowly. "And you knew the admiral . . ."

"I know what you're thinking, but it won't work," he said. "Not unless you can change both the weather and the approach of the English navy. We were unlucky on every front. There's nothing we can change."

"That's not true. A show about the armada aired on the BBC after they found the ship. The English had to deal with the same weather you did. It was fighting style that made the biggest difference. The

Spanish used an old-fashioned crescent shape while the English fired in a straight line from their broadsides. And when they knew they were losing, the surviving ships from the armada sailed around Ireland. That was mostly weather, I suppose, but most of the ships had jettisoned their anchors, hadn't they? So when the winds came up from the west, they were blown right into these rocks." She waved her hand out at the ocean.

"A show?" Fionn asked, his eyebrows wrinkled.

"I keep forgetting you're not from my time," Nora said. "Remember I told you about the box that shows moving pictures? It was like a lecture by various scholars, I reckon, but with pictures and computer-generated graphics to illustrate what happened."

"But none of these scholars were there, were they?"

"Well, no. O'course not. That's my point—*you* were. You know firsthand what went wrong. We can tell them what to do differently this time."

She had expected Fionn to argue, but instead he looked thoughtful. "There was one point where I think we could have won. Off the Lizard."

It was Nora's turn to be confused.

"The southernmost point of England, by Plymouth," he clarified. We knew there were many English ships in the port at Plymouth. If we had attacked suddenly, when they had no room for their broadside maneuver, we could have destroyed much of their fleet. But Philip's orders were for us to proceed directly to meet up with Parma's army in the Netherlands. We were then to escort them to England for the land invasion. So we sailed on, only to be trapped in the Channel by Howard and his brilliant broadside formation." He smiled wanly at the skeptical look on Nora's face. "It *was* brilliant, in hindsight. He and Drake were formidable foes."

"How'd you escape?"

The ghosts of drowned comrades seemed to move behind Fionn's eyes. "Not everyone died. Of the hundred and thirty or so ships, they say sixty-seven made it back to Spain, and about half the men. O'course, disease took many more lives after we were 'safe' in Spanish waters."

"There's nothing you could have done," Nora said, placing a gentle hand on his arm. "You couldn't control the weather, or the actions of the men in charge. But we've a second chance now. What else can you remember?"

He shook his head. "It was a very long time ago, but I've read some other accounts about it since. I might be able to come up with an alternate plan if I put some thought into it. The biggest challenge will be convincing Philip to go along with it. Like I said, many of us saw the flaws in the plan as it was in the making, but Philip refused to be persuaded."

"I don't think Philip is the problem. If he wins, he won't care that the admiral disobeyed his orders. And the admiral's the one in charge once they're at sea, right?"

Fionn nodded.

"And you were friends with him, so you were," Nora said.

"'Friends' is a strong word," Fionn said. "But we knew each other, aye. I think he respected me." Still he looked uncertain.

She gripped his shoulders so that he was forced to look at her. "Fionn, hindsight is all we have here. We can't be afraid to use it."

"There are still a thousand things that could go wrong."

Nora dropped her arms. "If you're not willing to at least try, why did you come back?"

"I just don't want to go on a fool's errand," he snapped, and he paced several feet away before stopping. Nora watched him silently, her heart sinking. This was one plan she couldn't pull off without him.

"Will you at least consider hearing my plan?" she asked tentatively.

"Isn't it obvious? You want me to go to Medina Sidonia and convince him to change his plans."

"Yes and no," she said. "You're not going to tell him—the other you is."

Fionn stopped at the head of the spiral staircase he was about to descend. "Nora, you know I can't talk to my past self. I'll think I've gone mad. You were panicked when you thought it might happen at my estate."

"I don't want you to speak to your past self. Both because of how he might react, and in case you're seen by someone else."

"Ah," he said, understanding dawning across his face. "So *you* plan to be my ambassador."

"Aye, I do. You said you think you've gone back to the Continent by now. Back to Lisbon?"

Fionn paced nervously. "Aye, I'm almost certain. I wouldn't have stayed away for so long."

"Grand so. We'll sail to Lisbon, and you'll tell me exactly what to say to . . . well, *you* about what to change in the Spanish strategy. Once I tell you what I know, you're sure to believe me. Who else in your life knows who you really are?"

"No one," he said, his eyes darkening. "And I liked it that way. I was a different man, Nora. I'm not sure how I would have received such a revelation. I can't guarantee that I won't . . . hurt you."

This surprised Nora. But several hundred years was time enough for a personality to change, to soften. "I can handle you," she said, forcing confidence into her voice. "But I'll be careful, I promise."

He frowned, then moved away from the top of the stairs and pulled her into a window alcove. "And if you can convince my past self? How d'you expect him to convince Medina Sidonia?" he asked in a hushed voice.

"Simple enough," Nora said, trying to ignore the rush of pleasure that came from being in a confined space with him. "You said he becomes admiral at the eleventh hour. So he's probably not admiral yet, is he? Santa Cruz is still alive."

Fionn frowned as he thought. "Yes, you're right. Santa Cruz would still be admiral at this point."

"And Medina Sidonia is a religious man, is he not?"

"He is . . ."

"And people in this age are very superstitious—I know that much. You'll tell him that you know he'll be named admiral because you had a vision from God. He'll laugh at you, no doubt. You said yourself that he didn't want the job, wasn't qualified for it. But your 'vision' will come true. And then he'll listen to anything you have to say."

She waited for his patronizing explanation for why this wouldn't work due to some unknown-to-her aspect of history. But he said nothing. She could tell he was running the scenario through his own mind, comparing it with his own experience with Medina Sidonia and the armada.

"It might work," he said at last. "If there is one person Medina Sidonia will take orders from over King Philip, it's God. And his appointment *was* a complete surprise to everyone, so he won't believe it was just a lucky guess on my part. O'course, I can't guarantee that my advice will change the outcome of the invasion. Anything could change—the men, the weather, Medina Sidonia could have a change of heart once at sea."

"But we have a chance," Nora said.

"Aye. I suppose we do."

She grinned, all the tension she'd absorbed since Red Hugh's capture draining out of her. "Then let's go find you."

Chapter Twenty-Four

Granuaile was hesitant to set out for Spain, for she would have to leave most of her fleet in Donegal Bay. But Nora and Fionn convinced her that time was of the essence. They needed to reach Medina Sidonia before Santa Cruz died.

Despite their hurry, it took them two weeks to stock the ships with food and water for a trip of unpredictable length. And Granuaile insisted on replenishing her supply of ammunition from O'Donnell's stock, "in case we run into the English, or pirates better armed than we are." It was the worst time of the year for sailing, a fact that weighed heavily on them all. Twice they set out, only to be beaten back by harsh winds. Granuaile opted to bring two ships on the journey, in the hopes that if one of them went down the other could rescue survivors.

Fionn enthusiastically joined the crew, but Granuaile insisted Nora share her quarters—and stay in them. It was too dangerous a voyage to risk any mistakes, the captain insisted, or to have Nora distracting the crew. She was given the job of timekeeper. Considering this involved turning over a giant hourglass every four hours, Nora was less than enthusiastic about her role.

Despite sharing the captain's cabin, she saw Granuaile only sporadically. When she wasn't on deck or inspecting the guns and stockpiles of fresh water and dried meat and biscuits, the captain was either sleeping or gambling with her men. O'Neill had been right: Granuaile loved to gamble. Nora often fell asleep to the sounds of raucous laughter, coarse jokes, and the exchange of coins.

One morning, however, she awoke to find Granuaile sitting at the table in the center of the room, watching her. "Is everything okay?" Nora asked groggily as she stumbled to her feet and went to check the hourglass.

"Your man Fionn," Granuaile said. "What is your relationship with him?"

Nora kept her back turned to the other woman as she made sure the hourglass was secure in its brass casing. They had a backup in case this one broke, but Nora figured if this was her only job, she might as well not screw it up. "We're friends, is all," she answered.

"I imagine something as intense as traveling through time would bring two people together," Granuaile remarked.

Why was she asking this? Sizing up the competition?

"Aye, we've grown quite close," Nora said, turning around. Granuaile's face was weathered and her hair salt and pepper. Yet her body was strong and tight, and her dark eyes spoke of nothing but passion and adventure. Aye, she could see the appeal. "Why d'you ask?"

Granuaile continued to consider her, and Nora had the impression she herself was the subject of the same scrutiny she had just given the other woman. "I just like to know who I'm throwing my lot in with," she said. Then she stood and left the room.

They reached Lisbon after two weeks, which Granuaile pointed out was little less than a miracle. They'd encountered a couple of storms, but nothing to blow them too far off course or drive them toward the rocky coast. Granuaile was in such good spirits she allowed Nora on the main deck to take in the view as they approached the harbor.

"There they are," Granuaile said, pointing at the vast array of ships that were anchored nearby. Nora's breath caught. There, in front of her, was the Spanish Armada, flags flying proudly in the breeze.

"They don't sail until summer," she whispered to Fionn. "Why are they all here now?"

"Because Philip wants them to sail sooner," he replied. "That's part of the problem. He insists that the men stay on their ships, but it's the worst place for them. They're dying by the hundreds."

"Dying of what?"

"You name it. Scurvy, typhus, dysentery, common-enough diseases for a seagoing man."

"Jesus."

"Aye."

"Do you know where to go? Where we'll find . . . you?"

"I had rooms near the royal palace." His mouth twisted at the memory. "I reckon that's where you'll find me."

"What's wrong?" she asked.

"Nothing," he said. "I've some business to attend to while you're busy."

"Business?" she asked. "Here?"

"Aye," he said, and his tone made it clear that she would get no further information out of him. He passed her a letter, sealed with a glob of red wax. "I've written down everything we discussed, all the ways he . . . *I* might change the outcome. It'll be easier this way. He should recognize his own signature. But he won't like some of my suggestions."

"Who? You, or Medina Sidonia?"

"Both."

Once safely anchored and on shore, Granuaile took her leave of them, determined to put in a good day's trading. Fionn gave Nora detailed instructions on how to find his rooms. "Perhaps I should lead you there," he said.

"No," she insisted. "What if we run into your past self and he screams bloody murder, thinks you're a ghost or devil or something? I think you should stay on the ship."

"I'll be careful," he said. "But so should you. I meant what I said. I was a harder man then. I might not believe you as readily as I did in Kilmainham."

"Tell me something only you would know, then."

He thought for a minute, his expression darkening. "When the Black Death passed through Ireland two hundred years ago, I pretended to be a priest so I could offer the last rites to those who were dying. All the priests within a hundred miles had died; I was the only survivor. Part of me hoped that regular contact with the sick would kill me, but I knew it wouldn't. I suppose it was penance, in a way. I could offer some small comfort to the plague's victims and their families."

Nora had been expecting something more mundane, like his favorite color or a childhood memory. "Right," she said. "Black Death. Got it. Well, wish me luck."

"You'll need it," he said, then turned and walked through the crowded port, away from her.

His directions had been clear, and she found her way to the building where he'd kept a room. Lisbon was a port city but had a very different feel than Dublin. The air was fresher, and sunlight and heat replaced the damp, chill drizzle of Ireland's largest city. The cobblestones beneath Nora's feet were reddish in tone, and the street was lined with deep-green bushes spotted with bright bursts of color. She passed the royal palace—one of many, Fionn had told her—admiring the soaring columns of marble and the grand outer stairs that led to massive carved doors. The scent of flowers helped mask the smell of the sewers, body odor, and animal waste.

Fionn's rooms were in a square stone building four stories high. Nora knocked nervously, her fingers making sweat marks on the letter in her grasp. A young man she assumed to be a servant opened the door. Fionn had warned her the servants would not be able to speak English or Irish. For a moment she froze, afraid she would not be able to remember which false name Fionn had been using at the time. *Shite.* The servant said something in Spanish that sounded very much like it meant, "What the hell do you want?"

"Robert O'Hanlon," she said with relief. She showed him the letter and pointed to the name written on the front. The servant gave her an appraising look. He took the letter and flipped it over, examining the seal on the back. He moved to close the door, but Nora shoved her way inside and took the letter back, then gestured to herself to indicate that she was to give the letter to Mr. O'Hanlon herself. The servant shrugged and led the way.

Nora was certain he could hear her heart hammering against her rib cage as they walked up a long, curved staircase that ran between columns in a huge, ornate entry hall. They climbed all the way to the fourth floor before the servant stopped outside a closed door. He smirked at her before leaving, shaking his head slightly as if indulging in some private joke. Nora watched him go, then leaned in to listen at the door. She heard muffled voices. *Ballix. He's not alone.*

She knocked lightly, and a man's voice shouted something in Spanish. She pushed on the latch, and the door swung open.

Fionn lay in a tangle of limbs on a wide four-poster bed. His gray hair was long, curling softly around his shoulders. A sheen of sweat covered his bare skin. He hadn't even bothered to cover his nakedness. Two women were in bed with him, a lithe, dun-haired woman and a curvy woman with raven hair that fell down to her ample arse. They, too, were naked, and staring at Nora in surprise. One of them said something to Fionn in Spanish, and they both laughed. Nora thought she recognized the word for "three."

Nora stared back at them, her senses assaulted by the exposed flesh, the pungent smell of sex and sweat, and the lascivious grin on Fionn's face. *This isn't my Fionn*, she told herself. Then, *There is no* my *Fionn*.

"Get out," she told the women, her voice deep and trembling. When they stared at her uncomprehendingly, she grabbed the dun-haired woman by the arm and yanked, dumping her onto the floor as she pointed to the door with her free hand. "Out!" Fionn's mouth opened in surprise, and the other woman shouted angrily at Nora in Spanish while clinging to Fionn's arm.

"Tell them to leave!" Nora snapped at Fionn, irrationally angry.

"You speak English. Who are you?" he asked, the woman still clinging to him. The dun-haired woman had picked herself up off the floor and was shooting a venomous glance at Nora as she wrapped a silk robe around her naked body.

"I'm a friend," she said, though her tone belied her words. "And a friend of Brigid's. I'm here to help you break your fucking curse."

This got his attention. He wrenched his arm out of the raven-haired beauty's grasp, his face pale. "What did you say?" His voice came out in a breath.

"Aye, I know about Diarmuid and Aengus Óg and all that." She looked around the room. "Where the hell is Bran?"

Fionn gaped at her for a moment longer, then spoke to the women in Spanish. They looked mutinous, but they left the room after gathering up their clothing.

"Put some fucking clothes on," Nora snapped. She turned away from him and took several deep breaths. So what if this past Fionn had been a ladies' man? It had nothing to do with her. And she needed him to trust her, or at least believe her. "Are you dressed?" she asked, forcing a more pleasant tone.

"I am," he said. "Who are you?"

She turned around. He was leaning back against the bed, dressed in a deep-red silk robe that tied around his waist.

"My name is Nora O'Reilly," she said. "I'm sorry about barging in here and how I spoke to your . . . friends. I was just surprised. I expected to find you alone."

"Who sent you?"

"Brigid sent me," she said. Technically, that was true.

He narrowed his eyes at her. "*Which* Brigid?"

"*The* Brigid," she said impatiently. "The Tuatha Dé Danann goddess."

He glared at her for a moment longer, then said, "I have no idea what you're talking about. Who are you, really? Did FitzGerald send you?"

"Don't play dumb," she said, firing up again. "I'm telling the fucking truth, and I don't have time for games."

"For your sake, I hope not," he said, his tone menacing. He stood straight and ambled over, coming so close she could smell the wine on his breath. He towered over her, his eyes searching her face. She met his gaze with equal intensity.

"What's that supposed to mean?" she asked, fighting the urge to step back.

He broke the gaze first. But instead of stepping back, he moved an inch forward and fingered a wisp of hair that was sticking out from under her hat. "The last time I saw Brigid, I received twenty lashes for the pleasure," he said.

Nora jerked her head away. She'd expected their mutual friendship with Brigid to be an asset, not a liability. "Why? I thought you two were friendly."

He scoffed and moved away. He picked up a goblet and glanced in it before tossing it away. It hit the ground with a clatter and rolled around, empty. "Only when it suits her," he said. "She's obviously too afraid to come herself. O'course, she's probably told you all manner of lies. That's what she deals in, Brigid. Lies and deception."

Nora didn't know what to say to this. She should have brought Bran, who could have convinced this Fionn that they were on the same side, that they wanted the same things. But Bran had gone with her Fionn, wherever he was.

"You're right," she said, lifting her chin. "Brigid didn't send me. She only made it possible for me to find you. Coming here was my idea. I don't know what happened between the two of you, and honestly I don't care. It has nothing to do with why I'm here."

Fionn had crossed the room and was now filling a fresh goblet with wine from a pitcher resting on a sideboard.

"I know who you are," she said. "I know you're the Fionn mac Cumhaill from the legends. I know Aengus Óg put you under a curse because you killed Diarmuid, and you cannot die until you save Ireland from her enemies. I know you've been trying . . . and failing. I know you can communicate with Bran, your wolfhound, and that she's actually your cousin."

"Did Brigid tell you all this?" he snarled, but he could not disguise the sudden flash of pain that crossed his features.

"No. You did."

He stared at her, nonplussed. After a few seconds' silence he said, "That's impossible. I've never seen you before. And I haven't told anyone who I am—no one who is still alive, that is." His lips curled back in a snarl.

"I swear it's true," Nora said. "Just hear me out. I know this is going to sound crazy, but remember, it's no more crazy than living for hundreds of years." She wasn't sure he was even listening to her. His dark gaze was fixed on some unseen point, and his thoughts were obviously elsewhere.

"Go on, then," he said, surprising her.

Nora crossed to the sideboard and poured herself a glass of wine, mostly to give herself time to think. There was no delicate way to say it. "I'm from the future."

He tore his gaze away from the spot on the floor he'd been glaring at. "You're mad."

"Just hear me out," she urged. "I'm from 2005, but Brigid sent me back in time to 1923, where I met you. She wanted us to help each other."

He gave her an incredulous, almost pitying look. "God, you really believe it, don't you? What was your name? Nora O'Reilly? Well, listen to me, Nora O'Reilly, there's something wrong with your head if Brigid has convinced you that you're from the future."

"She's not convinced me of anything!" Nora retorted, flaring up at once. "I had dreams about you for months; then I was sent back in time to track you down. It took a while to convince you of the truth, but you believed me. I'm only trying to help you. We want the same thing."

"And what is that?" he snapped.

"You want to save Ireland from the English so you can die and be with your friends and family in the Otherworld. I want to save Ireland to prevent the war my brother dies in."

"And I told you this, did I? I just opened my heart and shared all my secrets with a woman from the future?"

"Like I said, you took some convincing. I broke you out of jail. And then we tried to . . . well, we tried to change something in 1923, but it didn't work. So we asked Brigid to send us further back, and here were are."

"We?"

She was starting to regret her insistence on delivering the message instead of Fionn. "He's here. That is, you are. From 1923."

He sank down on the bed, his face white. "If you're telling the truth—and I hope to God you're not—then I'm still alive in 1923."

"Aye, you are. I'm sorry. But—"

"Three. Hundred. Years. That's over three hundred years from now." He closed his eyes and seemed to grow smaller where he sat hunched over his goblet of wine. "I haven't . . ."

"No, you haven't," she said gently. "But that's why I'm here. To change that."

He snapped himself out of his reverie. "I don't believe you," he said. "Everything you've said, Brigid could have told you. This isn't the first time she's played games with me. As if I didn't have enough to worry about without her interference."

He hadn't looked all that worried when Nora had burst in on him, but she chose not to point this out. "I'm not making this up, and I'm not touched in the head, either. I'm here to tell you how to defeat the English navy. D'you want to know or not?"

He looked up at this, eyes narrowed. "What do you mean? Are you a spy?"

"For Christ's sake, I'm not a spy! I told you who I am. I came here from the O'Donnells' castle in Donegal. Hugh O'Neill and Granuaile were there, too. Granuaile is the one who brought us here to find you."

"Granuaile? The pirate queen of Connacht is here?"

"Aye, she's down at the docks, trading."

"And my future self? Where is he? Why did he not come?"

"I told him it wasn't worth the risk of someone seeing you together. I don't know where he's gone; he just said he'd meet me back at the ship."

"So future me takes orders from a woman, does he?"

Nora bristled. "We're partners." He scoffed at this, and Nora's dislike of Past Fionn deepened. "We need you to take a message to Medina Sidonia."

Fionn looked up at this. "Why? What message?"

"We know you're friendly with him. Santa Cruz is going to die any day now, and Medina Sidonia will be appointed admiral of the armada. In our timeline, the armada loses, and badly. But we have information for the new admiral that can change everything." Nora quickly outlined their plan, undeterred by the look of disdainful disbelief on his face.

When she had outlined it as best she could, she passed him the letter Fionn had written while on their journey to Lisbon. "Once Medina Sidonia is appointed admiral, he'll be convinced that you really did have a vision from God. Then you can pretend this is the plan God gave you."

"Medina Sidonia as admiral? That's preposterous." All the same, he accepted the letter and ripped open the seal they had borrowed from Granuaile. He stared at the inky scrawl. "This is my handwriting."

"Aye, so it is."

He scanned the contents while Nora held her breath. Everything hinged on his willingness to deliver this message to the man who had the power to act against the king's wishes—and, in so doing, win the battle. She stayed as still as possible, not wanting to distract him. Cormac and Kat at Fionn's estate had obviously had the sense to keep quiet about their boss's doppelganger. She was grateful for their sakes, but it might have speeded things up here if he'd already known about a look-alike visiting his house.

Suddenly, he threw the letter onto the bed and stood. "I want to see him."

"Him?"

"My future self. If I'm going to risk making an arse of myself with Medina Sidonia, I need to be sure this isn't some elaborate joke. You could be an English spy, or maybe you're from the French. They'd enjoy watching our mutual destruction, I'm sure."

"How would a spy know everything about you?" Time for the coup de grâce. "He told me to tell you about the plague—the Black Death. He said he pretended to be a priest as penance. He said he also hoped it would kill him, but obviously that didn't happen. No one else could possibly know that."

"A game is being played here," he muttered as he pulled on a linen shirt and hose. "And I'm going to find out what it is."

"I told you, I don't know where he is," Nora insisted. "And if you come back to the docks and the sailors see two of you wandering about, what will they think?"

"I know exactly where he is," Fionn retorted. "If I know myself at all." He snatched the letter from the bed and tucked it into a pocket inside his vest.

She had no choice but to follow him as he swept from the room and down the marbled corridor to the grand staircase that curved between massive stone pillars. She had to nearly run to keep up. "Where are we going?" she asked, but he ignored her, his eyes set on the path ahead. They crossed a busy street filled with merchant's stalls and carts stacked with goods from all over Europe. He followed a side street, turned down one lane and then another, this one lined on both sides with stone houses pressed close together.

Nora saw him first.

"Wait," she said, tugging on Past Fionn's sleeve. "Are you sure you want to do this?" But he wasn't listening to her—he was staring at the man several houses in front of them, the man whose attention was fixed on the window. Bran paced nervously behind her master. When she saw Nora and Past Fionn, her hackles rose and she growled low.

"Bran?" Past Fionn said, crouching down. "But . . . I left her at my estate in the countryside. Is she from the future, too?"

The man at the window jerked around at the sound of his own voice.

"He insisted on coming to see you," Nora said apologetically, but neither man was paying any attention to her. Their identical stormy-blue eyes were fixed on each other, a pair of rams locking horns.

"I just wanted to see them again," the Fionn by the window croaked, his voice hoarse. "I had almost forgotten what they looked like. I just . . ."

The other Fionn continued to stare. "How is this possible?"

"Brigid," Nora and Future Fionn answered at the same time.

"Believe me now?" Nora asked the still-gaping man beside her. He turned slowly and looked at her as though seeing her for the first time. Fear mingled with his expression of shock. He nodded slowly as his gaze returned to his future self. "I believe you. And you need me to . . . to . . ."

"We need you to take these instructions to Medina Sidonia," she said gently, tapping the letter tucked into his pocket. "And then, hopefully, the Spanish will succeed in invading England, which will help free Ireland. If that happens, it may free you of your curse."

"What will happen to you?" he asked the other Fionn, who was still staring through the window.

"We'll die," Fionn said simply, not taking his eyes away. "And we'll see them all again."

"And if it doesn't work? If things continue as they did for you? What happens then?"

The Fionn at the window gave his former self a look that could only be described as pity. His face was drawn and haggard, and his eyes had a haunted look. "You'll find out."

"Papa?"

A small girl, maybe four years of age, had stuck her head outside the door and was looking up at Future Fionn with huge blue eyes. Her dark-brown hair tumbled past her shoulders, a tangled knot sticking out the back. Nora made to shove Past Fionn out of sight, but he beat her to it, ducking into the lane before the girl could see him. Nora watched from the shadows of the laneway, her heart breaking at the tormented expression on Future Fionn's face. Bran joined them in the shadows, giving Fionn and his daughter their privacy.

"Papa, what happened to your hair?" the girl asked.

Fionn ran his hand through it. "Oh. I . . . it's a wig," he said. "Just trying something new."

"I like it better long," she told him.

"Then the next time you see me, it will be long." His voice broke, and his hand shook as he reached out to touch his daughter's dark hair.

"Aren't you coming in?" she asked, reaching up and taking his hand.

"No," he said quickly. "I just . . . I wanted to see you. I love you so much." Tears began streaming down his cheeks.

"Papa, what's the matter?" the little girl asked. "Are you sad?"

"Yes, darling. But don't worry about me. I'll be all right. We all will." He dropped to his knees and scooped her into his arms, clutching her tight against his chest. The little girl kissed his cheeks where they were wet with tears.

"God be with you, Papa. Thank you for coming to visit me."

Nora could tell it was with great reluctance that he relinquished his hold on her. "Tell your mother I will be home this weekend, and after that, I won't be gone so much anymore."

The child nodded solemnly. "I will." She hugged him once more, then skipped back to the doorway and disappeared inside.

Nora hastily wiped her cheeks on her sleeves and then stepped out of the laneway and took Future Fionn gently by the arm. As soon as they were back in the shadows, he grabbed his past self by the throat and shoved him up against the stone wall.

"Fionn!" she cried. "Stop it!"

"Listen to me," he snarled at his reflection. "Stop whoring around. Live with your goddamn family. She's a good woman and deserves better." He released his hold, and the other Fionn rubbed his neck, gasping. Without another word, Fionn grabbed Nora's arm and marched her down the laneway, away from his past life.

Chapter Twenty-Five

Nora and Fionn spoke very little on the return voyage to Ireland. He threw himself into work on the ship, taking on double shifts and the most dangerous tasks. Much to Nora's relief, Granuaile relaxed her rules. Nora was allowed to work up on deck with the others, repairing ropes and scrubbing the floorboards with seawater. Granuaile had sent the ship that had sailed to Lisbon with them on to Donegal to order the rest of the fleet back to Clew Bay once repairs were finished. They would reattempt the voyage to Scotland when the winter storms had abated. Granuaile and the crew all seemed heartened by her decision.

"We're going home," she had announced to wild cheers.

Fionn took to spending hours in the crow's nest, scanning the horizon for approaching ships or storms. Bran would pace miserably at the foot of the rigging until Granuaile finally sent her below deck to take out her frustration on the rats. About a week into their voyage, a gale blew up suddenly, but Fionn stayed up in the crow's nest despite the scourge of lightning and rain. At the height of the gale, Nora thought she could hear him screaming, but perhaps it had just been the wind. No one could scream that loud.

The next day was calm, and the strong wind at their backs relaxed the tension in Granuaile's shoulders. Fionn was not in the crow's nest this day, but a cry from the watchman on duty caused them all to stop what they were doing and look toward their captain.

"English ships!" Granuaile shouted. "All men on deck, into your uniforms!"

At once, the men scurried below deck. When they emerged less than a minute later, they were pulling on navy jackets with brass buttons and tying their long hair behind their heads.

"English uniforms," Granuaile told Nora, tucking her own dark locks under a cap and pulling on an English captain's uniform. "Fionn, take the flag up." She handed Fionn a cross of Saint George sewn onto a white cloth. Without a word, he tucked it into his jacket and scampered up the rigging. "Nora, get below, for God's sake," Granuaile snapped.

Nora knew better than to argue with Granuaile when she was preparing for a possible battle. She joined Bran below deck, where they huddled together in Granuaile's cabin. And waited. After what must have been hours, the bell was struck for the changing of the shift, and Nora deemed it safe to venture above deck. The men coming off their shift were shedding their stolen uniforms as they sought empty floor space to grab the four hours of precious sleep they were allowed before their next shift.

"What happened? Is everything all right?" she asked one of the men as he passed her. He shied away as though she were some sort of specter, then nodded jerkily.

"Aye, the English ship passed us, and the captain says we're not being followed," he said before moving away quickly.

Nora's eyes immediately sought out the crow's nest when she emerged on the top deck. She could just make out the flash of gray that told her Fionn was up there, bringing down the Saint George's cross before they were attacked by one of Granuaile's own clansmen. Disaster averted—for now.

On the cold, lonely nights at sea, Nora found herself thinking of the Fionn she'd met in Lisbon. The image of him sprawled naked on the bed, whores draped over him like dirty laundry, was burned into her mind. No matter what she told herself, the Fionn she had met in Lisbon would eventually become Thomas Heaney, a freedom fighter on the anti-treaty side of the Irish Civil War. Past Fionn and *her* Fionn were one and the same.

Were beautiful women his Achilles's heel? It seemed possible. The curse that had given him eternal life was, after all, Aengus Óg's punishment for the crime of passion Fionn had committed. Grania had been engaged to Fionn, but she'd fallen in love with his best friend because of a charmed love spot on the man's forehead. Consumed by jealousy, Fionn had pretended to make peace with Diarmuid, only to kill him. How much of the man who'd murdered his best friend over a woman was still a part of him?

And what kind of a woman had Grania been to inspire such madness? They said Helen of Troy was "the face that launched a thousand ships," but Grania's face had launched over a thousand years of purgatory for one man. A wee voice in the back of Nora's head, one she hated, whispered, *Who could ever hope to compare to her?*

As they approached Connacht, once again sailing as far away from the coast as they could, a lighter, smaller boat approached them, flying the O'Malley colors. Signals were passed between the two ships, and then the smaller ship drew up beside them and a plank was thrown between the two decks. A portly man with a mottled complexion crossed the plank, and he and Granuaile clasped hands firmly before going down to her cabin to talk. Nora wished desperately she could follow them, but perhaps it was time to stop scheming. For now. She and Fionn had done what they could to facilitate the Spanish invasion of England, and all they could do now was wait for the outcome. The armada would not set sail for another three months—at least that's the way it had happened originally. Granuaile had offered to let them stay at her home in Carrickahowley.

"Is he all right?" Granuaile asked Nora after emerging from her conference with the other captain.

Nora glanced up at the crow's nest, where Fionn was silently watching the coastline as it drew nearer. "I don't know," she said honestly. "He had a strange experience in Lisbon. I think it did something to him."

Granuaile shook her head. "Before you two came along, I thought *I* had lived a most extraordinary life." She, too, cast her gaze to the crow's nest. "He's seen more than the rest of us. And suffered more, too. Give him time. He'll come back to you."

"Oh, we're not—" Nora started, but Granuaile waved her into silence.

"Not lovers?" she asked. "Maybe not in the flesh, though I reckon you want it, and badly. You've not taken your eyes off him the three weeks we've been at sea. You're worried for him, and rightly so. But how you truly feel about him is written across your face as clear as the stars across the sky. Don't let him keep you at bay much longer. In this world, if you want something, you have to fight for it. It's always worth it in the end."

Granuaile patted Nora's arm and then continued along the deck, inspecting the rigging and speaking with her sailors as they prepared to sail into Clew Bay. Nora moved to the prow of the ship and gazed ahead, her thoughts on Granuaile's advice.

She *did* want Fionn, despite what she'd seen in Lisbon, despite her confused thoughts about Grania. She could admit that much to herself. And he felt a certain attraction to her, she was sure of it. But he was afraid—he'd told her as much. Afraid that they would become close, and the same old scenario would play out: she would grow old and die while he stayed young and strong. The thought frightened her, too. But more than that were his words in front of the window in Lisbon. *What if we succeed?* the other Fionn had asked.

Then we die.

And wasn't that why they were here in the first place? To break his curse, so he could finally join those he had loved and lost through the centuries? Their end goal, the point of their entire mission, was to achieve his death. How could she love him, knowing that?

Granuaile's enemy Bingham was nowhere to be seen as they maneuvered through the gauntlet of tiny islands and rocky outcroppings that dotted Clew Bay. On the shore stood Carrickahowley, which the English called Rockfleet, a tall tower house similar in style to Doonbeg Castle. The tide was high, and the tower house seemed to rise out of the water that surrounded it on three sides.

Granuaile's men knew the routine; they were in familiar waters. And so the pirate queen left them to it and stood beside Nora at the prow, her eyes shining as they drew nearer to her home. "Did I ever tell you how I acquired this castle?" she asked Nora.

"No," Nora said, intrigued. Granuaile had never confided in her before.

"Carrickahowley belonged to my second husband, whom they called Richard-an-Iarainn, Iron Richard. He was a Burke of the MacWilliam Burkes." She grinned wickedly. "I divorced him after our first year together."

Nora raised her eyebrows. "Why? Was he an eejit?"

"No more so than any other man. I just wanted my freedom, is all. I longed to be out on the sea, and Richard wasn't a seafaring man. It was simple enough. I don't know how you do it where you're from, but under Brehon law all I had to do was say, "Richard-an-Iarainn, I dismiss you!" three times, and that was that. O'course, I'd locked him out of his castle first." She threw back her head and bellowed an infectious laugh.

"What'd he do?"

"I know he thought of fighting me for it, but 'tis a well-fortified keep, and most of his men had already come over to my side. They were inside the castle, ready to defend me. So he'd no choice but to ride away, his tail between his legs. Ach, he was a good sport about it in the end. Never challenged me for the castle or the men, and we stayed allies until he died a few years ago. I even helped him when he was angling for the MacWilliamship. Richard had been elected tánaiste by the clan, but the English had a mind to appoint someone else. So I sailed in with a ship full of redshanks, and the English backed down soon enough. 'Twas the proudest day of his life, becoming The MacWilliam. So I think I was forgiven, after all."

The fishermen and farmers who lived on the shores of Clew Bay cheered and greeted Granuaile as she strode up the kelp-strewn beach toward her fortress. Unlike Doonbeg, Carrickahowley had no windows, only thin arrow slits, and corner turrets topped either side of the fortress. They walked through a gate in the outer wall and circled the castle to reach the main entrance, which faced inland. A massive oak door framed by a chiseled Gothic archway stood before them, and a torch burned in a bracket on the stone wall beside it.

The doors opened as Granuaile approached. Of course, the caretakers of the castle had seen them coming; Carrickahowley was ideally located to observe the comings and goings of all ships in Clew Bay and beyond. Granuaile and a thin, elderly woman embraced with all the warmth of long-lost sisters. Then Granuaile beckoned Fionn and Nora to her side.

"Ciara, I've brought some visitors home," Granuaile said.

"Again?" Ciara asked. She was all bones and angles, and her skin was leathery. Her gray hair was braided and fastened in a looping wrap around her head. She wore a simple léine dyed saffron, topped with a fur shawl around her scrawny shoulders. She stood a foot shorter than Granuaile, who towered over most women and men in this age.

Granuaile rolled her eyes, then said, "Fionn, Nora, this is my housekeeper and dear friend Ciara. She'll help you settle in. When I'm away, she's in charge."

"Only when you're away?" Ciara asked, her light blue eyes twinkling.

Granuaile chuckled. "Fair enough. Fionn and Nora will be with us until summer, at least. I'll put them to work once we've settled. I'm afraid we all have to pitch in here," she said to them, almost apologetically.

"O'course," Nora said, who had no desire to lounge about for the next three months, waiting for news of the Spanish invasion. The time would pass quicker if they kept busy.

And there was plenty of work to be done. The O'Malley and Burke clans had borne the brunt of Richard Bingham's cruelty. Cattle had been captured or killed, fields burned, fathers and sons murdered. The English now controlled all trade. Boats laden with wool, iron, and fish no longer sailed from Clew Bay to France, Spain, or even other ports in Ireland. When they did, it was at great risk—a risk even Granuaile's brave and loyal captains were increasingly hesitant to take. Bingham showed no mercy to the families of those who displeased him.

True to her word, Granuaile soon found jobs for both Fionn and Nora. Fionn had apparently regaled Granuaile with stories of battles and campaigns won by him and his men, for she tasked him with making soldiers out of sailors, fishermen, and cattle farmers. Nora had half-expected to be made Granuaile's chambermaid, but their host had other plans for her.

"I don't want them to know you're from the future," Granuaile told her. "But maybe my clanspeople can benefit from your knowledge. Most of these families can't afford to send their children to the priests for schooling, but you could teach them English, reading, and writing. It's a chance they'd never get in any other clan." Granuaile puffed out her chest and lifted her chin. "I want people to say that the O'Malley clan is the most educated clan in Ireland. And you'll teach the girls, too. It was the greatest gift my father ever gave me, and I want every young girl in this túath to have the same opportunity I did."

And so Nora set up her tiny school in an old, abandoned stone cottage near the shore. The wains delighted at her strange accent and modern Irish, and she delighted in changing the past in this small way. Though she knew she was walking a fine line, she gave them the basic information they would need to survive what was to come. In addition to language, reading, and writing lessons, she taught them basic hygiene and better farming techniques. She also taught them a few of the simple prayers she had learned as a child, hoping faith in God would give them strength for the trials ahead.

They'd been in Clew Bay for two weeks when Nora finally cornered Fionn on the staircase of Carrickahowley. She hadn't wanted to push him, but enough was enough.

"Are you planning to ever speak to me again?" she demanded.

"I *do* speak to you," he retorted.

"Aye, about the weather and the food, and precious little else. I know seeing your daughter was hard on you. But you can't just . . . disappear."

"You have no idea what it's like," he said, shoving past her.

"Then tell me!" She followed him down the stairs and into the entrance hall. "After everything we've been through, d'you think I won't listen? I want to help you, for Christ's sake."

"You can't," he said, still avoiding her gaze. He pushed open the heavy door. A light drizzle was falling, but Nora ignored it. She grabbed his arm and yanked him to a halt.

"Stop running away from me!"

He jerked his arm free. "Leave me alone!"

"No."

"What?"

"No, I won't leave you alone. You've been alone for far too long—that's the problem. For once in your life, you have someone who knows who you are, who believes you, who fucking loves you. D'you think you're the only one who's felt pain and loss? You have to fight it, damn it!"

He drew close to her, so close she could see the slight tremble in his jaw. "You think you know everything. But you don't. You don't know anything about me."

She let him go this time, her face burning as if he'd slapped it.

Chapter Twenty-Six

Nora and Fionn didn't speak of it again. In fact, for several days, they didn't speak at all. Nora was picking samphire on the boulders jutting out of the sea early one morning when Fionn strode toward her, his figure a dark silhouette against the rising sun. She continued filling her wicker basket with the fleshy green plant, studiously ignoring him. Bingham's raids and constant harassment of the Irish farmers and fishermen meant that food was scarce, even for someone with Granuaile's means. The samphire that grew in abundance here was a welcome addition to their diet of oatmeal, oatcakes, oat bread, and fish.

"Can I help you?" Fionn asked when he got within voice range.

"I'm almost done," she replied coolly, indicating her nearly full basket. He waited in silence as she gathered a couple more handfuls of samphire, then held out his hand for the basket as she climbed carefully off the slippery boulder. She ignored the gesture and waded back to shore with the basket in hand. She'd grown used to the constant cold and wet of Clew Bay, but over the course of their short residence, the weather was beginning to warm. Tiny pink and purple flowers were starting to shoot up between the limestones that dotted the fields beyond the castle.

Granuaile had been wise to assign Fionn the task she'd given him. Over the last few weeks, his spine had straightened and fresh color had flooded his cheeks. He'd started to lose the haggard, defeated expression that had marred his beautiful features since their arrival in the sixteenth century. Despite her anger at him, Nora was grateful for the improvement. These humble men he was training were a far cry from the fabled Fianna, almost all of whom had possessed supernatural strength and abilities, but Fionn was doing something he excelled at. Under his firm but kind guidance, the men had begun to recover some of their lost dignity. Some even called him Lord of Carrickahowley.

Many of Granuaile's people had started to quietly question the role of the handsome man who was so often at her side. This wouldn't be the first time Granuaile had shown up with a younger lover. Many years ago, one of the old fisherwomen told Nora, there'd been a shipwreck in a storm off Clew Bay. A single man had been plucked alive from the debris, spotted while the locals scoured the water for any treasure the ship may have been carrying. After nursing the young man back to health, Granuaile had brought him into her home and then her bed. She had grown to love him, and her wrath had been terrible to behold when the MacMahon clan had killed him during a raid. She had delivered retribution on the MacMahons a hundred times over. Ever since, Granuaile's lovers had been treated with deference and respect.

Why had Fionn come to see her? To tell her that his relationship with Granuaile had changed? Granuaile had encouraged Nora to fight for him, but maybe it was too late; maybe their coldness to each other had shown the older woman that Fionn was free for the taking. Finally, Nora could bear the suspense no longer.

"Is everything all right?" she asked.

"Aye," he said quickly. Then he stopped. "No."

"What's wrong? Is it Granuaile? Is she okay?"

"Aye, she's grand. Well, she's a bit upset with me, I reckon."

"And why's that?"

"I suppose it has to do with you." He sat on a boulder that had just been lit by the rising sun. Nora had planned on going into the castle to put on the dry stockings she'd left by the fire to warm. But she stayed.

"With me? What have I done now? I've left you alone and minded my own damn business. Isn't that what you want?"

He rubbed the back of his neck. He'd not cut his hair since they'd arrived in this century, and it was now starting to curl around the base of his neck, daring her fingers to reach out and wrap themselves in the soft tendrils. Her own hair had grown into a shaggy bob, and while it wasn't yet long enough to be tied back in a ponytail, at least she could tuck it out of the way behind her ears. She folded her hands to keep them from twitching toward him. He lifted his chin and met her eyes. "I've come to say I'm sorry."

Nora cursed her heart, which had started bouncing around in her chest like an excitable toddler. "Oh, aye? For what? Being a stubborn arsehole?"

"You were right, Nora. We've been through so much together, you and I, yet I've treated you like a stranger since we arrived at Carrickahowley."

"Since we left Lisbon, actually," she pointed out.

"Aye."

"Why? I only wanted to help you. Why wouldn't you let me?"

"You know that I saw my family when we were in Lisbon. One of my families," he corrected. "It brought it all back—how it felt to lose them." Nora sat next to him on the boulder and pressed her hands into her lap.

"I tried to not fall in love with Maria, my wife," he continued. "But it happened, and then we had Sophie, my daughter, and wee Isabelle. They were grand children." Pride shone in his eyes. "And, as you saw, I was not my best self."

She hadn't told him that she'd walked in on him in bed with two naked women who were not his wife. As much as it rankled her, who was she to judge? There were many pieces of her past she did not look back on with pride. Perhaps he remembered, or maybe he had simply read the truth in the careful way she'd related her encounter with his former self.

"The time came, as it always does, when people started to question why I was not aging. Maria, especially, noticed."

"Could you not have told her the truth?" Nora asked.

He shook his head. "After we married, she became very religious, very superstitious. She could have accused me of witchcraft or some devilry. My children would have been tainted by association, suspected of being witches themselves."

Nora doubted that a woman who truly loved him would have acted in such a way, but perhaps her modern worldview impeded her from understanding. She remembered the tiny wains she had seen in Nigeria, cast out by their families for being "witches." She'd found a toddler digging through the trash, trying to survive, while the family and community shunned her. She'd brought the child to the feeding center, but it was too late. The parasites in the child's stomach could not be controlled, and she died a week later. Nora understood why Fionn would not have risked such a fate for his children.

"Aye, I see," she said, and he seemed to take heart in that.

"So I had to leave," he said. "I left her almost all of my money. I thought she would soon remarry, find someone to look after the girls." He cast Nora an apologetic glance. "Women were not as self-sufficient then as they are in your day."

"What happened to them?" she asked, knowing there could be no happy ending to this story.

"It doesn't matter," he said, the shadow passing back over his eyes, and she didn't press. "My point is that I was harshly reminded of what happens to the people I love . . . and what happens to me when I lose them. I was unprepared for the impact. But it does not excuse my appalling behavior."

"Thank you. I *was* hurt," Nora admitted. "But I do understand." She lifted her face to the weak morning sun, a hint of warmth promising a fine day. She stood and picked up the basket of samphire. "I need to get these to the cook before they start wilting."

"Wait." His hand shot out and grabbed her wrist.

She held her breath. She'd thought his story about Maria was meant to remind her that there was no future for the two of them. Unless . . .

"Did you mean it?" he asked. "When you said you loved me?"

Vulnerability made her want to pull away, to laugh off what she'd said and pretend she hadn't meant it, but Granuaile's advice echoed in her mind. *If you want something, you have to fight for it.*

She slowly sat back down. "I . . . I do. I think I have for some time."

His hand cupped her cheek, his eyes searching hers. "I am afraid." He didn't need to tell her that. The fear was evident in the wrinkle of his brow, the fine creases around his eyes, the set of his lips. But there was something else there as well. Longing.

"I've a question for you," she said.

"Anything."

"If we succeed, then you'll die. Is that right? You'll be free from your curse, and you'll just vanish or something?"

"I don't know about vanish," he said. "But aye, that's the general idea. Aengus Óg didn't exactly give me details, but Brigid did some investigating on my behalf, long ago. As far as I know, that's what will happen."

"Then I have the same problem as you," Nora said. "You're afraid that if you allow yourself to care about me, you'll have to watch me die one day. But I already care about you, and if we do what we set out to do, *I'll* be the one who watches *you* die. We're in the same situation."

"This is entirely new territory for me," he admitted, his face stricken. "Which is unexpected. What . . . what are we to do?"

"Well," Nora said slowly. "I can't tell you what to do. But for my part, we never have a guarantee that the people we care about won't be taken from us. So what if we know for certain that this won't last forever? I want to make the most of the time I have left. You only live once, even if it is for hundreds of years."

She expected him to laugh at this, but there was no time, because his lips were crushing hers. So great was her relief, her mouth widened into a smile under his. Her fingers unclasped in her lap and wrapped themselves in the thick curls at the base of his neck. He cupped her face with his hands, holding her close to him. Every cell in her body swelled with life, as though a warm torrent of sunshine were pouring through her, filling her up.

Behind them, a child giggled.

Nora gasped and pulled away, but Fionn pulled her onto his lap. Shooting a glance over his shoulder, he asked, "What are ye wee rascals up to?" The three children were crouched behind a nearby boulder and crept out one by one, their cheeks red and their eyes round.

Nora groaned. "O'course. I'm supposed to be teaching."

"And I'm supposed to be breaking in some new horses Granuaile acquired from who knows where," Fionn said, his hands still around her waist. "But I can think of many other things I'd rather be doing." The children giggled again, and Nora put her hands on Fionn's and slid out of his grasp.

"Later," she said, her eyes twinkling. "We've both jobs to do, and I should set a good example for my students, so I should." But she couldn't stop herself from leaning back down and kissing him again. Her head spun; this was really happening. *But he* will *die*, a wee voice in the back of her mind insisted as she pressed her lips against his and felt hot blood course through her body. *Then I'll enjoy him as much as I can*, she shot back stubbornly.

Word spread like wildfire, of course. By the time their first English class had ended, all the students were casting her knowing grins. There were a few concerned looks as well. If Fionn had been Granuaile's lover, then they would be right to worry about Nora's safety. But what woman would be mad enough to steal the pirate queen's lover while living in her home?

The makeshift school was dismissed just before lunch so the children could rejoin their families and participate in the daily struggle for survival. Nora packed up her few supplies—parchment and ink were too dear to be used for writing practice, so the children practiced their letters in the sand with pointed sticks—and headed back to Carrickahowley. Halfway there, she changed course, passing beside the tower house toward the field beyond. When he wasn't teaching the farmers and cottiers how to fight, Fionn had been showing Granuaile and her people a few modern farming methods.

She found him in a paddock with high stone walls, walking a beautiful black horse around in a circle. She let herself in by the gate and smiled at him. "That doesn't look so bad," she called.

He grinned back at her. "You should have seen her yesterday! I've tired her out for now."

"It's time to take a break, don't you think?"

"Done setting a good example for your students?" he asked, tying the horse to a sturdy post embedded in the ground.

"I am." She was grinning like an idiot, but she didn't care. He came over to her and kissed her on the cheek. He smelled of horse and sweat and salt, and she had never wanted him so badly.

"Then let's go," he murmured, nipping her ear lightly with his teeth.

They walked hand in hand back to the tower house, Nora's leather satchel with her quill and parchment slung over one shoulder. Bran came bounding out from behind the stable and nosed her way between them, panting.

"Not jealous, are you Bran?" Fionn asked. The hound barked in a way Nora could only describe as indignant, then ran in circles around them as they progressed up the hill. She broke off just as they neared the front entrance, intent on chasing a seagull that had dared land on the castle's lawn.

Fionn let go of Nora's hand to heave open the heavy oak door, and didn't take it back as they moved inside. Neither of them spoke until they reached the point at which they'd have to turn one way for his room and the opposite way for hers. Nora felt like a hapless teenager again.

"Ciara changed the linens yesterday," she said with a half grin, then turned and walked down the hall toward her room, trying to control her unsteady breathing. When she reached the door, she turned around. Fionn was still standing several paces away. "Aren't you coming?" she asked. Why was he hesitating? Was he about to change his mind again?

He took one step toward her, and then another. She pushed open the door, and he followed her inside.

"Are you sure?" he asked once the click of the latch had sounded behind them.

She turned to face him. "It sounds to me like *you're* the one who's unsure."

"I just don't want to hurt you," he said. "I care about you, Nora, I do. I don't want this to be some . . ."

"One-night stand?" She put her hands on his shoulders and let them glide down his arms, feeling the tautness of his muscles beneath the sleeves of his léine.

"Is that what you call it?" he asked, his breath hitching as she moved her hands to his leather belt and started unknotting it.

"Aye," she answered. "And I plan on having you for more than one night."

"But—"

She put her fingers on his lips to stop him. "Fionn. You're going to die. I'm going to die. Get over it, will ye?"

He responded by kissing the tips of her fingers, then moving his lips to her palm, her wrist, the tender skin on her forearm. Her other hand was still hooked in his belt, which she tugged loose. Then she wrapped both arms around his neck and kissed him deeply. When she finally pulled away, his expression was no longer hesitant—it was hungry.

"Ah, Nora," he breathed. "I have wanted you since the first moment I saw you."

"Even though you thought I was stark raving mad?" she teased.

"I still do," he said. He lifted one of her hands and waltzed her toward the bed. "Remember when we danced at the pub? I thought you were mad then. Mad and irresistible."

Nora laughed as she fell back onto the bed, bringing him with her. "Well, I won't tell you what I thought of you," she said, her eyes glowing. "Although I did think you were very handsome. I almost kissed you, you know—the first time you spoke to me in my dreams."

"That would hardly have been appropriate," he said in mock scandal, "seeing as how we were strangers. But now . . ." He grabbed the hem of her léine, a question in his eyes. She lifted her hands about her head in answer. He pulled the léine off, and Nora, who'd adopted the Gaelic custom of foregoing underclothes, sat naked in the center of the bed, her legs curled slightly underneath her.

"Good God," he whispered. "You should be painted."

She resisted the urge to cover herself, instead letting him map her body with his eyes. A cool breeze through the window brushed over her skin, and that small sensation was enough to nearly drive her over the edge. She grabbed him by the collar of his léine and pulled him in for a rough kiss. His stubble rasped against her skin, but she drew him closer still, the smell and taste of him swirling together. His hands cupped her naked breasts, and then his mouth was on each of them in turn, tasting and savoring and devouring. When he lifted his mouth to hers again, she pushed him onto his back with a twist of her arms. He must have read the desire in her eyes, because in two swift moments he had removed his léine and trews, leaving every inch of him exposed and open to her. She sat up and drew back on the bed, admiring him as he had admired her.

"You're amazing, so you are," she burst out, staring unabashedly at his naked body, taking in the cut of his muscles, the thin trail of hair that ran from his navel to the soft nest above his erection.

"Come here," he said, his voice gruff. His hand shot out and captured her wrist, tugging her on top of him. He kept her wrist pinned to the bed, his free hand behind her neck as she kissed him. She straddled him lightly, keeping her hips aloft, then brought his hand between her legs so he could feel how much she wanted him.

"Good Lord," he moaned, cupping her softly. No longer able to wait, she slid his hand out of the way and lowered herself onto him. She closed her eyes as he filled her, his hips rising to meet hers. Then she tightened her thighs around him, capturing him inside her, where he belonged.

They moved together slowly at first, savoring the electric sensations. Then Fionn grabbed her hips and thrust harder, pulling her closer with each rise. Her hands clutched his chest, her nails pressing into his skin. The storm in his eyes intensified, and his whole body tightened between her legs. Then he cried out in some ancient language as his release swept through him. Nora collapsed onto his chest, and they rolled onto their sides, facing each other, still coupled. Sweat glued their bodies together, their chests rising and falling in tandem. Fionn appeared lost for words. His mouth opened as if to speak, but then he just leaned forward and kissed her forehead, her nose, her cheeks, her chin. Laughing with joy, she tilted her head back so he could kiss her neck. After thoroughly kissing her head and neck, he settled his head on her shoulder, adjusted his hips so he slid out of her, and wrapped his arms around her waist. She lay still, reveling in the sensation of his warm body wrapped around hers, and listened to him breathe. She thought he was about to fall asleep when he slid his arm from around her shoulders down her body, tracing swirls and patterns on her ribs and stomach. Then he slipped his hand between her legs, finding her wetter than ever.

"Oh," she said in surprise.

"Oh?" he asked, hesitating.

"I thought we were done."

He lifted himself onto his elbow and grinned at her. "Ah, no, *a mhuirnín*, we're just beginning."

One hour and two orgasms of her own later, Nora slipped out of bed to visit the bogs. Fionn had fallen asleep beside her. She grinned as she pushed open the door and stepped into the hall. Her body ached with exertion and was rubbed raw all over by Fionn's stubble and grasping hands. God, how long had it been? Too long. Perhaps he would have energy for another go before they returned to their duties . . .

"Nora? Are you all right?" She had nearly collided with Granuaile.

"Aye, I'm grand, ta," Nora said, ducking her head so that Granuaile might not see her swollen lips and the evidence of Fionn's teeth on her neck. Had word reached her yet? How would she react?

Granuaile was not fooled. She grabbed Nora by the arm and yanked her close, inspecting her face. Then she gave a huge sniff, like a hound tracking a scent. She let Nora go with a bark of laughter and slapped her on the back. "So that's what you've been up to, is it! Please tell me you've your man Fionn in there, not some poor, hapless fisherman who won't know what's struck him."

Nora rubbed her arm where Granuaile had grabbed her. "I . . . yes. Fionn and I are . . . together." Granuaile's face split into a wide grin, showing her two missing teeth.

"Then all's as it should be."

"You're not bothered?"

"Bothered by two young people on a grand adventure taking some time to enjoy each other? Why would I be?"

Nora decided to take the bull by its horns. "I know you said I should fight for what I want. But, well, some of the folk say that *you* and Fionn, and I thought maybe . . ."

Granuaile looked pleased by this rumor but shook her head. "Ach, Nora, you don't think this old sack of bones can compare with a body as young and lovely as yourself? He's a real handsome man, I'll grant you that, and I'd have had him in my bed faster than a dropping anchor if he'd wanted it. But he wants *you*. It's been plain as day ever since he begged me to rescue you from Thomond. He wants you, and it scares him near half to death."

Chapter Twenty-Seven

As spring turned into summer, Carrickahowley started to feel like home. Fionn had moved into Nora's room after a week of daily visits. The rumors of a dangerous love triangle had died down quickly, for Nora, Fionn, and Granuaile were often together—eating and drinking, playing at cards, and inspecting the castle and its defenses.

Rumors about the armada continued to reach them through visiting merchants and fishing vessels. Nora and Fionn obsessed over each one, but it was impossible to sift fact from fiction. There was no way of knowing if Admiral Medina Sidonia had even received their message.

"I should have gone to him myself," Fionn said early one morning as he helped Nora gather samphire from the rocks.

"Only to have your other self contradict you the next time he saw his friend? We've been through this before. We did the best we could. Now we just have to wait."

But as much as she loved Carrickahowley, her students, and the happy rhythm of her new relationship with Fionn, Nora was restless. Her nerves were frayed with the waiting, with the uncertainty. If the armada set sail and won, would Fionn disappear from her arms? What would happen to her? Surely Brigid would intervene if they accomplished their goal and changed the future. Would the goddess return Nora to her own time? What would she find there? How would she be able to navigate a life so different from what her own had been?

Eamon would help her. Because if they succeeded, her brother would still be alive.

But Fionn would be dead.

It's what he wants, she told herself as she swept out the hut they used as a schoolroom on rainy days. The days were growing longer and warmer, which meant the armada would be setting sail any day now. Perhaps it had already happened. Nora's nails were bitten to the quick.

A knock on the stone doorway jolted her out of her thoughts. Fionn leaned against the weathered stone, arms crossed, his eyes fixed on her arse, which had been facing him as she bent over to sweep.

"What is it? Has it happened?" she asked breathlessly.

He shook his head. "Nothing." He wrapped his arms around her and cupped her bottom in his hands. "There's a storm coming, a mhuirnín."

"What kind of a storm?" she asked, the tension in her body lessening at his touch. "The bedroom kind?"

"Bedroom . . . schoolroom. You pick. Or . . . Granuaile is still away in Scotland. We've not done it there yet."

"I am *not* doing it in Granuaile's rooms!" she said. "The servants would tell, and then she'd kill us both. Or insist on joining in next time."

Fionn snorted.

"I choose bedroom," Nora said, running her nails lightly down his chest and feeling his nipples tighten through his léine. "*Ours.* You'll need something soft behind you when I'm done with you."

He cocked an eyebrow, and other parts stiffened against her. "Will I, now? Then we'd better get going. Also, there's an actual storm coming, so I wanted to fetch you before you got caught in it."

Nora leaned her broom against the wall and looked outside. The sky had changed while she'd been sweeping—once overcast, it was now a roiling dark gray. She was used to these sudden storms by now, but this one looked particularly intense. The wind had picked up as well, blowing toward them off the heaving ocean.

"I've changed my mind," she said, turning back to Fionn. "Let's stay here." She loved the intensity of a good storm.

"Here?" he asked, looking doubtful. "Are you sure? It might not be very comfortable."

"I don't want to be comfortable." She pushed him against the wall, kissing him with the ferocity of the wind that was screaming outside the door. Responding to her savagery, he crushed her lips as his hands roamed her body. The storm built outside the hut, the bay waves rising and crashing and the sky growing darker and thicker until it burst open, releasing a torrent of rain that battered the rushes above their sweating bodies.

When they had taken their fill of each other, they sat wrapped in a wool blanket in the doorway, watching the storm wear itself out at last.

"I've been wondering about something," Nora began, suddenly tentative. "What happened to Grania? The one you were engaged to before she ran off with Diarmuid." She'd wanted to let it go, but for some reason she'd been unable to stop thoughts of Grania from rising in her mind at the most inopportune moments. She couldn't help but wonder what had become of her, what she'd been like.

His eyes snapped to her face, and she noted that his chin rose slightly. "Why do you ask?"

She shrugged. "Just curious."

"Well . . . ," he began slowly. "After Diarmuid died, I married her."

Nora choked. "You *married* her? After you killed her husband?" A cold, sick feeling swept into the pit of her stomach.

"I know what you're thinking, but it wasn't like that," Fionn said, his voice pleading.

"Then how was it?" Nora said, wriggling out from under their shared blanket.

"She forgave me," he insisted. "She wanted it."

Nora couldn't believe what she was hearing. *She wanted it.* The defense of rape apologists in every age.

"I find that hard to believe," she said through gritted teeth. "If someone killed a person I cared about, I'd slit his throat myself. The last thing I'd do is marry him." She had almost said, *If someone killed you*, but stopped herself in time.

"You think I forced myself on her? Is that what you think of me?" He stood, his eyes flashing, and Nora scrambled to her feet to face him. "Grania was a different woman than you. And it was a different age. All she wanted was a good husband, someone with power and money. She'd been promised to me by her father, the High King. She forgave me. She was *happy* with me. After a time, she loved me. We loved each other."

From the look in his eyes, she knew it was true. Perhaps he still longed for Grania after all these years. Ridiculous, angry tears pricked at Nora's eyes. The affectionate glow they had been basking in was gone. She wished she'd never brought it up, wished she'd never given him a chance to disappoint her.

He picked up his clothes and stalked out into the dying storm. The wind blew the door shut, leaving Nora in the dark.

Shite. Why'd she flown off the handle like that, assuming the worst? Hadn't she ended up in bed with Mick O'Connor, who'd forced her brother to join the Provos? Mick hadn't killed Eamon, but neither was he entirely innocent in her brother's death. She at least owed it to Fionn to hear him out.

She shrugged into her léine and shoved her way out the door, framing an apology in her mind. The rain was still lashing down, and the rocks on the beach were slippery with fresh seaweed brought up by the waves. Fionn was down by the water's edge, and she carefully made her way toward him.

"Fionn!" she cried out, but he didn't turn. His eyes were fixed on the water. Finally, she reached him. "Fionn, we need to talk about this," she said, wiping the rain out of her eyes with the back of her hand. Then she caught sight of his face. This wasn't just about the fight.

"Look," he said, pointing. She followed his gaze and the direction of his finger.

The wreckage of three ships was just visible through the deluge. They'd been dashed against the hundreds of merciless rocks that filled Clew Bay. Debris bobbed on top of the waves: cracked barrels, jagged shards of wood . . . and bodies. A torn flag hung limply from the splintered mast of one of the ships. The red, white, and yellow of Spain.

"Jesus, Mary, and Joseph," Nora breathed.

"The ships of the Spanish Armada," Fionn said, his voice wooden. "Wrecked off the coast of Ireland. Exactly as it happened before."

Nora's legs trembled. So their plan hadn't worked, after all. Had the Fionn in Lisbon failed to deliver their instructions? Or perhaps Medina Sidonia had refused to believe Past Fionn. That brought her to the most frightening possibility of all: he'd followed their instructions to the letter, but the English had still defeated them.

She sank to her knees in the wet sand. She wanted to scream, to rage against the skeletal ruins. But a part of her considered the alternative—Fionn vanishing before her eyes on the beach—and rejected it with just as much vehemence.

"There are survivors," Fionn said, straightening up at once and moving into the water. Nora started after him. He was right. Some of the bodies were moving, wading toward them through the shallows. She counted ten, maybe a dozen. How many hundreds of men had those ships held? There was no time to think on it. She waded toward the closest man, who was struggling to stand though the water was only at his shoulders.

Granuaile's people streamed onto the beach, but no one else waded into the water to help the Spaniards. Ciara arrived as Nora was laying the half-drowned Spaniard down on the sand. The housekeeper's face was tight, and there was a long dagger clutched in her hand. "Spanish," she said. "We'll have to kill them."

Nora swiveled around to look at her. "*What?*"

"A messenger was here this morning. The governor of Connacht, Sir Bingham"—Ciara fairly spat the words—"has declared it treason to give assistance to the Spanish survivors. A crime punishable by death."

"But these are unarmed men!" Nora said. "Are we to do the English's bidding and slaughter them?" The onlookers watched the two women carefully. With Granuaile gone, whose word would carry more weight?

"We've no choice!" Ciara said, moving toward Nora's rescued Spaniard. "The English carry the heaviest stick; we must do what they say."

"The English will only have won when we stop fighting them!" Nora cried, seizing the older woman's wrist. "Your grandchildren are in my school, Ciara. D'you want them to know their only role in life is to do as a foreign queen orders them?"

"I want them to live," Ciara said, wrenching her arm out of Nora's grasp with surprising force.

"And what of these men?" Nora waved out at the sea, where Fionn was still struggling to drag men out of the water and bring them to shore. "They want to live as well. What about their wives and children? These people are not our enemies—the English are." Ciara looked unconvinced but made no further move to slash the Spaniard's throat. "No one needs to know," Nora urged. "We'll hide them in the castle, then smuggle them to safety."

Ciara nodded curtly, but instead of helping Nora with the wounded sailor, she turned and marched back to the castle. Nora faced the men and women who had gathered on the shore and raised her voice.

"Take whatever treasure you find. It's yours to keep. And bring the dead to shore so we can give them a proper burial. But bring any survivors to the castle. And quickly, before the English hear of it."

In the end, only nine living men were rescued from the water. It was a wonder they'd made it this far—the way their pasty skin hung on them reminded her of the starvation victims she'd seen all too often in her work. She confined them all to one room and tended to them herself, praying her vaccinations would protect her from the diseases they doubtless carried. To her surprise, Ciara insisted on helping her. A small chest of Spanish gold and a silver chalice had been found, but most of the clansfolk had come away with nothing but stripped timber—which, in this part of the country, was almost as valuable as the gold.

As Nora worked, the crushing disappointment of their failure to help the Spanish invade England mingled with the relief that Fionn was still alive. As soon as the last sailor had been dragged from the water, Fionn had gone off to send a messenger to Granuaile, telling her to stay where she was until she heard from them again, lest she arrive home only to be arrested by Bingham.

When Fionn returned to the sickroom, Nora pulled him toward the closest Spaniard. "Ask him what happened."

He nodded curtly as he knelt beside the injured man. "I've been wondering that myself." Nora stood nervously by while the two conversed in Spanish. There was a chance—a small chance—that the rest of the armada had successfully landed in England and launched their planned invasion. She watched their expressions, listening for familiar words that might give her some clue as to what they were saying. But she could make out nothing.

Finally, Fionn stood. He gave her a sorrowful glance, then shook his head.

"What happened?" she pressed.

He gave a short, sardonic laugh. "We changed history."

Her pulse quickened. "In what way?" she choked out.

He rubbed the back of his neck. "Medina Sidonia is dead."

She stared at him, uncomprehending.

He sighed, the weariness of centuries resting on him. "I told you about the Lizard, the point in the invasion where I thought we could have changed things. In our past, the English navy was trapped in the harbor by the incoming tide. The admiral and his generals held a council of war to decide how to proceed. Many, myself included, thought we should attack the English while they were in the harbor, but Medina Sidonia sailed on because he did not wish to counter Philip's orders."

"And this time?" Nora asked, fearing the answer.

"The admiral took my advice. He engaged the English in Plymouth Harbour, and a well-aimed cannon from the *Golden Lion* took his life. After Medina Sidonia died, his second-in-command took over. De Recalde and most of the men feared that God had struck Medina Sidonia down because he had disobeyed Philip's orders. So they fled the harbor and continued north, where everything unfolded more or less as it did for us."

Nora sank to the floor, stunned. She clutched her rosary, desperate for any source of strength and wisdom. It had been such a grand plan. But it had failed. Did that mean history—at least the major, nation-changing events—was set in stone?

No. Brigid had sent them here for a reason. "I won't give up," she said, her voice shaking. She looked to Fionn for comfort, wanting also to offer comfort in return, but he had already gone.

Chapter Twenty-Eight

Three days later, the soldiers arrived. Nora was down at the school when she heard the cry of alarm. She ran out of the hut and saw the cross of Saint George flying from three ships drawing toward them in Clew Bay. Shite. She put the eldest boy in charge, ordered him to lock the door behind her, and ran toward the castle.

She was too late. An advance party must have reached Carrickahowley by land before the ships had docked in the harbor. When Nora staggered into the entrance hall, Ciara was in the grips of a bearded soldier, bleeding copiously from the side of her head.

"Let her go!" Nora shouted. "What the hell are you doing?" The soldier had cut off Ciara's ear.

"Where are the Spanish?" the bearded man demanded, brandishing a bloody knife.

"I don't know what you're talking about," Nora said, trying to project an air of superiority. "I insist you let her go. She's only a servant—she knows nothing." Nora avoided Ciara's gaze and lifted her chin in defiance.

"Servants know everything," the man growled. He pinned Ciara to the ground and started sawing off her other ear.

"Stop! Stop!" Nora screamed, lunging at him. Another soldier grabbed her from behind and held her tight, pinning her arms to her sides. Ciara's screams reverberated off the stone walls. Then the doors burst open and Fionn ran in, brandishing a musket. But before he could decide whom to shoot, there was a knife at Nora's throat and two muskets pointed at Fionn's head.

"Let her go," he growled as he lowered the gun. "I'm the one you want. I'm in charge here."

The soldier who had cut off Ciara's ear plunged his dagger into the old woman's breast as casually as if he were cutting a steak. Nora's mouth dropped open in horror, but no sound came out.

"Actually, *I'm* in charge here," another man said, stepping into the pale light. Nora recognized the long, red-tipped nose and the pale face of Richard Bingham. She held her breath—would he recognize her despite her longer hair and plainer dress? His attention was fixed on Fionn—for now. He seemed to think he required no introduction. "I'm going to ask you two simple questions: Where is Grace O'Malley, and where are the Spanish you're harboring?"

Nora fought the urge to vomit.

"O'Malley isn't here," Fionn said. Two men were restraining him. "And the Spanish are in the churchyard. Go dig up the graves for all I care."

Bingham sidled up to Fionn. "And how do I know you're not hiding both of them?"

Fionn stared disdainfully down at the man, who was a good six inches shorter. "If you knew Granuaile at all, you'd know the last thing she would ever do is hide. If she were here, she'd have cut your balls off by now." A fist in his stomach doubled him over, preventing him from speaking any further.

"She's here," Bingham growled. "And we're not leaving until we find her."

"Search the seas, then," Fionn retorted, recovering his breath. "For all the good it'll do you. Granuaile has more friends than Elizabeth in these parts."

Bingham hammered several more blows into Fionn, then shouted at a cluster of soldiers, "You there! Search the building." He gestured to the soldiers closest to him. "You three come with me. We'll start questioning the natives." He stalked out of the castle, rubbing his knuckles, as the other men split up and began to search the place. Fionn and Nora were bound by their wrists and ankles and left under the watch of a soldier armed with a matchlock cavalier, which he kept pointed at them.

"Oh, Jesus," Nora said, looking at Ciara's body. A red puddle was spreading on the flagstones she had always kept so clean. "This is all my fault."

Fionn edged closer and brushed his knee against hers. "Don't believe that," he whispered. "You know whose fault it is."

He was right in principle, but she was the one who'd insisted they harbor the survivors. Now Ciara was dead, and Bingham's men were swarming the castle and the surrounding lands, bringing fresh hell to the people she'd begun to consider her own. Would her students be safe? Would the soldiers think to check a stone hut on the edge of the beach? She moaned. Of course they would. They were looking for hiding places.

"Are you all right?" Fionn asked.

"Better than you." He had a bloodied lip and a rapidly swelling eye. Their guard paced the hall, glancing nervously out the door over and over again, as though he expected to be swarmed by the Irish. Then the door banged open, and Bingham marched in with several of his men. And her students.

"What are you doing?" Nora said, trying and failing to get to her feet. "Those are but wains!"

Bingham's response was to grab one of the children—Failge, ten years old, a fisherman's son—and point his musket at the boy's head.

Bingham stared hard at Nora, his dark eyes narrow. She held her breath. Did he recognize her?

"Where is O'Malley?" he barked.

"Please, you don't have to do this!" she pleaded. "He's just a kid!"

He didn't give her a second chance. He pulled the trigger, and Failge dropped to the ground, half his face missing.

"No!" Nora screamed. "You fucking bastard!" The other children screamed and cried but were penned in by Bingham's men. He passed his musket to one of his men, who reloaded it. Then he grabbed another child, Geróit, seven, who was so frightened he'd wet himself.

"Where is she?" Bingham asked again, pressing the tip of his musket to the back of the boy's head.

"Scotland! She went to Scotland!" Nora said, the words burning her mouth.

"Very good," Bingham said. He gave the child a shove toward the door, then grabbed another. Saoirse, age eight. Had trouble reading but could draw beautifully. She was crying into her hands. Failge had been her brother. "Where are the Spaniards?" he asked, speaking so softly Nora could barely hear him over Saoirse's crying.

She choked as she fought to get out the words that would save Saoirse from her brother's fate. Fionn said it for her. "In a secret room on the second floor. Behind the tapestry with the tree on it."

"Go," Bingham said to a subordinate. He released the crying girl, who ran for the door. "Let them go," he said dismissively. He had what he'd come for. A moment later the other soldier returned.

"They're in there, sir, just as he said. What should we do with them?"

"Slit their throats," Bingham said. "Why waste bullets on Spanish papists?" Then he turned and considered Nora and Fionn. "But these two, however. Who are you? You might be of use to me."

So he still didn't recognize her. Nora, her lips pressed tight together, shook her head. What could they possibly say to appease this monster?

"We are travelers," Fionn said softly. "Guests in the home of Grace O'Malley. We are of no importance."

"I wouldn't say that," Bingham said. "You were harboring enemies of Her Majesty, and my men need a boost in morale. I think a good hanging should do it."

They were taken to Galway on one of the English ships anchored in Clew Bay. Nora was brought to the same jail as before, only this time she was thrown into a cell packed with other female prisoners. They were all filthy, and a single bucket served as their toilet. The other women didn't speak to her. Imprisoned for lesser crimes, they didn't want to risk being associated with the woman charged with treason.

On the third day, Nora was sitting crouched against the wall, knees drawn up around her face to ward off the stench, when a guard shouted her name. She stood stiffly and fought her way toward the barred door.

"I'm Nora O'Reilly," she said, her voice raspy from lack of use.

"Stand back, all you whores!" the guard shouted, thrusting his sword at them through the bars. The women skittered back like a group of rats. The guard opened the door and grabbed Nora's arm, pulling her out.

"What's going on?" she asked.

"Your time is up, traitor."

Nora's insides turned to liquid. This couldn't be happening. There had to be some rescue, some eleventh-hour salvation. Where was Fionn? Where was Brigid? Had Brigid really sent Nora back in time twice, only to let her hang at the end of an English rope? She fumbled at her neck for the tiny bone at the end of her rosary. *Jesus, Mary, Brigid,* she pleaded inside her mind. *One of you, hear me!*

The guard made to tie her hands together behind her back, but before he could do so Nora snapped the rosary off her neck and gathered it in her palm. She was dragged up a set of stone stairs and then pushed outside. Sunshine stabbed at her eyes. They were in front of the jail. A crowd had gathered, shouting, jeering, but Nora paid them no mind. Her eyes were fixed on the large wooden gallows that towered above her. She tried to twist away from the guard, but he only laughed and tightened his grip, prodding her in the back with the hilt of his sword. He marched her toward the gallows and then up the small set of stairs to the platform. A masked executioner stood at the ready.

"Nora!" Fionn was at the foot of the gallows, his wrists and ankles in chains. They'd brought him out to watch her die.

"Fionn," she breathed, feeling stronger at the sight of him. His clothes were torn and dirty, and bruises in shades of yellow and purple covered his face. But he was alive. At least one of them would survive this.

"Nora, you have an escape—use it!" he called out. A soldier hit him with the butt of his musket and told him to shut his mouth, but Fionn didn't take his eyes off her. "Run, Nora," he urged. "I know you can. Run!"

But where could she run?

"Any last words?" the executioner asked as he put the noose around her neck.

"*Sinn féin amháin*," she tried to say, but it came out in a whisper. What was Fionn on about?

"Sorry? I don't think the crowd heard you," the executioner said in a mocking tone.

Nora kept her eyes trained on Fionn. They were not going to make her cry, or beg, or speak like a frightened mouse. She squeezed the rosary hard, felt the relic dig into her palm. Then she stepped forward, the noose tightening around her neck. She took a last, final breath and spoke clear and loud, so that her cry of rebellion would be carried on the wind to every corner of Ireland. "Sinn féin amháin! Ourselves alone!"

Then the ground disappeared beneath her feet.

Chapter Twenty-Nine

Ow. That hurts.

Everything hurts.

Where am I?

This must be hell.

Or . . . purgatory?

Nora's thoughts oozed through her mind, sluggish and convoluted. She opened her eyes, only to immediately close them against the harsh brightness. Then her mind registered what her eyes had seen: a skeleton, covered in sores, mouth gaping, staring at her. She opened them again. It was still there, lying on a cot beside hers. The long hair seemed to indicate a woman, but the skin was drawn so tightly across her face it was hard to tell for sure.

"You've woken, thank God," a voice said. "Another day and they'd have made me send you out for burial with these poor souls." A woman pulled a sheet over the skeleton in the bed beside her.

Nora tried to speak, but her voice didn't seem to be connected to her thoughts. Was she dead? This was hardly how she'd imagined the afterlife. Her eyes followed the woman as she wrapped the emaciated body in the sheet and carried it effortlessly outside, as though it weighed no more than a loaf of bread.

Am I like that? She tried to sit up so she could examine her body, but even the thought of movement exhausted her. She compromised by lifting a hand in front of her face, fighting the sudden surge of pain. It was normal—thin rather than skeletal, and mercifully free of red sores. She let her hand drop and moved her head slightly to get a better view of the room around her. The walls were covered in chipped whitewash, and the roof's wooden timbers were exposed. The floor was bare stone. Rows of straw mattresses surrounded her, each with a gaunt, sticklike occupant. She took a deep breath through her nose. The reek of urine and feces stung the inside of her nostrils. This was a place of death.

She lifted a hand again and touched her neck. Now she remembered: she'd been on the gallows, about to die for helping the survivors of the Spanish Armada. She'd been clutching her rosary and the relic in her fist, but where were they now? She heaved her body upright, then fell back again as a swarm of dizziness overtook her. Her stomach lurched, but there was nothing to eject.

"For goodness' sake, please lie still." The woman who had carried the body away bustled back to Nora's side. She was tall and gangly, with brassy red hair tied back under a white cap and a long, drawn face. But her eyes were soft and kind, and the hands that brushed Nora's hair off her face were gentle.

"Where am I?" Nora croaked. Had they taken pity on her because she'd passed out on the gallows? Or were they just waiting until she regained consciousness to hang her?

"You're in the fever hospital of the Galway Workhouse," the woman said, lifting each of Nora's eyelids and then checking her pulse. Even the skin on her eyelids hurt. "We brought you in three days ago."

"Brought me? From where?"

"You tell me. We found you lying outside the gates, unconscious. Now, when was the last time you ate?"

"I . . . I don't know. In the jail, I suppose, if you can call that food."

"In jail, were you? Well, the food there's better than what they serve in here, to be sure. If you were in prison, you were getting a fair diet. And you don't appear to be starving, not compared with some of the poor souls I take in here. Do you know why you were unconscious?"

"I . . . I was . . ." She was about to say, *I was on the gallows*, but something wasn't right. The woman's uniform was a shin-length blue dress with a white apron over it. Her accent was Irish, but she was speaking English. There were medical instruments on a table under the window. *Oh, holy shite.* Nora's heart started pounding painfully. "What year is it?"

The nurse gave her a pitying look. "You weren't out for that long, dear. It's still 1846."

"No," Nora breathed, struggling to sit upright. She fought a wave of dizziness and kept her arms rigid on the sides of the bed until it had abated enough for her to open her eyes. The nurse was still there. "Are you sure?"

"O'course," the nurse answered slowly. "What's your name?"

"Nora O'Reilly." Fionn had told her to run, but she hadn't understood his meaning until now. She'd clutched the relic and stepped forward, ready to accept her fate as an Irish martyr. The floor beneath her feet had dropped, and the last thing she could remember was the feeling of falling through the air, waiting for her neck to snap.

She'd traveled through time.

"I had something on me, a rosary with a . . . a piece of bone attached to it. Is it here?"

The nurse shook her head. "No, love. You were found with naught but what you're wearing. We washed it, but there was nothing else on you."

Nora looked down, panic starting to build inside her. She was still wearing her léine and brat. "Are you sure? It's very important." How had she arrived at the workhouse? Was it in the same location as the sixteenth-century gallows? "How did I get here?"

"I don't know. Hundreds of people show up here every day, hoping to be admitted. We take in as many as we can, but half of them die in the night. All I know is you were lying outside the gates. You were lucky to have been brought to the infirmary."

Nora's brain, still sluggish, clunked through the dates scattered throughout her memory. "Ach, no. I'm in . . . This is the Great Hunger." Her face must have registered a fair amount of shock, because the nurse walked to a sideboard and brought back a glass of water.

"You could call it that," she said. "D'you have any family, Nora?"

Nora shook her head, then stopped because of the pain. She sipped the water gratefully. "No, but I'm not starving," she said. But for how long? She'd no money, no friends in this century, and no relic. If she failed to find it, she'd be stuck in one of the greatest disasters Ireland had ever known. She had to get out of here and find the relic. She started to move her legs to the side of the bed, but another wave of dizziness struck her so forcefully that she fell into the narrow space between her bed and the empty one next to it.

"For Christ's sake!" the nurse exclaimed, hurrying around to the other side of the bed and hauling Nora to a sitting position. She pushed her none too gently back onto the straw mattress. "You've only just regained consciousness. You've not eaten in at least three days, maybe more. Stay here while I find some stirabout for you. And don't leave that bed." She pointed a threatening finger at Nora, then bustled out of the room.

Nora waited for the world to stop spinning. This was worse than last time, she knew it. On the one hand, she'd been unconscious for three days, allowing her body to start the healing process. On the other hand, what if she didn't wake up next time?

"Brigid . . . ," she moaned. If the saint's relic had saved her from the gallows, why wasn't Brigid here to take care of her?

And why now? She could have traveled a year forward, a day forward, or even a week back so she could take Ciara's advice and refuse to hide the Spanish. Why 1846? It made no sense.

She had to find the relic.

She had to get back to Fionn.

His face swam to the forefront of her mind, and a great well of emptiness rose up in her stomach and blossomed through her chest. Before she could stop it, tears streamed down her face. A tight, physical pain clamped down on her lungs, threatening to suffocate her. What had happened to him? Was this it? The end to their mission? The end of their relationship? So many things had been left unsaid after their argument over his former wife, Grania.

She was about to make another attempt to get out of bed when a young, dun-haired woman with protruding cheekbones and pale, freckled skin approached her, carrying a tin cup of milk and a bowl of what could only be described as mush.

"I've brought you some stirabout," the girl said, avoiding eye contact. A shapeless bag of a dress hung limply from her bony shoulders, the hem ragged and torn. Despite the cold stone floor, she was barefoot, and red sores covered her legs. Patches of her hair were missing.

"Ta," Nora whispered. The girl looked like she needed it more than Nora did. "Are you a nurse?"

"No. My family's here in the workhouse. This is part of my job, helping in the infirmary."

"Your job?"

"You can't stay if you don't work," the girl said. She raised her eyes from the floor and looked at Nora curiously. "Didn't you know that?"

"No," Nora said. "I don't know anything about this place. I only just arrived."

The girl set the bowl on the floor so that she could help Nora sit up, then handed it to her. "Once you're well enough, you'll be moved to the women's wing," she said. "Then they'll give you a job—laundry or picking oakum or looking after the children."

"There are wains here?" Nora couldn't imagine a drearier place.

"Aye. My wee brother's in the boy's wing. He's five. They do a lot of the oakum picking, though I heard there's a bit of a school for them as well."

"You haven't seen him?"

She shook her head and looked back at the floor. "I've not seen any of my family. They split you up when you come in. I don't know why. You'd best eat that. It's even worse when it's cold."

Nora lifted the spoon to her lips and took a tentative sip. Disgusting, but she'd had worse. It tasted like a blend of potato, milk, and oatmeal, with the texture of glue. Thick and gooey, it stuck to the roof of her mouth, and she had to take a drink of milk to wash it down. "D'you want some?" Nora asked, holding the bowl toward the girl. The girl's eyes fixed on the offering, but then she shook her head and took a step back.

"Mrs. Warren said I wasn't to touch it," she said.

"I won't tell," Nora said. "Come on, I'm not really hungry. You have it." She shoved the bowl toward the girl, who took another step back, looking around to see if anyone was watching.

"They whip you if you break the rules," she whispered.

Nora stared at her. This poor waif was frightened to death of having a forbidden spoonful of this most unappetizing porridge. Nora didn't want to tempt her further. She pulled the bowl back close to her body and forced down another spoonful.

"What's your name?" she asked.

"Margaret," the girl whispered. "Do you need anything else? I should get back to Mrs. Warren."

"Is that the nurse who was with me? Tall, red hair?"

The girl nodded wordlessly.

"Thanks, Margaret."

Margaret left, casting one last longing look at the mush in Nora's bowl. Nora slowly ate it, hoping it would renew her strength enough to allow her to leave. But the effort of eating exhausted her, and she fell back against her thin pillow once she'd scraped the last sticky bits out of the bowl. The heaviness of sleep fell on her, and for once she welcomed it. Perhaps when she awoke, she'd have the wherewithal to find some answers.

But answers were elusive. For two days, Nora lay in the infirmary bed, too weak to leave. And all the while she knew her chances of finding her rosary and the relic were worsening. No one knew anything about how she had arrived at the workhouse. Perhaps some person had taken her here before walking away with her rosary. Or perhaps she'd dropped it and it was still lying in the dirt of the courtyard where the gallows had stood three hundred years ago. But as the hours passed, her hopes of finding her treasures grew less and less.

Unable to get out of bed, she had naught to do but think, surrounded by the dead and dying. The Great Hunger was something all Irish children knew about. Hell, it wasn't just the Irish. The legacy of the potato famine was taught in history classes all over the world, or at least in those countries where the Irish diaspora had landed. More than thirty million Americans claimed Irish heritage, and the great lot of them had arrived on coffin ships from a country that could no longer sustain them. Two years of blight in a row, combined with the cruel, racist economic policies of Ireland's English overlords and the complete lack of social networks, had led to the deaths of over a million men, women, and children. Two million more had fled the land of their ancestors. There'd been talk of labeling it genocide in recent years.

Genocide or not, after two days of being driven to near madness by her own confusion, eating naught but stirabout, and listening to the cries and moans of those dying of typhus, dysentery, and starvation around her, she wanted nothing more than to leave.

But where to go? The nurse wanted to transfer her to the women's wing of the workhouse. "If you leave, they won't let you come back," she warned her. "And you've said yourself you've no place to go."

"I can work," Nora said stubbornly. "I've medical skills. I'm a good organizer. I can teach school. I can—"

"Suit yourself," Mrs. Warren said, already moving toward the next bed. A young boy lay there, his eyes bulging out of sunken sockets.

I can find the relic and get the hell out of here.

"Wait," Nora said as Mrs. Warren headed toward the door. "I've a question. D'you know where the jail was in 1588? The gallows in particular?"

"I beg your pardon?"

"I know it's a strange question. But the jail . . . I'm assuming it's in a different place now than it was then. But maybe not. Was it here?"

"Why the devil d'you want to know something like that?"

"I can't say."

Mrs. Warren huffed, as though Nora were wasting her precious time. "I've no idea. The town jail is down by Nun's Island. I suppose it was in Blake's Castle at one time, but I've more important things to do than wonder about where things were three hundred years ago."

"Ta," Nora said, but Mrs. Warren had already walked away.

She left the workhouse by the front gates, presumably the same ones she'd been deposited at. She searched and searched every inch of ground, but there was no rosary.

Dressed in only her léine and brat, she shivered and clutched her arms around herself as she walked barefoot through the city. No one seemed to spare her a second glance, so inured were they to the sight of the destitute crawling the streets. She kept her eyes on the ground as she walked, in case the rosary and the relic had slipped from her limp fingers as her possible rescuer carried her to the workhouse. But the ground held nothing but dirt and sharp stones that dug into her feet. She tried to remember where the jail had been, where she and

Fionn had been taken. They'd ridden a few blocks east from the docks. Galway had grown since then, but she should limit her search to the medieval section of the city. She asked a merchant for directions to Blake's Castle. He reared away from her before pointing west. But that couldn't be right . . . She would have remembered a castle. They'd been kept in a smaller building. She continued up the narrow cobblestone streets, keeping her eyes peeled for any glimpse of wooden beads and a thin finger bone. A cart rattled by her, six coffins piled in the back, headed outside the city.

Nothing.

She walked for hours, ignoring the ache of hunger in her stomach and the searing pain in her legs. That relic was everything—if she couldn't find it, she would be stuck here forever, unless Brigid intervened. But Brigid didn't seem to be in the intervening kind of mood these days.

She limped down a laneway but froze at the sight of three mangy dogs several feet ahead. They were growling at each other, their ribs pressing against matted coats. They were fighting over something, some object one of the dogs had gripped in its teeth. Another made a lunge for it, and it fell to the muddy ground. It was a human head.

Nora pressed her dirty fingers firmly to her mouth to hold back the bile. She took a step away from the half-eaten face that leered at her, the mouth torn open.

The dogs took note of her and abandoned their rivalry, crouching low, growls broadcasting their intent. Nora cast one last horrified glance at the abandoned head, then turned and ran. The dogs gave chase, but another cart careened past as Nora reached the other side of the street, and the animals retreated to their grisly feast. Nora didn't stop running.

Finally she stumbled into a churchyard, nerves and body frayed like the hem of wee Margaret's pathetic dress. She would find no help here, not when the entire city was overrun with the starving and destitute. But she had to start thinking about survival. Shaking, she sank down onto a broken slab that had fallen over in the churchyard, clinging to the mantra that had saved her before. *Food, shelter, clothing.* It was the same situation she'd found herself in when she'd first arrived in 1923—skint, no friends, no place to go. But she'd survived then, and she would survive now. Only this time there were no helpful Brigidine Sisters, no envelopes of cash, no kind Gillies family to take her in.

She thought about finding the Brigidine Sisters, but how? She was on the other side of the country from Kildare. She ran through the options in her mind. Did trains run between the two cities? Could she sneak aboard one of the train cars? What about ships? Perhaps she could become a stowaway, steal aboard a ship from Galway to Dublin, then make her way to Kildare. Or work on board to pay her fare. Surely the Sisters would help her if she could find them.

The sun was setting. Despite the crushing need to lie down and rest, she straightened her spine and headed back onto the street. She'd seen the worst of humanity in her years as a relief worker. She could handle Galway in the nineteenth century, whatever it had to throw at her. This was hardly the first time she'd been in the midst of widespread famine. She needed to use the skills that had been drilled into her. She could help with relief efforts, share what she knew about how to organize people and supplies.

If she couldn't leave, that was.

Chapter Thirty

Nora walked by dark shop windows. The merchants were all home for the night, their doors barred to the paupers flooding their city. Up ahead, light spilled onto the sidewalk—the pubs would still be open, at least. She could wash dishes or wait tables with the best of them in exchange for a bed for the night. She pinched some color into her cheeks and pushed open the door. The smell of something amazing—some kind of stew or meat pie, perhaps. The famine had not reached the wealthy Anglo-Irish landlords of Galway City, who could afford the elevated food prices and didn't rely on the blighted potato.

"No beggars!" a man called from behind the bar. It took a moment for Nora to realize he was addressing her.

"I'm not a beggar," she said, affecting her most genteel accent. "But I've just been attacked by a band of them near the workhouse." The lie made her cheeks burn, but she needed the proprietor to think she belonged here. She settled on a stool at the bar. "I heard it was so much worse out here, so I brought a cart of food from Limerick. But they swarmed me, stole my cart and all my belongings. Ungrateful souls." She shook her head. "I'm looking for help, but everywhere's closed. Where can I find the city officials? I want to report this."

The barman looked at her suspiciously. "They'll all have gone home for the night. Why'd you not go to hospital?"

"I'm not hurt, except for my feet," she said. "And I don't know where it is. I tried to tell the people running the workhouse, but they were busy dealing with the riot."

"A riot at the workhouse?" he said. "I didn't think those poor souls had it in them. Would they rather be out on the street, starvin'?"

"Perhaps," Nora said. She raised her head and gave the barkeep an endearing smile. "Can you help a lady for the night?"

He looked uncertain. "It's not my business to go handing out charity."

"It's not charity. I'll be certain to pay you once my things have been returned to me, or I can write for my brother in Limerick."

"What's your name, honey?" He leaned forward, his eyes flicking to the neckline of her léine.

"Nora O'Reilly."

"Listen, Nora, if I gave free food and board to everyone who walked in here with a sob story, I'd be out of business. I'm sorry for your trouble, but I've got a full house of paying customers."

"I can sleep on the floor," she said, her confident veneer slipping slightly. "And I'm happy to do some work to earn my night's rest. Put me to work in your kitchen, or I can help you with your bookkeeping. I'm good with numbers."

"Aye, I can tell from your speech that you're no country waif, and I'm inclined to believe you. But the fact remains that I just don't have space. Nor can I afford to ask a paying customer to leave so as you can have his room. And I'll not have a lady sleeping on my floors."

"You'd rather I slept in the street?" Nora said, her temper flaring. She ached all over, and the bottoms of her feet were raw and bleeding. A pulsing pain was spreading through her neck and skull. She just needed a place to lie down before she renewed her search for the relic in the morning.

Some of the other patrons were starting to stare, but Nora ignored them. She kept her eyes fixed on the barman, trying to goad him into helping her with the force of her will. But he leaned forward and said, "You rode all the way from Limerick yourself, did ye?"

"Aye." She didn't let her gaze waver.

"And where were you planning on sleeping, then? No friends, no relations here in the city?"

"I was going to pay for a room for the night, o'course, until my money was stolen. God, I tried to bring some charity to these poor, starving folk and this is the thanks I get? To be attacked, stripped of my goods and my horse and cart, and now denied a simple night's rest in safety?"

"Sorry, miss. You'll have to try somewhere else. My inn is full."

"She can 'ave my room," a voice slurred from behind her. A slumped figure sat alone at a wooden table, surrounded by empty mugs of beer. His silver hair hung in his face in dank, greasy strands, and a thick beard covered his cheeks and jaw.

"Fionn," she breathed, sliding off her stool at once. She winced as her raw feet touched the bare floor, but it didn't slow her pace as she spanned the short distance to the chair opposite him.

He looked up at the sound of his name, and his eyes were afraid through the curtain of gray hair. "How'd you—"

"Are you sure, Mr. Madden?" the barkeep asked. "You might not be thinking so straight right now."

Fionn brushed his hair out of his eyes and raised his head, though he didn't take his eyes off Nora—nor did she take her eyes off him. "You heard me."

The barkeeper was uneasy. "You're a decent man, Mr. Madden, and you've done a good deal for the poor of this city. You'll promise me the lady's safety?"

"You weren't so worried about her safety when you were about to kick her out on the street," Fionn said, his words sliding together.

The barkeep grumbled something under his breath and then moved to the other side of the room to mop up a recently vacated table.

"Fionn, are you all right?" Nora said, peering at him. He was obviously drunk, but it was undeniably him. She wanted to cry with relief, wanted to wrap her arms around him. How was this possible? Had he followed her here from the gallows in 1588? Or was this . . . *oh*. This wasn't *her* Fionn. It was . . .

"How d'you know that name?" he demanded.

"I . . . Hang on." She pinched the bridge of her nose and closed her eyes. How did this work? Had she started a new timeline by traveling to 1846? Or was this the same Fionn she'd met in Lisbon? Or the one who would go back in time with her in another eighty years? "D'you recognize me?" she asked. She wasn't sure he'd recognize his own mother in the state he was in, but she had to ask. She leaned in closer. "Look at my face. My name is Nora O'Reilly. We've met before, I think. In Lisbon."

"Lisbon!" he snorted. "I've not been there in some time."

"I know," she said gently. "It was a long time ago. I came to ask for your help with the armada. Do you remember?"

He squinted at her. "The Spanish Armada?"

"Aye. I was with . . . your other self." She leaned in close. "From the future."

Was it just her imagination, or did his complexion lighten? "No," he said, drawing back in his chair. "No. That was just a dream."

"Fionn," she said, keeping her voice down. "It wasn't a dream. You know that."

"It was!" he said loudly. "A fit of madness, maybe. But it wasn't true. It can't be true." To her surprise, he put his face in his hands and sobbed like a small child.

She laid a tentative hand on his shoulder, but he shook it off viciously. "Don't touch me!"

Nora sat quite still, unsure of how to respond.

"I shouldna have come here," he said, his voice muffled by his hand.

"Why not?"

He lifted his face and glared at her with bleary, red-rimmed eyes. "I don't usually frequent this pub, but a *friend* told me to come tonight. Like the fool I am, I obeyed."

Brigid. Nora's heart leapt. So she *was* watching them. She sagged forward with relief, then took a great gulp of beer.

"Ach, not a friend, exactly," Fionn continued, spilling some beer onto his beard and wiping it with his sleeve. "A voice in my head. But it's not the first time. I'm not crazy, y'know."

"I . . . I know." Nora's spirits sank. It was probably Brigid, aye, but how was Nora supposed to track down a voice in his head? How was she supposed to demand Brigid set things right unless she could see her face to face? "D'you believe me now?" she asked. "It wasn't a dream. I was real then, and I'm real now. I can travel through time, remember?"

He didn't answer, only waved the bartender over for another drink. "And one for the lady," he muttered. "And whatever food's hot." Then he raised his eyes to Nora once more. "So I suppose the rubbish you gave the barkeep isn't true, is it? You're not here to feed the poor. Which is well enough because I've been tryin' and tryin', and nothin' works. I can throw money at it all day long, and it makes not a piss of difference, pardon my language."

"It's quite all right," she said, her heart squeezing. How many times had her Fionn apologized for swearing? "And it's not your fault. I know you're doing everything you can."

"They're all dyin'," he said, slumping forward onto his arms. She leaned toward him so she could hear his muffled voice. "Everyone."

"People you know?" she asked gently.

"Everyone. And I dunno who t'blame. English, sure. Potatoes—well, those were brought over by the English, weren't they? But it was our people who latched on to them so firmly. And why not? It kept them alive for generations, no matter how hard the bastards tried to wipe 'em out. But now they're all dyin' or leavin', and if all the Irish people leave, then what will be left for me to save? How can I save them when they're all dead or in America?" He raised his head, and Nora flinched at the look in his eyes.

"And now you're here," he said, his lip curling up in a snarl. "Why did you come?"

"It was an acci—" But before she could finish the word, Fionn had grabbed her one-handed by the throat and pulled her across the table. "Why did you come here? To throw it in my face? To remind me that everything I do is pointless? That I'll still be here in the goddamn next century?"

"Stop," she gasped, trying to pry his hand from her neck. The barkeep set down his tray of beer and meat pies with a clatter and rushed to her aid. He pried Fionn off her and looked set to throw him physically from the premises, but Nora waved her hand. "It's grand, so it is," she said. "Let him be."

But Fionn would not stay. He shoved his chair back with a force that sent it skidding into the next table. He stumbled in the direction of the barkeep, who grabbed his arm and turned him toward the door. With a look of utter loathing on his face, Fionn threw his key and a fistful of coins onto the table, then staggered out of the pub.

"I am so sorry, Miss O'Reilly," the barkeep said, his cheeks flushed.

"It's grand, so it is," Nora said, her eyes fixed on the door. Should she go after him? Not the wisest decision, given the state he was in. But why had Brigid—if she was indeed the voice in his head—arranged this meeting? Was Nora supposed to help Fionn, or was it the other way around?

Fionn. Her Fionn, whose fire and spirit were tempered by wisdom and experience. Who fought against his demons—and helped her do the same.

"I have to go back," she whispered to herself. But there was no relic, no Brigid. Only a healthy dose of fear about what another trip through time would do to her already-ravaged body. But she knew now there was no other option; she needed to return to the man she loved. She pictured him in her mind's eye, his straight, proud back, the soft fullness of his lips when he crushed them against hers, the storm that swelled in his eyes when he looked at her. She felt a sudden pull, as though a magnet inside her chest was being drawn to him. A wave of dizziness, the sensation of falling . . .

She gasped and grasped the edge of the table to steady herself. What was happening? She didn't have the relic. Was Brigid disguised as one of the patrons? But she knew somehow that this wasn't coming from Brigid or any outside source. She could feel it deep inside her. The pull to another time.

"Are you all right, miss?" the bartender asked, his eyes flicking between her and the direction Fionn had gone.

"Aye, grand so," she tossed back. She picked up the key Fionn had thrown on the table. "I'll be taking this room tonight, then."

"Aye, I suppose so," he said. "I'll just go tidy it up for you."

"There's no need." She stood, her legs shaking. The tag on the key read *2*. She hobbled on her sore feet to the stairway and up to the landing, where the doors were marked with simple brass numbers. The second door on the left opened to the turn of her key. Before she could slip into the room, she was blocked by a growling mass of brown fur.

"Bran!" she exclaimed, and the wolfhound backed away, her head tilted to one side. "Bran, it's me, Nora. Right, you've not met me yet. But I know you can understand me. Fionn's not here, but he'll come back for you." Nora eased into the room and showed Bran the key. "He'll be grand, so he will. He just needs to sleep it off. God, it's good to see you again. How are ye? Fionn's in rough shape, isn't he?" She dropped to her knees to be eye level with the hound. Bran stared at her for several long seconds, and Nora could almost see the wheels turning in her head. "Bran," she said softly. "Just trust me. I'm here to help."

That appeared to do the trick. Bran stepped forward and nuzzled Nora with her long snout. Nora wrapped her arms around the hound and squeezed, grateful for the familiar, comforting presence. Then she let go and sat on the edge of the bed. She closed her eyes and thought of Fionn, *her* Fionn: helping her gather samphire in the early mornings; shouting commands and swinging a long, glinting blade as he trained Granuaile's men; lying naked in her arms as their bodies melted into each other.

The pull came again, stronger than before, but this time she gave herself over to it.

Chapter Thirty-One

It was becoming too familiar, this sensation of dying, of muscles being ripped from bone, of breath from body. Nora floated through it, noting a tear here, a stab there. Then she tumbled back into nothing.

The second time she awoke, there was a light in her face. A blur of movement, but it made her dizzy, and she closed her eyes.

Why am I here? The thought floated through her mind, curious, searching. There was something she was supposed to do. Wake up? But why? It was dark and cool, and she was at peace.

The third time, she tried to focus on the moving figures. They swayed in and out of her vision, carried on waves of thought and memory. It was too soon. If she awoke, the pain would break her.

Then there was a familiar voice, and her chest swelled. His voice spoke again, then grew softer, then disappeared.

Wait, I'm here. She tried to open her eyes, tried to call out to him, but there was only silence and darkness. She fought it—now she *wanted* to wake up; she *wanted* to know whose voice had called to her. But the pain . . .

The pain could go fuck itself.

She laughed, inside her mind. So crude, so west Belfast. She must be getting better.

The fourth time, she kept her eyes open. She tried to speak, but it was impossible to make the connection between her thoughts and her voice. So she forced her eyes to stay open until someone came, until someone noticed her. She couldn't move, couldn't turn her head to see around her. Above was gray stone flecked with white. She could be anywhere. Or any time.

Time. She'd traveled through time again. Her own particular brand of sadism. Her eyelids started to droop. *No. Stay open*. But the darkness was calling to her, welcoming her.

A gasp, followed by a shatter. Not from her—it was still beyond her to make such noises. Someone was in the room.

"*Dar Dia*, Miss O'Reilly, you're awake!"

O'Reilly. Aye, that was her name.

"Can you hear me?" The speaker was a young woman, thin and wiry, with fair skin and a smattering of freckles across her cheeks and forehead.

Aye, I can hear you. She concentrated on her lips, willed them to move, angry with their stubborn disobedience.

"I'm going to fetch the mistress. Oh, please stay awake. We've missed you so." There was something familiar about this girl. She knew her somehow.

That was a good sign. She was somewhere with friends. It was important to stay awake—though now the agony of her determination was making itself known. Was that sweat on her forehead? She tried to move her fingers—they fluttered feebly before settling back down on the bed. Toes, check. Why couldn't she speak? Maybe just a short rest . . .

It was dark the next time she opened her eyes. A torch burned in a bracket on the wall, illuminating the rough stone behind it. She opened her mouth. It was dry. Push. She forced air from her lungs over her vocal cords. It felt as if her breath were made of acid. But she was sure she'd made a sound. There was a stirring; then something wet and soft was on her face.

"Bran." It came out like a rasp, as though she'd smoked a pack a day for seventy years. Bran's tongue was rough against Nora's cheek, her hot breath warming her face. Tears leaked from the corners of Nora's eyes. The hound licked her again, then barked into the air and ran to the door, which was closed. She barked three more times, and the sound stabbed through the front of Nora's skull. But she didn't mind. Let the dog bark, if it brought Fionn to her.

But it wasn't Fionn who crashed through the door moments later. "So you've come back to us, have you?" Granuaile crossed the room, her eyes fixed on Nora. As she drew closer, Nora noticed that she looked different. Her face was more lined, and her hair had gone almost completely gray. She was still beautiful, still filled the room with her presence. But she seemed more tired.

"He's coming," Granuaile said in answer to Nora's unspoken question. "I sent someone to wake him. He'll be so happy to see you." The tightness in her face did not reflect her words. Nora opened her mouth to ask one of the thousand questions that had burst into her mind, but her words died on her lips when the door opened again.

There he was, framed in the doorway. Her heart leapt painfully at the sight of him. That same pull that had brought her here swelled in her chest. He was wearing only a léine, and he'd dressed in a hurry: it was on backward. His chin was covered in a neatly trimmed gray beard, but otherwise he was just as he had been—just as he always would be. *Her* Fionn.

But he did not move toward her. He stood in place, his legs braced as through in preparation to flee. Granuaile moved silently toward the door, and some secret message passed between them as she stepped around him and closed the door behind her.

The click of the latch sent Fionn to her side. He grabbed her hand and held it to his chest. "How are you feeling?" he asked, his eyes searching her face. She ignored the question; her health was not what she wanted to discuss.

"It worked," she whispered, her lips dry and cracked. "I came back to you."

Without releasing her hand, Fionn pulled up a chair beside her bed and sat down. She wanted him to kiss her, to take her in his arms, to weep for joy that she'd escaped the noose and found her way back to him. But he did none of those things, only gripped her hand and stared down at her with a mix of confusion and fear. Was he still angry with her for her accusations about Grania? Wasn't her narrow escape from death enough to put that behind them?

"Nora . . . ," he started, his eyes fixed on her hand instead of her face. "What happened? One minute you were on the gallows, and then you disappeared. Where did you go? Did you go to another time?"

She nodded, the infinitesimal movement making her wince. "You were right," she whispered. "You told me to run, so I did. Only, I didn't know where I was going. When I woke up, I was in 1846."

"The Great Famine?" he asked, his steely eyes widening.

"Aye. It was horrible. I think someone brought me to the workhouse infirmary. They took care of me until I was well enough to leave."

"You were like this?" Fionn asked, gesturing to her slack body.

"Aye. Apparently I was unconscious for three days. It seems to get worse each time. How long was I out this time? And how did I get here?"

"Thanks to your English lessons, one of your students is a merchant now in Galway." Fionn's smile was sad, and there was a storm behind his eyes. "He found you unconscious in a pub. Apparently, it created quite a stir. You just showed up in someone's room. They thought you were dead. He recognized you at once. Brought you here a week ago."

"A merchant? Who?" This made no sense. Her students were mere wains. Unless . . . The truth gleamed in Fionn's eyes. Of course, he hadn't aged. But Granuaile had. Everyone else had. "What year is it?"

He hesitated, then said, "Fifteen ninety-three. You've been gone for five years."

Her hand went limp in his. *Five years.* "But how? I was thinking about you, about us . . ." She remembered what she had wanted to tell him. "Fionn, I did it myself. I think . . . I think it's been me all along."

"What d'you mean?"

"The time travel. I lost the relic somewhere in 1846. I had it in my hands on the gallows, but it was gone when I woke up in the workhouse. I couldn't find it. But I met you—"

He gave her a sharp look. "Me?"

"Aye." She smiled faintly at the memory. "You were so drunk. You said a friend inside your head had told you to meet me at the pub. I think it was Brigid. It's almost like she's directing us, only it wasn't *her* I felt inside, if that makes sense. She didn't send me back here; she just showed me I could do it myself. And it worked."

Fionn's expression was tortured. "You should get some rest," he said. She started to ask him to stay with her, but before she could get the words out, he had slipped his fingers from hers and left the room.

In the morning, she managed to prop herself up against the feather pillows. Like the other rooms in Carrickahowley, there were no windows beyond the thin arrow slits that punctured the walls. A fire had been lit in the hearth. Her head was clearer this morning than it had been the previous night, so she played her conversation with Fionn over in her mind.

Of course he'd been surprised to see her—it had been five years. He'd probably thought she was never coming back. A chill settled on her heart. Perhaps his feelings had changed. Why had she come back so late?

This was much closer to the year Brigid had originally intended to send them. Back in Kildare, Brigid had told her to think of 1592, but they'd ended up in 1587 instead. Could that have something to do with it?

A headache blossomed in the front of Nora's skull. She was thirsty, hungry, and in need of the bogs. That last one she decided to manage herself, and to her relief, did so without falling over. She was just crawling back into bed when the door opened.

"How's our miracle girl?" Granuaile asked.

"A bit better this morning, ta," Nora said. "Granuaile, what's happened in the past five years? What have I missed?"

"I think Fionn had best answer your questions," Granuaile said. "I was just checking to see if you were awake. Are you hungry?"

"Aye."

"Then I'll send him in with some food—and some answers."

Sure enough, the door opened again a few minutes later, and Fionn backed into the room with a tray. He gave her a tentative smile, which she returned. Five years. There was a lot to talk about.

"You're looking better," he said.

"I'm feeling better," she replied. "A bit. I wish it didn't take such a toll on me."

"Well, it's not natural, is it?"

"It doesn't affect *you*," she pointed out.

"Aye. Well, I've only done it the once. Here." He handed her a mug of ale and placed the tray on the foot of the bed. A half loaf of grainy bread and some soft cheese. "I'm sorry it's not more," he said. "It's been a difficult couple of years. We've been on the move a lot. It was lucky we were back here when Padraig brought you in. We'd been up on Achill Island for the past few months."

"How'd you escape Bingham? They were going to hang you."

"They thought they were. Let's just say that your sudden disappearance from the gallows caused a bit of a disturbance. Most of the soldiers fled in terror. It wasn't hard to escape amidst the chaos."

She took a mouthful of bread and chewed slowly. It hadn't been very well milled, and there were hard bits of grain throughout. "Why Achill Island? What's been going on?"

Fionn sank back into the chair beside the bed and regarded her carefully. "A lot has happened since you . . . left. Bingham has become intolerable. He's terrorized the people of Connacht. The O'Malleys and Burkes in particular."

"How is Granuaile handling all this?"

"She's had a hard time of it. You remember that Bingham had her son Owen killed?"

"Aye, that happened before we arrived."

"Her next-eldest son, Murrough, went over to the English."

"Ach, no."

"Aye. Sided with Bingham, the same man who killed his own brother. She ransacked Murrough's castle to teach him a lesson, but she'll never forgive him."

"I don't blame her."

"Bingham burned most of Connacht. It's as bad as we saw in Munster, maybe worse. Most of the people are dead or gone. And he captured her fleet. She has but one ship now, and that one was stolen from the English."

"So what is she doing?" If Nora knew Granuaile at all, the older woman was not sitting idle.

"She's been writing to the queen."

Something stirred in Nora's memory. "Queen Elizabeth?"

"Aye. They've become quite the correspondents. Apparently Elizabeth is fascinated with Gráinne's story. Who wouldn't be?"

Nora paused, digesting this. Something stood out to her.

"You call her by her proper name now. Gráinne." It was an observation, not a question. She lifted her chin and looked him in the eye, daring him to tell her the truth. The magnetic pull she'd felt toward him was gone, replaced by a growing tightness in her chest.

He looked away, out the tiny arrow slit in the stone wall. Then he wrenched his gaze back to hers. "You deserve the truth. We found comfort in each other, for a time. We grew close. And aye, we were lovers. But that part of our relationship has been over for more than a year. We still need each other, but in different ways."

The roar of the ocean filled Nora's ears. She became intensely fascinated by the mug in her hands. She cursed her fair skin, which was turning an ugly, blotchy red, betraying her desire to appear calm. What had she thought would happen? That he'd take her in his arms like the cover of some trashy romance novel? That he would have waited indefinitely for her?

"Nora, I know what you must think of me right now. But please, you have to understand. I thought you were . . ."

"Dead?" The word came out more harshly than she'd intended, but she let the word ring clearly in the cold air.

"No. I knew you'd just gone to some other time. I didn't expect you'd come back."

"How could you think that? You thought I would just . . . leave you? Leave what we'd started?"

"I just had a feeling that you could transport yourself without Brigid's help. That's why I told you to run. I knew you could escape that way. And I figured you wouldn't come back once you knew. That you'd go save your brother."

It was as though he had drawn back his fist and punched her square in the face. For a moment she could do nothing but stare—not breathe, not speak, not think. She closed her mouth, then gingerly got out of bed and crossed to the tiny slit of a window. Pressing her forehead against the cool stone, she stared down at the bay without seeing it.

What have I done?

It had not even occurred to her to go to 1991. All her thoughts had been for Fionn. In fact, she'd barely thought of Eamon at all since they'd arrived in the sixteenth century. She'd been so caught up in the ruthless politics, the extreme culture shock, and the constant threat of death. Even in their relatively peaceful months at Carrickahowley, she'd been thinking of *Fionn's* mission, *his* curse, *his* freedom.

And now she'd thrown away the chance to save Eamon by going to Fionn, only to discover he'd fallen for another woman in her absence.

It may not have worked. It didn't work for Roger, or Lynch, or the armada.

But I should have tried again. I should still try.

She took a deep, shuddering breath before turning back toward Fionn, her hand on the stone wall to steady herself. "I could have," she admitted. "And I suppose, in light of . . . well, I should have. But the truth is, I wanted to help you. I thought we could work better together." It was partially true. She didn't need to add to her humiliation by admitting that her desire to be with Fionn had crowded out all thoughts of her long-dead brother.

She limped back to the bed, aching body and soul. Fionn moved to help her, but she waved him away. She pulled the blanket up around her shoulders. "I'm going to rest now. Thanks for the food."

"Nora, I think we should talk about this," he said, though he looked terrified at the prospect.

"We will. Later." She sighed. "After all, we've plenty of time."

He had reached the door when she called out to him. He was back at her side in a moment. "How'd you know?" she asked. "When I was on the gallows. How'd you know I could time travel without Brigid? Had she told you?" Had the two of them conspired to keep it a secret? What else wasn't she being told?

"No," he said, dropping to one knee so that he was level with her. "I just suspected. Despite her, uh, flamboyant nature, Brigid likes to work in the background, to give people the opportunity to take care of themselves. It would be just like her to make you believe she was the one orchestrating everything, when in reality you had it in you all along."

"But why? Why go to all that bother?"

He hesitated, then picked up her hand from where it lay on the sheet. She didn't draw it away, but neither did she return his gentle squeeze. "Would you have ever done it without her?"

She gave a short laugh. "What, try to travel through time? Probably not."

"Well, then, there's your answer. However it works, I'm glad you came and found me."

She didn't know if he was referring to 1923, or just now. And was afraid to ask.

Chapter Thirty-Two

Three days later, Nora had recovered her strength enough to venture outside the castle. She was perched on what remained of her tiny school, destroyed by Bingham's soldiers, when Fionn found her. She'd come out here to clear her mind. It was a fair summer day, but she couldn't seem to get warm despite the shawl on her shoulders. Perhaps it was the sight of the ruined school, the burned-out huts of her former students and their families, and the overflowing graveyard. So much had changed.

Fionn sat beside her, the silence between them as expansive as the ocean. Finally, Nora spoke, her voice sounding strange to her own ears. "How long?"

"How long . . . what?" he asked. He spared her the briefest of glances out of the corner of his eye.

"How long were you with Granuaile?"

"Does it matter?"

A laugh escaped her lips on a wisp of breath. "I suppose not."

"Two years."

She nodded slowly, her eyes fixed on the horizon ahead. Two years. Much, much longer than she and Fionn had been together.

"Do you love her?" She wanted to take the words back as soon as they filled the space between them. "Never mind. I don't want to know."

"I told you, we found comfort in each other for a time. It was never . . . It wasn't like you and me. It wasn't real. Nora, I'm sorry. I thought you were never coming back. I didn't know if you even wanted to come back."

"Why would you think that?" She turned her eyes on him, willing them to stay dry.

His brow wrinkled. "Because we'd just quarreled. I thought you were disgusted with me."

"Oh, ballix." Nora put her head forward into her hands. "I was wrong; I knew it as soon as you left the hut. I came down to the beach to apologize, but then the Spanish came, and there just wasn't time. God, I'm sorry. I've done my share of sleeping with the enemy—who am I to judge you?"

His brow remained wrinkled in confusion. "Gráinne is not the enemy—" he started, but she cut him off.

"I wasn't talking about Granuaile. I was talking about Grania, Diarmuid's wife. Though it's ironic that they should have such similar names."

She smiled sadly and returned her gaze to the sea. Bran splashed in the shallow water and barked at the seagulls that screeched at her from overhead. "We're a couple of hotheads, so we are. God knows it's gotten me in trouble most of my life, but I can't seem to figure out how to be any different." She let a moment of silence slip between them, then said, "Did I ever tell you about Mick?"

He shook his head.

"He's the one who got me into the Provos, the new IRA I told you about."

"I remember."

"He was such a bastard in so many ways—brash, controlling. Loved his bloody power trips, so he did. Thought he could change the course of Ireland single-handedly."

"Sounds like just your type."

She grinned at this. "Aye, mebbe. I loved him and I hated him. Without him, Eamon might still be alive. But he thought he was doing what was right for Ireland, and you can't fault him for that." A cormorant landed and picked at an empty shell, then flew away, disappointed. "All I'm saying is that I think I understand. It's possible Grania did love you, as you say, even if you were responsible for the death of someone else she loved. Love's never as straightforward as we'd like it to be. Anyway, that's what I meant to say after our fight. I suppose five years late is better than never."

He seemed to take this as encouragement, because he cleared his throat and asked, "And how are you feeling about what happened with Gráinne—Granuaile?"

"I don't know," she said. "It hurts. I came back with different expectations, to say the least. But if there's one thing I've learned during this whole mad experience, it's perspective. I saw dogs fighting over someone's head." She shivered at the memory and pulled her shawl tighter. "Remember the woman we saw in Munster, on our way here? She'd been eating nettles, and her face and hands were green. She was mad with starvation. Almost three hundred years, and people were still starving. Still mad from hunger. Only, in 1846 there were more people to starve."

And I'm starting to doubt that we can change anything. But that was too depressing of an idea to voice.

"If I had known you were coming back . . ."

"It's grand," she said quickly. "Like I said, perspective. There are bigger things at stake."

"So what are you going to do?"

What *was* she going to do? Despair and hopelessness threatened to smother the revolutionary fire that had directed so much of her life.

"Well," she said, forcing some conviction into her voice. "We keep trying. I suppose there's naught really to do until the Battle of Kinsale. It's only eight years away. We can at least tell O'Neill and Red Hugh how they lose. O'course, they might not listen to us. I don't know, Fionn. I'm just . . . shattered. We've fought so hard; we've given so much. Honestly, I don't know what there is left for us to do."

"I've an idea," Fionn said. It took her a moment to realize that he'd spoken, so lost was she in her despair.

"*You* have an idea?"

"I know," he said with a self-deprecating laugh. "But I reckon it's my turn. It's a bit mad, though."

"Grand so," she said, now curious. "Let's hear it."

"Gráinne—Granuaile—is going to see the queen."

Nora gaped at him. "The queen of England?"

"No, the queen of Tír na nÓg. O'course the queen of England."

"But . . . why? How?"

"Remember I said she'd been writing to her?"

"Aye."

"Bingham doesn't like that. He thinks she's telling lies to Elizabeth to discredit him."

Nora snorted. "He's an eejit if he thinks Elizabeth won't hear about how he's treated her 'subjects' here. Whether she cares or not is another question."

"He took Tibbot."

A heartbeat of silence. "Ach, no." Sympathy for Granuaile bloomed in Nora's chest. To have her child in the hands of that monster . . .

"Aye. He's been charged with treason. And we know what the punishment for that is."

"You think it was because she wrote those letters?"

He nodded. "She feels that she's established a bit of a rapport with Elizabeth, even though they're technically sworn enemies. But I also think she would see all of Ireland burn before she'd let anything happen to her son. She's determined to meet with Elizabeth face to face and demand Tibbot's release."

Nora let out a long, slow breath. "Jesus. D'you think she'll do it? I don't imagine they hand out audiences with the queen to just anyone."

"Have you ever known Granuaile to set her mind to something and fail? The two of you have that in common."

Nora laughed, but there was no pleasure in it. "I've done naught *but* fail. You're right, though—in fact, I have a vague memory that this meeting did happen. Christ, I wish I'd paid more attention in school. But this sounds familiar somehow—the meeting of the two queens."

"D'you remember what came of it?"

Nora shook her head. "So that's your plan? To tag along? For what? D'you think Elizabeth will let Ireland be free just because you ask her?"

His eyes scanned the empty beach; then he moved closer to her, leaning in so that his lips brushed her ear.

"This is between you and me, and you and me alone. Granuaile knows nothing of it."

"Of what?"

"We're not going to ask the queen anything. We're going to kill her."

Chapter Thirty-Three

"You were dead on. It *is* a mad idea," Nora said. They'd retired to one of the castle's massive fireplaces and were warming a pot of mead, clutching their empty mugs expectantly. Bran had settled herself close to the fire, rolling over occasionally to warm another side.

"Hear me out," Fionn said. "It's practically the same plan we had with the Spanish Armada, only we wanted them to do the dirty work. That was our problem—leaving it to someone else. The timing's better now anyway."

"How d'you figure?"

"O'Neill and O'Donnell weren't ready back in '88; we saw that clear enough. Red Hugh was in prison, and O'Neill was still faffin' about, trying to secure his earldom. But they've finally started to mobilize. I know because I was there—I am there, I suppose, helping them."

"Wait—" Nora held up a hand. "You're there? But the other you wouldn't have met them before, so won't they suspect when you act like you don't know them?"

"Aye, I anticipated that. I sent myself a letter, explaining the situation."

"Tell me more about O'Neill and O'Donnell. What's happening now?"

"As you said, we're close to the start of the Nine Years' War, which ends with the Battle of Kinsale."

"Which we lose."

"Which we lose," he agreed. "*However*, we win many other battles—the Battle of Clontibret, the Yellow Ford, Curlew Pass. We come *this close* to winning the whole war." He held his fingers a few millimeters apart.

"And you think that if we kill the queen, it will make a difference?"

"It will make all the difference. She's still not named a successor. Her death is England's greatest nightmare."

"But we know that James of Scotland will succeed her, and he's no better for Ireland."

"That's not for another ten years, so it's far from settled at this point. There will be infighting, several claimants for the throne, maybe even a civil war." He learned forward. "King Philip is preparing another armada. If Elizabeth dies, he'll see it as the perfect opportunity to invade, to put a Catholic on the throne. Even if he doesn't succeed, all the lords will withdraw their men from Ireland to fight for their preferred claimant for the throne. Like I said, we came so close to winning last time. If we act now, we'll have a completely different future."

"And you'll be free," she said, so quietly she wasn't sure he heard her.

"Aye," he said. "And there will be no war, no Troubles, as you call them, in Ulster. Your brother will still be alive. Isn't that what you want?"

I don't know what I want anymore. But she nodded her head. Is this what she sounded like when she had her heart set on a plan? So convinced of its virtues that she was blind to its faults?

"Think about it," he continued. "Brigid wanted us to come to meet Granuaile in 1592. A year ago. This meeting is what she must've had in mind."

"You can't possibly know that," Nora murmured. "Besides, she didn't send us. I did. Apparently."

"Yes, but she told you when to go. Even if she's not the one doing the time traveling, she had a reason for wanting us to come here."

Nora sipped her mead and watched the low flames dance in the fireplace. It needed another sod of turf, but she didn't feel like moving. What *was* Brigid's role in all of this? What did the goddess want from them?

"How do you think you came by this ability?" Fionn asked.

Nora was surprised at the sudden change in conversation but grateful for it all the same. One did not choose to assassinate the queen of England lightly. This was much more dangerous than any of their previous plans. Maybe Fionn couldn't die, but what did he think would happen to the rest of them if they were caught? She was prepared to give her life for Ireland—she always had been—but she also wasn't eager to rush into a situation that would likely end in slow, torturous deaths for herself, Granuaile, and everyone they loved.

"I've no idea," she said. "It was just a feeling, deep in my chest. I felt drawn to—well, to come back here. But I don't know how to turn it on and off, or if I even can." The thought was unsettling. What if she lost control and kept spontaneously disappearing, waking up in some strange era, at the mercy of whoever found her? "Listen, Fionn. Your plan might work, but it's too dangerous. They can still torture you. Maybe I should try to time travel again."

"To save your brother?"

"I thought of that, but it wouldn't help you. If I can, I'd like to do both. We know Kinsale is the deciding battle—there must be something I can do there. Make sure the Spanish show up at the right end of the country, for starters."

Fionn shook his head firmly. "Absolutely not."

"Why?" she said, affronted. She'd listened calmly to his harebrained idea, and now he was dismissing hers out of hand.

"Because I've seen what happens to you when you time travel!" He sounded appalled at the very idea. "D'you think I'm going to let you go through that again?"

"*Let me?*" Nora rose to her feet, her fatigue forgotten. "It's my own life. I can make my own choices."

"I know you can," he said, raising his hands in a position of surrender as she glowered down at him. "But Kinsale is as complicated as the armada, if not more so. There are too many moving parts, too many people involved. You think you can get to O'Neill, O'Donnell, Tyrrell, and Juan del Águila and convince them all to do what you tell them? What if you end up in the wrong year again? And even if you do end up in the right year, how d'you know you'll be in any shape to tell them anything? You were near dead when you were brought here from Galway. I can't go through that again, Nora."

"You'd rather I run the risk of being drawn and quartered? Because that's what will happen if we're caught trying to kill the queen."

"I don't want that, either," he said, getting to his feet and crossing his arms. "Which is why you'll be staying here."

There was a beat of silence, then Nora spoke. "You're fucking kidding me."

"I'm not. You don't have to be involved. As long as history changes, you'll get what you want—no war in the north. But *you* don't have to be the one who changes it. *I* do. *I* have to save Ireland. It's the only way I can lift my curse. *I'll* go with Granuaile, and *I* will kill the queen."

She folded her arms and gave him a scathing look. "Like hell you will."

"Nora—"

"No, you listen to me," she said, jabbing a finger in his face. "It doesn't matter that I was gone for five years, or that you were with Granuaile. You and I are a package deal. D'you think for a second that I'm going to sit back here, minding my own business, while you're off tryin' to kill the most powerful woman in the world? Jesus Christ. You'll need all the help you can get."

"Seems to me you thought it was a bad idea. Now you're all keen to join in."

"I *do* think it's a bad idea. But if you're dead set on it, I'm not staying behind. And maybe you're right. We've tried working through other people and beating around the bush. Maybe it's time to be a wee bit foolhardy."

"And if I refuse to bring you with me?"

"Then I'll do things my own way," she said menacingly. "If I can escape Bingham's gallows, I can escape you."

Before he could argue further, she grabbed a fistful of his léine and pulled him into her. She kissed him fiercely, possessively, giving him neither time nor breath to object. Then she let him go with a thrust of her hand and stalked out of the castle.

Three days later, they set sail for London on the *Queen Medb*, each person on board keenly aware that they might not see Ireland again. Granuaile's crew was a mix of her loyal sailors and kinsmen as well as others who wished to plead their case with Queen Elizabeth. She introduced Nora and Fionn as "my dear friends and companions" to her first husband's cousin, the O'Flaherty chieftain Sir Murrough-ne Doe, who was acting as her second-in-command.

Nora's joy at being Fionn's partner in crime again warred with her guilt over keeping their plan hidden from Granuaile, who had risked so much for both of them. Though she had made no further advances toward Fionn since her impulsive kiss three days ago, she stood fast to the fact that they were in this together, whether he liked it or not. She laughed at Granuaile's suggestion that she stay below and insisted on being taught everything there was to know about sailing a galley in the unpredictable waters of the North Atlantic.

On one of the few occasions she was off duty at the same time as Fionn, Nora brought up the subject of the queen's assassination. "Have you thought about how to do it?" she asked him as they watched the south coast of Ireland sail past.

"Poison, I reckon," he said.

She nodded. "That's what I was thinking, too. Arsenic is probably best."

He cocked an eyebrow at her. "Why d'you think that?"

"It's the only one I know much about," she admitted. "At least, the only one that's readily available in this century. No one uses poison much anymore. Forensic science has made it too easy to trace. I think that happens after your time," she added.

"Well, they certainly use it with abandon in this era," he said. "But how'd you learn about arsenic?"

"A village in Bangladesh," she said, her face tightening at the memory. "The water was dirty, and the kids kept getting sick from worms and parasites. Malnutrition, stunted growth, all that. Some NGOs came in and dug a well to get to the clean water." She shook her head. "They had good intentions, but they dug too deep and ended up tapping water from formations that were naturally high in arsenic. Thousands were poisoned. My team was called in, but it was too late. Most of the people died."

"I'm sorry. That's horrible."

"Aye. Anyway, my point is that I had to do my research. Arsenic's easy to come by—rat poison will do. And the symptoms are similar to food poisoning—stomach cramps, diarrhea, vomiting. Should give us time to get away before she dies."

They were passing Cork now, the same port where they'd been forced to put ashore for repairs after their encounter with pirates. Now *they* were the pirates.

She hesitated. "I suppose you've thought about how to get by the food tasters? I'm assuming Elizabeth hasn't survived this long without them."

"I have."

"You're going to drink it, too."

He nodded. "I, too, have seen victims of poisoning firsthand. It won't be pleasant, but at least we know it won't kill me."

She laughed mirthlessly. "Ironic, isn't it? Your curse is the one thing that could help you break it."

"How does one get an audience with the queen, exactly?" Nora asked as she, Fionn, and Granuaile played cards in the captain's cabin. The two women had not talked about Fionn. It was in the past, Nora kept telling herself. She had to stay focused on the future.

"I've asked the Earl of Thomond to arrange it," Granuaile said placidly. "You remember him, don't you, Nora?"

Nora nearly spat out her ale. "*What?* Why would Donough O'Brien help you?"

"Well, for starters, he had no idea I was the one who broke you out of Doonbeg. It's not like I was flyin' the O'Malley flag while firing round shot at him." Granuaile studied her cards. "And he owes me. I've handled some of his . . . less-than-aboveboard trading, let's say. He's spent most of his life at court; it shouldn't be too hard for him to affect an introduction. O'course, if he doesn't come through, we have a backup plan sitting right here."

Nora looked between Granuaile and Fionn. "Sorry?"

Fionn gave Granuaile an exasperated look, but the intimacy in it was enough to make Nora's hands tighten around her deck. Granuaile winked at Fionn and said, "Her Majesty has a taste for handsome young men. I think she'll be quite keen to meet The O'Malley here, don't you?"

"The O'Malley?" Nora stared at Fionn. Was this something else he'd kept from her?

"It's just a ruse," he said quickly. "The real O'Malley is about my age, but—"

"Ugly as the hind end of a cow and a cripple to boot," Granuaile interjected gleefully. "But Elizabeth doesn't know that."

"So, you're just going to pimp him out? Throw him at Elizabeth in the hopes she'll . . . what?" She was being overly aggressive, she knew, but it rankled that they'd made this plan without her. To be fair, Granuaile didn't know that Nora and Fionn planned on assassinating the queen. But that was as it should be. The pirate queen would never let them go through with it, not with Tibbot in Bingham's custody. Nora felt a renewed twinge of guilt at the thought of their deception, but they were trying to save thousands, maybe millions of lives.

"In the hopes that she'll grant me a meeting," Granuaile replied, some stiffness returning to her voice. "Although if Fionn should choose to enjoy the affections of the queen of England, that's his own choice, is it not?" She laid down her cards. She had won. Again.

"O'course, I have no desire to do any such thing," Fionn said casually, laying down his own hand. "But I can flatter the old woman if it will help you get your son back."

"Grand so," Nora said. Now that she'd calmed down, it made perfect sense. Fionn was incredibly handsome, well educated, multilingual, and a master storyteller. He was just Elizabeth's type. And if he could get her alone, it would be that much easier for him to poison her.

"What if Thomond recognizes you as the bard?" she asked Fionn.

"I kept my face partly covered. And in case you've forgotten, his attention wasn't fixed on *me*. If he recognizes me at all, he'll assume it was from some gathering of the clans, or at court. However, he will no doubt recognize you if he sees you."

"Not if I'm dressed as a servant and keep a low profile. These nobles don't give servants a second glance. I'll just fade into the background."

"Mmm," Granuaile said as she shuffled the deck. "That might work. And Elizabeth will certainly take no note of a lowly Irish servant girl. She sees beautiful young women as a threat, but only those who are highborn."

"I don't like it, Nora," Fionn said. "It's too risky."

Nora, her lips pressed together in a thin line, said nothing. She knew he had a point, but there were few things she hated more than being left behind while others took action. She reached absentmindedly for her rosary, only to feel bare flesh under the neckline of her léine. Whoever had given her this ability to time travel—God, Brigid, or some other being she had yet to encounter—had obviously chosen the wrong person.

Days later, they navigated their way up the Thames, the tension on board crackling like sails in a brisk wind. Nora hung over the rail, gawping at Elizabeth's London.

"Gibbets ahead!" one of the men called out. In one motion, caps were doffed and heads bowed. Nora leaned farther out to see what all the fuss was about, then drew back with a hand over her mouth. Blackened bodies hung in iron cages suspended over the river. Some were finely dressed, brass buttons catching the morning light, bare feet swaying slightly in the wind. Others had been stripped naked, whether by man or weather Nora could not tell. As they passed under one such poor soul, the sun reflected off a sticky black resin that coated his skin. Bran, who stood sentry beside her, bared her teeth and growled.

"The tarred ones are lucky, you could say," Granuaile said, her broad captain's hat clutched to her chest. "The birds will leave them alone. Once the tide has washed over them three times, they're cut down—at least, that's for the common ones. This poor fella . . ." She pointed toward a half-decomposed body swinging from the end of a gallows. "He's naught but carrion feed."

"Who are they?" Nora asked, unable to take her eyes off the ruined bodies.

"Pirates," Granuaile said, crossing herself. "May they rest in peace." Then she winked at Nora. "And may we not end up beside them."

Nora fought the sudden urge to vomit. "You must be mad to come here," she said, her voice faint.

"Once you've children of your own, you'll understand. I'd gladly march myself to the Tower or the Execution Dock if it meant savin' one of their lives. Even Murrough, traitorous child though he is. But Tibbot . . . ach, he has a special place in my heart. Did I tell you how he was born?"

Nora shook her head, and Granuaile's eyes took on that faraway look she had when remembering her past adventures. "We'd made a good haul off the coast of Scotland and were bound for home. Some of my men hadn't wanted me to come on the voyage at all, being so great with child. But I'd not been on the sea in over two months, and a little adventure is exactly what I needed—though it turned out to be more than I'd reckoned for. Wouldn't you know, I gave birth on the ship. In the middle of a ragin' storm, no less, with no woman to aid me and all my men terrified of seein' their captain in pain. Jesus, they were hardy souls against man and nature, but show them what actually happens between a woman's legs and they're as squeamish as city folk. Well, I'd done this before, so I more or less handled it myself, though my quartermaster brought me hot water and clean linens as he could find them."

"You gave birth to Tibbot on your ship?" Nora asked, barely noticing the city they were passing as they inched their way down the Thames.

Granuaile nodded, a proud blush spreading across her cheeks. "Aye, my Tibbot came out screaming and hollering as though he wanted to drown out the wind. We were only a week from home, so I thought I'd stay below, just me and my boy, and let the men handle the ship. O'course, I didn't reckon on us being attacked. That changed my plans a wee bit."

"Who attacked you? The English?"

"Not this time. 'Twas those damned Barbary pirates. Vicious barbarians, with no code of honor. Why spare a sailor when you can hack him to pieces?" She shook her head. "No, it was the worst possible scenario—my men up against those animals, and me with a babe at my breast."

"What happened?" Nora asked, entranced.

"I could tell we were losing. And if we lost, they'd spare no one—not even a suckling babe. They'd dash his brains out just for the sport of it. So I had no choice. I hid the babe in a drawer, did up the front of my dress, and hauled my sore arse onto the deck, a musket in each hand. New mother or no, I was the captain, and my men needed me like never before. I daresay I fought more fiercely that day than I had before or have since. My child's life was at stake. My men rallied around me, and together we beat off the savages and took their ship as our own. Then I returned below deck and pulled wee Tibbot from his hiding place, and he's had the name Tibbot ne Long—Tibbot of the Ships—ever since." She gave Nora a piercing look. "There's naught I wouldn't do for him. Aye, I know Elizabeth is dangerous, probably more dangerous than the Barbary pirates. But it doesn't matter. What matters is saving my son's life. If I end up swinging in a gibbet but convince the queen to let my son go free, I'll consider it a success."

The likelihood of Tibbot going free if Granuaile was tried and convicted as a pirate was slim, but this wasn't the time to say so. Nora had never known such devotion in a mother. Her own mother had lost herself in her grief after the murder of Nora's father. What would it have been like to have a mother like Granuaile, someone who was willing to stand between her children and the entire English army? Something stirred deep in her gut, a longing she'd never allowed herself to feel.

"Time to arm ourselves for battle," Granuaile said. "I'll need your help for this one."

Chapter Thirty-Four

Nora followed Granuaile below deck to her cabin. The older woman opened a heavy chest filled to the brim with clothing. She replaced her trews and jacket with a low-necked linen smock and a pair of silk stockings held up by a garter. She laced up her corset herself; then Nora tightened the laces, averting her eyes when Granuaile lifted her breasts so that they spilled over the top. Next Granuaile brought out a willow-bent farthingale of red taffeta, which Nora slipped over her head and tied to the corset, then topped with a bumroll to give the skirt some extra swing.

"How they wear these things day in and day out is beyond me," Granuaile muttered, holding on to Nora's shoulders for balance as she stepped into a green satin kirtle.

"If the queen's so jealous, won't she mind you being dressed so fine?" Nora asked, peering into the huge chest to see what could possibly be left. Granuaile pointed at an embroidered partlet, which Nora helped her into and then tied under her arms. A large ruff was attached to the neckband, and Granuaile scratched where it rubbed against her skin.

"She may. But I am coming to her as an equal, not a subject. And I mean for her to know it." She crossed the room and opened a large wardrobe, then brought out a gown the likes of which Nora had never seen. Every square inch of the deep-emerald fabric seemed to sparkle with gold thread, pearls, and tiny, glittering jewels. Nora helped her slide her arms into the sleeves and then did up the hooks and eyes in front. Granuaile shook out the skirt and adjusted the shoulder rolls at the top of each arm, then looked down at herself in satisfaction.

"Bring me that box," she said, pointing to a smaller chest in the wall cabinet. She unlocked it with a delicate silver key, then lifted the lid. A heavy gold neck torc lay on a cushion of velvet. "A gift from Hugh O'Neill," she said, placing the torc around her neck. She fastened on teardrop-shaped pearl earrings and slid several sparkling rings onto her rough fingers. "And these are the profits of privateering. I could have sold them, o'course. I sold almost everything else. But I had a feeling the queen of England and the queen of Connacht would finally meet face to face one day." She brushed out her thick gray hair and then deftly wove it into a series of knots at the back of her head.

A knock on the door, and Fionn entered with Granuaile's cousin-in-law, The O'Flaherty.

"Dar Dia, woman, where's my captain?" O'Flaherty asked, looking at Granuaile with an amusing mixture of admiration and disgust.

"You look spectacular," Fionn added, and Nora couldn't deny it. Standing tall and regal, her gray hair swept up to reveal high cheekbones and sparkling dark eyes, the pirate captain looked every bit a queen. If there had been any doubt that she would be Elizabeth's equal in this meeting, it was gone. But then Granuaile snorted in a decidedly nonregal fashion and said, "Ach, that's enough, both of you. Are we drawing near to Greenwich?"

"Aye," O'Flaherty said. "Will you come above?"

Granuaile nodded sharply and swept toward the door. Nora followed behind, and together they managed to squeeze the farthingale through the narrow passage and up the ladder. "I should have dressed on deck," Granuaile grumbled as she inched forward, careful not to step on the hem of the embroidered gown. "Thomond was to watch for us. Send a boy ashore to tell him we've arrived. Good God, I can barely move in this thing."

They'd sailed through the medieval city and were now in the countryside, drawing near to one of Elizabeth's other palaces, where she went to escape the plague that burned through the city each summer. Nora had never seen Greenwich Palace—she was quite sure it no longer existed. She caught Fionn's eye and moved toward him.

"What happens now?" she asked.

"I 'borrowed' a supply of rat poison from the quartermaster," he said in a low voice. "I've brought a fine bottle of whiskey we can poison—a gift from the Irish." His jaw was set grimly as they watched the palace draw near. "But we may only have one chance."

Granuaile was deep in conversation with O'Flaherty, oblivious to their scheming. Fionn, perhaps sensing Nora's nerves, turned and gripped her by both shoulders. "Freedom, Nora," he said bracingly. "It's within our grasp. We've come so far together. Do not lose heart now."

"O'course not," she said, her shoulders tingling from his touch. "You should go change as well. If you plan to woo Elizabeth, you'll need to dress better than that."

He smiled reassuringly at her, then headed to the lower decks. Nora had no need to change. She'd resigned herself to staying behind during their initial meeting with Donough O'Brien. Afterward she'd behave as unremarkable as possible on the off chance she ran into him unexpectedly.

Nora and Bran watched from the *Queen Medb* as Granuaile and Fionn disembarked onto the landing platform to meet the earl. Thomond came striding across the wide green lawns of Greenwich Palace, dressed in a costume of red, black, and gold, a cape billowing out from behind him. He wore a ridiculously wide-brimmed, plumed hat, but it somehow suited him. Nora cursed the guilt that squeezed her heart. She'd been this man's prisoner—of course she'd tried to escape. Still, she knew she had hurt him in the doing, and for that she was sorry.

She held her breath as Thomond drew nearer to where Fionn and Granuaile stood waiting. If he recognized Fionn, everything would be lost. Out of all the Irish lords Granuaile could have prevailed upon to help her . . .

But it seemed Fionn was right. He was dressed in the finest clothing Granuaile had ever stolen, a far cry from the simple léine and brat he'd worn to Doonbeg. Thomond gave Fionn only a passing glance before he kissed Granuaile on both cheeks.

"My lord Thomond. May I introduce to you the new O'Malley, my cousin's son Fionnbhar O'Malley," Granuaile said, her words carrying easily to the ship where Nora stood watching.

"A new O'Malley! Good God, have I been away from Ireland so long? You've made your submission already, then?" he asked shrewdly.

"It was my first act as The O'Malley," Fionn said. "But I hope to have the opportunity to offer my service and submission to Her Majesty in person."

"Hmm, yes, we'll see about that," Thomond demurred. "You are not the only of our countrymen to beg an audience with Her Majesty."

"Oh?" Granuaile asked in surprise. "Who else is here?"

"You didn't know? I was surprised when he came here without you, to tell you the truth. Your own son's brother-in-law."

"Donogh O'Connor Sligo?" Granuaile exclaimed. "What the devil is he doing here? Has he come to plead for Tibbot's life as well?"

Thomond looked uncomfortable. "I believe his petition is of a more . . . personal nature."

"Christ on the cross! He's come seeking more lands and titles for himself while his sister's husband is at the mercy of that tyrant Bingham?" Granuaile's face flushed with anger as she jabbed a finger at

Thomond. "Tell him he'd best stay far clear of me. If I find him, I will cut him down like the weasel he is."

"Now, now, Grace," Thomond said. "You'll need to control that legendary temper of yours if you wish to meet with Her Majesty. All of London is not big enough to hold both your personalities, I fear."

"And is it arranged?" Granuaile said, straightening her ruff, which she'd knocked askew.

"It is," Thomond answered, looking quite pleased with himself. "And it was no easy matter. Her Majesty has hundreds of petitioners waiting for a chance to speak with her. But she seemed quite intrigued when I mentioned to her that you were on your way and desired an audience. Of course, I did not know the exact date of your arrival, but the groundwork has been laid. The next step will be to speak with Lord Burghley, and then await her summons."

"And how long am I expected to wait?" Granuaile asked, stiffening.

"As I said, Her Majesty has many petitioners, and her mood can be . . . well, changeable, as I'm sure you know." He lowered his voice so that Nora could barely hear him. "If you ask me, the queen is quite anxious to meet with you—but equally anxious to not appear eager. Have patience, my dear woman. I have said it will happen, and therefore it will happen."

"Then we will remain on our ship until Her Majesty desires the pleasure of our company," Granuaile said.

"Are you certain?" Thomond said. "I have a room ready for you."

"My thanks, Your Lordship," Granuaile said with a minuscule nod of her chin. "But I prefer the company of my men while I wait. And I should make good use of this time by ensuring we are ready for the journey home."

"As you wish. I'll send word as soon as I know anything further."

Farewell pleasantries were exchanged, and then Fionn and Granuaile made their way back up the gangplank.

"I can't believe I got dressed in this ridiculous outfit for that," Granuaile grumbled as Nora held out a hand to help her back on board.

"At least he's set things in motion," Nora said. "Maybe it won't be too long. You were right," she told Fionn. "He didn't seem to recognize you at all."

"Thomond has a good eye for pretty ladies, but not for anything else around him," Fionn said.

"Why do you want to stay on the ship?" Nora asked Granuaile. "I would have thought you'd fancy staying in the palace."

"I'm sure it's grand, but there are two things I've learned from dealing with the English: always watch your back, and always have an escape plan. I know Bingham has been whispering in Elizabeth's ear, so I'd rather not sleep where her servants can easily cut my throat. We're doing this on my terms, or not at all. She'll bend, you wait and see. Now help me get out of this damned dress."

And so they settled in to wait—for how long, none of them knew. When they weren't working on repairing masts and reinforcing the keels, most of the crew went ashore in search of brothels and alehouses. Nora, Fionn, and Granuaile whiled away the time by playing at cards or strolling along the banks of the Thames, Bran by their side, but they spoke only of small things. The magnitude of what they were about to attempt hung heavy over Nora and Fionn, and Granuaile fretted that every day they waited was another day her son was in the hands of the Butcher of Connacht.

On the third day, a messenger arrived from Thomond. It was time.

Nora helped Granuaile back into her massive dress, and Fionn changed into a velvet doublet of silver and crimson. Nora would be accompanying them in the guise of Granuaile's lady-in-waiting. Fionn had argued against it, but in the end Nora had prevailed. "If the worst happens and he does recognize me, I'll just tell him that I escaped when the pirates were attacking Doonbeg. I eventually found you and entered into your service. There's no way he can fault you for that. And it's not like he's going to leave the court to haul a servant back to Ireland."

Once they were ready, Thomond's messenger led them up from the banks of the Thames and to the palace. "His Lordship is in the tilt-yard," the messenger said, waving them past him. Thomond was leaning against a stone wall, watching two gentlemen ride at each other with blunted lances. He smiled and clapped his hands when he saw them approach. Nora slowed her pace and slipped behind a large rhododendron blazing with pink blossoms.

"My dear Grace! And Chief O'Malley," he said. "You look resplendent." He kissed Granuaile on both cheeks. "I heard from Burghley this morning. Her Majesty has consented to give you an audience in her presence chamber. You are most fortunate. There are those who have been waiting many months for such an honor."

Nora resisted the urge to roll her eyes. She failed to be impressed by the accident of birth that created kings and queens and set them above ordinary folk. Still, she must play her part. She followed the others dutifully into the palace, keeping her head down and staying several steps behind. It was beautiful, to be sure, but there were signs of ill keep. The tapestries on the walls were faded and in need of a good beating, and they had to step around a puddle that was spreading on the stone floor from a leak in the roof far above.

Courtiers milled around them in a sort of malaise that Nora suspected came from having absolutely nothing to do but wait for Elizabeth to take notice of them. They arrived at a set of tall oak doors, guarded by a pair of men dressed in long red coats, swords swinging in scabbards at their sides.

"Grace O'Malley of Ireland, at Her Majesty's invitation, and The O'Malley of Mayo to offer his submission," Thomond said, and the guards parted to let them through.

Finely dressed men and women lounged about inside the presence chamber. Some leaned against walls; others huddled around small windows. They seemed only half-attentive to those around them; the other half was always attuned to the only person in the room who mattered, less she cast her rays in their direction.

There was only one chair in the room, and on it sat Gloriana herself, Queen Elizabeth, who had wrought so much destruction, so much death, so much suffering on Nora's people. In a red-veiled instant, Nora saw the skeletal woman who had crawled in the Munster dirt, the blank-eyed wains rotting with their mothers in the bowels of the Galway jail, the ruined homes of the peaceful fishermen who had tried to eke out survival for their families on Clew Bay. She hated the woman on the gilded chair in front of her, hated her fame, hated her success, hated her legacy.

Before Elizabeth could catch her staring, Nora dropped her gaze to the ground. Several deep breaths later, she raised her eyes slightly. The queen was beckoning to Thomond, who offered Granuaile his arm. "You'll have to stay back until she expressly summons you, I'm afraid," he said to Fionn, once again completely ignoring Nora, who had tried to hide herself behind a marble pillar.

The queen's attire was so extreme as to be ridiculous. Her sleeves were at least a foot wide, and her starched ruff extended beyond her shoulders. Gems and precious jewels hung from her as though she'd been dipped in them. Her bright-red hair, so obviously a wig, was crowned with a gold tiara set with emeralds and small rubies in the shape of the sun. Her face was unnaturally white, as though already dead. She was garish, like a child playing at dress up, so enamored with the fantasy of her own beauty that she failed to see the mockery she was making of herself. Granuaile, on the other hand, breathed elegance and refinement as she sailed forward on Thomond's arm.

The ever-watching court grew silent, their attention captured by this newcomer, calculating how her arrival might impede or advance their own interests. Elizabeth stood as Granuaile approached, holding out a hand so that her subject might kiss it. But Granuaile held out her own hand. A collective gasp arose from the courtiers, followed by silence as they held their breath, waiting to see how Elizabeth would rage at this interloper.

To the astonishment of everyone in the room, Elizabeth reached forward and grasped Granuaile's hand in her own. Then the regent sat back down and beckoned Granuaile in close.

Nora and Fionn weren't the only ones who edged forward, hoping to overhear the exchange between the two women. But the man beside Elizabeth—Lord Burghley, Nora surmised—cleared his throat softly, and the courtiers at once fell into feigned conversation with those around them.

"You don't have super hearing, I suppose?" Nora whispered to Fionn.

He snorted. "If I'd been able to keep any of my former abilities, that wouldn't have been first on my list. Although now I'd pay dearly for it."

"Has the queen noticed you, d'you think?"

"I saw her watching me earlier. We exchanged a quick glance. Whether anything will come out of it . . ."

"It has to!" Nora said, then lowered her voice. "We'll never get her to drink anything in this room full of people."

"Shhh. Her lapdogs have well-trained ears," he cautioned.

"Aye, sorry. Maybe you should go talk to her."

"One does not just 'go talk to' Queen Elizabeth. I must wait for an invitation, something Granuaile said she would try to secure."

"Does she know why?"

"No, but she trusts me."

A burst of laughter from the front of the room made them jerk their heads toward the two women. Elizabeth's head was thrown back, exposing her blackened teeth, and Granuaile roared in laughter at some private jest between them.

"That's a good sign, so it is," Nora muttered. She wasn't so sure a moment later, when Granuaile let loose a loud, honking sneeze. She patted down her dress, no doubt wondering if a handkerchief was hidden anywhere inside it. There was another collected murmur from the room as the queen of England offered her own handkerchief to this rebel, this pirate. It was better than any play, any joust for entertainment value. The courtiers abandoned all pretense of conversation as they watched these two remarkable women.

Granuaile didn't disappoint. She blew her nose, said something to the queen, then strode to the nearest fireplace and tossed the handkerchief into the flames.

Elizabeth's pale face reddened. "That was a gift! You were supposed to keep it!" she said in a voice loud enough to be heard by everyone in the room. There was a stir; now the Irishwoman would be at the receiving end of the legendary temper that they themselves had too often witnessed.

But it was Granuaile's turn to look offended. "Keep a rag I've just blown my nose into? The Irish have better standards of cleanliness than the English, so it would seem."

"Oh, for Christ's sake," Nora moaned under her breath. What was Granuaile playing at?

The queen seemed as shocked as her courtiers, but her recovery was much quicker. Her eyes narrowed, but not in hostility. It was as though she were trying to discover what sort of creature stood before her. Granuaile was an enigma. She motioned for the Irishwoman to come close again, and they resumed their hushed conversation. This time, no one but Burghley was within earshot.

Nora let out her breath, and Fionn relaxed beside her. "What is she doing?" she whispered to him.

"Showing the queen that they are equals," he said, pride coloring his words. "Granuaile didn't come here to grovel. She came to deal."

"And what is she offering in return?"

"That remains to be seen. If she can manage it, nothing at all."

There was another shocking burst of laughter from the two women; then Granuaile waved at Fionn and beckoned him over. He strode to her side in an instant, every bit the obedient courtier.

"My kinsman and chieftain of our clan, Fionnbhar O'Malley, Your Majesty," Granuaile said. "He has been begging me for the opportunity to meet you."

Fionn swept into a low, stately bow before stooping to kiss Elizabeth's proffered hand. "I have heard many tales of your beauty, Your Majesty, but they are but specters when compared with the truth of your countenance. I am not worthy to stand in the light of your sun."

Nora had to turn away, lest anyone notice the expression on her face.

Fionn and the queen conversed quietly for several moments, and at one point he got down on one knee—to offer his fake submission, no doubt. Then he rose, and he and Granuaile backed away from the queen. Thomond quickly joined them, looking at Granuaile with new-found respect.

"We have received Her Majesty's permission to leave the room," Granuaile told him, her eyes twinkling. "Will you join me on board my ship for some refreshments, Donough?"

He demurred, stating that he needed to attend to some business with one of the other courtiers.

"Very well," Granuaile said. "Then I shall offer you my thanks for affecting this introduction. I believe it will be a fruitful relationship indeed." And with that, she took Fionn's arm and swept from the room, every eye fixed on the woman who had gone head to head with the queen of England in her own presence chamber—and won.

"What happened?" Nora asked, hurrying to keep up with Granuaile's long, purposeful strides.

"Wait. Ears grow on the walls in this place."

They walked in silence down to the ship. Even then, Granuaile insisted on getting out of her elaborate dress before satisfying Nora's curiosity. She called for a bottle of wine and three goblets. Once the cabin boy had left, she sank down into a chair.

"To my son's freedom," she said, lifting her goblet in the air.

"To Tibbot," Fionn said. "And the queen of Connacht."

"To Tibbot," Nora said. Once they'd all had a drink, she asked, "Did she grant you his freedom?" Had it really been that easy? If they had truly concluded their business, there would be little chance for Fionn to get the queen alone.

"Not yet, but she will," Granuaile answered, and Nora relaxed and took another drink.

"What did she say?"

"She wishes to hear more of my story. She has granted me a private audience. I'll press my case to her then. Today was just the introduction."

"You seemed to get along well," Nora observed.

"We are both women in a man's world; we've that in common. But her desire is to build an empire. Mine is to protect my family. In that we are very different. But I think we understand each other."

"And you?" Nora turned to Fionn. "That was quite the speech you gave her—not worthy to stand in her sun and so much rubbish."

He shrugged. "Elizabeth is notoriously vain, and grows more so as her beauty fades. It is impossible to flatter her too much."

"What did you speak about? I couldn't hear the rest."

"More flattery. A little groveling. All things she craves in abundance. I am a novelty to her."

It was impossible to say more while Granuaile sat across the table from them. Nora had a feeling that Granuaile suspected Fionn's desire to meet the queen had a hidden motive—after all, she was well aware that they were trying to change the future. But for now, she seemed content to let their plan—whatever it was—play out, so long as it did not interfere with her own.

Chapter Thirty-Five

Another summons came the next day. "Her Majesty wishes you to ride out with her," the messenger told Granuaile. "And The O'Malley also." An hour later, Granuaile and Fionn were riding beside the queen on borrowed horses, while Nora trailed behind with the servants and other members of the court. She tried to sort through her emotions as she watched the trio from a distance. It wasn't jealousy, exactly. She had no desire to pander to the queen's vanity or even be near the old bag. She just felt . . . alone. She missed Fionn, missed the intimacy of his touch, missed the wonder with which he had once regarded her. There was so much they hadn't talked about, yet he had not sought another private audience with her. Had he truly stopped caring for her in the five years she was gone?

Perhaps his actions—or the lack thereof—spoke plainly enough. When she was being completely honest with herself, the idea that he would rather break his curse and die than live and be with her was excruciating.

"I'm being an eejit," she whispered to Bran as she stroked the wolfhound's thick dun fir later that night. "He's lived and suffered long enough; he deserves a peaceful death and whatever comes after." He was

Fionn mac bloody Cumhaill. Of course he'd prefer to go on to whatever awaited gods and heroes than to stay with some mere mortal, a girl from west Belfast with a dangerous skill she didn't understand. Bran nuzzled closer and licked her cheek. "And you will go with him, I suppose," Nora said. "If it works." The uncertainty was killing her. Would their plan succeed? Or would it fail in some unexpected way like all their other plans had done? Only time would tell.

And so she stayed quiet when, a few days later, another summons came—this one for Fionn alone. And then another. The word started to spread that Elizabeth had a new favorite. Granuaile, of course, was delighted. She, too, had enjoyed a private audience with the queen and was now waiting for Burghley to draw up the documents that would grant Tibbot his freedom.

Finally the letter arrived. Granuaile read it carefully, her expression growing more and more jubilant. "It's settled," she said, folding the letter carefully. "We can go home."

"Then I suppose I should pay Her Majesty one last visit to take my leave," Fionn said, giving Nora a meaningful look.

"If you must," Granuaile said dismissively. "But I've achieved what I came for and have no desire to step foot again on English soil for the rest of my life. But go, take your leave. She's grown so fond of you I fear she'd send a fleet after us if you left without saying good-bye."

Fionn nodded grimly and left the room. Nora watched him go, then was gripped with a sudden fear.

"Wait!" she cried as she ran after him. He lingered in the dark passageway. She pulled him into her tiny cabin. "Fionn, are you sure? What if you get caught?"

What if it works?

"I'll be careful," he said. "We've shared a drink before; she'll not suspect I've poisoned this one."

"Aye, but what if you're caught?" she repeated. "They'll torture you."

"True, they likely will. But if it saves my country, it doesn't matter what they do to me. I'll be free soon enough."

She wanted to stop him, to say that she didn't want him to be free. They could pick a time period, any time period, and live out their lives together. But she knew it would be only her life she'd be living out. Fionn would continue to exist in this state of limbo, never aging, never changing.

"And you'll have your brother back," he added. "Isn't that what you want?"

"Yes, o'course," she said. But the memory of Eamon, beloved though he was, did not fill her with the kind of burning fire it once did.

"Well, I suppose this might be good-bye, then," she said, pushing past the lump in her throat. Bran joined them, whining softly. Fionn bent down and took the hound's head in his hands. He whispered something to her that Nora didn't understand. Then Bran sat on her haunches at Nora's feet, her ancient, sorrowful eyes fixed on her master.

"I made you something," Fionn said to Nora. "Wait here." He left the cabin and returned a moment later with a package of square linen. "Open it."

She undid the tie around it and unfolded the linen. Lying on the white cloth was a wooden rosary. It had been hand carved, each bead polished and smooth. A tiny cross hung from the end, a ruby embedded in each point. She couldn't hold back now; the tears ran hot down her face as she gripped it.

"I know it's not the same as the one your brother made for you," he said. "But I know how much it meant to you, and I thought you might like a replacement."

"It's beautiful," she said. "Thank you." There was so much more to say, but it would only end with her begging him to stay with her. And he wanted to go.

"Well, I'll be off, then," he said.

She nodded. "Good luck." She expected him to just walk away, but instead he wrapped his arms around her. A shudder went through his body, and he kissed the top of her head.

"I love you, Nora," he said, and then he let go abruptly and strode from the room. Bran whined but sat unmoving at Nora's feet.

Nora's silent prayers were interrupted several minutes later by the door opening. Granuaile never bothered to knock. The older woman's eyes swept over Nora, taking in her wet, blotchy complexion and the rosary clutched in her hands. Her eyes flicked to the hound, then back to Nora.

"Is he gone, then?"

"Aye."

"He's coming back."

"Aye." *Or not.*

Granuaile sat herself in the only chair in the room and rested a booted foot on the opposite knee. She was still holding the letter she'd received from the queen.

"You must be pleased," Nora said, gesturing toward the letter. Better to talk of Granuaile's triumph than to have this awkward silence spread thick between them.

"I am. As pleased as one can be when one makes a deal with the devil."

Nora looked up. "What kind of deal?"

"Her Majesty has granted me many things—the freedom of my son and my other relations who are being held with him. Our ancestral lands granted back to us—not to truly possess, o'course, but to live on and use, recognizing that all of Ireland now belongs to her. The right to a pension from both of my husbands' estates. And the freedom to maintain myself and my people by land and by sea, which is basically an admission that she doesn't care who I raid, so long as it's not her."

"And in return?"

"In return I have offered to fight against Elizabeth's enemies in Ireland."

"*You what?*"

"Can you not see it, Nora? Elizabeth has won. All we can do is gain as many concessions from her as we can."

"So that's it? You're giving up?"

Granuaile folded her arms across her leather vest. "I wouldn't call it that. I'll still continue my fight against Bingham, because he is a cruel and heartless monster. But I will be very surprised if he's not recalled and sent to some godforsaken post after my conversation with the queen. Times are changing, Nora, and sometimes the only respite is to change with them. Now, are you going to tell me what the two of you are up to?"

"What do you mean?"

"I'm an old woman, or nearly so. I've known chieftains and earls and beggars and whores. I've met sailors and merchants from all over the world and crossed swords with more than I care to remember. I've even made the acquaintance of one of the Old Ones, our friend Brigid. I might not know the intricacies of what the future holds. But I know people. And I know you and Fionn have been planning something to do with this voyage. Why should it matter to him to meet a queen he has cause to hate? Why pretend to adore her? I got what I came for. What did *he* come for?"

Nora's eyes filled with ridiculous tears again, and she brushed them away angrily. Did it matter now if Granuaile knew the truth? She had her son's freedom clutched in her hands.

"Death," Nora answered. "He came for death."

Granuaile unfolded her arms and leaned forward. "Death?" Her voice was suddenly small, not the booming, confident voice of a woman who had just claimed everything she wanted from the queen of England through sheer force of will.

"Did he tell you who he really is?"

Another flicker of uncertainty. "A man from the future. He told me that when he was trying to convince me to rescue you from Doonbeg. We didn't talk about it much . . . after you left."

"He *is* a man from the future. And the past." Nora put her face in her hands. Would Fionn be furious at her for telling Granuaile? Why had he not told her himself? But she could no longer bear the burden alone. "We told you that Brigid sent us here to change Ireland's past. We both had our reasons. My brother Eamon dies in a war in Ulster four hundred years from now. That war starts now. I thought if I could stop it from happening, Eamon would still be alive."

"And Fionn?" Granuaile asked quietly.

Nora hesitated. It was his story, not hers. And yet it had become hers, intimately so. "His name is really Fionn mac Cumhaill. *The* Fionn mac Cumhaill, from the legends. He's under a curse," she said. "He's lived for hundreds of years, and he can't die until he saves Ireland. That's what he's trying to do. That's what he wants."

Granuaile leaned back in her chair. "I knew he was more than he said. But this . . . I did not imagine this." She did not question the truth of it but stared at Nora for several long seconds. "He's going to kill her."

"Aye."

For a long moment the two women just looked at each other. Then Granuaile stood and crossed the room to the door, wrenching it open. "O'Flaherty!" she bellowed. "Raise anchor!"

"What are you doing?" Nora said, getting to her feet. "We can't leave yet."

"Will he return?"

"I . . . I don't know."

"If they catch him, they will throw him in the Tower. Then they'll come after us. What will happen if he succeeds?"

"He'll die."

Granuaile closed the door and turned to face Nora. "And what the devil are you doing here, on this ship, while he goes off to fulfill this destiny of his?"

"I'm just . . . waiting." She hated the way those words echoed in the room, in her heart. But there was nothing else she could do.

"You're just waiting." Granuaile crossed the room, her hands on her hips. "I'm sorry about your brother. And I'm sorry about Fionn's curse. He didn't tell me. But I understand loss and desperation. Ah, yes, I've felt them both keenly." She crossed to the porthole in the side of the cabin and peered out the foggy glass. "I'm no goddess, and I don't have the ability to travel to different times. But one thing I know for certain: you cannot change the past. What's done is done, whether it be good or evil. Do you think I'd not give anything to see my Owen's face again? But he's gone, and nothing you or I or the gods do can change that. There would be no meaning in life if there was no meaning in death."

Her eyes fell on a roughly drawn map pinned on the wall. "The Ireland of my fathers is slipping away, I know that. The old ways will soon be gone, and it breaks my heart. I've done what I can; I've fought the English with everything I have. But it wasn't enough. We cannot stop the storm that is coming. All we can do is ready our ships and weather it the best we can."

"I can still fight," Nora said, but her voice betrayed her.

"You can, but you'll never win. You've picked the wrong enemy, Nora. The only one you'll never defeat. *Time.*"

Nora struggled against the rising tide of despair. Had it truly all been for nothing? She had suspected as much ever since she'd staggered around famine-ridden Galway, surrounded by the dead and dying, maybe even before then. But she'd refused to believe that this grand endeavor of theirs had been a lie, a joke, a quixotic quest from the beginning.

"But that doesn't mean you stop fighting, not completely," Granuaile said, reading the hopelessness on Nora's face. "We might not win the war, but we can still protect those we love. I can't bring back Owen, but I can do everything in my power to save Tibbot." She paused, pressing her lips together. "And *you* have someone who needs saving. You *know* he's going to fail. I can see it in your eyes."

"But if I'm wrong?" Nora said in a whisper. "He *wants* to die. How can I take that from him? How can I ask him . . . ?"

"To choose life?" Granuaile finished for her. "To choose *you*? Do you not know him at all? He might say he wishes for death, but what he really wants is a life worth living. *You* can give him that."

Nora stared at her. Could this be true? Her mind immediately supplied her with all the reasons why she should just let him go, why they would never work. But her heart burned and ached and strained against her chest with such intensity she was afraid she might disappear, she might go back in time to when they were happy together. Granuaile was right, though it pained her revolutionary soul to admit it. They could not change the past. They could not alter the course of Irish history.

But she could save the man she loved from torture and imprisonment and loneliness.

Granuaile cleared her throat. "You might be used to having all the time in the world, dear, but if they take him to the Tower, we will never get him out."

"Right," Nora gasped. "Wait for us!" she called over her shoulder as she scrambled up the ladder toward the top deck, praying she was not too late.

Chapter Thirty-Six

Nora dashed toward the palace, Bran at her side. A plan—a crazy, desperate plan—took shape in her mind. She'd grabbed a coil of rope from the ship, and now she bent down and tied it around Bran's neck. "Sorry, girl," she whispered. "It's just for show." A guard at the doorway held up his hand when they reached him.

"I'm delivering a parting gift to Her Majesty," she said, indicating the wolfhound. "From Grace O'Malley and the O'Malley chieftain." By now, everyone knew of Granuaile and her kinsman. The O'Malley's newfound favor with the queen had been cause for much gossip and jealousy.

"Take it to the kennels," the guard said with a jerk of his head.

"I'm under strict instructions to bring the hound in for Her Majesty's inspection. 'Tis an extremely valuable gift, and The O'Malley does not want the kennel master to touch her until Her Majesty has given her approval."

The lie was enough. The guard's scowl did not fall, but he let Nora through.

"Where is he? Can you smell him?" Nora whispered. They were headed in the general direction of the presence chamber. But if Fionn had hoped to share a quiet drink with the queen, surely he would have chosen somewhere more private. But where?

Bran kept her nose to the ground and her ears pricked for a hint of her master's voice. What was going on inside the hound's head? Was she communicating with Fionn even now?

She ignored the scandalized looks from the courtiers and petitioners who were lounging in groups of two and three. Bran tugged on the rope, and Nora eagerly followed. They were stopped outside the door to the presence chamber, where two large Gentlemen Pensioners stood with their bayonets and bored expressions.

"I've a gift for the queen from Grace O'Malley and The O'Malley chieftain," she repeated.

"The queen is in her privy chamber, not to be disturbed," one of the guards said gruffly.

"I've been ordered to take the hound directly to her."

"Her Majesty is *not* to be disturbed."

"Can I not wait in the presence chamber, then?"

"No."

Nora led Bran a few paces away, then knelt down and whispered in her ear. "Can you contact him? Tell him that he must come out at once."

She waited, pretending she was fixing the hound's makeshift collar and inspecting her fur. After a few moments Bran whined softly.

"What's the matter?" The hound whined again, giving Nora a sorrowful look. "Is he not coming? Why the hell not?" She cast a panicked look at the closed door of the presence chamber, which stood between her and the privy chamber.

The solution strode toward her, his cape billowing behind him. A flicker of hesitation; then she threw caution to the wind.

"Donough!"

The Earl of Thomond stopped midstride, caught off guard by the familiar address. Then he drew closer, and his expression changed from one of offense to one of stark astonishment. "Nora!" he exclaimed, a hand flying to his chest. His narrow eyes bulged as he took her in. "What . . . I thought I'd never see you again! I thought you'd been taken!" His voice shook slightly.

"I left," she admitted. "In all the chaos, I suppose I saw my chance." He leaned forward, as though he couldn't quite believe what she was saying.

"You . . . left? Of your own accord? But why?"

Apparently he'd been more enamored of her than she'd realized—and had believed she felt the same way.

There isn't time for this. But she did need his help. "I was afraid Bingham wouldn't believe you. I couldn't risk ending up back in prison."

Thomond's expression turned sour as he digested this. "I would have protected you."

"I know you would have," she said softly. "I was afraid. I'm sorry."

"But whatever are you doing here at Greenwich?"

"I found Grace O'Malley. I've entered into her service, and I'm here with her now."

He nodded uncertainly. "Yes, I'm the one who arranged her meeting with Her Majesty. Were you—" He peered more closely at her. "You've been with her all this time, as her servant! And yet I didn't recognize you."

"I wanted it that way," she said. "I didn't want to hurt you." She paused. "Donough, I know you probably don't want to see me right now, and I understand. But I have something for you."

His hand cupped her cheek, and for a moment she thought he might kiss her right then and there, in front of all the other courtiers. But he remembered himself. "What is it?"

"It's this wolfhound. Granuaile is on her ship, making ready to depart while the weather is fair. But she told me to come deliver the hound to you as a gift of thanks for your assistance."

Thomond bent down and examined Bran with great interest. "She is remarkable," he said, stroking her long fur. "I've not seen a hound like her. It is a very valuable gift."

"She is a pure Irish wolfhound of the greatest ancestry. And now she belongs to you. However . . ."

"However?"

"The person who offers this hound as a gift to Her Majesty will bring themselves great honor."

"Ah."

"You don't have to, o'course—it's just a suggestion. But it might help bring you favor. I remember you saying you wanted County Clare to be transferred from the jurisdiction of Connacht to Munster. Perhaps this will help pave the way."

"'Pave the way.' You have so many odd expressions, Miss O'Reilly. But you are politically astute. Very well, I accept," he said, taking the rope from Nora. "I will bring the hound to Her Majesty straightaway." He walked toward the Gentlemen Pensioners at the door, who nodded to him deferentially. "Will you accompany me?" he said, turning back to her.

"O'course." And with that, they were inside the presence chamber.

The queen was not in her gilded chair of state, but dozens of courtiers still milled about in anticipation of her return. A guard stood outside an ornate door at the other end of the hall. Nora's heart beat furiously. If Fionn would not come out in response to a mental plea from Bran, how could she reach him without getting herself killed in the process?

Casting a terrified look at Bran, who stood obediently by Thomond's side, she raised her voice and said, "The plague! The plague has come to Greenwich!"

Thomond spun around. "What are you doing?" But his remonstrance was drowned out by the sudden exclamations of horror around them, by the swirl of skirts and the buzz of frantic activity. The chamber erupted into chaos as courtiers vied for the doorway or shouted questions to each other from across the room. Thomond lost his grip on Bran and was shunted toward the door by several of his friends, who ignored his protests. The guards, hearing the commotion, burst into the room, bayonets at the ready.

If they could hear it, she knew Fionn could, too. Not a moment later, the door of the privy chamber opened and Fionn burst out, looking around with wide eyes. "See to Her Majesty," he told the guard who had remained at the privy chamber door.

Nora caught him by the wrist and pulled him close. "Have you done it?" she demanded.

"Not yet, but—"

"Good. Let's get out of here." She pulled him toward the door, pushing through the crush of courtiers dressed in silk skirts and velvet doublets, moving past Thomond, who was struggling against the friends who were dragging him in the opposite direction of Nora. The sixteenth-century equivalent of yelling "fire" in a cinema had created the perfect diversion. They emerged into the corridor, where the fear of plague was spreading quicker than any flame.

"Nora, what—?" Fionn stopped short, bent over and gasping. "Is there really a plague?"

"No," she said, trying to urge him forward.

"But—"

"Listen," she said, grabbing his face so he had to look at her. "I'll explain everything, but we have to get out of here first."

Then he vomited on the floor.

Her face paled. "Oh, God, *you* drank it, didn't you?"

He nodded, sweat breaking out across his face. "She hadn't . . . touched her glass yet," he groaned.

"Come on," she said, taking him by the arm. Bran ran up beside them, the rope trailing behind her, Thomond nowhere in sight. They were given a wide berth as they hurried through the corridors, Fionn retching as he ran, his complexion turning the color of stale oatmeal. The wide green lawn opened up in front of them, and farther down the river the masts of the *Queen Medb* stood ready and waiting.

"Stop," Fionn said, pulling her to a halt. The palace loomed behind them, and there was still a danger that soldiers would pour out of it, ready to take them both to the Tower.

"Not until we're on the ship," she said.

He grabbed her arm in a fierce grip. "What are you doing? This could be our last chance!"

"I'm saving you!"

"From what?"

"From death. From torture. Pick one."

He stared at her, unmoving, as though trying to decipher her words.

"Right, if this is where we're going to do it," she said, speaking quickly. "I didn't want to believe it, but I think Brigid lied to us. Or maybe she just let us lie to ourselves. We *can't* change the past, not really. It's impossible. The future of Ireland is set, no matter what we do. We can't stop my brother from being murdered, and we can't break your curse—at least not this way. If you really, truly want it, I will help you—we'll go to the future, to my time, and try again there. But the truth is, I don't *want* you to break your curse. I want you to *live*." His hand had grown slack on her arm, and she slid out of his grasp and took a step back, her eyes challenging him. "You said you love me. And I love you, more than I've ever loved anyone. *We're worth fighting for.* Don't you believe that?"

He winced, and her heart plummeted. But then he waved his hand. "It's not you," he gasped. "It's the arsenic. Not you. I thought . . . I thought your brother meant everything to you. I wanted to bring him back for you."

Nora let out a slow breath. "Eamon did mean everything to me. I loved him. I will always love him. But he's gone. I can't bring him back. And the best way I can honor his memory is by living a life he'd be proud of." She gave Fionn a tentative smile. "He was a big fan of yours, you know. I think he'd be happy for us."

Fionn wrapped his arms around her, and she melted into his chest. "God, I'm a fool," he said. "I thought I was doing what you wanted, and here I was doing the opposite."

She pulled back so she could see his face. "Tell me the truth. Do you really want to die? Because if that's what you want, we'll find a way to break your curse together."

"I used to want that, more than anything," he admitted. "But something tells me there's a little more life to be lived yet."

"Then let's get the hell out of here."

Chapter Thirty-Seven

It was a much happier captain and crew that sailed back to Clew Bay. Granuaile locked her precious letter from the queen in the same chest that held her jewelry. Once they had safely sailed out of English waters, she opened a keg for the crew, then she, Fionn, and Nora gathered in her cabin and toasted with a French claret she'd been saving for victory.

"Are you certain? You really think it's impossible to change the past?" Fionn asked.

"I *wish* it were possible," Nora said. "Though who knows what other problems we could create. Change isn't always for the best. What if we'd managed to depose Elizabeth? Someone even worse could have taken her place. I've started to look at it this way: time is like a river. Over hundreds, maybe thousands of years, it can change course slightly, become broader or narrower or branch off in different directions. But that takes a massive amount of force—an earthquake, a flood, or thousands of years. No one person can go back and change the course of the river once it has carved its path. All the things we've been trying to do—save Lynch, help the armada, assassinate the queen. We're like pebbles throwing ourselves into the Shannon. We can have an effect on individual lives—like yours, for example," she said to Granuaile. "But we're simply not big enough to change the course of the river once its path has been determined."

Fionn leaned back in his chair, chewing on his lip. "That begs several questions, the foremost of which is: Why did Brigid send us here in the first place? What was the point, if there was nothing we could change?"

"I've been thinking about that, too. Technically, going further back in time was my idea," Nora said, though she was loath to defend Brigid at the moment. "And if we're right about my ability to time travel, *I* brought us here, not her. But that doesn't answer why she suggested this particular time period."

"Brigid always has her reasons, though rarely does she deign to share them," Granuaile said. "But *my* question is this: What are the two of you going to do now?"

Nora glanced at Fionn, who looked as uncertain as she felt. "I suppose that's something we need to talk about," she said. "I've a few ideas."

"O'course you do," Granuaile said. "Well, I'll be sad to see you gone, to be sure, but I'll take you anywhere you need to go, so long as it's sailing distance. I don't think this old galleon could make it to the New World."

"Now that's something I haven't considered," Nora said thoughtfully. "Can you imagine? Going to America at this time in history?"

"No thanks," Fionn said. "I've had my share of colonialism, if you don't mind."

"Fair point."

An hour later, Granuaile went up top to make sure at least some of her sailors were still sober, and Fionn and Nora retired to Nora's tiny cabin.

"Why'd you stop me?" Fionn asked as soon as he'd closed the door.

"I told you why," Nora said, surprised.

"You said it wouldn't change anything. But I still could have killed her."

"Why?" she asked. Something in his tone bothered her. "Why take that risk knowing it wouldn't make a difference?"

"I thought you of all people would understand. After what Elizabeth has done, after all the horror she's brought to Ireland, why does she deserve to live?"

Nora sank down onto the bed. "Maybe she doesn't. I'm hardly one to talk; I'm a former terrorist, after all. But I think there's a difference between killing to gain a country's freedom and killing for revenge. You're a freedom fighter, not an assassin."

"And what are you?"

She stretched out on the bed and watched him, this tormented, conflicted, beautiful man. "I'm a woman who hasn't been laid in a very, very long time."

"That's quite the change in conversation," he said, but he came toward her, a grin spreading across his face. He sat beside her on the bed, and she wove her fingers through his.

"The truth is, even if poisoning the queen could have saved Ireland, I still would have stopped you. Because you'd be lost to me either way—dead or locked in the Tower. I've already lost one man I love, and I can't bring him back. I'm not going to lose you, too. Now are you going to just sit there, or are you going to kiss me?"

He kissed her, long and deep, his hands pulling her closer. Before she could stop them, tears rose to the surface. She tasted the salt in her mouth even as she pressed her lips against Fionn's.

"What is it, a mhuirnín?" he asked, drawing back and wiping a tear away with his thumb.

She shook her head, trying to steady her breathing. "It's just . . . I had so much hope. I thought I could save him. I can't imagine how you must be feeling. You've been waiting for hundreds of years for this second chance, and now to find out that it won't work . . ."

He cupped her face in his hands. "Believe me. I want to stay. I want to live. I want to be with you."

She chose to believe him—and to ignore the inevitable implications. Like Fionn's other partners, she would grow old and weak while he stayed young and virile. But when had she ever thought that far ahead? He was here, and he loved her.

"I love you," she said, and drew him back toward her. He sealed their words with his lips, then tugged off his boots and lifted his linen shirt over his head. As soon as his chest was bare, she kissed it. She ran her nails along his sides as she teased his skin with her tongue. He made a guttural sound in the back of his throat and roughly disrobed her before attacking her throat with his mouth. She arched against him, the rasping of his beard on her skin driving her mad, making her crave the feel of him everywhere. Nothing else mattered—neither past nor future could intrude on this moment as he spread her legs with his hands and moved inside her, filling her. She wrapped her arms around his shoulders, bringing him closer as their hips pressed hungrily together, desperate to be reunited.

"D'you forgive me for stopping you?" she asked, her lips brushing his ear.

"You could burn this country to the ground and I would forgive you right now," he said.

She smiled and closed her eyes, then tilted her head back as he thrust deeper into her.

"Brigid!" he cried.

Her eyes flew open. "What did you say?"

But it had been no mere slip of the tongue. Brigid was standing in their room, leaning against the wall as casually as though she were watching a game of cards. She was dressed in full Elizabethan regalia, complete with a massive starched ruff and a floor-length midnight-blue gown studded with diamonds. A delicate silver tiara glittered among the waves of dark curls elaborately arranged on top of her head.

Nora scrambled back on the bed and grasped for whatever fabric was nearby to cover her. Fionn had no such modesty; he swung around to face Brigid completely naked, though considerably more limp than he had been moments before.

"You have got to be kidding me," Nora said. "We've been wanting to speak with you for ages, and *this* is when you turn up?"

"I do have a talent for choosing my moments, don't I?" Brigid said, the corner of her wide mouth tilting.

"What do you want?" Fionn snapped, his expression dark. "Come to play with us some more?"

"Whatever do you mean?" Brigid said, sliding onto the room's only chair in one fluid movement.

Fionn grabbed his léine off the floor and yanked it over his head. "We know the truth—Nora time traveled away from here, and back, without you—and it nearly killed her. Why pretend you were the one doing it? Why tell us to find Granuaile?"

"So many questions," she purred.

"Aye, and we'd like some answers, so we would," Nora said, still wrapped in the sheets from the bed.

"I take it you haven't enjoyed your trip to the sixteenth century?" Brigid asked maddeningly.

"Oh, aye, it's been grand, so it has!" Nora burst out. "What with being jailed, shipwrecked, and nearly hung."

"Pity," Brigid said. "I thought something good must have come out of it, given what I walked in on."

Nora fell silent.

"What happens between us is none of your business," Fionn said. "What are you playing at, Brigid?"

"You should be thanking me," Brigid said, her voice darkening. Nora had only ever seen the goddess in a playful, coquettish mood. What would she be like when she was angry? "Did I not bring the two of you together? Did I not send Nora to you in the first place?"

"Aye, and I'm grateful for that," Nora said. It would do no good to infuriate the goddess. If she left in anger, they'd never get answers to their questions.

"Very grateful," Fionn echoed, softening his voice.

"We've realized we can't change the past," Nora said. "At least, nothing we've done yet has seemed to work." She told Brigid her theory about time being a great river, and the two of them mere pebbles tossed into it. "D'you agree? Is that how it works?"

"I'm impressed," Brigid said. "And I suspect you are right, although—shocking as this may seem—I don't know all the secrets of the universe, ancient and powerful though I am. Obviously, I, too, can travel through time. But when I return to the present, it is just as I left it."

"Then why'd you let us believe we could change things? All that talk about second chances?"

"You take things so literally, dear. It's very boring. Do you think there is only one reason for traveling to the past? Are there not other lessons to be learned, experiences to be had? Was it really such a waste of time, if you'll forgive the expression?"

"Why did you want us to meet Granuaile?" Fionn asked. "*That* was your idea."

"Because she's a fascinating woman who never got her due, in her own lifetime or since," Brigid snapped. "Must I have some sinister reason for arranging a meeting of two of my favorite people?"

"That was it?" Fionn asked, nonplussed. "You just wanted us to meet?"

"Well, I have to admit I didn't intend for you to take things quite so far as you did," Brigid said, reproach in her voice. "That was *not* part of the plan."

"So there *was* a plan," Nora said.

"You act like I completely abandoned you," Brigid said, her voice cool. "I would like to point out that you're both quite capable of taking care of yourselves. Your reliance on me is a smidgen unbecoming, to be honest. But here I am, and the two of you seem to be getting along just grand." She stood and adjusted her skirt.

"You're not leaving?" Nora demanded.

"Well, you don't exactly seem thrilled to see me. I thought I'd look in on Granuaile, maybe have a drink with her. At least *she's* a laugh."

"Wait," Nora said. She scrambled to her feet, still clutching the sheets around her. "There's still a way you can help us."

Brigid arched a dark eyebrow. "And why would I want to do that?"

"Because you just said Fionn is one of your favorite people. And I know there's more you're not telling us."

"Well spotted," Brigid said dryly.

"What do you know about Fionn's curse?"

"No more than he does, surely."

"When I first started dreaming about Fionn, he was asking me to help him. And *you* put those dreams in my head. You told me as much. So why add that bit? You wanted me to help him break his curse. If it's not by going back in time and changing the past, then how?"

"Are you in such a hurry for him to die?" Brigid asked, eyeing Nora's swollen lips and the rash around her neck from Fionn's stubble.

"I'm just trying to figure out what I'm doing here."

"I'm not sure if this expression has been coined yet in 1593, so let me be the first to say it: don't look a gift horse in the mouth."

"What's that supposed to mean?"

Brigid rolled her eyes. "Come now, Nora, you're smarter than this."

Nora ignored the taunt. "O'course I'm glad Fionn and I met, and no, I don't want him to die. But because I care about him, I want to help him. And I think you've information that could help me do that."

"Such as?"

"Is there a way to get out of this deal with Aengus Óg?"

Brigid appraised Nora with a shrewd eye.

Then Fionn spoke up. "It's not a deal, Nora. It's a curse. A punishment. I appreciate what you're trying to do, but there's no way out but to fulfill his terms, which I'm beginning to think are impossible." He took her hand in his. "And besides, I told you, I *want* to live."

"I know," she said, lifting his hand and studying it. "But you've had this hanging over you for long enough."

"So, you want . . . ," he started uncertainly.

"I want the best of both worlds," she said. "I want you to be free from your curse, and I want you to live a natural but long life." She smiled up at him, the stubborn blossom of hope taking root in her chest. "Is that so much to ask?"

"You have guts, I'll give you that," Brigid said slowly.

Nora swiveled to face her, still holding Fionn's hand. "Can you make that happen?"

"No, of course not. I can think of much better things to do with Fionn mac Cumhaill than curse him. And since it's not my curse, I can't touch it. Only Aengus Óg could do that."

"Aengus Óg would rather become mortal than forgive me for what I did to Diarmuid," Fionn said, the familiar note of defeat slipping into his voice.

"Hush," Nora said, her mind spinning with conflicting thoughts. Perhaps they couldn't change Ireland's future, but could they change Fionn's? "What if you never killed Diarmuid at all?"

"I know what you're thinking, but it won't work," Brigid said. "You'd be surprised at how volatile your man Fionn was back then. I highly doubt you'd be able to sway him. Killing Diarmuid was a crime of passion, as they say. And"—Brigid held up a jewel-encrusted hand to forestall Nora's objection—"Aengus Óg's relationship to time is different than yours, as is mine. He already knows what has happened, even if by some miracle you managed to change it, which you've already determined is impossible."

"She's right," Fionn said softly. "But it *was* a noble thought."

Nora knew in her heart this was true. Nor would it result in what they both wanted: a normal life for Fionn, a life in which they could grow old together. "Then we've only one choice. We must find Aengus Óg and ask him to lift the curse. Where is he?"

Fionn snorted. "Not here, if that's what you're thinking. All the Tuatha Dé Danann—except Brigid, of course—disappeared from the mortal world centuries ago. To find him, you'd have to go to Tír na nÓg, and I can't take you there."

"Can *you*?" Nora asked Brigid, but the goddess shook her head.

"Not unless you never want to return. And even then I can't guarantee you'll survive the passage."

Nora's jaw stiffened. "Right. When?"

"When what?" Fionn asked.

"When was Aengus Óg last seen in this world?"

"No." Fionn stepped between Nora and Brigid. "Absolutely not."

"I know what I'm doing, Fionn."

"No, you don't. You could die."

"You're exaggerating," she said, though she knew he wasn't. "If being unconscious and sick for a few days is what it takes to give you a normal sort of life, then I'd risk it a thousand times."

"I can't let you do that."

"It's *my* life. I'll do what I want with it. I'll track down Aengus Óg on my own, so I will. You can come with me or no."

"I do not know for certain when he left Erin," Brigid said. "But I do know he was still here during the reign of the king known as Brian Boru. You would do well to seek him then."

"No!" Fionn said, twisting around to face her. "She's not going."

"How long have you known Nora, Fionn?" Brigid asked.

"Long enough to know I don't want to see her die."

Brigid took a step toward him, so that they were only inches apart. "I have known you your entire life. Eighteen hundred years. I have seen you take lovers and leave them, have families and leave them, and isolate yourself from the world for fear of losing anyone ever again. And I don't blame you. No, I understand. It comes with immortality. But here is a woman who understands you, who believes you, and who has already risked everything to help you." She put a white hand on his cheek. "Let her help you, Fionn. Even gods can change their minds. If you have the courage to find him, Aengus Óg will give you a fair hearing."

"The reign of Brian Boru," Nora said. "So around the turn of the millennium. Are you certain?"

Brigid didn't deign to answer.

"Let's do it," Nora urged Fionn.

"If something happened to you . . ."

"I'll be grand. I promise." She grabbed his hand and closed her eyes.

"Not here!" Fionn said quickly. "Not unless we want to appear in the middle of the ocean."

"Right," Nora said, opening her eyes and blushing. "I suppose I jumped the gun a wee bit. We should prepare this time. We can bring back muskets, ammunition, food, whatever passes for medicine here." On an impulse, she hugged Brigid around the neck. "Thank you."

"Yes, yes," Brigid said. "Now if you'll excuse me, I believe I can hear Granuaile uncorking another bottle of wine."

Historical Note

My goal with this novel has been twofold: to tell a good story, and to strive for historical accuracy. It is my hope that I have achieved both.

In two notable areas I have taken some artistic liberties (besides the time travel, legendary warriors, and ancient deities, that is). First, we do not know which of the O'Malley friends and agents smoothed Granuaile's way at court, though some speculate it could have been Black Tom Butler, the Earl of Ormond. In the absence of historical certainty, I have chosen the Earl of Thomond as a worthy candidate.

Second, professional historians generally agree on the lack of hard evidence that Granuaile met Elizabeth I. What *is* known for certain is that she went to London, was at the court, and achieved her aim of getting her son released and her status and lands guaranteed. However, the story of the face-to-face meeting and the burning of the handkerchief grew up after the fact and may or may not be true.

Acknowledgments

Many thanks to Dr. Áine Sheehan at University College Cork for her invaluable assistance as I strove for historical accuracy. Any errors that remain are mine alone.

I am also grateful to Erika Holt, Janice Hillmer, Jody Johnston, and Janelle de Jager for their thoughtful critiques and encouragement.

As always, I am indebted to the team at 47North: Adrienne Procaccini, Angela Polidoro, Kim Cowser, and everyone else who had a hand in bringing this book to life.

About the Author

Photo © 2015 F8 Photography

Jodi McIsaac is the author of several novels, including *A Cure for Madness* and the Thin Veil series. She grew up in New Brunswick, on Canada's east coast. After abandoning her Olympic speed skating dream, she wrote speeches for a politician, volunteered in a refugee camp, waited tables in Belfast, earned a couple of university degrees, and started a boutique copywriting agency. She loves running, geek culture, and whiskey. *Summon the Queen* is the second installment in the Revolutionary series, following *Bury the Living*.